The
Last Light
Spoken

Barry Grills

Books by Barry Grills

Fiction
The Last Light Spoken (Fluid Grouse Enterprises)
Cock-Eyed Voice: Stories (Fluid Grouse Enterprises)
Too Late The Hunter (Fluid Grouse Enterprises)
Oblivion (Fluid Grouse Enterprises)
I And You, And Me And Her (Fluid Grouse Enterprises)
Roadkill (Fluid Grouse Enterprises)

Non Fiction
Every Wolf's Howl (Freehand Books)
A New Day Dawns (with Jim Brown) (Quarry Press)
Falling Into You (Quarry Press)
Ironic (Quarry Press)
Snowbird (Quarry Press)

The
Last Light
Spoken

Barry Grills

FLUID
GROUSE
enterprises

Barry Grills

Library and Archives Canada Cataloguing in Publication

Grills, Barry, 1948-   , author
The Last Light Spoken / Barry Grills

Cover Design: Jennifer Rouse Barbeau
Cover Photo: Jennifer Rouse Barbeau
Author Photo: Liz Lott

ISBN:
978-1-7751389-9-0

For my parents

Barry Grills

ACKNOWLEDGMENTS

The Last Light Spoken is a novel that was a relatively solitary project. Still, there are some people to thank for helping me along the way. My friend of many years, Hugh Chandler, was kind enough to read an earlier version of the manuscript; he was consulted to consider its historical and geographical accuracy because our acquaintance and friendship began in a village much like the one in which most of the novel is set at the beginning of the 1960s. Thank you, Hugh. My wife and partner, writer Jennifer Rouse Barbeau, also went through the novel a couple of times, editing or making notes along the way. She is also responsible for both the book and cover designs, for which I am grateful. Bringing this book to market has been seriously hindered by the Covid-19 pandemic which continues into its third year on this planet. We press on with hopeful gratitude.

Barry Grills

Love is the last light spoken

Dylan Thomas
Ceremony After A Fire Raid

PROLOGUE

Back then, that summer, we called ourselves The Skeleton Club. There were four of us, each of us points of a compass, different but the same. We were eleven years old and going into Grade Six, and there was something tenuous about our relationship, as if different and same argued gently inside us for sole proprietorship of our souls. It was the summer of our lives when we knew for the first time that we were beings on the move and there is a powerful force in the world called change . . .

REMEMBERING MY MANNERS, I stop reading and glance up from the manuscript, tucking it back into its envelope. Your young widow, Melanie, watches me, and I find myself wondering what she must think of you and me, of our cloudy ancient history. She has given me this manuscript of your story at your grave site, of all places, at the junction where present comes to a screeching halt at the stop sign of the future.

"Thank you, Melanie," I say, feeling awkward taking something creative of yours from a woman I hardly know, nor would have sought to know. She is bony, pierced and tattooed, heavily made up in black lipstick and eye shadow. Young. To me, hardly more than a child.

I haven't even decided if I'm truly grateful for her gift, or whether I'm just being polite. Politeness is so devious a talent, so unapologetic over its lack of soul. I hold the envelope in my fingers, noticing how it turns golden in the sunshine. I didn't ask you for this manuscript, Phillip, nor did I ask your young widow for it. But you mentioned it to me that night we had dinner, while we talked and sipped single malt scotch in your small home on your small Muskoka lake. You told me how you wrote the story as a kind of whimsical catharsis, dealing with the important incidents it recalled for you and me. "Ironic, really, that I would write this story and you wouldn't," you said. I said nothing to this. You must have mentioned something to Melanie about these remarks afterwards to inspire her to bring me this story on the day you are being committed to the ground.

"Am I to keep it?" I ask. "Or do you want it back? Is this the only copy?"

She shrugs, I suspect, because she doesn't care. "I think he would have wanted you to keep it."

"Are you sure?"

She nods, then can't hold her judgment back. "It's all way before my time, isn't it?" she says. And I feel the familiar jab of a modern young woman's disdain.

"Yes, I suppose it is."

"Even when he wrote it," she is saying. "Even that was before my time."

"Yes."

"He told me you'd find it interesting. Because it's about you and him together when you were kids."

"Yes," I tell her. "Things happened back then, Melanie, when he and I were children. I write about them myself sometimes, just wrestling with what it all means. You haven't read the story?"

"No."

"It was a big deal for us, Melanie. It really was. You know, what went on back then."

I don't mean to be cryptic with her—she doesn't seem intrigued by anything ominous in my words anyway—but the incidents themselves are cryptic, having grown increasingly so over the years, I think. Then again, I've come to believe time seals everything in its own peculiar, protective code. We rationalize, embellish, and reshape events before we get to their telling. Everything about our days is in code, I have learned, now that I am in my early sixties and living out what remains of my human years.

I glance again at the envelope, considering the night I visited you and Melanie a month or so ago. Remembering this, I am struck by the harsh reality of a man's dying, it's end of grammatical tense. And I keep peering in the direction of your casket where they've lowered it into the ground and will shortly cover it with dirt, as soon as this pathetically sparse clump of mourners lingering here at the grave site finally departs.

You have no family in Muskoka, just a casual friend or two, as far as I can see. Most of the people here today seem to be Melanie's friends. They're young, of course, either preppy in suits or ties or dressed in pierced, tattered, or tattooed black. I guess I'm the only true emissary from your generation, Phillip. Your parents are dead. You had no siblings. To hear you tell it, people knew you only fleetingly, you moved around so much, at least until you bought your A-frame on the lake a half decade ago. I conjectured the night I visited you that you enjoyed playing the role of posse-pursued outlaw to the hilt. In a way, you and I switched places over the years. When we were children, I was the one who judged our society harshly. You seemed so innocent to me then. Now I wonder if we reversed ourselves as we grew older. Today, a few days after your death, I see myself as the innocent one, while you arrived at the grave a cynic. Hard to know for sure. You died well before I could even wish to figure out the nature of our associated incongruities.

I feel guilty at this moment because I still own a present tense, because I can enjoy a reasonably confident glimpse into the future. Worse yet, I feel I escaped our childhood in an unscathed way that you never could. It makes me ashamed somehow, like I've been taking a privilege in life for granted, a privilege you never knew.

I feel your Melanie watching me. Even when I return the glance, she continues to stare at me. She possesses the usual rude demeanour I attribute to her youth. To me, new millennium young people flex the rudeness muscle as often as they can, as a you-can't-make-me posture. Melanie is a pretty woman, I suppose, but I am too old to appreciate a right ear pierced with a complex network of earrings and chains, a stripe of blood-like crimson dyed into her jet black hair. Young women like these seem damaged to me, by their fashion and jewellry, and by their refusal to acknowledge that anything could have happened before their birth. I am a curmudgeon about this; I've earned the privilege. I wondered the night I saw you last why you'd married a young woman like Melanie. And I wondered even more why a woman like her had married a strange, old desperado like you. Friendship, I supposed then. I noticed something easy about the two of you that night, as if neither one of you had any serious expectations of the other. Maybe ease was what you needed, Phillip, after so many years of sanguine searching.

Heart attack, Melanie said on her cellphone when she called me a couple of days ago to tell me you were dead. "I found him down on the end of the dock. On his towel. I thought he was sleeping."

"I'm so sorry, Melanie," I said. "It must be a terrible shock." Somehow I didn't want to believe her, just on principle I guess. I knew you were barely sixty. I found solace in the usual platitudes. I've known other deaths during my life—one reaches an age when we attend more and more funerals. I know the ceremony death seems to demand of us. I know what I'm supposed to say.

"Yes," her voice kept saying with an unapologetic calm, as I stumbled through my regrets.

"Did he have a history of heart attacks? Did he know he had a heart condition? He never mentioned anything the night I was over there."

"He knew," Melanie replied. "Phillip was in a state of

denial. We almost never talked about it. He took medication but he never let me see him do it. When he remembered to, he wore his nitro patch. I pretended not to notice it on his upper arm."

"Jesus, he never said a word."

Your young wife—this one talking to me on my landline—this young wife—didn't understand anything about death, I remember thinking at the time. Ignorance inspiring her state of calm. What some people used to call bliss. I'm not sure it's bliss, though. Ignorance is too flat to be bliss. No, ignorance is just all that inevitability life has in store for us, the events we haven't acknowledged yet, the things that are going to happen to us down the road apiece, the places where we are going to happen to others and, in our happening, wreak some havoc of some kind. We're like scarred up wedges of beach repeatedly harassed by tiny tsunamis—surprises, shocks, enticements, tragedies—events we can't escape. Life, I suppose, for want of a better word.

I probably thought most of these things when Melanie— how old is she? Twenty-six, twenty-seven? Maybe even younger?—called to tell me you were dead. So young to be married to a man now gone. So unaware that a small version of her own inevitability was charging towards her in the way inevitability careens towards each one of us, some snorting bull with a sword jammed into its bleeding shoulder. We don't know much when we are younger. And when we've grown to be a lot older, all we've learned is that we will never know.

"Sometimes," Melanie was saying, "when we made love, he would gasp. In pain, you know? I would see the pain. It never held him back, but I would see the pain. Whaddyuh call it?"

"Angina?"

"Yeah. Angina. I would see it hurting him."

"Yes," was all I said.

"Anyway, I wanted you to know about Phillip. I wanted you to know he was dead."

Calm, practical, young, your Melanie.

Even now, here at the grave site, she exudes the same

calm. I am struck again by her youth. She is dressed like a widow—a small pillbox hat pinned to the jet black side of her hair, black dress and jacket—but it looks wrong somehow, like she's so young she can't truly have lost anyone, not even a parent, let alone a husband. Like she's got to grow up a few more years before she's allowed to go to a funeral, before she can even think about aspiring to widowhood.

"Are you okay?" I ask her, annoyed by the various two-sided doubloons of envy and impatience I feel about her youth.

She nods.

"Thank you for bringing the story." Crisply I salute her with the envelope.

"I think he would have wanted you to have it."

"Thank you," I say again.

As we fall silent, I notice the cemetery making cemetery noises, a breeze rustling some leaves on a maple not far away, an insect's hum, the twitter of some birds, the intrusive, rattling honk of a passing raven somewhere high overhead. It's the end of August. Summer still wants to pretend it's going to last forever.

"What are you going to do now, Melanie?" I ask at last.

"Nothing."

"Nothing?"

"There's money. I have time to take my time."

"Good."

I wonder if I should suggest I check on her now and then, but I'm a man around sixty and she's a young woman under thirty. Something about trying to be friends with her would be misconstrued, I'm sure. By people living here in small town Muskoka. By her. Even by me. I'm not you, Phillip. My life as a quest, as a flight from pain, is more cautious than yours could ever be. And I hate being judged hastily by the people who share this planet with me. That night I visited you, I decided you revelled in the banditry of it. Now, with little else to say to your young wife, I extend my hand to her. She shakes it briskly.

"You have my number, if you need it," I say, knowing she'll never call, relieved that she probably won't.

"Yes," the young woman says.

"I'm so sorry, Melanie," I add.

"Thank you," she replies.

She smiles a little at me, then turns away towards the black-suited men from the funeral home who are standing by the hearse, waiting for us to be done. They will look after her, I know, better than I can or wish to. And afterwards, after this business of dying is taken care of, she and her murder of crowlike friends—the ones who have come here in tattered black to share her grief—will have a party celebrating the long, secure future still remaining to her and them.

I turn away, walking towards my car, thinking how many wives you've left behind, Phillip. The other ones, I mean, Melanie's predecessors, the ones you mentioned the night I visited you, the ones who had your children, who fell in love with you, who fell out of love with you, until one or the other of you felt compelled to leave someone behind. These wives are all widows too, because, as far as I know, most of them remain alive. They're widows to me because I view marriage as deeply permanent, regardless of how it comes to an end. Divorce or death. It doesn't matter. It brings to an end a state of connubial transformation. I've never married, myself. I guess I've never wanted to be a part of this process, to perpetuate an institution that people like me are tempted to idealize too much. Maybe I don't want to learn that I am wrong. Maybe I want to keep pretending I am right.

Your children didn't come to your funeral. I'm not surprised by this—you had explained about your children recently, the last time I saw you. We were talking then, I believe, about the great capacity humans have for alienation.

I asked you, though, how a man comes to marry so much in life, the night I visited you a month or so ago, the night we celebrated our awkward, ambivalent reunion over dinner and some drinks.

"Just trying to get it right," you said. "Believing in it, I guess."

"It? You mean marriage?"

"No," you said with some surprise. "I mean love."

WHEN I RAN INTO YOU ON THE STREET in Huntsville, downtown on the bridge across the Muskoka River, that July day earlier this summer, I recognized you right away. We hadn't seen each other in five decades, but I knew it was you, all right. I could still see the pre-adolescent version of you I had known so many years before in the middle-aged man standing before me now.

"Phillip? Phillip Barrett?"

"Yes?"

"It's me," I said. "Gary."

"Gary?"

"Gary Burnside."

"Shit," you said. "I don't believe it."

It was the day of the bathtub derby in Huntsville. There'd been a parade. The races in the river basin were about to begin. Hundreds of people milled about, talking, laughing, buying, cajoling.

You and I shook hands. We nearly embraced, although we didn't in the end because, I suppose, five decades is a very long time to squeeze inside a hug.

"What are you doing here?" you asked me.

"I live here."

"Where?"

"Dorset. On the edge with Haliburton."

"Jesus," you said. "The place I bought is near Baysville."

We were jostled by passing strangers. One of them glared at us for being in the way.

"Looks like we're going to have to move," I said.

But you stood there firmly, the taller and larger of us, making the crowd meander around us like a stream around an island.

"I've read your novels," you said then. "I didn't connect the Gary Burnside of literature with my Gary Burnside at first, but once I did . . ."

". . . Thanks," I said.

"I still have them all. They're waiting for your autograph."

I nodded.

"Are you married? Do you have family?"

"No. You?"

"Married again." You turned and began to point into the crowd down on the wharf. Then you stopped in mid-gesture, as if it didn't ultimately matter. "My boys are grown up," you murmured as an afterthought.

"How many?"

"Two."

"Do they live in Muskoka too?" I asked.

"No," you said distantly. "Down south. We're . . . out of touch."

"Oh."

Someone started making announcements over the PA system. We waited a moment before trying again to speak.

"We have a lot to talk about," you said.

"A lot to catch up on. How many years has it been?"

"Almost fifty," you said, as if you'd only tallied up the years a few hours ago this morning, preparing yourself for the possibility that we might meet.

I nodded.

"I have a card," you said. And you reached for your wallet, retrieved one, and gave it to me.

I gazed at it. "You write too? What a coincid . . . ."

". . . Journalism. Newspaper and magazine pieces. Not at the same level as you, Gary."

I never know what to say to a comparison like that. "Oh, pshaw," seemed as good as anything.

"I want you to come and see me," you said. "I have a place on Grandview Lake."

"Okay."

"Some evening when we can watch the sun go down."

"Okay."

"For dinner," you said with a grin. "I do the cooking. You're safe."

"Okay. I'll call."

17

"My young wife can't cook—that's all I meant by that."

I said nothing to this. Were you bragging or complaining? I felt briefly miffed at you. Too much information or something, I guess.

"Great to see you, Gary."

"Great to see you too."

"You'll call?"

I nodded. "I'll call."

You placed your hand on my shoulder a moment, then moved into the milling crowd. I noticed then that your hair was tied back into a swan-coloured ponytail.

It seemed important at the time, the ponytail, underscoring our differences, the way we had perhaps accepted our times in a contrasting way. But it doesn't matter now. Zeitgeist. Paradigm. Ponytails. Time laughs at everything we human beings believe is important.

I NEARLY DIDN'T CALL, OF COURSE. One reaches an age when turning over rocks is liable to unearth a scorpion. Fifty years, you'd said. A lot of gap to fill in between our friendship then and any camaraderie that might lie ahead in the future. Then again, I was curious, not just about you and what had happened to you over the years, but why fate had brought us together again with our connected, respective states of youth so many years behind us. And I sensed something about that time lay unresolved. Closure is the word we use these days. Denouement. I discovered, in some dismay, that I probably needed this kind of final wrapping up. Now and then, once or twice a year, I would wake up in a sweat, a victim of the same old nightmare. Flames . . . acrid smoke . . . the odor of the burning and melting of sacrificial flesh. Maybe my unexpected, even extraordinary encounter with you heralded a kind of vital exorcism. For both of us.

So I telephoned you after all. We made a date. You gave me directions. I was to come to dinner. I took wine. And I wondered casually what I was getting into.

Strangely enough, Melanie didn't eat with us. "I have a

date with friends," she said. "I've already eaten." At some point a half hour later I noticed she was gone.

"Melanie . . ." I said to you somewhat later, in search of some kind of explanation.

"I'm crazy about her," you said. "Number four."

"Number four?"

"Wife number four."

"Oh."

"I don't know, Gary," you said. "Love has slapped me around at times. Like I've always needed some kind of beating for feeling things the way I did."

I watched you sip your scotch. By this time we'd eaten and cleaned up the dishes. Now we were filling in a few of the gaps so many years represent, sitting around your living room, watching the sun go down on the other side of the lake through a large picture window. Grandview was the name of the lake, you'd said. I could see now that the sunset was the reason for its moniker.

"Melanie remind you of anyone?" you asked me then.

"I don't know," I said, not wanting to say "no," not wanting to say, "yes."

"You sure?"

"Sorry."

"Kimberley."

I felt your eyes on me.

"You remember Kimberley, don't you?"

I nodded. "Absolutely," I said.

"But you didn't notice the resemblance?"

"I wasn't looking for it."

"Well," you said resignedly, bringing more scotch to your lips. "Maybe it's just me remembering too hard."

We talked about Meridian a bit, the village where we'd lived when we were kids. Neither one of us ever went back there for any reason. In fact, it seemed we shared a commitment to stay away from the place.

"I hear it's all built up, of course."

"Yeah. I hear that too," I said.

"So what about you?" you said. "Never married. What's that all about?"

I shrugged.

"Gay?"

I shook my head. "Just geeky."

You grinned.

"I'm told I'm hard to reach," I confessed, surprising myself with this admission.

"Me too. But it hasn't stopped me from trying to marry and settle down."

"Engaged once," I admitted. "Nearly engaged another time." Another shrug.

"But you get laid, don't you?"

"I get laid," I said with some embarrassment. "When the occasion presents itself."

"Viagra?"

"Never touch the stuff."

"Good. Apparently it would mess with my nitroglycerin." You grinned, joking I thought then.

I don't know how much we truly talked about. Certainly we kept coming back to Meridian, as a bond between us, as the village we once knew. Memories of this place occupied us most of the evening. You mentioned the fire that, while it didn't directly change the personalities of the people in our lives, seemed to redirect events that happened to them afterwards.

"I wrote a story about it," you said. "I'll have to dig it out of my files and let you have a look."

"Yes," was all I said.

Eventually I left. Melanie wasn't home yet, but I thought it was getting late. You and I promised to get together again, although I wasn't sure whether or not we truly meant to.

I drove through the pitch-black woods on the way to the highway, thinking how I couldn't remember whether or not Melanie looked like Kimberley. But I hadn't loved Kimberley in the shockingly deep way you had. And I hadn't felt the pain you must have felt back then, when society and fate finally caught up with you and shamed you for your feelings.

It struck me at that point how much feeling there had always been in your life, in contrast to the little I have felt. Some of us lean heavily towards feeling; others of us prefer to think our ways through life. At that moment, driving through the Muskoka darkness, I felt like some kind of Narziss to your passionate, ponytailed Goldmund. As Narziss, I felt trapped inside some wisdom that was emotionally incomplete.

IN THE DAYS AFTER YOUR FUNERAL, I go over your story, The Skeleton Club, a dozen times. And I break out a brand new scribbler and make hundreds of speculative notes. Until just a couple of months ago, I had not seen you for half a century. Yet something new in me wants to tell the truth about Meridian. I don't know why, except that the place and our childhood both intrigue me again. And writing novels about various pleasant agonies and various necessary truths, as I see them at least, is what I have always wanted to do with my life.

Besides, you are dead at last, Phillip, murdered by a defective heart. You cannot argue with me, although your version rests inside the ambitious short story you wrote, which sits on the right corner of my writing desk, something your widow remembered among the papers you left behind.

I seem to recall making you a promise back then, when we were just children. As I begin to write whatever it is I will write, I convince myself that writing it will help me keep my promise to you. And as I write and try to remember, I begin to believe, as writers do, that I can understand virtually anything, utilizing memory and imagination to reveal what lived inside your head, what hurt inside your heart.

ONE

. . . The skeleton that served as our mascot belonged to Dwight who was albino blonde and wore horn-rimmed glasses endlessly wrapped in white tape at one joint or another, or right in the middle just above his nose. Dwight was tall and bookish, thin, with a gravely intelligent mind. We knew he took advanced tutoring in subjects like algebra but this was something he refused to admit; he was shame-faced enough in the classroom whenever he turned in one hundred per cent on a test, which was nearly all the time.

The skeleton, about a foot long, was the same colour as Dwight's hair, its plastic yellowing here and there in tantalizingly bleached authenticity. It wouldn't stand, couldn't sit, but there was an eyebolt fastened to the top of the skull so that Irving—we called him Irving— could swing from a cord on a nearby tree branch or from the light fixture in Dwight's bedroom . . .

AT THE TIME, YOU THOUGHT MERIDIAN was perfect—perfection for a child isn't complicated. It would happen—years later during adulthood—that perfection became complex, a tiresome labyrinth of right and left turns, of going on and turning back, of pressing your nose against obstacles until it hurt, then falling back bloodied into the obscurity of human struggle.

But as a child, unaware of the impossibility of perfection, you decided Meridian approached perfection somehow, because it was your place. Eventually you and the village knew each other well. Its various cogs and wheels meshed effortlessly with your boyish perception and undemanding expectation. All familiarity was comfortable, all adventure sensory. You delighted in a perfectly sunny summer's day and a perfectly executed dive from the popular wooden raft in Brannigan's Cove just up the river from where you lived in Meridian that first year or two. There were other delights too, the usual pleasures, childish, attainable, innocent. The apparent ease in feeling, the fleeting nature of angst, the ardent simplicity in time and imagination. Meridian was enough. Enough, back then, was perfection.

Meridian was then on a major highway to Ottawa. At the end of the 1950s, highways went through towns instead of around them. There was a social element to a highway, an egalitarian ease in the way it brought the outside world into the centre of the community, before the focus of travel grew to reflect getting from Point A to Point B with as little interruption or delay as possible.

You liked highway travel as a boy. There was always a chance that your parents would stop at Benny's Fish and Chip Wagon, and, while there, something new and interesting would happen. It was in the going, not in the arriving that you found pleasure. Although you had no idea whether or not there was magic up ahead, it seemed promising enough just to be going in some direction.

No wonder, as a child, changing residence from one community to another was, itself, a collaboration with possibility. Too young to be included in your parents' reasons for moving, you assumed instinctively that only opportunity lay ahead. You liked the future as much as the present. Your past was best forgotten. So that when you and your parents moved to Meridian at the end of the school year in 1956, you decided without evidence of any kind that living there was going to be fun.

YOUR FATHER WAS IN A GOOD MOOD the day he drove you and your mother around the village in his 1949 Chevrolet, a couple of weeks before you moved. His mood prevailed even though your mother was subdued, a little anxious, a little unresponsive. It was a pleasant June day of crisp, blue sky and pillowy, drifting clouds. From your place in the back seat, you gaped in silence at the highlights of the tour, leaving conversation to your parents; you were skilled in knowing this was one of those times it was best to remain silent.

There was a tension in the car. Although you could sense it, you didn't understand it entirely. You simply left it there to loiter like a vagrant at the edge of your growing excitement. You supposed, though, that it was the move that made your parents awkward with one another. You were aware of what lay ahead, two more weeks of school back in South Clarion, the village where you'd lived for five years, then the frenzy of packing, left almost entirely to your mother, much to her chagrin. But once you moved, it was likely things would improve again after you arrived in Meridian to stay.

Certainly the village looked large enough to kindle possibility. You heard your father tell your mother it was twice the size of South Clarion, although, to you, it seemed much larger than that.

"There's more to do here," your father said, navigating his black torpedo-shaped sedan down one silent, well-groomed street after another.

"Like what?" your mother asked.

"Clubs, ball teams, choral groups."

You'd heard bits and pieces of this discussion before, the day your father had returned from Meridian the first time, having spent the day accepting his new job, renting a home and registering you for school. Today's tour, like the debate over the promised activities, was an opportunity to reinforce your father's view that he had been right to decide to move. Being proved right, you already knew, was something your father especially cherished.

"See?" he said. "There's the bowling alley. There's the curling club. And there's the hockey rink. Phillip can play hockey here."

"I guess so," your mother said.

Hockey, you reflected. Did they want you to play hockey?

"Do you think Phillip will be happy here?" your mother asked now, glancing into the back seat at you, looking pretty in the way she could when she appeared perplexed.

"Of course. It's perfect for a boy like Phillip."

You almost spoke up at that point to reassure them both, but you felt uncertain of yourself. For an interminably long time you'd been a child. As far as you knew, you were going to be a child much longer still.

You sensed this move was important where your father was concerned. Normally he was not a man to shilly-shally, as he liked to put it himself, but the tour of Meridian that day was unusually thorough. You concluded he must be hopeful life would be better here.

He parked across the street from the Anglican church so that your mother could have a look at the place where they would worship. The building didn't make much of an impression on you. All churches tended to look the same to you, formidable and cold, their crosses clinging to a front wall or stabbing at the sky from the top of a weathered steeple. This church was made of stone, with a thick stone balustrade housing the wooden stairs outside leading up in both directions to the front doors. The church hall was in the basement, your father said, and you noticed its entrance around the side. Although it was daytime, the outside light had been left on over the door and the naked bulb glowed forlornly under a metal hood as it waited again for the purpose it derived from darkness.

Church was important to your parents. Both of them sang in the choir in South Clarion and assumed they'd be asked to do so here as well.

"I hope they're not snooty," your mother said of the

congregation. "I couldn't bear it if they thought they were better than us."

"Oh Carol, let's not be silly, okay?" Then more gently your father added. "Why would they think they're better than us?"

"It's just that it's so close to Ottawa."

"Won't matter where Ottawa is," your father said as he put the car in gear and drove away.

He took you by your school. It seemed terrifyingly large and square in the distance, situated in the centre of an unusually large piece of open property. Red Brick, three storeys. The school yard consisted of two large fields separated by a ditch. A row of pines grew along sections of this shallow ditch. At each end of the outer field you could see the backstop of a waiting ball diamond.

"Whaddyuh think, Phillip?" your mother asked, her lips tight as she spoke.

"Looks great," you said, gazing at the school to make certain what you said was true.

"Of course it's great," your father said. "You're going to love it here."

He drove by the grocery store where he would be working as the butcher. Red & White Food Lockers, it was called. Posters listing the specials for the week clung to every window. Each parking space, angled towards the building, was filled with a car or pickup.

"Joe Langley, the store manager, lives right next door," your father explained, pointing out a humble insulbrick house on the other side of a driveway to the left of the store. Lilacs grew along the driveway separating house from business. The porch on the house had once been white but the paint was peeling badly. Your mother noticed this but didn't mention it.

"What about our house?" she asked at that point. "Don't we get to see where we're going to be living?"

"Huh? Oh! Of course, well, the outside of it anyway. The owners haven't moved out yet. We don't want to look pushy."

He drove away and shortly stopped on the gravel

shoulder at the edge of another street. You and your mother peered over the crest of a steep hill at a pale green and white bungalow, and at the river just beyond.

"I hope they mow the lawn before we come here to live."

"I'm sure they will, Carol," your father said with a bit of an edge in his voice.

"It's on the water," you said, more or less to change the subject.

This pleased your father. "I'll teach you to fish," he said. "And swim."

"Okay."

"I just wish we could stay in this house longer than two years," your mother now lamented, interrupting the accommodation you had reached with your father. "We've moved so much, Bert. I'm so tired of it."

Your father said nothing. You glanced at his fists wrapped around the steering wheel. His knuckles were white and huge, enough to remind you he'd been a fighter when he was a boy. He'd been raised in the country, he often reminded his friends. "Farm boys," he would say, "all know how to fight."

"We'll find another place to live when the time comes," he was saying now. "There are lots of places here to rent. Maybe by then we can buy."

"Don't get me wrong, Bert. It's just when I think about moving, the packing, the cleaning . . ."

". . . I know. I know."

The way you understood it, the owner of the bungalow was in the air force and had been transferred out west for two years. When he and his family returned, you'd have to move out again.

Your mother had mentioned this to you a few days before, back home in South Clarion, the evening your father was working late. She'd sat you on the couch beside her—the house in South Clarion sulky and brooding, jammed with cartons and piles of newspaper—to explain her laments. You thought she might have been crying earlier, although she didn't mention it. Instead she just complained about packing and scrubbing, about leaving people behind. She put her hand on your knee afterwards and gave you a sad little smile until you felt sorry for her.

"You understand what I mean, don't you, Phillip?"

"Sure," you'd said, relieved that you could satisfy her in this way.

The tour now over, your father put the Chevrolet in gear and drove the seventy-five miles back to South Clarion. As you drew closer to the village, you thought the tension between your parents had now begun to recede.

BECAUSE YOU FELT YOU SHOULD, you tried to feel sad about leaving South Clarion. On moving day several of your parents' friends came over to say goodbye. Some of the men helped with the move, lugging furniture out the front door, across the wooden porch, and into a livestock truck your father had borrowed from a farmer a few miles away. The truck had been swept clean for the move but still gave off the rich aroma of cow manure.

Your mother cried that day, off and on it seemed, and you thought you should cry too, to keep her company. But you couldn't. So you kept out of everyone's way. You sat down on the steps at the edge of the wide porch and watched the men laugh, grunt and swear as they carried furniture and boxes up a ramp to stack them in the truck. No one acknowledged you until they moved your parents' upright Heintzmann towards the truck. The grunting and cursing increased and your father told you to get out of the way. "Kids," he remarked to his friends, knowing they would understand.

You supposed you couldn't be sad about leaving South Clarion because Meridian seemed so promising. It had a river instead of a creek, ball diamonds with lights, and intriguing stores and shops on both sides of the highway running through the centre of town. You'd had lunch the day of the tour in a restaurant right downtown. There'd been a large ice drink cooler and a clock on the wall that said Coca-Cola on its face, and a jukebox in the corner, although someone had unplugged it and you could see the snake of the cord in a coiled pool not far away. South Clarion, on the other hand, didn't even have a restaurant although there was a general store.

Granted, you'd liked playing along the shore of the creek the previous summer, catching tadpoles and letting them go again, poking at a discarded snakeskin with a stick, wondering why the yellow and black colouring had turned blue where it lay tangled on the branches of the underbrush. But you weren't going to miss the creek any longer, the way you might have missed it once.

It had relinquished its mystique the previous September when Danny Clemens had suggested skipping school to hang around under the bridge. You'd ended up getting caught when your mother passed by overhead on her way to the general store. Enraged, she dragged both of you through the village, depositing Danny with his mother and tugging you back to school. She pushed you into your classroom and demanded in front of everyone that you be given the strap. When your teacher didn't want to, your mother ordered you into the teacher's office where—despite Miss Robinson's urgent protests that you were one of her best pupils and never caused her any trouble—she gave you the strap herself. After that you didn't go back to the creek very often; the creek seemed an accomplice to your pain.

Although there'd been other lickings prior to this, you remembered this one at school because it filled you with so much shame. Afterwards, when you sat down at your desk, your face felt wet and hot with tears and embarrassment. Your classmates wouldn't look at you and this only made it worse. For a while Miss Robinson stood by your desk after your mother left, to make sure you were all right, to be certain that what she liked about you didn't completely shatter.

That licking at school was probably the worst. Or maybe the one the previous year, one morning when you were in church.

Your father this time. Sunday morning. Both your

parents wearing choir gowns, sitting in the loft at the front of the church. You were in the front pew, hardly old enough for school, a clip-on tie fastened to the collar of your shirt, the metal clip sticking into your throat now that it had popped undone. The pain made you dizzy and you began to squirm. You kept trying to disengage the clip from your flesh, inserting your fingers into the shirt because the metal was very sharp, aware that during the service you weren't allowed to remove the tie. The pain and dizziness increased, you couldn't stop fidgeting, not even when your parents looked down from the choir loft, your mother from the soprano section, your father from the tenor, transmitting angry glances to warn you to behave.

But you couldn't help it. The metal clip kept digging at your throat and now you'd begun to gasp. You felt lonely and tortured. No one sat in the pew beside you. There was no one nearby to understand what was wrong with you.

Shortly, his face beet red in embarrassment, your father stood up and left the loft in the middle of the sermon. Taking you roughly by the arm, he marched you down the aisle as quickly as he could. You couldn't talk, couldn't explain yourself, the metal clip still cut into your throat.

In the vestibule at the front of the church he gave you a licking, reminding you with a hiss that this was church and you should stifle your sobs of pain. Afterwards—it was all by now a painful blur—he marched you back up the aisle past rows of wooden people, the wooden congregation gazing at their minister from their rigid, wooden pews. Your father sat you down again while the minister continued his sermon. The entire room gazed at Rev. Collins like a workshop of human carvings. The clip cut into your flesh again and you breathed deeply through your nose, desperate to behave.

Somehow you didn't faint. Your heart ignored the pain in your throat. How could the physical agony compete with the sensation of being so ashamed? It was one of those days you realized that shame is more powerful than pain. And life can—and often will—resort to being unfair.

Afterwards the deep scratches at your throat cleared up your innocence. Your parents confessed, less to you than to each other, what a shame the incident had been. But your mother put the tie back into a drawer with your socks and underwear until she remembered to buy you another one before Sunday rolled around again.

These were the two lickings that were probably the worst. Because there were people around to see—friends, guests and neighbours. Like your parents' friends were supposed to approve of this kind of discipline. You sensed, at a very young age, approval from their peers was deeply important to your parents.

TWO

. . . The club was actually born that spring, while the last restless days of school were still unfolding, when all of us spent more time looking out the window where the sun was greening the grass than we did with our books. Just Dwight and me at first; we were The Skeleton Club. Then Chuck joined, fat Chuck who never wore bluejeans and who took the oath of secrecy in the woods behind the school, wearing an expression of tolerant disdain, Irving held by a string in one hand over his head, his other hand placed over his heart, mumbling "I swear" in embarrassment at the end of the ceremony. Billy, Chuck's cousin, also joined The Skeleton Club because Billy belonged to whatever Chuck did. Billy was fat as well, though not as fat as Chuck. In obesity too, he could only attempt to catch up to his older cousin . . .

PERHAPS MERIDIAN ONLY SEEMED PERFECT because South Clarion hadn't been. Or maybe, growing up a little more, you'd begun to learn how to survive in a world less fair than your parents had told you it would be.

Even Meridian, those first few years, demanded passing a number of tests. Eric Petersen, for instance, dogged you all the way home from school most of that first September in Grade Three, knocking your books out of your hands, pushing you around, trying to make you cry. Until one day, provoked beyond the limits of your frustration, you punched him in the nose. The instinctive blow didn't do much damage, but blood trickled out of one nostril. He was transformed instantly into something fragile, standing there with his hands over his face, tears running down his cheeks, glistening in the cracks between his fingers. At that point the war between you, the skirmishes you hadn't understood in the first place, abruptly ended. Eventually you even became friends.

There were tests on the home front too, so difficult to understand as a child, from the place you were compelled to occupy on the periphery of events. The night two men from South Clarion came to call not long after darkness fell, for instance. They were noisy and drunk, and you got up out of bed to go to your window, alarmed because your father was still at work. You saw the dust settling where their pickup had rolled to a stop. The two men were familiar to you, one of them dark, the other blonde; they'd helped your parents on moving day in South Clarion. After you heard your mother sit them down in the kitchen, hushing their boisterous conversation, you climbed back into bed, knowing she'd be in to check on you. You kept your eyes closed, pretending to be asleep, when she peeked into your room, and you didn't open them again until you heard the scraping of chairs from the kitchen, your mother's laughter, the rise and fall of drunken voices.

Eventually your father came home—you heard his car pull into the driveway. A brief silence followed. Then the murmur of conversation gradually crescendoed into cries. "Get the hell out of my house," your father yelled.

After that you heard truck doors slamming shut, your father's last angry profanity. The two men departed in name-calling protest, their tires spinning in the gravel. And at the top of the hill, there was a squeal of rubber on the pavement and the sound of the retreating engine. Then silence— ominous, deep, ultimately nearly suffocating. In the aftermath, if your parents were talking, they were conversing only in whispers.

Your bedroom door opened afterwards. Like a good son,

you feigned sleep, even with a narrow ribbon of light bathing your face, prying at your eyelids. Eventually you slept and next morning everything was so normal it was like you'd only dreamed the events of the night before.

Your father taught you to swim the following summer at the bottom of the yard. He climbed the concrete wall at the water's edge and threw you into the river. You submerged and floundered at first, then rose terrified to the surface, paddling clumsily with arms and legs, your terror gradually giving way to a powerful exhilaration. "A person swims when he has to," your father said, standing on the concrete wall, his arms crossed, his head nodding in self-satisfaction. "Even animals know how to swim. Right?"

"Yes," you gasped from the water. "Yes."

You began to play organized baseball the following year and your father began to coach. Only nine, you were the youngest and smallest on the team, condemned by ineptitude to stand in the lonely wasteland of the outfield where nothing ever happened and you couldn't do any harm. You daydreamed intensely out there in the distance, an old hand-me-down trapper on your left hand, its thumb warped by time and dampness. Sometimes you turned to gaze at a second diamond in the distance, the one beyond the bleachers, watching tiny youngsters there, playing a ball game of their own, one that tended to make more sense than the one you competed in yourself, because it was far away, because you were not participating.

"Phillip! Phillip!" your father cried one night, his voice barging into your reflections.

When you turned from the game being played on the other diamond, you saw his face was urgent, even angry. He gestured frantically towards the darkness overhead.

"Phillip! Look up!"

And you glanced up, a being separate from all the confusion taking place in your own infield, where runners sped from bag to bag and voices cried out in delight, cheering one another on.

There, over your head, was a fly ball suffering desperately from gravity, shining silver in the glow of the lights flooding the diamond in the August darkness. You didn't move except to raise the trapper over your head to shield yourself from harm. The ball forced the bent thumb of your glove aside, nestling comfortably in the pocket it had opened.

It was the third out, you learned later, the last inning, a victory for your teammates. Bewildered by the ceremony of it all, you cowered as your team ran from the infield towards you, arriving amid noisy cheers, determined to carry you from right field in celebration. Your father beamed proudly from his station at the dugout. He seemed so satisfied, you didn't have the heart to tell him you didn't understand what had actually happened, that the amazing catch was just an accident.

It was a major turning point in your childhood. You never did play hockey—you found skating with a stick outside in the bitter winter elements a cold, clumsy, and spiteful exercise. But baseball grew to be a passion. The next spring, a year older and much taller, you spent two Saturdays in May caddying at the Jewish golf course until, with the money you'd earned, you could buy a fielder's glove and a catcher's mitt for the summer of baseball ahead. It was the spring you and I became friends. You practiced throwing and catching with me each afternoon after school. Your father and coach put you behind the plate. You'd been promoted to the infield.

MERIDIAN GREW TO BE HOME. The first two years there, your father introduced you to life along a river shore. He bought a small rowboat and motor and taught you how to fish. You passed the time some evenings trolling for bass or anchored in the bulrushes, fishing for mudcats.

For your father, fishing was a tribute to the ceremony of silence, watching the bobber, studying the line, instructions to you whispered in a prayerlike monotone as grave as being in church. You'd return to the house before dark, braving the last few minutes of a mosquito-infested twilight, having said less than a dozen words. But you enjoyed the silence as much as your father did—it was life's truce between the skirmishes you now realized punctuated the act of being alive.

Fishing with your father didn't last. The owners of your bungalow along the river returned, you had to move away from the water's edge, and your father sold the boat because he didn't need it any longer. Your father was fickle with his hobbies. He loved them passionately at first, then became quickly bored with them. He would treat his pastimes this way as long as he lived, you mentioned to me that night in Muskoka just before you died.

Your family rented another house, a two-storey stucco structure directly across the street from the Anglican church all of you attended. This house had a stone wall along the driveway and you would sit on top of it, whiling away the hours in a vast array of reflections. You liked this house, it seemed more accommodating than the bungalow on the river had been, safer somehow, more secure, more permanent.

Or perhaps it was just that as each season passed, the village grew more familiar, shrank a little bit as you grew bigger to fit inside it. Your favourite summer haunt was the pair of ball diamonds where you played Little League and your father played competitive softball with the men—pitching for Meridian with a ferocity you found similar to his anger. You gathered here with friends and spent your meagre allowance at the canteen, buying potato chips from Fat Hilda, splitting the foil bag down the side to sprinkle liberal doses of vinegar and noisy squirts of ketchup all over them. While the men played softball in front of the bleachers packed with loyal, catcalling Meridians, you and your friends gathered some distance from the stands, wrestling, talking and laughing, the best way you could figure out to be children those days, to be seen and never heard.

On summer afternoons, it was the river that called to you. Bicycling the two miles to Brannigan's Cove, wearing a bathing suit and t-shirt, you'd wade out from the beach, then swim over a thick patch of clutching, weaving river weeds until you reached the deeper water and a wooden raft beyond. From the raft you dove endlessly into the deep cobalt mystery of the river, clawing for its bottom, feeling courageous in the deeps. Even when a rain shower came up and your friends went home, you'd stay behind on the raft alone, diving, swimming, reaching stubbornly for the bottom. Finally, only when you were exhausted, would you pedal wearily home.

YOUR PARENTS JOINED EVERYTHING IN TOWN, it seemed. Your father not only played softball but signed up for a five-pin bowling league and took up curling as well. He joined Meridian's new Kiwanis Club which held its luncheon meetings in the village's only reasonably fine restaurant, The White Pelican. Your mother wasn't quite so independent. Save for regular morning coffee klatches with the women along your street, her interests were strictly musical. As they had in South Clarion, your parents enlisted in the St. Luke's Anglican Church choir and, later on, the new Meridian Choral Society.

For as long as you could remember, singing and music had been an integral part of life in the Barrett household. Your parents took turns playing the piano jammed tightly along a wall in their tiny living room. Even upstairs in your room or outside where the music seeped through an open window, you knew, by their contrasting rhythms and skills, which parent had sat down on the long piano bench to play. Your mother, everyone said, possessed the most raw talent, playing by ear as well as note. Your father played by note only, stubbornly plodding through complex sonatas and études, repeating entire bars until each mistake had been corrected. Although he had a fine voice, his musicianship was as much the result of determination as it was any kind of visible gift.

Whenever guests came over for the evening, everyone gathered at the piano to sing, your mother's fingers dancing nimbly over the keys. Your father would stand at her left shoulder, turning the pages of the sheet music, singing harmonies, sometimes acting as the conductor of the concert. Your parents even settled their differences of opinion with music, ending long, antagonistic silences with a necessary rehearsal of an anthem scheduled for the following Sunday.

You too were required to sing, not only at social gatherings at home, but as part of the school choir and as a soloist in Ottawa area music festivals. You hated performing in public. With butterflies twitching in your stomach, you'd climb the stairs to the stage, trembling in terror. After the festival adjudicator rang his bell for you to begin, you dashed through your piece of music so that you could hurry from the stage. Fortunately for you—and to everyone's dismay—your voice began to change shortly after your eleventh birthday. Your parents and the music teacher concurred that your days as a competing soprano were over.

After this, while you matured precociously, music evolved into a spectator sport for you. On a tiny portable record player that skipped whimsically across the surface of your tiny collection of 78s and 45s—until you taped a lead fishing sinker to the arm—you listened happily to the gentler side of rock 'n' roll, the only music your parents would accept. You'd become enamoured of Elvis Presley's Jailhouse Rock, but one night, just before the eight p.m. musical curfew your parents had imposed, your bedroom door burst open and noisily struck the wall. Your father stood there a moment, veins popping with rage. Then, without a word, he stormed to the record player, dragged the arm over the record with a ziiuuup, picked up the 78 and broke it over his knee. Afterwards he turned and stomped out of the room without explanation, slamming the door shut behind him.

Resigned, you went to the record player and turned the power off. Calmly you went to the bathroom and brushed your teeth. Then you went to bed, determined not to cry, determined not to admit you would never get used to the sudden eruption of your father's anger. You left the shards of Jailhouse Rock on the floor until next morning when it didn't hurt so much to have to pick them up. You were learning,

Phillip Barrett, it was wise to sublimate your pain.

BY THE TIME MERIDIAN CELEBRATED its centennial in 1959, your father was well established in the community. He was heavily involved that year—under the auspices of the Kiwanis Club—with some of the planning for the celebration's various events. Like most of the men in Meridian, he grew a beard—it emerged on his face dark and impenetrable—to compete in the centennial beard-growing contest. He attended organizational meetings frequently in the period leading up to the festivities and, during the four days of the July celebration, was busy helping to oversee its various activities.

Your mother complained about his busy schedule one day that spring, after you came home from school and the two of you were alone for lunch. Sitting at the kitchen table while you ate chicken noodle soup, she drank coffee and smoked cigarettes, her hair a stern network of bobbypins and curlers. She gazed at you that day as if she wasn't sure who you were or where you'd come from.

"You're a good-looking boy," she said at last.

You blushed.

"Phillip, you have to say 'thank you' when someone tells you you're good-looking. Even if it's only your mother. We've raised you better than that." Annoyed, she crushed her cigarette into the rubble of orange butts already in the ashtray.

"Sorry, Mom," you replied. "I was embarrassed."

"Don't be embarrassed. There's nothing to be embarrassed about. Just say, 'thank you.'"

"Thank you," you murmured uncomfortably.

"Your father is a good-looking man too," she mused. "Maybe that's why he always does exactly what he pleases."

You didn't know what to say. Nothing came to mind. You were aware only that you felt awkward. Talking with your mother wasn't like talking with your own friends, when your words came out with an ease you didn't have to think about. It was difficult to know exactly what she expected.

You felt like a traitor whenever she criticized your father. He was your father after all.

"Someday," your mother said, " you being good-looking, a woman will want to marry you. I want you to remember, when you get married, you have to know how to give and take. When you get married you have to share things fairly. You can't just be thinking about what you want to do." Glancing at you intently, she reached out and took your hand. "I'm trying to teach you things your father never had a chance to learn, with his upbringing on the farm. You see what I'm saying?"

"Yes, Mom," you said, wishing she'd remove her hand.

She did, but only to light another cigarette. "It's not easy living with your father. Sure, he works hard, doesn't drink, always does the best he can, but we don't have much and he gets too involved in things. He's a good man but he's so independent." She drifted off a moment. "Can I be honest with you, Phillip?"

"Sure, Mom."

"There were other men I could've married. I was popular. Sometimes I wonder . . ." She fell silent, then forced herself to leave her reverie behind. "Never forget that you're father's such a decent man," she concluded after a moment.

"I know, Mom."

"Anyway, the point is, when you get married, make your wife your main concern. And remember, when I get mad at you, it's because your mother's been through a lot. You won't understand these things until you grow up. But take my word for it."

"Okay, Mom."

"You're a good boy, Phillip."

Having said this, she glanced at the electric clock humming above the refrigerator, its cord twisted and brown. "You'd better get back to school. You're going to be late."

Both of you got up together. She turned towards the sink. With her back to you she seemed thinner, browbeaten in some way. Yet, as she rinsed out your soup bowl under the tap, she began to hum a song. You left the house wondering, without knowing how, if you'd cheered her up somehow.

THE CENTENNIAL CELEBRATION early that summer seemed so large to you it was nearly overwhelming. The entertainment, the costumes, the parades and picnics, the midway, the crowds.

Cautious about heights, you'd never been on a ferris wheel before. I talked you into it, suggesting, once you got used to it, the ferris wheel would be fun. But when our turn arrived to wait at the top for the lower gondola to be loaded, an acrophobia set in so terrifying you panicked. I panicked as well . . . you were rocking the gondola so much. I wrestled with you to restrain you, telling you to knock it off. Your panic seemed to last forever and I noticed people were staring at us from below. When our gondola reached the bottom again, the tattooed carney operating the ride shut it down and ordered us out. You were shaky and hesitant, so he grabbed you by the arm and dragged you down the wooden platform before pushing you towards the exit.

"Hey!" I said. "Leave him alone!"

But the carnie ignored me. "Don't come back here, kid," he said. "I see your face around here again, I'll kick your arse." He turned to me. "You too, kid."

Some of the local teenagers lined up nearby to board the ride began to laugh at us. "Asshole," someone murmured, and everyone laughed harder still.

You didn't like the crowds, you said later. The crowds seemed violent and mean. I learned you sometimes perceived a hostility in a crowd that I have never felt in quite the same way.

Hostility the next night too, when the singer from Country Hoedown performed in the ball diamond, you and a crowd of strangers pressing against the stage. As the singer performed, some in the audience began to toss nickels onto the stage. They bounced and clattered on the plywood there while everybody laughed. When he finished his last song, the singer bent down, scooped up a few of the nickels and tossed them back into the crowd. Then he departed, heading for a small trailer not far away, leaving the band to fend for itself.

"Should kick the shit out of him," a young man standing beside you said.

"Yeah," a couple of voices chimed in.

Frightened again, mystified by the anger all around you, you slipped quickly out of the crowd. There was no policeman there to mitigate your fear. Meridian, you'd overhead your father say proudly more than once, preferred to police itself.

In the end, nothing happened to the singer. But there were times, you realized, when people gathered into crowds, that Meridian wasn't so perfect after all. Sometimes Meridian was an angry place. Sometimes it conveyed a confusing spite.

THREE

. . . *Of course you'd have to know our village, the way Highway Sixteen hurried through it as if it couldn't wait to leave town, stores on both sides of the street, barely a dozen in all, not counting the car dealership and the ball diamond at the west end of town. You'd have to know there was a river that was only a river from April until May, before it shrank to a creek again. And you'd have to know most of the houses were constructed on streets running diagonally to the highway, except for my house and a half dozen others located directly along the road, all of them fronted by paint-peeling porches where people sat most summer evenings to watch the traffic go by.*

We thought we understood the village well. We'd been there forever; no one seemed to move in and no one ever left. We'd learned there were stores that were amenable to kids, others where we weren't as welcome. We didn't go into Stedman's, for instance, unless our mothers were with us. We didn't go into the restaurant that everyone called The Tea Room because that was where the teenagers hung out. We didn't go into D'Angelo's either, where the Colonial bus pulled in a couple of times a day, because Mr. D'Angelo wasn't partial to kids. And we never went into Winston's, the feed and implement store, because it was getting terribly rundown and there wasn't much to look at anymore . . .

YOU SAW KIMBERLEY FOR THE FIRST TIME at the

43

end of that same summer. By then the centennial celebrations were over and three weeks had passed since Findlay's General Store had burned down one night, taking the life of Mrs. Findlay and driving the remaining Findlay family permanently out of town. The fire, Mrs. Findlay's death, and the confusing aftermath were on every tongue for a few days after the tragedy until, quite suddenly, as if by mutual agreement, it was rarely mentioned again. As September loomed, the silence deepened even further. In fact, at Basil's Barber Shop, which, for the men, served the function of oral local newspaper, the topic never again came up. Yet it lingered in the silence at the edge of every conversation, a ghost exiled to the fringes of an otherwise corporeal social gathering. Silence—in the barber shop where everything that happened in Meridian was discussed, analyzed and ultimately acted upon—was unusual, especially where tragedy was concerned. But this time it was as if there was an unspoken pact behind the notion that everyone should let the topic drop. As a child, you did so unquestioningly, carried along on the relentless tide that is adult human convention.

On the Saturday morning that Kimberley eventually walked by, the men discussed other subjects instead; Joey Smallwood, who had just won another election in Newfoundland, Nikita Kruschev—regarded as Mephisto himself—and Fidel Castro, the man everyone had begun to change his viewpoint about, thanks to the influence the U.S. media had on Canadian public opinion. On this day in particular, you sat in the barbershop waiting your turn, wondering what Castro had done to cause him to fall out of favour so quickly. Not long ago, everyone in Meridian had seemed to like him. You found adult changes of heart confusing. Sometimes adults made about as much sense as the weather.

Today's haircut was to be your back-to-school model. The brushcut you'd endured at the beginning of June had grown out and today's cut, short-back-and-sides, would replace it. This was the pattern your parents had adopted in recent years, longer hair on top in the winter months and the despised brushcut at the beginning of summer.

Still, you enjoyed the barbershop, the pleasant scents of talc and aftershave, and an array of grooming items you never saw anywhere else—straight razors and the belt on which they were sharpened, electric clippers, scissors of various shapes and sizes, bottles of lotions and potions provocatively coloured green or yellow, and the gigantic mirror along the main wall which, in reflection, doubled the size of the room. All of these devices attracted you. Granted, most of the men smoked, but the door was open and it drifted lazily outside, pipe, cigar, and cigarette smoke floating seductively by your nostrils on its way to infinity.

You liked men here in the barbershop more than anywhere else. Here they were relaxed and patient. Here they had more time, grew unusually jovial or reflective. You suspected they visited the barbershop to enjoy the wait for their turn more than the trim or the shave they were waiting for. And sometimes after the cut, men would remain for one more pipe of Sail and the remainder of a particularly compelling conversation. You thought tobacco was mystical then, in the way it gave discussion syntax. Men smoked to get to the end of a discussion.

Basil Grisham, the barber, was a short, trim man in his early fifties. You were secretly amused by his baldness, the way a bald barber seemed like a pilot with no airplane to fly. But bald he was, with a grey fringe around his head just above his ears. He wore a white smock with several combs and a pen nestled in the front pocket. His shoes were tan and soft, as comfortable as sneakers. And his polyester slacks didn't have cuffs like the trousers the other men wore. Cuffs were on the way out and Basil Grisham knew it. He was a bit of a dandy; everything fit his tiny body so perfectly. He was the only middle-aged man you knew who didn't have a paunch.

"H'lo, John" or "H'lo, Fred," he'd say when someone entered the shop. "H'lo, Bert. H'lo, Phillip." Like he'd taken the hell out of hello, where it had never belonged in the first place.

John MacLean, Meridian's most well-to-do farmer, was in the chair this morning. When he talked with Grisham he spoke directly into the mirror so that what he said bounced back again to include the other men waiting their turn in chairs along the windows, the sun exploding brightly across the red-tiled floor. Except for your father and Jim Connelly, the manager of the Bank of Nova Scotia, the rest of the men were farmers too, Conservatives every one of them.

This summer was a happy time for Conservatives. There was a mood among the men that what could be counted on could, indeed, be counted on, which, perhaps, is what conservatism is all about—a guarantee that nothing much should, or would, change. Leslie Frost had taken seventy-one seats in the Ontario Legislature in June, the Queen of England and the Duke of Edinburgh were touring the country, and John Diefenbaker was still prime minister. Diefenbaker had cancelled the Avro Arrow project and there was hardly anyone who didn't know someone who knew someone else who had lost a job because of it. But still, the Avro Arrow sacrilege aside, the world nonetheless exuded a comforting solidity and this was what mattered most.

MacLean was one of the few men who still retained the beard he'd grown for the Meridian centennial beard-growing contest. Most of the other men, your father included, had removed their beards the day after the contest was over. It was a permissible oddity that MacLean would break the rules, because he enjoyed a relative wealth and respect in the community. Otherwise, in those days, a man with a beard was believed to be rebellious. And rebelliousness was something that shouldn't be encouraged.

"You gonna keep that patch of grey on your face?" Don Stuart asked from his chair not far from the door.

"You bet I am," MacLean replied, "until Olive won't kiss me anymore."

Everyone laughed.

"Keep me warm this winter," he added, encouraged by the guffaws.

This inspired someone to predict that the winter of 1959-1960 was going to be a harsh one. No one argued with him.

"Saw Rhonda ride past the other day on the stallion," George Manson mentioned to MacLean afterwards.

MacLean nodded and, with practised ease, Grisham's scissors stopped snipping for a second to accommodate the movement.

MacLean was known less for the size of his herd of Holsteins than he was for his Palomino horses. And he'd become respected in recent years for the outstanding blonde good looks of his daughter Rhonda too. There was something about MacLean that seemed anointed, coronated by destiny, like he had a more profound right to beautiful things than other people did, offspring included.

"S'pect someone will be taking her off your hands before too long, John. S'pect there's a line up."

"Well," reported MacLean, "I thought it might be young Marty Brickman, but it seems Rhonda broke it off. That's what Olive says."

"Nice boy, Brickman," Grisham said.

MacLean sighed. "I know. Rhonda can be stubborn. When she takes a notion, there's no talkin' her out of it."

Each man fell silent, toying privately with various provocative, but unsubstantiated rumours he'd heard about Rhonda MacLean. But someone eased the silence by suggesting, "things'll work out just fine—it's just a matter of giving it time."

More or less to show he was master of the conversation as well as his daughter, MacLean adroitly changed the topic by bringing up his dog, a greyhound named Bailey. "He's been growling and snapping at people," he told the other men. "I'm wondering if I'll have to put him down. If I do, Olive'll have a conniption."

Everyone murmured their assent. A dog gone vicious wasn't good for much except patrolling a junk yard.

Feeling safe about mentioning his daughter again, sensing he had unsettled the other men in the barbershop in some nebulous, comforting way, MacLean announced that Rhonda would be working with Jim Connelly at the bank in a couple of weeks. He spoke this news into the mirror on the wall in front of him, his grey eyes falling on the image of Connelly reflected there. In the medium of the mirror their gazes locked for a second.

Not that everyone didn't already know the story behind the arrangement. Don Stuart's wife, Blanche, a longtime teller at the bank, had already spread the news that MacLean had been in to see Connelly and, him being a large depositor, how the two men had come to an agreement which would give MacLean's daughter her first job. Rhonda had just graduated from business school in Ottawa. Apparently she was qualified. If only, well, if only she'd stop being Rhonda MacLean. Still, with this background information secretly behind them, the men grunted and nodded benignly after John MacLean made his announcement, each one of them affirming that it was nice that Rhonda had found a job.

Done cutting MacLean's hair, Grisham took the brush to the back of his neck, removing the residue of what he had trimmed. Then the farmer got up, hitched up his trousers, and strolled over to your father for a moment.

"How you been keeping, Bert?" he asked.

"I'm fine, John."

"And you, young master Phillip?" This with a wink.

"Fine, thank you," you said.

"Polite boy," he said to your father in a complimentary way. Then he winked again. "Nice looking too."

"Thank you," you murmured uncomfortably, remembering what your mother had told you a couple of months before.

"Growing like a weed," your father said.

"Stand up, Son," instructed MacLean.

Glancing nervously at your father, you stood up.

"Nearly as tall as me."

"Can't keep him in clothes," your father said.

MacLean winked at your father again. "Nice looking

boy," he said before he went out the door.

"Who's next?" the barber asked as he put down the broom he'd used to sweep MacLean's leavings into the corner.

"Your turn, Phillip," your father said.

You headed for the chair.

It was then that Kimberley Smith walked by on the sidewalk just outside.

"There's the Smith girl," murmured Don Stuart, who happened to be sitting sideways in his chair at the window.

Everyone turned to look.

You didn't have time to see much yourself, only a glimpse of her, mostly from the back. Later, it would seem more of an illusion than an actual sighting as she passed— tanned legs, pastel pink shorts, a white jersey, chestnut hair cut relatively short. Then she was gone.

"Pretty little thing," mused Stuart aloud.

And most of the men grunted in thoughtful agreement.

"Of course I don't think their real name is Smith," someone said. "Word around Meridian is they might be Jews."

"Jews?" said Stuart.

Your father did not comment. He'd fought with the air force in the last few months of the war and one of the reasons he'd done so, he said now, was because of what, it had been discovered, the Nazis had done to the Jews. When people criticized Jews, your father only nodded, waiting for the topic to move on. But he joined in when people complained about Quebec. He admitted he didn't have much use for the people in Quebec.

"Heard the same thing myself," said Grisham about the apparent Jewishness of the Smiths, snapping the hair out of the white gown he intended to clip around your neck and gesturing to you to sit up straighter in the chair.

"It's all pretty mysterious, I hear," continued Stuart, running his fingers through his thick, brown hair. "When it's mysterious, you get the rumours. That's just the way it goes until people know what's fact. No one knows how he comes to be taking over the Supertest station here, whether he bought it, leases it or what."

"Are they going to live in the trailer?" your father asked.

"Yup. Right down there on the lot."

Your father's reflection in the mirror nodded. "Short back and sides this time, Basil," he remembered to tell the barber.

As the clack of the scissors continued, you overheard the story about the Smiths, how, indeed, they were probably German Jews and would be residing in the mobile home anchored at the edge of the service station lot. As for the Smith girl, no one could recall her first name, although some mentioned she'd be going into your Grade in school despite being three years your senior. It was getting around that she'd been held back in school because of illness, but others thought, because they were foreigners, she had some education to make up.

Everyone agreed, though, amid an awkward chuckle or two, that she looked pretty mature to be going into Grade Six.

"Noticed that, did you?" someone quipped while everyone began to laugh.

"Yup," said Don Stuart at the end of the outburst. "She's a pretty little thing. No doubt about it."

After that, the men quieted down a bit. Jim Connelly glanced through a copy of Field & Stream and your father discussed crops, drought, and the hard winter everyone expected with the farmers waiting their turn. Raised on a farm himself, your father felt sure of himself with farmers. He'd told you some time ago, that if his father hadn't been so mean, he wouldn't have left the farm to work. Had he stayed, he said, life would have been different for you, a better life, although he never specified in what way it would be better. But his regret at how things had turned out was visible on his face, whenever he mentioned it.

After he was done with you, Grisham cut your father's hair, scissoring through the tall, tight curls until they piled up black on the floor beside the chair.

Jim Connelly was next and he eased his long frame into the chair carefully just before you and your father left to walk the short distance home. You were impressed by Connelly, reputed to be the tallest man in Meridian. And he had a finely trimmed dark moustache you particularly liked. Catching you looking at him in awe, he smiled tentatively into the mirror. You glanced away, embarrassed. His own son Gerald was going into Grade Six too in a week or so and Gerald was tall as well. In fact, you and Gerald were now the tallest boys in your grade.

You followed your father out the door. The sun washed you warmly. You stood there a moment, enjoying it on your face, until your father began to fret that both of you would be late getting home for lunch. Behind you, in the barbershop, there was another burst of laughter. Your father snapped his head around, wondering, you supposed, what it was he'd missed. Then, without a word, the two of you walked home.

IN THE FEW DAYS OF SUMMER remaining that year, you didn't see "the Smith girl" again. You were busy visiting your favourite haunts, now melancholy with summer's imminent conclusion.

On the morning shift you and your friends gathered at Wetherby's Gift Shop, looking through comic books on the rack, sometimes buying chips and soda. When Mr. Wetherby said, "Okay, boys," in a friendly way, which was always what he said when you'd loitered at the magazine rack too long, you'd go outside and sit on his sprawling concrete steps, eating your chips and drinking your sodas, discussing a wide assortment of what ifs and wouldn't-it-be-neat-ifs with your friends.

From there, you could glance across the street at the soot-blackened concrete block foundation that was all that remained of Findlay's General Store. Some of the older boys had been seen sifting through the wreckage but your mother had already warned that you'd get a licking if she caught you playing there. "You'll get your clothes filthy," she said by way of explanation.

Although mornings were spent downtown, afternoons were still reserved for swimming at Brannigan's Cove. It was already cool, the river chilling down, and you knew diving from the raft would soon be curtailed by the weather until summer arrived again next year. Next summer, you had to admit, seemed an eternity away.

By the end of August baseball was over too, but you attended the Meridian Marauders games to watch your father pitch, because his team was in the playdowns again. He pitched well that summer, although it made you strangely nervous to watch him in action. It was the intensity of his play, the way he seemed so angry, the way he seemed to become more of who he was in front of the Marauders fans, that prompted you to keep a kind of distance. Still, all of this was normal, and normal was familiar, and familiar was agreeable comfort. You loved Meridian—Meridian was comfortable. Sort of, anyway.

FOUR

. . . But Fargo's was a different matter. It was headquarters for all the kids in town. At Fargo's you could stand in front of the magazine rack and leaf through the comics after you bought your gum or a bag of chips and a soft drink. In summer, some of us would sit on the steps outside, deciding what we were going to do that day. Mr. Fargo kept his eye on us, a pair of glasses sagging professorially on his nose, but there was a twinkle in his gaze and he whistled the same hymn day after day, hour after hour. Jesu, Joy Of Man's Desiring.

I lived just a few doors up the street and his steps were one of my ritual haunts.

"Mornin', Richie," he'd say to me some days, squinting in the sunlight, ready to sweep the concrete for the day.

"Hello, Mr. Fargo."

"Dust from the traffic," he'd say. "It just keeps comin' back."

I nodded. Chores and dust. One seemed to create the other. I suspected even then that this was a repetition in life I would know as long as I lived . . .

AUTUMN CAME TO MERIDIAN. September, then October. The river assumed a deeper shade of blue as the angle of the sun grew sharper, the water turning grey and finally white in its headlong dash over the dam at the old flour mill, which was still a few years away from being designated an historic site and remained in relative disrepair. The river was the barometer of the seasons, its colourful shades, its cycle of freezing and thawing. You'd see it in the distance through the changing and falling leaves on your way to school that year, as you turned the corner by the bank and walked the last long street to class, crossing the bridge half a mile down from the dam. Here the river seemed frail, held back by the rocks in its bed, until it shrank to a trickle.

You liked autumn. It was the beginning of things, when life got going again. And sometimes you wondered if this sense of things getting underway was the same for everyone.

IN THE BANK JIM CONNELLY began his morning by setting up his desk. Generally he was the first to arrive at work and the last to go at the end of the day. Arranging the surface of his desk seemed the best way to organize his mind for the rituals of his day. He would reposition his calendar on the right corner of the polished oak surface, not far from an onyx stand containing two fountain pens and a bottle of black ink, a Christmas gift from his wife Betty the year he was promoted to manager. In front of him he placed file folders containing loan applications, sorting them alphabetically, a good a way as any to give them priority. Loan applications that had been denied found their way to the top so that he'd be sure to deal with them first. Get the difficult part of the day out of the way as soon as possible was his motto. Procrastination, he believed, was the root of all evil.

He set the keys to the front door on the other corner of his desk. The keys passed down through the ranks of the employees as the bank gradually eased itself into full operation each day. When Mabel Flannigan, the head teller, arrived Connelly let her in. Then Mabel took the keys and let Blanche Stuart in. Blanche, in turn, let Rhonda MacLean inside. It was Rhonda's job to unlock the door at ten to admit the first customers gathered outside on the steps, where they fidgeted the wait away with gossip or proclamations about the weather. The bank had been doing things this way for years. Over time even the faces in the process didn't vary much from day to day. Most of the people in Meridian—as most people are wont to do—lived by ritual alone.

By autumn Connelly was aware Rhonda MacLean didn't fit the mould of a bank employee well. She was capable enough, but he'd observed that she didn't reflect the sobriety the position traditionally required. For one thing, due to arrive at nine, she was sometimes a minute or two late. For another, she was more gregarious than Mabel and Blanche, and hadn't embraced the hushed, worshipful tones appropriate to an institution whose only preoccupation is money.

Connelly found these characteristics forgivable. What troubled him, though, was the ostentatious nature of her good looks. It seemed out of place in a bank in a town this size, distracting, even alien. Shapely and vaguely irreverent blondes, he thought ruefully, represented a threat to banking tradition, so ancient and honourable a practice. Or was it that Blanche and Mabel, comfortably middle-aged and stocky, aggravated the contrast? Strictly business were Blanche and Mabel; valuable employees too. Connelly felt torn. Although he found Rhonda a refreshing change, he was careful not to let it show. He felt a small, but mysterious guilt that, in appreciating Rhonda, he was betraying something sacred about banking.

He would ponder frequently the first week of her employ, when he had beckoned her into his office and indicated as paternally as he could the top of her cashmere sweater.

"Your button's undone."

"Huh?"

"The top button on your sweater."

"Oh," she said with a bit of a disingenuous blush.

He'd noticed that people could see the first half inch or so of the swell of her well-formed breasts, which simply wouldn't do. This was a bank. Bad enough that she was given to flirtatiousness. Bad enough that some of the younger men lined up to be served at her wicket regardless of the length of the line. And when Blanche or Mabel asked if they could help, the men switched lines grudgingly, as if the stern goodwill of the other tellers represented betrayal of some kind.

She did the button up with just the hint of a smile. Impertinence really. Both of them knew the button hadn't come undone by accident, that she'd worn it to work that way.

She'd made the incident even more awkward by standing in front of his desk a moment or two, her hands still positioned at the top of the sweater, pale blue with rhinestones. He'd noticed her delicate fingers, a silver ring, how long her nails were, gleaming with red polish.

"That's all," he'd said, feeling embarrassed. "There wasn't anything else." He felt bad about how cold he sounded. "Thank you," he'd added to soften his brusqueness, the good deed coming phlegmy out of his throat, which didn't help at all.

"You're welcome," Rhonda had said as she turned to go.

He liked to blame everything on her youth and the damned good hiding she probably had never received when she was younger. Wealth, good looks, and social standing gave her a confidence she hadn't truly earned. And with these other traits, he thought, came a disturbingly precocious knowledge of men.

After the sweater-button incident, what bothered him most was not the certainty that he was going to remember the upper edge of her breasts more than once that day—each time, in fact, he didn't want to. No, what bothered him most was the possibility she was going to know he was remembering. This was what was infuriating.

ONE DAY THAT SAME AUTUMN—it was a Thursday—Eldora Diamond, known to many in town as The Cat Woman, walked from her home on the main highway at the edge of Meridian's small downtown core to the Supertest station to introduce herself to Mrs. Smith. Her destination, five minutes' walk, was the intersection of the highway and Church Street, so named because the Anglican Church was the most imposing building along its length. In the distance, as she approached, she could see the GM car dealership, its network of pennants dangling sadly against the blue sky. Across the road, she knew, was her destination. Eldora had been putting off this hospitable venture for nearly a month because, in Meridian, it was easier not to bother. Generally newcomers were left to themselves until their newness sorted itself out in a process of arduous integration.

Eldora, a relative newcomer herself and a keen observer of human and social nature, knew the village wasn't friendly. It maintained a caste system with which she was already familiar. Eldora, who wrote poetry and published it with a respected house in Toronto, had been aware of Meridian's reserve for the three years she had resided here. It amused her to think she had the system down pat.

The foundation of this rigid hierarchal arrangement was the network of families who'd lived in the area for at least two generations. These were acknowledged to be the movers and shakers, elevated in status by the longevity of their history. Most of them had Scottish or British names. It went without saying that all of them were white. There wasn't even a Chinese restaurant in town, not that anyone would have patronized it. In villages like Meridian, the assumption that people's vanished pets made it into the recipes of oriental restaurants remained accepted as fact.

The next rung on the ladder was occupied by newcomers who, because of their perceived talents, appeal or potential, were construed to be up and comers. These were the people responsible for the future of Meridian. As such, it was their duty to maintain and entrench the village's existing values, gradually taking their honoured place among those already possessing a history here.

At this point the classes of residency grew fuzzier, the people less well received. There was a small group deemed riff-raff who, despite the length of their history in the area, were condemned immutably to a state of riff-raffism based on some ancient sin or other no one talked about. The only escape from the tag was to leave town.

Finally, there existed an even smaller group, barely a dozen lost souls in all, best described as "odd." This was the place in the caste to which Eldora Diamond, The Cat Woman, had been relegated. Not exactly shunned, she was nonetheless removed from the mainstream of village life because she was deemed arty, eccentric and maybe even crazy. Why else would she keep so many cats and wear her hair the way she did?

In truth, there were no more than half a dozen cats, all of them Persians. But there was more to it than just the felines. Her hair—long and black, tied in a ponytail each morning, reaching down to the small of her back—was an affront to the status quo. Eldora also had a refined and articulate way of speaking, uncommon in a village this size. Although it was known she had an artistic aptitude, no one in Meridian knew she was a poet of some repute. Many thought, instead, she had been a ballet dancer in her youth, or perhaps an opera singer. There were rumours that she had a university education, which, for a woman, was presumptuous at that time in a town like Meridian.

Worse yet, there was a skeleton in her closet. Her father had been divorced. It was the late Neville Diamond's only perceived oddity but it was a powerful one in Meridian. His second marriage, to a Meredith McCormick, had brought him to the village in the first place. At the point of her husband's true acceptance by the village, Mrs. Diamond had died, leaving her husband on his own. Then he died too, three years later, mostly of a broken heart.

Eldora lived in Meridian because she had inherited her father's house, a comfortable structure in which she could enjoy the quiet of village life. Still, the locals were known to wonder why she didn't live in Toronto; she was so clearly a Toronto type of woman. Had she been asked about this, she would have replied that poets are poets anywhere, often taking root in unusual places as long as they can write. But no one ever asked and she doubted anyone ever would.

One more thing: Eldora Diamond was a beauty. Her beauty was of a classical nature—shiny black hair, large dark eyes and prominent, perfect cheekbones emphasized by the way she tied her hair back so tightly. She knew this about herself just as she knew classical beauty in Meridian was an oddity. People there were more used to pretty, cute, good looking, or other pleasing variations of beauty. Classical beauty, she'd learned, wasn't to everyone's taste, indeed wasn't even always perceived or understood.

Of all the things she was on the day she went to visit Mrs. Smith, Eldora was mostly known to be The Cat Woman. She'd heard so herself. A couple of teenagers loitering on the corner near her front door one evening several months ago had referred to her as such through her open windows, whether inadvertently or not. Two men walking home from the bowling alley had come along and told the kids to get home before they got their asses kicked, but Eldora knew the teenagers hadn't invented this Cat Woman business themselves. The opinions of the hierarchy were passed on from generation to generation; the children merely parroted them.

Knowing there was so much status quo to overcome in life, Eldora, at forty, was philosophical about it. While the status quo must indeed be overcome most of the time, usually it was so devoid of substance that overcoming it hardly seemed worth the trouble. She wrestled with this particular irony often.

On the day she walked to the Supertest station to welcome the Smiths to town, the weather was filled with promise: windless, sunny, unseasonably warm. The leaves had all changed and the village was a concert of colour—yellows, oranges, and reds. Thanksgiving was just around the corner. It was a forward thinking kind of day. Regardless of the outcome, Eldora knew she would be pleased with herself that at least she had made the effort.

As she crossed the oil-splattered asphalt of the service station lot and climbed the three bleached wooden steps to the mobile home to knock gently on the door, she noticed a man in coveralls, whom she took to be Mr. Smith, pumping gas into a powder blue '59 Chevrolet. When she turned to look at him, the sun caught the chrome on the car's wide, horizontal fins. Blinded, she had to glance away. He did not smile or wave; he seemed lost in private reverie. Eldora was deeply struck and surprised by the bleakness of his expression.

She heard footsteps inside the trailer.

When the storm door opened, Eldora was forced backwards to make room. She retreated down a step so that Mrs. Smith, several inches shorter than her, could maneuver around the door. This artificial advantage in height added to the woman's sternness.

"Yes?" said Mrs. Smith.

She wore no makeup and her face was deeply lined. Her dark hair was streaked with grey. It was set in tight curls held in place by a network of bobby pins.

"I'm Eldora Diamond. I was passing and I decided to pop in and introduce myself."

"I see."

Though daunted by this response and Mrs. Smith's stern expression, Eldora plunged on. "I'm a relative newcomer to Meridian myself. I thought I'd invite you to tea some afternoon soon. Perhaps we could get to know one another."

"Oh," said Mrs. Smith, brightening just a smidgen. "I see."

Silence.

"Anyway," said Eldora, not knowing what to say next. "That was all, I suppose."

"This is very kind of you," said Mrs. Smith, her German accent now obvious.

Eldora heard Mr. Smith behind her at the bottom of the steps and, somewhat startled, she turned.

"This is my husband, Karl," said Mrs. Smith.

Eldora smiled. He nodded curtly. His age was difficult to fix. Late fifties maybe. Weathered just enough to blur the issue. And he limped, aging him.

"My goodness," she said then. "I'm in the way."

"This is all right," said Mrs. Smith.

But Eldora leaned back against the railing and Mr. Smith took the opportunity to slip by. As theatre, the scene was badly blocked. Mrs. Smith had to go inside, closing the door, to let him in.

"Have I come at a bad time?" asked Eldora when she reappeared.

"Oh no. Everything is good."

"Well perhaps we could have tea some afternoon soon."

"I call you. On the telephone."

"Yes. Okay. Again, my name's Eldora Diamond. I live just a couple of blocks up the street."

"Yes. Good. I call you."

"I'll look forward to it."

Mrs. Smith smiled, although it was a tired vagrant of a smile, just passing through with nowhere else to go.

"Well, until then, then," said Eldora, turning to leave, the "then-then" echoing badly behind her.

"Goodbye. And thank you."

As Eldora crossed the car-stained asphalt of the Supertest station lot, she heard the wooden inner door close behind her. The aluminum storm door slammed shut all by itself.

THAT SAME DAY, John MacLean's newly cantankerous greyhound attacked the driver of the Meridian Feed Store truck as he was getting down from the cab in the sprawling front driveway of the prosperous MacLean farm. Billy Kinney, a lanky eighteen-year old, new on the job, had only just touched the dirt of the driveway with his new tan cowboy boots, clipboard in hand, when Bailey dashed around the front of the truck and lunged at his coveralls. The coveralls tore not far from the thigh as Kinney scurried back into the truck and slammed the door.

The dog, barking and snarling now, jumped up at the door, trying to leap in through the window.

"Bailey!" called MacLean in some alarm. "Get outta there."

When the dog didn't relent, the farmer hurried forward

and kicked it solidly in the rear end. The dog yelped, disappearing around the corner of the house.

"You okay, Billy?" MacLean asked, glancing into the cab of the truck. "Goddamned dog. I don't know what's wrong with him these days."

More frightened than he wanted to admit, Kinney didn't reply.

"He didn't bite you, did he, Billy?"

"Tore my coveralls a bit."

"I'm sorry, Billy. I'll replace them, of course."

"Okay, Mr. MacLean. No harm done."

"Jesus," said MacLean. "I hope I don't have to put him down. Olive loves that stupid dog."

"I'm all right, Mr. MacLean. Honestly."

Thoughtfully the farmer nodded. "Okay, hand me down that clipboard."

Kinney passed it through the window.

"All right," MacLean said after he'd checked the invoice. "Just take it down to the main door at the barn. I'll get two of the fellas to unload it for you."

"Right, Mr. MacLean."

"You're sure you're okay, Billy?"

The colour returning to his face, Kinney managed a smile. "Just startled me," he said. "No harm done."

MacLean moved away, muttering "damn fool dog" as he did so.

ELSEWHERE THAT SAME AFTERNOON, Miss Bertha Cartwright rearranged the seating of her Grades Six and Seven pupils. There was a brief enjoyable hubbub while she stood at the front of the class, calling each student by name and directing them to a new seat, the Grade Seven students first, your Grade next.

"Phillip Barrett, I want you at the front where I can keep an eye on you," she said in the midst of the exercise. And she tapped the desk in question with her hand, the one closest to her own.

This was a surprise, both to you and to me. You were

not and had never been a discipline problem. The move to the front, you later surmised, had less to do with your behavior and more to do with the fact that Miss Cartwright didn't like you, a dislike you didn't understand. You were polite and treated her with respect. Whatever was at the root of her feelings, it had little to do with your behavior.

Although puzzled and offended, you took your new seat, convinced her dislike had something to do with you and me being best friends. How did you put it when we finally talked about it at recess? Like you weren't a good enough student to be best friends with the best student in the school? Was this why? You asked. Did teachers actually think this way?

"She's such an old maid," your mother had complained last spring, while you were in Grade Five, after a painful parent-teacher interview.

"Now, Carol," your father had said, not wanting you to witness this disrespect.

We students all called her The Owl but you liked her the least of all of us. Often you lamented that your future didn't look bright. The way things were set up at the school at present, you not only had the rest of Grade Six to put up with her, but Grade Seven as well. I had to agree your prospects seemed dismal, although mine were just as bleak.

When at last the dust settled on the new classroom seating arrangement and The Owl turned to the blackboard to write out an assignment for the Grade Sevens, you glanced back from your new perch at the front to see what I thought about this new development. I noticed, though, that Kimberley Smith caught your eye first. I saw her gently smile at you. It was such a kind and benevolent gesture, I knew this was why you smiled back.

"Phillip Barrett! Face the front this instant!"

You snapped your head around.

Miss Cartwright hovered sternly over your desk. But most of the class was laughing so hard, she let it go at that.

You blushed with embarrassment. The laughter of the class. Kimberley's delicate smile. But I knew something new and important had passed between you and the strange, new girl who was spending her first year in our school.

"BOY," SAID ONE OF THE MEN in the barber shop that day as Kimberley and Maggie Mathieson, her best friend, passed the shop on their way home from school. "They sure didn't make them like that when I was in elementary school."

None of his companions replied. It wasn't that they disapproved of the comment; it was just that most of them had been thinking the same thing themselves and there wasn't very much they could add.

Unaware of this, the two girls made their way to The Tea Room, which Maggie's family owned. There, they hurried around back, climbed the wooden stairs to the second floor, and went inside to listen to records until Kimberley had to go home.

Neither one of them had noticed the men in the barber shop, the ones who had noticed them. Not that the men had paid much attention to Maggie; it was Kimberley whom they saw. Kimberley was older, would be fourteen the following March. Kimberley, they'd noticed, was destined to be gorgeous.

INCIDENTS MUCH LATER THAT DAY made your father briefly famous, which pleased him very much. His notoriety focused attention on his implacability and courage, his loyalty to his employer and his combative prowess. Bert Barrett could ask for nothing better from an accommodating destiny.

It was bowling night, as it was on Thursday every week. Your father had been officially promoted to assistant manager the previous Monday and he was feeling good about himself. It had become a muggy evening for October. The sunshine of the day had given way to cloudy skies and, walking home from the bowling lanes, Bert Barrett undid his autumn jacket.

When he arrived home, he found his wife sitting at the

kitchen table with a mug of hot milk. In front of her was an ashtray filled with cigarette butts, the room smoky despite a nearby open window. Bert hung up his jacket and sat down at the table opposite her, lighting a cigarette of his own.

Your mother Carol had been sorting out her Christmas order in the Simpsons-Sears catalogue and was now fretting over your fragile family economy. Her mood was one of grieving.

"What's the matter?" asked Bert.

"Christmas is coming. We have no money. And you're out bowling with your friends, having a good time."

"I'll be getting a Christmas bonus."

"A turkey? What's a turkey going to pay for?"

"It's a turkey," he explained, "that we don't have to pay for ourselves."

This logic did not deter her. She arrived at the nub of the matter. "Did you talk to Joe Langley about a larger raise for being his assistant manager?"

"Joe's out of town until Monday. He's got a hockey tournament."

"Well it really gets my goat that he gives you a measly five bucks a week to be assistant manager when you still have to be meat manager too."

"Carol, it's a small store."

"So? You're still going to talk to him, aren't you?"

"Probably."

"Probably?"

Now your father grew angry. "That's enough, Carol. You've made your point. Why don't you leave my job to me?"

Thoughtfully your mother stubbed out her cigarette. "Sometimes," she said, "I hate this town. We don't get anywhere here. Things don't get better."

Bert was out of patience. On the way home it had occurred to him that they might make love tonight. Now he felt foolish, betrayed by his previous notion.

"Carol, it's late and we've been through all this before. I'm going to bed." He got up and headed for the stairs.

This was around ten p.m. By one a.m., both of them

were asleep. When the telephone rang, the sound was so intrusive it went off like a fire alarm.

Carol answered it, then passed the phone to her husband. "It's Doreen Langley."

His boss's wife was unnerved. She could hear, she said, someone next door at the grocery store. She thought they were trying to break in. Joe was away. What should she do?

"I'll be right there," said Bert. "In the meantime, call the police, the OPP. Tell them to keep quiet and not come in with their sirens going."

After he hung up, as he dressed, he explained what was happening.

"Shouldn't you leave this to the police?"

"I'll be all right," he said.

"Be careful," your mother said. "You're all I've got, Bert."

By the time your father trotted the two minutes to the store, then hid in the dense lilacs and other shrubbery at the edge of the driveway, he was pumped up with adrenalin. Indeed, two young men were trying to pry their way through the back door of the store's warehouse. Silently Bert remained hidden in the bushes, waiting for the police to arrive.

Later he would learn from Doreen Langley that, yes, she'd asked the police to arrive without sirens, but for reasons eluding everyone, when the two black and whites arrived on the scene, their red lights were flashing and their sirens were wailing hysterically into the night.

Hearing the sirens, the two thieves dropped their crowbar and dashed down the driveway. Afraid they would escape, Bert decided to give chase.

When the two young men heard him pursuing them, they split up. Bert dashed after the one on the right and the police arrived in time to nab the one who had turned left. Bert tackled his quarry on the remaining fringe of lawn where Findlay's store had been located before the tragic fire. There wasn't much of a struggle. Bert sat on him in silence, neither of them exchanging a word—sharing an odd embarrassment to find themselves in such close contact—until two police officers showed up to take the young man away.

By the next day the entire village knew the story of what your father had done. Several people told him that they never would have given chase themselves, if it had been their choice. Still, they had to admit he had courage.

As it turned out, the two teenagers were never charged with the crime. This, for your father, became the main thrust whenever he told the story. Never mind that he had witnessed, chased, tackled and held onto one of the "delinquents." The point to consider was that two obvious wrongdoers had escaped their actions without punishment.

"How do the police expect to catch criminals and have them punished when they come into town with their sirens wailing like that?" he wanted to know. He liked answering his own question. "Because they wanted them to get away. Because it's less trouble that way."

Many people in Meridian agreed with him. This was just one example of how the world was going to hell in a handcart.

FIVE

... After school let out, The Skeleton Club evolved into something more than the casual meeting it had been while we were still in the classroom. We decided we needed a clubhouse and were given permission to use a portion of our porch that stretched around the side of the house. We scrounged an assortment of dilapidated materials, including an old bathroom door my father had removed a couple of years before and had consigned to the garage, and three or four cardboard boxes – the large kind with White Swan written on the side – from Brown's Groceteria, around the corner from Fargo's. We barricaded the end of the porch, cut in a window, painted Skeleton Club on the cardboard walls and moved inside where we sweltered in the frequently humid July sunshine.

Here, Irving the skeleton presided over every imagining, dangling mutely from a bolt on the porch where my mother had once hung a planter of geraniums ...

HALLOWEEN ARRIVED AS IT ALWAYS DID, Phillip, impolitely barging in on your pre-adolescence. By 1959 you found dressing up an ordeal. Halloween, in some unfortunate way, filled you with shame and humiliation.

This year your mother had conceived of the notion that you should dress up as Zorro. She had come up with a black shirt and large red belt which matched some black trousers you sometimes wore to school. She had also been going through the toybox you no longer visited and discovered an old black cowboy hat and a plastic sword superficially resembling the rapier Zorro would have used. Inspired, she set about sewing a large satin cape out of an old evening dress she owned. The evening dress, she said, had been her wedding dress before she dyed it black.

You hoped by now that your Halloweens were definitely numbered, especially the dressing up to go out trick-or-treating. You were feeling too grown up for it and had never enjoyed it much as a child either. The self-conscious ringing of the doorbell, the polite begging for candy, everyone telling you how wonderful you looked, and stumbling around in the chilly dark in an outfit you found clumsy or confining all contributed to your embarrassment. Halloween, you suspected, had been conceived by parents to make fools of their children. Besides, most of the loot you gathered on Halloween ended up in the trash.

As for portraying Zorro, you had mixed emotions. It was a step up from the old woman costume you'd worn the two years previously. And the pirate and clown outfits you'd donned in the early days remained an uncomfortable memory. Maybe being Zorro would be okay; if it was required that you go out on Halloween, you might just as well dress up as a swashbuckler with a weakness for the underdog.

But on the day you were required to dress up for school, your mother had not yet finished sewing the cape, which would be ready for your rounds the next night. There was no alternative but to dress up as the old woman again. In the end you went to class, tripping over a long flowered dress, a fox stole twitching around your shoulders, a kerchief wrapped around your head, and makeup plastered on your cheeks. You felt foolish and betrayed.

You'd worked up the courage to mention your Halloween reservations a couple of days before, you told me, but your mother hadn't listened.

"Oh Phillip," she said. "Let's not be silly. It's Halloween.

People go to a lot of trouble to make Halloween fun for kids."

"I know. But . . ."

". . . And all your friends will be out. What will people think if you're not there?"

You fell silent, disappointed that she didn't understand.

"You see what I mean, don't you?" she said.

You'd nodded but the gesture was a lie.

And now here it was, Halloween again. And you stumbling off to school dressed up as a little old lady, hiking up the dress so that it didn't drag in the dirt and knowing at recess that you were going to have to stand around doing nothing so that the costume wasn't damaged.

As for tomorrow, Saturday, October 31, when darkness fell, well at least you'd be dressed up as Zorro and not some little old lady. For my part, I would be wearing a spaceman costume and, accordingly, endured an awkward shame all of my own. Together we decided we'd grit our teeth and find a way to get through it.

PEOPLE WHO DID BUSINESS at the Bank of Nova Scotia the day before Halloween that year were astonished to find the employees of the bank, Jim Connelly included, dressed up in costume. This was a first in Meridian and, although many people approved of this break with banking routine, there were others, of course, who did not. To some it was as sacrilegious as wearing costumes to church.

No one was surprised when the news got out that the costume business had been Rhonda MacLean's idea. What was surprising was that Jim Connelly went along with it.

"I was floored when Mr. Connelly agreed with the idea," whispered Blanche Stuart to a friend on the other side of her teller's cage.

"You don't suppose he's sweet on the MacLean girl, do you?" her friend replied with more than a hint of malice.

"Well, I'll say this: you know what men are like around a pretty woman. Their brains turn to mush."

In truth, Connelly himself wondered why he'd relented

so easily. It was the most provocative decision he'd made in years, as far as he was concerned. Yet, when Rhonda had tapped on the door at the end of the day a week ago, to tell him of the plan, he'd given in despite an instinct to say no. She'd asked him to suggest the idea to Mabel and Blanche as well, because she felt the scheme would have more respectability coming from him. He'd even agreed to this, resisting the feeling that conspiring with Rhonda in this way possessed its own intriguing appeal.

"I think some of the customers will get a kick out of it," he told his senior tellers. "At least we can try it and see what happens."

Neither one of them knew what they would wear.

"I'm going to wear my centennial costume," Connelly said as a suggestion.

So it was, on the Friday before Halloween, that Jim Connelly, Mabel and Blanche all wore their centennial outfits to the bank. Connelly's suit had once belonged to his grandfather, also a banker, and it reflected what had been the fashion during the previous century. Mabel and Blanche displayed long dresses and matching bonnets in the style of the homesteading women who had helped to found Meridian a hundred years ago.

But Rhonda didn't come to work in a centennial period costume. No, she arrived dressed in a full clown's outfit, large shoes, short trousers, and off-coloured suspenders, a jacket that flared at the hips, a top hat, red curly wig, and face paint. No one could deny, even in an outfit such as this, she managed to look fetching.

This was Connelly's opinion, at least, when she popped into his office that morning to ask him what he thought of her costume. Of course he was careful how he said so.

"Terrific costume, Rhonda. Very imaginative."

"This is fun," she said. "Thank you, Mr. Connelly. I think the customers are enjoying it."

"You're welcome," he replied, infected by her exuberance.

The pants, he noticed, as she turned to go, were tight

around her buttocks. The suspenders, he remembered, had tended to push her breasts together in a delightful emphasis.

Halloween then, was the day Jim Connelly began to wonder occasionally what it, the troubling it—romance, love, sex, pain, torture and skin—the it with Rhonda MacLean, would actually be like.

BEING ZORRO ON HALLOWEEN wasn't so bad. You kept the plastic sword inside the big red belt your mother thought necessary to your outfit and headed out as soon as darkness began to fall. You met me at the corner where the ruins of Findlay's General Store were located, me shining and shimmering in my spaceman suit. (I insisted you refer to me as an astronaut rather than a spaceman, after I made a long, deferential speech about the virtues of the American space program in which, back then, I hoped one day to be employed.) I had mapped out a route, which was the kind of thing I did as a child, and we followed it rigidly, making our rounds.

The streets of Meridian were sprinkled with trick-or-treaters—witches, ghosts in sheets, cowboys, little old men and little old ladies, ballerinas, clowns and even, in one case, a larger boy dressed from head to foot in a gorilla suit. Although we were impressed with his costume, you complained bitterly when you noticed he was collecting his loot in a pillowcase. This, by your definition, was greed and you had no patience for it.

Although you'd accepted your lot for the night, you continued to feel shy and self-conscious each time you climbed the steps of someone's porch to knock on the door or ring the bell. The hollowed-out pumpkins placed in accommodating windows or on porch banisters—their eyes and mouths flickering hospitably—couldn't make you comfortable. No accommodating welcome, "Come in, come in" and "What do we have here? Zorro and a spaceman?" could overcome your sense of intrusion. You felt vulnerable, condemned to observe a ceremony you didn't understand, conscripted into ritual purely for ritual's sake.

As we negotiated my carefully conceived, step-saving route from house to house, we discovered evidence of pranks everywhere we went. Downtown windows had been thoroughly soaped, garbage cans had been overturned, and some of the trees had been decorated with rolls of toilet paper. We were torn between fear and excitement. If Halloween represented no actual paranormal reason to be afraid, it at least offered the apprehension wicked older kids could inspire. Police cars patrolled the village with a visible regularity, but we observed only one incident of legitimate vandalism: a fire we noticed burning in the distance across the highway on the crest of the hill at the eastern edge of town. By the time we glimpsed the distant flames, the police were already there, their red lights flashing into the deep, thick darkness. So we merely continued on our rounds.

Although there were two pumpkins lit up in the windows of The Cat Woman's home, signalling that we were welcome, both of us came to a halt at the end of her sidewalk to discuss the situation. I remember standing there using your cape to polish the dew and sweat from my horn-rimmed glasses while we considered what was the best thing to do. It was now quite dark and we'd walked what seemed a great distance. Our shopping bags of candy were already heavy.

"Whaddyuh think?" I asked as I repositioned my glasses.

"The Cat Woman?"

"Yeah."

"I dunno," you said. "What'd your parents say?"

"They didn't say anything. What about yours?"

You considered this a moment. Neither your mother nor your father had warned you away from any particular house this Halloween, but your mother had referred to The Cat Woman in the past a number of times as "odd" and "not married." Was there an implication in her words to keep away?

"She has a lotta cats," you murmured finally.

"How many cats do you have to own to be called The Cat Woman anyway?" I wondered aloud.

You didn't know. "About fifty. Maybe even a hundred,"

you ventured finally.

"Yeah? And a black one for Halloween, I'll bet," I said.

As we stood there, mired in our conundrum, we noticed two classmates approaching along the sidewalk. We recognized Maggie Mathieson right away because she wore no mask. She was dressed in white leotards and a shimmering blouse. She carried a fairy's wand with a star on its tip. The other one, we discovered, was Kimberley Smith dressed as a Gypsy. They stopped to say "hi" in the middle of our Cat Woman debate.

"Have you been in yet?" asked Maggie.

"We were just working out whether we should or not," I said.

"Are you going in?" you asked the two girls.

"Sure."

"You can come in with us," said Kimberley.

"I dunno," you murmured.

"Oh, c'mon," said Maggie impatiently.

She and Kimberley started up the sidewalk. I followed. What were we afraid of anyway?

Feeling compromised, I know, you grudgingly brought up the rear.

"Kimberley," The Cat Woman said at the door. "How nice of you to come!" She gazed at the four of us one by one, with a warm and appreciative scrutiny. "Come in."

Inside we smelled cat urine, but only a trace emanating from a litter box in the corner.

"Come down to the kitchen," our hostess said. "I have some special treats."

We followed her down the hall and into a large kitchen eerily lit by more than a dozen candles. On the stove, a large pot aromatic of apples and cinnamon extinguished what remained of the delicate odour of cats we'd noticed at the door. On the table there were two large plates of chocolate brownies and a bowl of Halloween candy.

"I haven't had many visitors," our hostess said. "Must be the Cat Woman business, eh?"

"How many cats do you have anyway?" I asked, vaguely

embarrassed that she knew what everyone called her.

"Six."

"That's not many," you put in, as embarrassed by it all as I was.

"Not for a cat woman anyway," The Cat Woman said.

She invited all of us to sit down at the kitchen table for a brownie and some apple cider. Everyone laughed when the sword cinched to your waist caught on a chair and you nearly toppled to the floor.

"I'm afraid I've made too much," our hostess said as she served us. But she joined us at the table, clearly pleased that we were there.

"So, am I to guess who everyone is? I know Maggie, of course." She turned to you and smiled. "I think I know who Zorro is. I'll bet you're that good looking Barrett boy I've heard so much about. Right?"

You blushed and stammered an embarrassed thank you, not knowing what else to say.

"Yes," said Kimberley then. "This is Phillip."

"Of course. Phillip Barrett. I know your father from the grocery store." She turned to me. "I'm at a loss on the astronaut, though."

"Gary Burnside," I said.

"Oh yes."

"And thanks for not calling me a spaceman."

"You're welcome," The Cat Woman said.

After that, while she served us another brownie, she began to talk about Halloweens she'd known when she was young. She explained about All Hallows Eve too, about greater and lesser sabbats in the witch's calendar.

"You don't believe in witches, do you?" I asked, feeling a new and deeper trepidation.

"Well, maybe I do," The Cat Woman said. "There are some people in town, I suspect, who wonder if I'm a witch myself."

There was an awkward silence after this. It seemed unfair to think of The Cat Woman as a witch. We'd decided that we liked her. Yet I knew adults told stories to hide themselves from children. I was suspicious about any information that seemed dishonest to me, whether it originated with an adult or not.

"See?" said Kimberley after all of us were outside again, gathered at the end of her sidewalk.

"She's a nice lady," you admitted. "And I didn't see a single cat."

Kimberley smiled—the expression dazzled under her mask.

You couldn't help yourself, I noticed. You smiled back, aware for the first time that Kimberley was very pretty. You didn't have to tell me this; I could see it for myself.

HALLOWEEN WAS ALSO THE NIGHT John MacLean killed his dog, a story Meridian told itself several times that year in the months that followed.

The incident took place early that night when MacLean's young grandson showed up to trick or treat at the family homestead. Rodney Fielding was six and his mother, Janice, MacLean's elder daughter, had been calling on friends with her son all evening. This was young Rodney's first Halloween. When she drove down her father's long driveway, it was to be her last stop. The MacLeans wanted to see their grandson in his new cowboy costume.

Olive and John MacLean strolled outside to meet their daughter when they recognized the car's headlights coming up the driveway. No sooner had the 1959 Chrysler New Yorker come to a halt when Rodney was out the door, packing twin pistols and wearing a cowboy hat tied in place with a cord. "I'm the Cisco Kid," he cried, pulling his pistols out of their holsters. "Pow! Pow!" the youngster said as he "shot" his grandparents who, still laughing, feigned injury.

Then Bailey the greyhound rocketed around the corner.

"Pow! Pow!" said Rodney as he aimed his pistols in the dog's direction.

It seemed innocent enough; boy and dog knew one another. But Bailey lunged at the little boy, took an arm in his teeth, pulled him down at the edge of the driveway and began to drag him over the lawn, snarling.

Janice screamed, joined almost instantly by Olive. Rodney, to this point in a state of shock, began to scream as well.

Everything happened quickly then. Although no one could remember why the pitchfork was leaning against a tree a couple of yards away—whether an employee had left it there fortuitously—John MacLean soon had it in both hands and was advancing on his dog.

"Bailey!" he commanded. "Let go!"

But the dog ignored him.

In close now, MacLean took a deep breath, considered the angle he must employ, then, with tremendous calm and force, bent down and jammed the pitchfork upwards into the dog's chest.

The dog wheezed and collapsed.

Although Bailey was already dead—MacLean later termed it an incredibly lucky thrust—he slammed the tines of the fork twice more into the dog. The second time, one of the tips entered bone and, when it would not easily release, MacLean just left it there, jutting out of the dog's carcass. He hurried into the house with his wailing grandson. His wife and his daughter—both of them sobbing hysterically—followed along behind.

There were teeth marks in Rodney's arm but, to everyone's relief, the skin was not seriously broken. MacLean assumed this was because the dog had locked on and not let go again, not tearing the flesh as much as he could have.

"It was quite a shock," MacLean told your father at Red & White Food Lockers a couple of days later.

For his part, Bert just stood behind the meat counter, repeatedly shaking his head. Although the large rump roast MacLean had ordered lay on top of the display counter, wrapped in brown paper, priced, and secured with a white cord, both men ignored it, caught up in the drama of what had happened.

"You know," said MacLean, locking gazes with your father, "I think it's because it's family. Something instinctive kicks in. I think that's what makes us do what we do. Because it's family, we know we have to do it."

"You bet it is."

"No one hurts my family. It's instinct. A problem comes up and I handle it. The instinct kicks in."

Solemnly Bert nodded. "There's a code involved. Even dogs can violate it. Sometimes a good swift kick in the ass just isn't enough for the job. Sometimes you have to go the distance."

"That's right," agreed MacLean. "It is a code, isn't it? A standard of behavior. Dogs are part of it too. Old Bailey broke the rules. I didn't have any choice."

All of which your father repeated word for word at the dinner table that night after he sat down to eat with you and your mother.

"Sooner or later," he said meaningfully, "we learn to behave or face the consequences." Then he glanced at you to make certain you understood.

Feeling uneasy, all you could do was meet his gaze until he looked away.

SIX

. . . It was my idea to make The Skeleton Club a detective agency, a suggestion I raised a day or two after the clubhouse was completed.

"A detective agency," mocked Chuck. "Jeezus."

"Wait a minute," said Dwight. "Why not? Like The Hardy Boys."

"Like The Secret Seven," said Billy.

"Yeah," I said.

Chuck looked each of us over, aware the tide of opinion was running against him. "I suppose so," he said at last.

"Skeleton Club Private Investigations," I suggested.

"Incorporated," added Dwight. "It helps at tax time to be incorporated."

We looked at him in awe; Dwight seemed aware of complexities in life the rest of us would never understand.

"We'll need business cards," he said in the silence.

And we all nodded solemnly. . .

YOU WONDERED HOW IT CAME ABOUT, in view of your mother's opinions about The Cat Woman, that you were dispatched one Saturday afternoon not long after Halloween to rake up the leaves in her back yard. It wasn't that you minded—you were to be paid for your efforts. It was just that taking money from a woman your mother thought was best shunned seemed inconsistent. Your mother had told you the line between odd and crazy was thin, "as thin as a length of thread," was how she had put it. You supposed your parents had found a way for it to be all right for her to be crazy, if she was paying you to rake her lawn.

No doubt this was your father's influence. Working hard and getting paid for it resided atop his list of virtues. It had been him that The Cat Woman had approached about having her yard raked. Business was business, your father often said. If The Cat Woman needed some yard work done, you'd better get over there Saturday afternoon and do it.

As for how you felt about it, The Cat Woman had been nice to you on Halloween. Owning six cats hardly qualified as crazy. Raking her lawn seemed like a great way to make some money—at home you had to do it for free.

What you didn't know was that Eldora Diamond usually raked her own leaves. This year, though, she'd been called away to visit an ailing friend the day after Halloween and, now that she was back and her friend was doing much better, she had galley proofs to go over for her latest book, a long narrative poem she called The Fox, after D.H. Lawrence's novella. With the deadline for galley revisions quickly approaching, she felt she needed help with her yard work.

So it was that Saturday afternoon, while you tackled the leaves in her garden, she sat at the kitchen table, carefully reading the blue lines of what she'd spent the last year or more writing. Two of her cats shared her lap, peering onto the table as if going over some of the stanzas too. Now and then, distracted by your labours occasionally visible through her kitchen window, Eldora would glance up and watch you work, amused by your determination. You looked to her like a young old man, grim and innocent, mature and immature, gangly but fluid.

You were concentrating. It was a crisp, sunny, cold November day. You wore ear muffs and gloves, but your hands sweated inside the wool. You'd divided the yard into sections to make a game of the work, counting how many strokes each section demanded to produce its own pile of rustling, brown leaves. There were three mature maples at the rear of the yard and a tall, arrogant elm up near the house. It seemed they'd dropped a mountain of leaves for you to rake into submission.

"We'll burn them in the incinerator," The Cat Woman explained when you first arrived. "I love the smell of burning leaves, don't you?"

You nodded, remembering the odor from your past. It was linked provocatively to your idea of autumn's passing. Even as a young man, you were fascinated by the routine process of Canada's changing seasons.

Kimberley came into the back yard as you were finishing up. By then the pile of leaves had risen to a formidable size. Engrossed in the satisfaction of what you had accomplished, you didn't hear the click of the gate as she entered the yard. She suddenly appeared beside you like a genie out of a bottle.

"Hi, Phillip."

"Hi."

"Wow," she said then. "What a huge pile of leaves."

Unexpectedly you blushed. "Yeah," you replied, turning away until the blush was gone, not knowing what else to say. This was different than school. It wasn't like you could borrow a pencil from her as an excuse for standing here beside her. The awkwardness in the moment continued. You stood there leaning on the rake and she stood there gazing at the imposing pile of leaves, your silence stretching out.

You noticed again that she was pretty, wondering what made it so. She wore a bulky sweater with a turtleneck collar, zippered up the front. Someone had knitted a band of black evergreens around the bottom. Her ear muffs were white, adding colour to her face. You felt confused noticing she was pretty. It didn't seem like a thought. It felt as if it had entered your mind through your skin, like a sound, a taste, a smell.

You glanced at her again and discovered she was smiling. It was similar to the smile you'd seen the day Miss Cartwright moved you to the front of the classroom, delicate, shy and pensive. You felt warmed but ignorant, as if at this moment she knew a hundred things you were unable to know yourself.

You smiled back anyway.

"She's going to burn these leaves, isn't she?"

"Yeah." Even with only one word to master, your voice cracked, splitting the syllable of your answer into two contrasting octaves.

Kimberley smiled again.

The Cat Woman came outside. "Look at you two," she said as she stepped down from the back porch. "What a handsome pair."

This time both of you blushed.

"How are you, Kimberley?" asked The Cat Woman.

"Fine, thank you."

"Everything all right?"

"Oh, sure."

As they smiled at one another, the smile was so private you felt yourself outside their friendship, set apart but privileged to witness it.

"I'll bet you're thirsty," The Cat Woman said then. "What about you, Kimberley? Would you like some lemonade?"

When she returned with a tray of glasses, she set it down on her picnic table, then pressed two dollars into your hand.

"Thank you, Phillip, for a job well done."

"Thank you," you murmured back.

As you and Kimberley sipped at your lemonade, The Cat Woman filled her incinerator and set the first batch of leaves on fire. There was a lazy gust of smoke and then a sigh of flames. Fascinated, the three of you stood nearby, silently watching them burn.

"What is it about fire that makes people like us smile?" The Cat Woman mused at last.

You didn't know how to answer her, nor did Kimberley. But what The Cat Woman said was true: all three of you were smiling at the edge of the dancing flames.

LATER KIMBERLEY AND THE CAT WOMAN talked

about you after you went home, how you were such a nice boy and obviously quite shy. Kimberley played with Eldora's cats, not wanting to leave even when it began to grow late.

When at last she walked home, she found her mother cooking dinner in the tiny kitchen in the mobile home. Her father sat in impenetrable silence at the table by the window, in case someone drove up wanting gas. Her mother turned and smiled when she arrived but she didn't say anything. Her father, deep in thought, didn't notice her at all. She went into her bedroom and sat in a small chair positioned by her window. There she sat until supper, gazing up the quiet street towards the church.

"The war," she remembered her mother saying to explain her father's moods of silence. But she couldn't imagine the war and it didn't explain anything for her. Sometimes her father noticed her, surprised that she was there. And afterwards he'd nod as if satisfied with the mystery of what she'd become.

"It was not so good for your father and me," her mother sometimes said. Then she would brighten and added, "Life is going to be better for you. You are so pretty, Kim. Being pretty will also help."

Kimberley's window looked up your street towards the Anglican church. Your house, she knew, was directly across the road. As she sat there looking out at night falling so quickly, she recalled how earnest you'd been as you raked Eldora's leaves. She smiled as she remembered the way you'd blushed, the way your changing voice had stumbled over your few words. She sat there wondering what you were doing at this moment, if somehow you could sense she sat here at her window, wondering where you were.

THE FIRST SNOWFALL OF THE YEAR arrived a couple of weeks later. It fell perfectly, floating and pirouetting out of a windless evening. You noticed it had begun to snow from your bedroom window. You could see it whitening the street, dancing inside the rays of the streetlight on the corner of the property where the Dunnings lived, next door to St. Luke's. The ground had been frozen for days and the air was very cold. Even your breath on the window pane turned to frost on the glass. You'd seen this kind of snow before and knew it was here to stay. You were fickle about the seasons, in love with their beginnings and bored when they were late departing.

Soon Mr. Dunning emerged across the street to shovel his driveway. "To keep ahead of the storm," was what he always said. Not long afterwards your father showed up too, although shovelling snow usually made him impatient.

You dashed downstairs. "Can I go out in the snow?"

"I suppose," your mother said, glancing at the kitchen clock.

Outside, your father shovelled furiously. His dark curly hair had turned white at the tips; he was not a man to wear a hat.

"Need some help, Dad?" you asked.

He glanced at you in surprise. "That's okay, Phillip," he said.

"Can I go over to the church?"

"I guess so," he replied.

On the church steps you danced and spun inside the storm, holding your arms outstretched to catch the snow on your limbs. You began to imagine that you were a trapper known as Yukon Phil, with dogs and a sled and a rifle, and bad guys to drive from your private mountain. Soon tiring of this, though, you gazed down the street, noticing lights in all the windows and how their feeble glow spilled into the falling snow like yellow gauze. In the distance you saw Kimberley's trailer on the Supertest station lot. You imagined you saw her in one of its windows and wondered if she'd noticed you pretending to be Yukon Phil. You felt a little embarrassed by your childishness. Thinking of Kimberley, you began to wish you'd been acting more grown up.

THE NEXT DAY, SATURDAY, you succumbed to snow madness. Even downtown it was beautiful, a foot of powder still clean and white where it hadn't yet been plowed or shovelled. It was too powdery for snowballs, but perfect to wrestle in. You made an angel or two with friends before—playing tag—you drifted towards the site of the Findlay fire. The snowfall had bleached the site of its soot and blackened timber. Now it lay clean and unmarked, an enticingly playful landscape for your game of tag.

This was what you were doing when your mother came along on her way to the grocery store. Engrossed in the competition, snow flying underneath your running feet, you didn't see her coming until it was too late.

Suddenly, to your dismay, she grabbed you by the arm and pulled you from the concrete. Then she began to lace your rear end with her other hand, her black pursing swinging up and down her arm.

"I told . . . you . . . not to . . . play . . . here!" she cried in a shrill voice as she gave you your licking.

In the distance, your friends stood there gaping.

You wore long johns, jeans and snow pants; you were too well padded to feel any real physical pain. Realizing this, she took you by both arms and shook you instead.

"You . . . disobeyed me . . . Phillip."

"Mom? Look, it's clean, it's not dirty snow," you pleaded desperately. Couldn't she see how white it was, that she was making a mistake?

She gazed at you then, as if considering this, then slapped your face hard. It stung so fiercely in the cold, tears gathered in your eyes.

"I told you to stay away from this place, Phillip. Didn't I?"

You nodded.

"Now get home. When I get back, you'd better be in your room."

Disheartened, you nodded again.

She pushed you away, then stomped towards the Red & White.

Your friends stood there looking at you. A couple of them shrugged before they turned away.

Embarrassed and confused, you headed for home.

THE EYESORE OF THE FINDLAY PLACE came up

three days later at the luncheon meeting of the Meridian Kiwanis Club. Someone stood up, addressing the club president formally and lamenting that the mess of the burned-out Findlay place remained for all to see. "It's a blight on the community," he said. "It reflects badly on all of us."

There was enthusiastic agreement.

Your father, having heard about the licking you'd received the previous Saturday, stood up then and reminded the rest of the Kiwanians that it was unsafe for the children in town to leave the mess around much longer.

Now that the subject was out in the open, the discussion intensified. After a great deal of shared disgust about "the blemish, the indignity and the degradation" the site represented, a special committee was struck to ensure that, by spring, ownership of the property would be clarified so that the mess was cleaned up by Dominion Day. By the end of their deliberations, the Kiwanians had resolved to look into the feasibility of transforming the site into a park. An amended motion to that effect was passed unanimously.

A further amendment proposed by Rev. Evers, the new United Church minister, however, that there be a tasteful marker placed in the park, acknowledging Mrs. Findlay's tragic death in the fire, went down to nervous defeat. A majority of the Kiwanians felt, under the circumstances, that any declaration about Mrs. Findlay's shocking fate was inappropriate at this time.

SEVEN

. . . There was some question of what Skeleton Club Private Investigations Inc. would do exactly, raised, of course, by Chuck.

"Solve mysteries," I explained.

"What mysteries?"

"Any that come up," I replied, glancing at Dwight for help.

"Like what?" persisted Chuck. "I mean, shit . . ."

"They're usually right under our noses," Dwight said calmly, as if he'd been a detective before. "Things look innocent on the surface, but underneath . . ." and his voice trailed off mysteriously . . .

DURING THAT PERIOD OF HASTE, confusion, and irritability leading up to Christmas that year, your mother took you into Ottawa with her one Saturday to finish her shopping.

"We'll have a special day together," she said the night before, when she told you where you were going.

"Okay, Mom," you replied as cheerfully as you could, resenting the ritual of occasions deemed special by those who knew better than you. When had special occasions ever lived up to their billing?

It was cold and sunny the morning you departed. You had shopping of your own to do, something for each parent, but as you prepared to leave for Ottawa it was clear to you that you'd have preferred to make your purchases in Meridian in your own way and time. Imprisoned in the car you felt powerless, manipulated by the demands of your mother's expectations.

The highway was clear, the sky overhead intensely blue. Although she didn't like the cold—the Chevrolet's heater faltered at the best of times—your mother was in an exuberant mood.

"I've been looking forward to this, Phillip," she said. "You and I don't get to spend a whole day together very often."

"Me too, Mom," you replied to please her.

"You're getting so grown up," she gushed. "So tall and so . . ."

. . . Don't say it, Mother, please . . .

". . . good looking. I'm really proud of you, Phillip."

"Thank you," you murmured quietly.

If she detected your embarrassment, she gave no sign. "I consider this part of your birthday celebration," she said. "Something special to let you know I know you're growing up."

You nodded. Your eleventh birthday, more than a week old, seemed an epoch ago. You had to concentrate to remember it. Boston cream pie for dessert, a card about, yes, how much you were growing up, and a plastic model of a Corvette you'd planned to begin assembling today or tomorrow. Even though your mother wanted to take you to a restaurant for supper and then to a movie, you felt confined by her generosity, guilty, undeserving.

She'd asked you last night which movie you wanted to see but you'd left it up to her.

"I thought you'd want to see Ben Hur," she said with some surprise.

"Sure. That sounds great."

"The chariot race? I hear a lot about the chariot race. They say it's worth the price of admission alone."

You'd settled on Ben Hur, if there wasn't still a lineup. Your mother was adamant that she wasn't going to stand outside in the cold just to see a movie.

"You realize," she was reminding you now, as you drove along the highway, "that we owe all this to your grandparents. They sent us some extra Christmas money this year, just to help out." Her voice dropped to a conspiratorial whisper. "More than a week's pay where your father works."

"That's great, Mom." You had no idea what your father made or why, but you sensed sometimes that it wasn't enough.

"So I thought the little bit a movie and supper would cost was in the budget. Whaddyuh think?"

"Sounds like fun," you said.

The grandparents she was referring to were her parents. Your father's parents never sent money. You supposed this had to do with what your father termed "the rift." But, you were frequently reminded, your mother's parents were considered kind and generous. "Not like your father's parents."

Your father claimed, himself, that his father was a sonofabitch. "He didn't want my mother to have me. He wanted her to have an abortion."

Not knowing what an abortion was, you'd asked the only question you could. "How'd you know your father didn't want you?"

"Your grandmother told me," he'd said, as if you should have known already.

Your father's parents never visited; they were said to be too busy on the farm they owned not far from Port Frances. Your mother's parents also lived in Port Frances but they were now retired—your grandfather from the railroad, your grandmother from having the house to herself. They'd been to Meridian to visit a couple of times, but once a year was all they could manage. Beyond some distant cousins, your mother had no other family.

Your father, on the other hand, had two brothers with children of their own, but it was rare that you actually saw any of the "Barrett Brood," as your mother referred to them.

"We live so far away," your father sometimes said. "It's the price you pay when you try to lead your own life."

Your mother said the fact you had no siblings was a

special bond you and she shared. "You don't regret not having brothers or sisters, do you?" she asked once.

"I don't know," you said because you didn't.

"After the pain of childbirth, I decided you'd be the last."

"Oh," was all you said, not wanting to know exactly what she meant, wanting to convey somehow that you hadn't meant to hurt her.

Your mother was explaining now, as she drove towards Ottawa, how difficult it had been to claim this Saturday for herself. "There are so many parties this year. Our calendar is nearly full."

"You and Dad must be popular."

"I've never been to so many parties, that's for sure," she admitted with a smile. "We're booked right up until New Year's."

You wondered if their parties made them nervous the way parties frightened you. You'd only attended one or two but you'd been nervous both times, your stomach full of butterflies, sweat a mysterious dew in the palms of your hands. "Meridian is a friendly place, all right," you said, merely to have something to say.

Your mother now reached the outskirts of Ottawa and the first series of traffic lights. She didn't drive as fluidly as your father. She tended to pop the clutch, shifting gears like hiccoughs. Your father, though, sometimes used his pinky to shift from second to third, this last shift a mere formality in a world of smoothly meshing gears.

"Our next car had better be one of those automatics," your mother said, like she was spying on your thoughts.

OTTAWA WAS FLAMBOYANTLY FESTIVE, even garish, for Christmas. Dazed by it all, you peered out the window, shocked by the traffic and noise, the haste of harried shoppers. The stores were ablaze with lights and decorations, as if now that Christmas was here, they were bent on making up for lost time. You burrowed into this cacophony like a nervous chipmunk, buying your father a pair of slippers and your mother a small, carved jewellery box, just to have your errands accomplished. Then, when you met your mother again at the entrance to Eaton's, there was nothing left to do but lug your gifts around while your mother stewed and fretted over what she needed to buy.

"I hate giving presents that people don't want," she muttered at one point, as she caught you trying to stifle your boredom.

You pretended to be more interested in the choices she must make after her complaint, aware that her anxiety was incongruous with her instructions to be grateful for every gift you ever received.

Sometimes she let you sit on a shopping centre bench where you could watch all the people pass, while she carried on alone. The passing shoppers frowned, grimaced, and often ignored the monotone of season's greetings that concluded every purchase or conversation. Even though these strangers seemed unhappy, you envied their confidence. The women dragged toddlers around yet still able to know where they were going and how best to get there; the men passed like distant giants in large fur hats your mother claimed (erroneously) were made out of beaver. You envied the way they ignored this Christmas assault on the senses, the background blur of adult voices, crying children, and jingling bells, the way Bing Crosby sang White Christmas from brassy loudspeakers in virtually every store. You wondered at one point, feeling separate from the passing throng, if growing up successfully depended on what you learned to ignore.

Gradually you and your mother worked your way downtown through the salt, sand, and slush on the streets, the mixture now hissing like soup in the rising temperatures and heavy wheels of the passing cars. She parked on a windblown lot not far from the Parliament Buildings, complaining that the wind from the river would probably chill both of you to the bone.

Walking along the busy streets, you shortly came to a halt in front of a large window where an elaborate network of electric trains had been set up on the other side of the glass.

"Wow," your mother said when you pointed it out to her.

She agreed to let you remain outside in front of the window after a cautionary instruction to be there when she got back. Vaguely you nodded, already mesmerized by this mystical, miniature world of trains, tunnels, bridges, stations, mountains, trees, buildings, and people walking tiny dogs. The more you stood there watching the endless motion in the scene—trains passing over or under roadways, through tunnels and into a dense woods—the more this tiny world seemed preferable to your own. The window display seemed a scale model of how life should actually be: controlled, sensitive, defined, maybe even perfect. It just made sense. The snow on the mountains was white and perfect, the trains travelled back and forth on an unfailing schedule. You began to imagine what it would be like to live in this window display, with the tiny people as your friends, and everything in your world certain and kind. Several minutes passed as you lingered on the fringes of this enticement. In this way, you transported yourself to the other side of the glass where you had your own train to catch.

Then a couple behind you began to quarrel, their voices so jagged they tugged you out of your imaginary spell. Confused, you turned towards the unhappy interruption.

"Oh, Peter," a red-haired woman lamented, her face framed by a fur-lined hood. "I just can't take your attitude any longer." Afraid she might cry, she tried to cover her face with her hands, her leather gloves so snug they seemed constructed of blackened flesh.

But the man who was arguing with her, his face white with fury, grabbed her by the wrists. "Midge! Can't you just shut up? Just shut up, for Chrissakes! Just for one day, okay?"

Before you could remember you shouldn't be staring, the woman glanced at you with painfully brilliant blue eyes. It felt as if you'd been caught de-materializing from inside the electric train world and materializing into this one where she was upset. You felt like a conductor with Canadian National. If you cried, "all aboard" at this moment, the man might let go of her wrists.

He did, but only to glare at you for not minding your own business.

As you guiltily turned away, you glimpsed him slap the woman's face. The sound of the blow echoed sharply in the cold. Hearing the woman gasp, you gazed stubbornly at the window display again, helpless, frightened, and flushed. You counted to one hundred, not daring to listen any longer, not daring to notice if they cast a reflection in the glass. Then, when you reached one hundred, you carefully turned around. You felt giddy with relief when you discovered they were gone.

This time, when you tried to enter the railroad world on the other side of the glass, it didn't work at all. The electric train world was still perfect and still made sense, but it was now plainly artificial. Although you tried for several minutes to make it real again, you ended up standing at the window without seeing anything. You were left to shiver in the cold until your mother returned.

CONFLICT THAT DAY WAS NOT OVER. In a small but busy restaurant a few doors down from the theatre, your mother took a dislike to the waitress serving you. You glanced at the waitress, surprised by your mother's opinion, not understanding the nature of the problem. She was probably your mother's age, although her face was deeply lined. She looked tired; even you could see that much. She wore the name Vera on a name tag.

"You'd think they'd get people to work in these restaurants with more personality," your mother muttered after Vera departed with your order.

You nodded.

"I used to waitress in a place like this when I was only fifteen. It was just as busy too. But at least I knew how to smile. At least I wasn't a sourpuss."

Nervously you remained silent.

Your mother lit a cigarette and puffed on it vigorously until she could gradually relax her pique.

Vera returned with your order, a hot turkey sandwich for you and a burger and fries for your mother, and set the plates on the table rather sharply. When she rushed away without comment, your mother glared after her. "This is the last time we patronize this place," she said.

You never knew what to say in the middle of this kind of conflict. You felt like a sponge, stupid and uninformed, absorbing only enough knowledge to know that something was wrong.

"Are you going to eat that?"

"Sorry, Mom," you said.

The hot turkey sandwich was fine, although your mother observed the gravy probably came out of a can. She hardly touched her food and hurried you through yours. As you both got up to go, she remarked that she wasn't leaving a tip.

When you glanced at Vera on the way out the door, she was still hurrying from table to table, barely holding her own. You felt guilty about your mother's malice, although you surmised Vera had no doubt already given up on the tip your mother hadn't left behind.

YOU ENJOYED BEN HUR, except for a few moments during the galley scenes when, to your dismay, your mother held your hand. It was, you decided, a dumb thing for her to do. You felt smothered by her touch, alarmed in the theatre's darkness. And your face felt broiled by the heat of your embarrassment.

After she let go of your hand, you were left to fret that she was angry with you. As you were leaving the theatre, you told her the movie had been great. You overdid it a little but she smiled, pleased with your gratitude.

YOU WERE ON HAND THE NEXT NIGHT—obliged to be part of the audience—when the Meridian Choral Society presented The Messiah. St. Luke's Anglican Church was jammed for the occasion. Because it was a big night, your mother insisted you wear a real necktie for the first time, one you borrowed from your father. He'd shown you how to tie it two days previously and, the evening of the performance, it was merely a matter of slipping it over your head, trapping it inside your collar, and making adjustments to the knot. You felt pleased with yourself, tall and businesslike.

The performance seemed very long and it transmitted its own nervousness, a kind of awkward intensity. But after it was over, the audience got to its feet in one fluid motion and applauded vigorously. You stood up too, knowing that you should follow everyone's lead.

Afterwards, Mrs. Wadkins, the minister's wife, accosted you and your parents at the door of the hall to tell them, yet again, what a wonderful performance it had been. Her husband, Paul, the choral society's director, was very proud of the group. Your parents politely expressed their thanks.

Mrs. Wadkins, a short, stocky, grey-haired woman with eyeglasses arching sharply upwards at their outer edges, then turned to you, smiled and leaned close. "And what did you think of the performance, Phillip?"

A wash of bad breath charged across the tiny distance between you. When she didn't move away, you held your breath. "It was great," you managed to stammer.

"And don't you look nice tonight," she added, a second gust of gingivitis soiling the air between you.

As you said "Thank you," you partially turned away, remembering, of all things, a sign you'd read in a gift shop somewhere, stating, "halitosis is better than no breath at all." Recalling this, embarrassed and trapped, a nearly maniacal glee drove you onwards towards the verge of laughter. You clenched your teeth to prevent this unexpected hysteria.

But the torture grew worse. "You're such a nice looking young man," Mrs. Wadkins said.

You were about to thank her again but you were out of wind, breathless in your purgatory of poison gas and imminent giddiness. Besides, Mrs. Wadkins turned away to respond to a remark from Betty Connelly, who was approaching with her husband, Jim.

You gasped for air and glanced at your mother whose mouth was clamped in fury. You felt a familiar, caustic uneasiness drift into the cavern of your belly.

"I'm so embarrassed!" your mother cried the moment the three of you were back home. She grabbed your arm and spun you around to face her.

"Mom . . ."

". . . The minister's wife compliments you and you stand there like a dummy. It was so rude and thoughtless. She'll think your father and I don't know how to raise you properly."

"Mom?"

"I could swat you silly, Phillip, for ruining the night that way."

"Mom, it was her bad breath. I thought I was going to be sick. I said thank you the first time."

"I'm so embarrassed," was her response.

Feeling wronged, you continued to plead your case. "And then she turned to answer Mrs. Connelly and I didn't want to interrupt."

There was silence after this remark.

You felt reduced by the panic you'd heard in your voice. You no longer felt tall or businesslike. You'd shrivelled up somehow.

Your mother glared at you a moment, then caught you by surprise. "Well, that's Betty Connelly for you," she said out of the blue.

The banker's wife, like your mother, was a soprano. They competed fiercely for solo parts in choral society performances and her name had come up in vain on numerous other occasions.

You pressed your advantage. "I'm sorry, Mom. I was going to say thank you but I didn't get a chance. I know what I'm s'posed to do."

Your father had rushed to the bathroom upon your arrival home. Now he had returned and stood in the living room doorway, looking menacing and conveying support for his angry wife.

"Everything's fine, Bert," your mother said, noting him there. "We've talked it all out. I'm satisfied."

"Mom?"

"What?"

"I wish people wouldn't do that all the time."

"What? Compliment you?"

"Yeah."

"Why?"

"Because I get embarrassed."

"Oh Phillip," your mother said with a careless flick of her hand. "When are you going to learn to feel good about yourself?"

EIGHT

. . . But what are we going to do?" cried Chuck, now hopelessly frustrated by the lack of specifics in our conversation.

"We follow people," said Dwight. "We take notes on what they say, what they do, where they go."

"You mean grown-ups?"

"Yeah."

"What if they get pissed off?"

"Then we know they've got something to hide."

Silence. This was a notion we hadn't considered before. Grown-ups with something to hide. Secrets. Troubles. Perhaps even lies they told one another. At that moment I was painfully aware that I'd believed forever that adults didn't lie. Dwight, it was now apparent, suffered from no such illusion. . .

MERIDIAN, AS YOUR MOTHER HAPPILY REPORTED, was the setting for several parties that year. Barely had December arrived than the invitations went out for various gatherings held until New Year's Eve. All of them, no one mentioned, adhered to Meridian's small-town caste system. And everyone on the positive side of the system was grateful for it.

Eldora Diamond was excluded from everyone's party list, not that she would have attended anyway. With a writer's intuition and some experience of her own, she knew small town parties suffered from too much double standard. To Eldora, they were celebrations turned aggrieved, settings for the sniff of scandal and the sniff of disapproval that scandal's enticement was designed to provoke. These were gatherings resembling annual meetings where no one can decide how good or bad it is that the secretary has forgotten the agenda. Not for Eldora Diamond to attend a party of people who called her The Cat Woman behind her back. Not for her to suggest that sin in conventional society thrives best inside a party structure where it finds a simple program it can follow, set up in virtue's name. Which was exactly how she put it that Christmas when she attended a reception in Toronto at her publisher's house and drank one cocktail too many.

In Meridian, Joe Langley hosted the annual Red & White Food Lockers party in his home next door, as was his habit. He and his generous paunch greeted everyone at the door with a polite but casual thank-you for bringing their own liquor. In a practical sense, he'd learned this was a wise request, because usually his employees drank too much each year. No harm done in most cases. Everyone lived close by and had walked to the event, carrying their shoes in a paper bag so that they could change from the boots they wore through the deep December snow.

It was Langley's wife Doreen who incited the sniff of scandal with your parents that year, though. You heard your mother and father chewing it over the next day after church, while they were preparing lunch.

The mock outrage and argument didn't interfere with the ritual of Sunday lunch. As usual, your mother prepared something for you and herself while your father made his own, the more exotic fare—beef tongue sandwiches or cream of oyster soup—he preferred on the Sabbath. These were items your mother despised. Shielded by her good taste, you had no opportunity to learn to like them either.

As they conducted the post mortem on Joe Langley's party, they sparred amiably with one another, stirring separate pots from their stations in front of the stove. Apparently, as near as you could tell, Doreen Langley had consumed too much liquor and spent more than an hour sitting in your father's lap, while he helplessly failed to find a way to discourage her. Your mother, while outraged by this territorial transgression, was heard to admit that it was also an endorsement of her taste in husbands, "Doreen being your boss's wife." Your father had little imagination at times like these; he fell to his previously stated moral credo with enthusiasm: you heard him repeat that he would no more violate his marital obligations than shit in the middle of the street. Yes, your mother said, your father was clearly the victim of another unscrupulous woman who was probably ashamed of herself now that she was sober.

You knew your mother's opinion of the sexes didn't vary much. She'd voiced them in your presence several times by now. Women, she maintained, tended towards shamelessness. Men, on the other hand, were little boys in grown-up costume. If not sexually innocent, men still stood by stupidly while female immorality merely manipulated them. And how would you—a dewy-cheeked youngster—know when the right woman came along? "When we're done bringing you up, you'll know the difference, Phillip," she had said on another occasion.

Waiting in the living room for your lunch to be prepared, you barely listened to the conversation your parents conducted, although you remembered another reason Doreen Langley was no threat to your mother. If not fat, she was at least quite chunky. Your father was outspoken that he liked his women slim. "The nearer the bone, the sweeter the meat," he was fond of saying, chuckling afterwards. Your mother, who seemed to smoke sometimes more than she ate, chuckled appreciatively too. And why not? She was thin. She was to her husband's taste.

AS WAS THEIR RECENT PRACTISE, the employees of the Meridian branch of The Bank of Nova Scotia attended two Christmas parties that year; one in nearby Ottawa, the other at Jim Connelly's home. The first event was the regional party hosted by the Ottawa main branch in the banquet hall at The Rideau Inn on the first Friday of December. It was the only opportunity for the staffs of the smaller Ottawa area branches to mix with one another and their various managers in the company of the staff from the main branch.

As a banker all his life and a loyal employee of The Bank of Nova Scotia, Connelly had attended several such events before. He'd seen various vice-presidents show up, take an honoured place at the head table and, as dessert was being served, present a dry, faltering yet morale-boosting speech followed by disingenuous, polite applause. During infrequent philosophical moments, Connelly described the annual Christmas ball as an event perched precariously "on the long telephone wire" between urban formality and grassroots provincialism. As such, the mix of country and city employees remained comfortably awkward each year. Each branch manned its own round table and, by the time everyone had loosened up, generally it was time to go home.

The year of Rhonda MacLean's first Christmas with the bank, there was a pervasive tension at the Meridian table, represented by its full complement of staff and guests. Connelly presided with his wife, Betty. Blanche and Mabel had brought their husbands, both of whom wore identical charcoal suits. Rhonda was accompanied by a handsome young man named Nick whom, she stressed more than once, was just a friend. Nick's last name wasn't mentioned and no accent was detected, but Connelly was convinced he was Italian or Portuguese, a sulky little bastard who didn't intend to have much fun at this particular event.

Rhonda wore a long, blue gown. Although the dress didn't cling too much to her well-proportioned figure and its neckline plunged only barely below the threshold of modesty, it still plunged and clung enough to offend the other three women at the table. This was a provocation aggravated even further, Connelly observed, when some of the men from other tables—returning to their wives with drinks purchased at the cash bar at the back—indulged in lingering glances and comradely nudges of appreciation as they passed the Meridian table.

Rhonda, he thought, seemed oblivious to the attention. In a fatherly way, he noted that she ignored the leering men. If she was a catalyst for some of the gloom and doom at his table, she didn't intend to be and this was good enough for him. Feeling sorry and remotely responsible for the tension at his table, though, he endeavored to be cheerful, encouraging everyone to enjoy themselves. It was an exhausting process that mostly failed. Connelly found himself blaming Nick. Nick didn't want to dance and, as the evening wore on, he slumped more and more deeply into his chair, surveying everything around him with Byronic disdain. With Nick glued to his seat, Rhonda, who wanted to dance, filled her card with the husbands at her table. Blanche and Mabel bristled each time their husbands danced with her and Betty noticed that Rhonda only asked her husband to dance when the music was slow. Eventually Connelly began to plead with fate to conclude the evening as quickly as possible.

By the time his wish was imminent, he knew Betty was seething. A tall, attractive woman in her own right, as far as he was concerned, he wished she'd find the means to help him through this awkward night. But when a private moment presented itself, she leaned towards her husband and clenched her teeth. "Your Rhonda MacLean is a spoiled little tart who's headed for a comeuppance if she doesn't watch herself."

Your Rhonda MacLean? Connelly was at a loss. His wife's remarks had arrived without preamble. He didn't know how to respond or why, purely from habit, he felt a ritual guilt. Knowing he was expected to reply, he nodded in an agreement he didn't actually feel. He kept nodding until, apparently satisfied, his wife turned away again.

At the end of the evening, just as the orchestra broke into its last waltz, allowing the evening to stumble to a thankful halt, Rhonda and Connelly came out of their respective bathrooms at the same moment and walked together down the hall towards the banquet room.

"I'm sorry, Mr. Connelly, for Nick and his behaviour."

"That's okay," said Connelly, a little embarrassed by her words.

"No, it's not," she said sternly. "I guess it just shows how immature some men can be sometimes."

Not knowing what else to do, Connelly merely nodded.

As they approached the entrance to the banquet hall, their shoes echoing on the imitation marble floor, Rhonda suddenly clutched his arm, bringing them to a stop. "Thank you for dancing with me so much," she said. "It was very sweet."

"My pleasure," he replied with a smile, feeling awkward still.

She gazed at him for a moment, then glanced beyond him briefly. "You're under the mistletoe," she remarked with a giggle.

Alarmed, he turned and saw the decoration hanging from the doorway more than a yard away. As tall as he was, he'd been ducking it all night long.

With unexpected impetuosity, Rhonda reached up and deftly kissed him on the lips. Then, blushing provocatively, she slipped into the banquet hall, leaving him behind in the moment's wreckage.

Caught by surprise, rooted to the spot, feeling guilty again, Connelly glanced up and down the hall behind him to see if there had been a witness to the kiss. Satisfied that there had not, he took a deep breath, composed himself and strolled as casually as he could back into the Christmas fray. By the time he reached his table, Rhonda and Nick had left. Their sudden departure added a strange, new poignancy to the incident near the mistletoe. To his sincere chagrin, he was distracted by Rhonda's kiss and what it might mean all the way home in the car.

THE GATHERING OF STAFF and favoured bank depositors at Connelly's home a few weeks later was anticlimactic. The event took place exactly as it had during previous years, despite the presence of Rhonda MacLean. It was intended that guests drop in for punch and appetizers. Prominent bank customers, a handful of friends and Connelly's staff began to show up around eight and then took turns arriving and departing—as if by secret code—until somewhere around ten-thirty. The Connellys' living room was comparatively small. As latecomers appeared, early birds departed, tacitly withdrawing to give more space to the arriving newcomers.

This was Betty's night. The various appetizer recipes were hers and each year she added a new one to replace a tired old favourite. Although she never got her hair done for the main branch Christmas party in Ottawa, she always visited the Meridian Beauty Parlor the morning of the gathering in her home. Beyond consulting with her husband over which customers of the bank warranted an invitation, she handpicked the other guests. It was rumoured that year that her rivalry with your mother in the choral society was what denied your parents their invitation.

Rhonda arrived on the arm of her influential father. Asked where his wife Olive was, MacLean said she had "too much baking to do." There was to be a large gathering of the MacLean clan when Christmas finally arrived the following weekend. Connelly was relieved that Rhonda appeared dressed in a loose-fitting sweater and a long skirt, the very definition of modesty. Not that she didn't remain alluring. With as little as a cursory glance, Connelly now realized it wasn't what Rhonda wore or didn't wear, what plunged or didn't plunge, even what was buttoned or unbuttoned, that defined her sexual mystique. It was something else he couldn't define, exuding from within. He wondered how it was she managed to be always a breath away from his endless male imagination, the one locked inside the closet he wished he would never visit.

If this second social encounter of the season reminded her of her kiss, she showed no signs of it. By the time she and her father departed, Connelly couldn't tell if he was disappointed by her "forgetfulness" or not. It was an ambivalence he despised. One of the virtues he prized most about himself was his steely self-control.

CHRISTMAS ARRIVED AT LAST, different for everyone even while its traditions remained the same. With no relatives in Canada, Kimberley spent a quiet Christmas with her parents in the mobile home on the Supertest station lot. It was a Christmas like so many of their Christmases, playing itself out between past and present like an angler with his fishing line. Kimberley's father would never get used to Christmas. He brooded deeply that day over what they'd lost at the end of the war and what might or might not lie ahead. It was a relief when he could open the station again on Boxing Day. But customers were few. He spent hours peering out the trailer window, trapped inside his thoughts, morose and deeply puzzled.

Kimberley too spent some time at her window, gazing up the snowbanked street in the direction of the Anglican church, anticipating anything, although she had no idea what that anything might be. Maggie Mathieson rescued her on Boxing Day. They spent time at Maggie's home above The Tea Room, listening to the new records both had found under their respective trees the previous morning. Just before dark they strolled up the street by your house and discovered that you were away, because snow had drifted in around the edge of the big stone wall at the edge of your driveway, and now lay undisturbed.

THIS WAS THE YEAR you visited relatives in Port Frances, first your mother's parents on Christmas Eve and Christmas morning, then the larger, noisier Barrett gathering at the homestead where your father had grown up. This was the Christmas you received your electric train.

The locomotive and four cars weren't at all like the ones you'd seen in the window the day you shopped in Ottawa with your mother, longer trains built to realistic scale. No, this was a toy version, less expensive, larger, but satisfactory enough to you. The locomotive featured a large lamp, which glowed brightly in the darkness. When you squirted drops from a small bottle of fluid included with the kit into the smokestack, smoke puffed into the air in wispy, short-lived clouds.

That night, in a dark room in the large farmhouse where, you were frequently reminded, you might have lived, under different circumstances, you set up the train not far from the Christmas tree and laid your head on the tracks in the darkness to enjoy the sight of the approaching locomotive light. The stack puffing clouds of white smoke and the brilliant green light on the front of the train were irresistible. But you suffered a painful gash when the cowcatcher collided with your forehead when you failed to get out of the way in time.

Everyone laughed afterwards because no one understood how fascinating it had been to watch the locomotive and its lamp approaching down the tracks. It was your first brush with the world's disdain for creativity and imagination. Imagination was simply stupid; you had the bloody gash and everyone's laughter to prove it.

NINE

. . . "It's not like on television," Dwight was saying. "All that shooting, murders and stuff. Being a detective is more like, uh, just work. You watch what goes on and make a lot of notes. You just keep an eye on things."

We painted another sign on the side of the clubhouse that afternoon. Skeleton Club Private Investigations, Inc. And Dwight typed our business cards that night, distributing them the next day at our first caseload meeting . . .

AS IT TURNED OUT, the rest of that winter was as harsh as the people of Meridian had anticipated. January and February were the worst. Snowfalls were extraordinarily heavy. Gradually the snowbanks at the edges of the streets rose higher and higher, pushing the Ottawa Valley horizon further and further away. Village houses, stores, and shops cowered behind these large banks of snow and ice like defenders behind the walls of a fortress. The siege reflected an ongoing cycle of snow, soot and sand, thaws and freezes, slush and crust, as the temperatures dropped and soared repeatedly.

The people of Meridian endured, waiting winter out with a ritual resolve, sharing bowling nights, hockey games, or curling bonspiels to pass the time. The more sedate attended choir practices, church suppers, and euchre and bridge tournaments. Your parents and the rest of The Meridian Choral Society began to prepare for a major performance celebrating Easter and rehearsal nights were scheduled once a week. The local Kiwanis Club began to see itself as a powerful political force, and it met officially and unofficially, regardless of the weather. Your father became engrossed in the continuous planning, organizing and gossip of the club, convinced that the club and its work were important to the community's well-being, especially the plan to build a park where the Findlay fire had taken place.

You were often restless that winter. It was a darker season this year, the daylight hours grey and half-hearted, as if night was a state of illness from which daytime couldn't quite recover. Winter was like an old black and white photograph, colourless and still, cars idling grey exhaust against the grey backdrop of the snow-entombed village. Human voices sounded strangled in the cold, jubilation compressed into a hopeless whisper by the frigid pallor of each day.

Nothing happened that winter in Meridian. No one died, no one married, certainly no one contemplated divorce. No businesses changed hands and no one ran afoul of the law. If this had been the case, you would have inevitably heard about it. It was a small world after all, a goldfish bowl.

One Saturday afternoon you glanced at a copy of The Ottawa Citizen and began to read it in earnest. You eventually learned to devour all the information in a daily newspaper available to you each week, happy to know there was a world outside this winter prison where summer seemed an eternity away. None of what you read touched you in any meaningful way but it was gratifying to know the names and the places and a little bit of what had happened. Antonio Barette, the new Quebec premier. The Canadian Government demanding amendments to the British North America Act to reduce tinkering in Canadian affairs by the British Parliament. Charles De Gaulle's ongoing struggle with Algeria. Barbara

Wagner and Robert Paul figure skating their way to gold medals in the Squaw Valley winter Olympics. Mysterious names and deaths and awards. Albert Camus, a winner of the Nobel Prize for literature, killed in a traffic accident. Richard Eugene Hickock and multiple murders, apparently on whimsy. James Hoffa and unionism as gangsterism. Lady Chatterley's Lover acquitted of indecency, although a U.S. judge studying the case said it contained "words written in public toilets."

You overheard a friend of your mother's say a copy of Lawrence's book was making the rounds in the village. Your mother admitted, with an embarrassed giggle, that she'd seen it. Then she said, with a naughty wink, there was too much writing between the dirty parts.

On Saturday afternoons you gathered with friends to skate at Meridian's outdoor rink. Listlessly, not feeling part of the activities in any meaningful way, you stumbled round and round the boards, past the rickety bleachers, tinny loudspeakers at each end of the rink gasping mucousy versions of Patti Page, Rosemary Clooney, Johnny Horton, and Marty Robbins, static clinging frantically to every note. If it was cold, you'd find your way to the canteen after a number of turns, limping inside on dull skate blades and weak ankles to warm your stinging toes. You rarely purchased anything. The hotdogs were steamed, the buns soggy. The hot chocolate was a bitter mixture of boiling water, powder and evaporated milk.

Yet you went each week, mostly just to watch the older kids make adolescent romance, holding hands as they skated by, preoccupied by the intrigue they put clumsily on display. You watched messengers hurry back and forth announcing frequent changes of heart, break ups, make ups. Each skating trip was a long afternoon of theatre and romantic conflict in which victims felt love and loneliness about a changing variety of partners several times each hour.

Sometimes in the middle of the week, once we were excused from school, you and I constructed tunnels in the giant snowbanks at the edges of my driveway, shoring up the crusty snow with bits of lumber scrounged from my back yard. We'd dig for a while, then sit in the somber network of tunnels until our feet got cold.

Snowbanks were empires too. During recess at school, you and I and the rest of our Grade waged war and defended our territory. The Grade Eight students claimed the highest peak; the Grade Sevens defended a lesser ridge. Our Grade Six snowbank was the smallest while the Grade Five boys dared to defend no hill at all. No territory was gained, no territory lost, but the battles took place each day regardless.

One week at the end of January, the girls in the senior Grades rebelled and tried to conquer one of the hills. They were speedily rebuffed, but not until Neil Donoghue, a brawny Grade Eight boy, pitched Kimberley from the top of his sacred snowbank. She fell to the parking lot ice with a painful thud. Before you could think better of it, you rushed to her side, knelt beside her and noticed tears forming in her eyes.

"Are you all right?"

She grimaced but nodded.

"You aren't going to cry, are you?"

"I don't think so," she replied.

But you were the enemy. With angry, laughing chats of "boys are such mean pigs," the other girls came to her rescue, pushing you out of the way, hissing further insults.

You retreated up your hill and gazed after her as she was led away. When Kimberley glanced in your direction, she caught you looking at her and you quickly turned away.

THIS WAS THE WINTER when Eldora Diamond began the novel she'd been putting off for years. She wrote a close friend in Toronto that she felt intimidated by the project. "I'm a poet," she wrote. "Ideas are like bricks for me. I'm not so good at weaving them into the novel form. One poem, one brick. Too many bricks in a novel. Actually, if I can mix a metaphor or two, I feel sometimes like I'm standing at the edge of a cliff, trying to ranch lemmings. Millions of them get away; they just fall over the edge. But I won't procrastinate, Nora. I promise you I won't."

By then she and Gertrude Smith often got together for tea, usually once a week. Eldora hosted these in her home as an alternative to the cramped quarters of the trailer on the Supertest station lot. Gertrude accepted this. Her husband's somber moods and silences were worse during the winter months. By times Eldora reflected on her friendship with Gertrude in terms of attrition, because they had so little in common. Mostly their bond could be found in the circumstance of their status in Meridian as strangers. Even so, this seemed to bind them together. Meridian did not seem as cold when they associated, even when winter locked it in. If tea every week eased their mutual exile, well it was bond enough for Eldora.

And of course there was Kimberley, Eldora's very special friend. Kimberley was sweet, bright, sensitive and charming, the daughter or the sister Eldora had never had. She looked forward to Kimberley's visits, to the way that they could talk.

"My mother says they're going to move me ahead in school next fall," Kimberley announced in February during one of her visits.

"Really? They want you to skip Grade Seven?"

Kimberley nodded. "If I keep up my marks and I want to."

It was Thursday evening and they sat at Eldora's kitchen table. Kimberley had brought her valentines over and was filling them out for class the next day. Valentine's Day wasn't until Saturday and the school was celebrating early. An hour had been set aside at the end of the day for cupcakes, cookies, and candied hearts. The previous day's art lesson had focused on the decorating of paper bags, now taped to each desk to receive classmate valentines. It was these Kimberley now punched out of perforated sheets so she could write something on each one.

"This skipping ahead, is this because you're doing so well?"

"I guess so. And because of my age, I suppose."

"I don't imagine they want to hold you back."

"No."

"How do you feel about it?"

"I guess it's a good idea."

Eldora sipped tea. Kimberley's Ovaltine cooled, forgotten beside her rising pile of valentines.

"But you don't sound sure."

"I'll miss my friends."

"Maggie?"

"Yes."

"But it's just across the hall."

"I know."

"Of course," added Eldora, remembering her own days in elementary school, "just across the hall can be a long way until you make new friends."

"What do you think?" Kimberley asked.

As Eldora considered the question she felt torn. There was poignancy in the dilemma she knew that she could share. Kimberley, nearly fourteen, was stuck between two poles. Her friends in school at one pole, her physical maturity at the other. Sooner or later she'd have to catch up with herself.

"Eldora?"

"You're growing up faster than your friends right now. In the end I think you'll be glad they put you ahead."

They fell silent then, considering what had been said.

For purely selfish reasons, Eldora wished she could stop time. "Never mind," she said. "I'm sure it'll all work out."

"I hope so," Kimberley said, although she sounded doubtful.

"So who gets the 'I love you' valentine?" Eldora wanted to know.

Kimberley blushed deeply.

"Isn't there always one valentine in the set that says, 'I love you' on it?"

Still blushing, Kimberley laughed and nodded.

"So who gets that one?"

"There's more here than I need," was Kimberley's reply.

"Oh. So no one gets the special one?"

"I guess not."

"Have you done Phillip Barrett's yet?"

This time Kimberley's blush was even deeper. She reached for your valentine and showed it to her friend. It was as innocuous as the others.

"I remember a boy I particularly liked in Grade Six," mused Eldora. "His name was Gabriel, but everyone called him Gabe. He had brown eyes. He was tall and very sweet. Gabe would have rushed over to make sure I was all right too, if a bigger boy had thrown me off a snowbank. We don't forget boys like that."

"Are you saying you gave him the 'I love you' valentine?"

Eldora sighed. "I don't remember. Love is a risky business. 'I love you' is a risky thing to say, even on a valentine."

Kimberley nodded thoughtfully.

IT WASN'T UNTIL YOU ARRIVED HOME from school the next afternoon that you discovered Kimberley Smith had given you two valentines. The picture on the first one showed a cowboy with a blazing red heart where his sheriff's badge should have been. You turned it over. "To my favourite friend who's a boy. Your friend, Kimberley," it said. The second one was the irksome "I love you" valentine, the very same one of Cupid and his bow you'd tossed into the trash under the sink last night when you'd filled out your valentines.

You almost didn't notice this second valentine. You'd felt impatient about this St. Valentine's Day business, deciding that this was another occasion requiring mandatory ceremony, another adult-conceived event vaguely designed to embarrass children. Last night too. Filling out your valentines because you knew you had to, you'd felt trapped and humiliated, because the world knew so much more than you did about just about everything.

Now this. Cupid pointing his arrow at a heart in the corner saying, "I love you" in white letters. You turned it over again. "To Phillip, from Kimberley." Poor Kimberley, you thought. She must have made a mistake.

Then your mother entered the kitchen, surprised to find you there.

"Valentines," she said testily, the way she would greet a group of termites. "Oh to be a kid and be remembered on Valentine's Day."

You didn't know what to say to that remark.

"I suppose you'll want to keep them as souvenirs."

"Nah," you replied quickly.

"Just as long as you don't leave them all over the kitchen table."

"I won't, Mom."

After she departed, feeling bold, you stuffed Kimberley's valentines into your shirt pocket. The others you consigned to the trash. Upstairs in your room you contemplated where best to hide what you'd saved. But gradually you began to feel hopeless. You didn't own a personal hiding place, never previously believing you needed one. Feeling ashamed and foolish now, you took Kimberley's valentines downstairs and put them in the garbage too. Then, to your dismay, the pang of sadness you felt drove you back upstairs.

AT FIRST JIM CONNELLY tucked his valentine, the one from Rhonda MacLean, into the middle drawer of his desk, the only drawer requiring a key. Alone in the bank at the end of the day, he felt sheepish and dishonest. For putting the valentine into the locked drawer. For even bothering. For wanting so much to keep it. For wondering why all of this mattered so much when he'd prefer it did not.

Deliberately he unlocked the drawer again and retrieved Rhonda's valentine, to remind himself of how harmless it actually was. Lushly designed with red roses of felt on an extremely glossy paper, it said, "To someone who has been an inspiration to me. Thinking of you on Valentine's Day, Rhonda."

As valentines went, it was rather insipid. He suspected thousands of managers and bosses had received one just like it today, with Valentine's Day set for tomorrow. He stood it up on the corner of his desk so that it would be there Monday for everyone to see. That way, whatever it was he'd initially wanted to hide wouldn't look like it was hidden.

Rhonda had delayed leaving the bank until after Blanche and Mabel left for the day before she'd come to his office to give him the card. She'd seemed a little flushed and awkward, although the more he thought about this the less sure of his observation he actually was. She'd handed him the card, then retreated back to the doorway, standing there patiently while he opened the envelope.

"Well thank you, Rhonda," he said after he'd finished reading the card. "This was very thoughtful of you."

"You're welcome," she replied.

They'd both faltered at that point, not knowing what else to say, although it felt like something else could or should be said. But she'd left and he'd stayed at his desk, not daring to look at the card again until after she was gone. Now, when he finally got up to go, he glanced at the valentine again. Yes, he'd leave it here until Monday. He believed intuitively that he couldn't take it home. Betty would not have been happy about it.

TEN

. . . Our July string of cases was heavy but not very exciting. We found out what Old Man Clapp kept in his barn at the edge of the creek, namely ancient newspapers and magazines. We discovered that Mrs. Durbin went to the doctor every week, although we could not explain this apparent excess, and that Mrs. Elkins's regular rendezvous at Reverend Howard's home was for a weekly game of bridge with Mrs. Howard and her two sisters.

Nonetheless, we met every day but Sunday in the clubhouse on my porch, Irving dangling silently nearby. Dwight now handled our various cases, assuming the role of chief of detectives. He read his notes and ours aloud, chastising Chuck for his sloppy penmanship, then filed the details of each case in a small metal box he'd brought from home. He gave each case a title and insisted that they be referred to by name. Old Man Clapp's newspaper collection, for example, became The Case of the Forbidden Barn. Even Chuck contributed a title for the Elkins case: The Mystery of Elkins's Bridge . . .

THE LONG, HARSH WINTER OF 1960 eventually came to an end. Eldora Diamond noted it in her journal one morning as she drank coffee at her kitchen table. The sun was angling towards the window and several long, narrow icicles hanging from her eaves dripped gladly in its rays.

"What is it about spring?" she wrote. "The madness of possibility? Is this what we anticipate so much?"

She felt powerfully philosophical, knowing she'd laugh at these words later on. She kept writing anyway, just for the fun of it. "The village will be euphoric: communally euphoric, that is. It's euphoria that permits the madness of possibility. Euphoria doesn't seduce; it just gives a careless permission. It's the madness of possibility that seduces. Guards are let down and the insanity slips by our careless sentries. Then what?" She glanced out the window again. "Then all hell breaks loose. Then all life breaks loose."

ON THE LAST FRIDAY IN MARCH, the sun shone warmly and the gurgle of spring run-off accompanied you home from school. Me too that year, I remember. I lived closer to the school. On days like this, I didn't have as much as you did to distract me. But you took your time this day, stopping at each drain along the street where muddy streams of water and floating bits of flotsam fell through the rusty steel grates, escaping towards the river. When you encountered large ponds trapped by ice or dips in the roadway, you dug a trench to the drain with the toe of your boot, intrigued and satisfied by the results of your handiwork.

Halfway home, you undid your winter coat. A balmy March wind tousled the fabric of your shirt and danced a chilly celebration along your perspiring flesh. You felt bold with your coat undone; your mother had told you to keep it zipped, not wanting you to catch cold. She'd been stern about it too. Guiltily and frequently, you glanced up the street in case she happened along to catch you disobeying her. You did the coat up again a few hundred yards from home.

"Boy, it's nice out, Mom," you said when you found her in the kitchen.

"Maybe spring's here at last," she replied, not sounding very convinced, glancing at you briefly over her shoulder.

"Fish and chips tonight?"

"Your favourite," she replied, cutting potatoes into

french fries.

A bowl of bubbly batter had already been mixed. You could smell the cod it covered. Your father's dinner lay on a nearby plate, coated with flour. He ate liver and onions on Friday nights these days, going back a few months to an argument they'd had about your mother making fish on Fridays when the family wasn't Catholic and "damned grateful for the fact."

"It's not because it's Catholic," your mother answered sharply. "I just like fish and chips on Fridays, that's all."

"But it looks Catholic."

"Well, so what?"

"What if someone stops by? They'll think we're secretly Catholics."

Your mother nearly laughed, although she didn't dare— your father was pretty angry.

"Phillip loves fish and chips," she said, stifling her mirth.

"Can't he love them on some other day of the week?"

Gradually they had worked themselves towards a stubborn compromise. Your father, they decided, would eat something else on Friday nights, liver and onions, his favourite. That way it would be clear he wasn't Catholic. The arrangement didn't make much sense. You figured, if someone popped in to assume—because you were eating fish on Fridays—that you and your mother were secretly Catholics, they would make the assumption anyway, whether your father ate something else or not. The compromise remained in effect, though, even on a day as nice as this one.

You slipped out of the kitchen and into the living room awhile. Then you went to your room where you played Conway Twitty's It's Only Make Believe twice through, singing along, your voice cracking on the high notes. But you grew bored because you wanted to be outdoors. As an excuse, you asked your mother if you could shovel away some of the slush and snow piled at the edge of your yard.

"If you keep your coat zipped up, Phillip."

"Okay, Mom."

Outside you immersed yourself in your work, constructing a network of canals, dikes and levees to clear away the run-off. While you were engrossed in these endeavours, Kimberley Smith and Maggie Mathieson passed by on the other side of the street.

"Hi, Phillip," called Kimberley.

"Hi, Phillip," called Maggie too.

Both of them were grinning broadly; you felt a faint embarrassment. Coolly you kept silent and only waved.

They giggled anyway.

It wasn't all that long until they walked by again, still on the other side of the street, going back the way they'd come.

"Hi, Phillip."

"Hi, Phillip."

You smiled this time when you waved.

When they came by the third time, they crossed the street to talk to you.

"What are you doing?" asked Maggie.

"Making canals for the run-off," you replied, feeling sweaty and awkward standing there on the sidewalk. You glanced down at your feet, idly moving slush around with the toe of your boot.

"It sure is nice out, though, isn't it?" said Kimberley.

"Yeah."

"Winter's too long," she added for good measure.

"Yeah."

When you glanced up at her then, you were astonished by an unexpected sensation of wonder and enchantment that virtually took your breath away. As she smiled at you, the feeling belted you in the stomach. You felt something normal about you vanish, like a skin you were shedding. For a moment you wondered, with a powerful dread, if you might faint.

Maggie Mathieson disappeared. You gazed at Kimberley, absorbing how pretty she looked, how soft with the sun behind her, glowing red where it touched her hair. Like a soft-focus photograph, she seemed perfectly beautiful. You remained conscious of the sun and blue sky in the background, an intermittent gentle breeze, but these natural enhancements now seemed entirely dependent on Kimberley. As if all of this was hers, the breeze here only to tousle her hair, the sunlight to silhouette her face, the sky to touch her shoulders on its way to endlessness. You felt dazed by what you saw, compelled to cling to it for as long as you could.

Maggie said something. You said something back. Then Kimberley said something. You said something back. You straddled two dimensions, neither one giving way to the other. Part of you talked normally about school, classmates, songs, pop stars, and movies. But another part of you was somewhere else where only Kimberley was real, Kimberley and the unexpected enchantment she inspired.

It remained this way for a long time as you stood there on the sidewalk, talking to them, like having a dream and being awake at the same time. Or caught between the edges of the two, unable to sort them out. This is crazy, you kept thinking, but crazy it remained. It was Kimberley. No doubt about it. Wasn't she the prettiest girl you'd ever seen? Crazy or not, you didn't want to give it up, this painful, exquisite moment of rabbit fur and quills in which you were so completely trussed.

"Phillip? I think your mother's calling you." Kimberley's voice, or maybe Maggie's, crying down some great, long tunnel.

"Huh?"

"Your mother. She's calling you."

You turned as the two girls chortled, and you began to sober up.

Your mother was standing in the doorway. "For God's sake, Phillip. Dinner's ready."

"Okay, Mom."

"I guess I'd better go in," you said to your friends.

Kimberley smiled a smile that made you ache.

They left at some point while you were still lost in the mist of your confusion.

"Didn't you hear me calling you?" your mother asked when you went inside.

"Sorry, Mom, I didn't."

"Too distracted by those silly girls, I guess."

"I don't know," you said with a bemused shrug.

"Wash your hands for dinner."

You turned to go but she spoke again. "So which one has the crush on you?"

You blushed, not knowing what to say.

"Maybe both of them," your mother murmured, more or less to herself. "Wash your hands. We're waiting for you."

"So now it starts," you heard her tell your father as you headed for the bathroom.

You'd lost time to Kimberley's spell. Your father's car was in the driveway. You had no idea how long he'd been home. It was later than you thought; you could remember it in the angle of the sun. Suppertime already. Being mesmerized by Kimberley had lasted more than an hour.

IT WAS QUIET ABOUT THAT TIME in The Bank of Nova Scotia a couple of streets away. Jim Connelly noticed the stillness after Rhonda let Mabel and Blanche out and locked the door behind them. There were sounds as he and Rhonda finished up for the week but these were peculiarly amplified and solitary, as if they held a life of their own inside the pervasive silence, Rhonda at her adding machine, doing her tally, the scratch of her pen as she jotted down numbers, the tinkle of the keys when she dropped them on the floor, her sigh of exasperation.

He interrupted his own calculations to glance down the narrow hallway towards the vault. The sun crept in there and died in dancing, dusty sunbeams. He pretended for a moment that the sunbeams too had sound.

He picked up a pair of metal cases, two of several to return to the vault.

"Can I help you with those?" Rhonda asked from his office doorway.

"That's okay," he said. "Finish your tally."

"I'm done."

"Oh, okay then."

Rhonda backed out of his office to give him room to get by. She smiled at him.

It took three or four trips. The hallway was so narrow they had to turn sideways to get by one another, continually excusing themselves.

There was no doubt Connelly's senses were acute. Not just sounds, but the scent of Rhonda's perfume, the quickly waning light, a tangle in her hair where it had been pushed behind her ear. Something else too, something palpable between their bodies as they passed in the narrow hallway. They hesitated there in their close proximity one last time.

"I guess that's it then," he said, knowing full well it was.

She smiled at him again, moving closer to him there.

He gave in and they embraced. They kissed. She opened her mouth for the kiss and Connelly staggered willingly inside. And he believed at that unexpected moment that no kiss had ever tasted sweeter.

Then, feeling a rush of guilt and confusion as powerful as his delight, he stepped away from her. "Jesus," he said in dismay. "What in hell are we doing?"

"It's called kissing," Rhonda said, leaning towards him again.

"I know what it's called," he snapped. "But what the hell are we doing?"

"It felt like you wanted to. I sure did."

"How old are you?" he croaked.

"Old enough," she said.

"Oh shit," he muttered, turning away, retreating the remaining few paces back to his office. He was—and had been—uncomfortably erect in his pants.

In his office, he sat down at his desk and leaned forward on his elbows. He felt a profound trembling in his hands, dancing off the ends of his fingers. He listened in the quiet, for what he wasn't sure. Rhonda had gone to the vault he knew; he could hear her being in there. He realized that she was waiting, and that time—for some kind of something or some kind of nothing—was running out. He felt like a quiz show guest where the audience is hushed, waiting for him to answer the question before the clock runs down. He got up and stumbled down the hall towards the vault, not knowing yet what he was going to say to straighten things out, but believing without question that he was going to say it.

Rhonda was leaning against the heavy wooden table in the middle of the vault, naked to the waist. Both hands calmly clutched the tabletop. Her breasts, he saw, were more perfect than he'd imagined and he realized, with a crash of defeat, that he'd imagined them dozens of times over the past few months. Her blouse and a black bra lay over the only chair at the table, telling him as much as anything else ever could that this was real.

He took two more steps towards her, intending still to say something stern, but when he opened his mouth to speak, all that came out was a phlegmy rendition of her name.

It was frantic, their kisses rough and bruising. She stroked his tongue with hers, back and forth, back and forth with maddening expertise. His hands went for her breasts, then his lips, his tongue polishing her flesh. He hiked up her skirt with both hands, parted her nyloned legs, stroked the smooth flesh above her stockings, moving ever upwards. She'd undone his trousers, pulling his clothing down to his knees. She had him in her fingers and he'd never been so erect. It was like they'd done all of this before. Him and Rhonda, familiar with one another. He'd never felt so skilled and sure. As if feeling frantic was all you needed to make love fluid and certain of itself.

Her panties were caught in her garter belt, so he simply moved them out of the way to slip easily inside her. He and Rhonda leaned against and half lay down on the old accounting table, which groaned in ancient protest, its dignity offended.

Rhonda climaxed after only a few ecstatic thrusts.

"Oh, God," answered Connelly.

"Not inside me," she gasped. "Not inside me."

Understanding her meaning, grateful for the reminder,

he cried out and withdrew at the last moment, jism spurting up her belly, through the cleft between her breasts, nearly splashing to her neck.

"Rhonda, I'm sorry," he whispered afterwards, deeply ashamed of this carnage.

"Don't be silly," she said with a smile. "It's natural, you know."

He wasn't reassured. He felt foolish and ungallant, childish really, as she wiped both of them clean with tissues she retrieved from a pocket on the side of her skirt.

He pulled up his trousers. She put on her bra and blouse.

He couldn't comprehend what he might say from the several possibilities available to him.

"Don't worry," she said during his silence. "I'm not going to tell anyone."

He merely looked at her, stymied by her words.

She seemed about to leave, to just go.

"Rhonda, are we . . . ?"

". . . Yes," she said. "We are."

He stood there a moment longer, puzzled by their exchange, trying to figure out which question he hadn't finished asking and which one of these she'd answered.

"You'll have to lock the door behind me," she reminded him.

"Yes."

She reached up and embraced him, kissing him delicately.

He was surprised and unexpectedly relieved that she still tasted so sweet.

At the front door, he unlocked the catch and opened it for her.

"See you Monday," she said as she slipped outside, her fingers whispering over the front of his trousers where his retreating penis lay, so that this touch was the last thing to depart, leaving him behind.

Connelly stood there much too long before he remembered to close the door. Still, he took time to verify that the quiet Meridian street was entirely empty.

AFTER YOU WENT TO BED THAT NIGHT you couldn't sleep. Images of Kimberley drifted into the folds of your thoughts, keeping you awake. You were mesmerized again by her image in your mind and the way the memory of her smile felt locked inside your belly. When you closed your eyes, it was like a photograph: Kimberley looking at you and smiling, the day a perfect setting around her, spring needing to touch her shoulders, to be a background to her beauty.

You supposed this endless agony was what people were referring to when they talked about love. You couldn't say for sure. You'd never known anything like this before. Nor was there a living soul you felt sure enough of to ask, not even me at this moment, although I know you believed I was so smart back then I probably might know. So you suffered in solitude, yearning over something exquisite you could never have defined. Even if this was love, so early in your life, how were you supposed to know what to do about it? All you could accept was that you felt like velvet cloth, caressed but suffocated. Love was going to be strange, you concluded, because even when it felt bad, it felt pretty good.

You heard your parents come to bed after the Friday night news. You heard them take turns in the bathroom, then their bedroom door close. You thought you heard them whispering somewhere outside your suffering, but you couldn't forget Kimberley long enough to listen to make sure. An inability to focus on anything else seemed to be another side-effect of falling so deeply in love.

THEY WERE TALKING across the hall from you.

"I suppose it's time Phillip was acquainted with the facts of life."

"Oh, Carol," your father said with his characteristic exasperation, "he's only eleven years old."

"And, in six months or so, he'll be twelve. I mean, Bert, look at him. He's so mature for his age."

Your father only sighed.

"Better he learn these things early, how to be a

gentleman and how to behave. Or would you have him learn about sex on the street from somebody cheap?"

"All right. Do you want me to talk to him?"

"Do you want to?"

"I hadn't planned on it so soon, that's all. I feel embarrassed just thinking about it."

"I suppose I could have a talk with him then."

Your father was surprised by this. "No, Carol. If there's going to be a talk, it has to be man-to-man."

"Yes, you're right."

"Jesus," he said then. "Are you sure it's not too early?"

"We won't accomplish anything putting it off, Bert. Say, maybe we should give him a book. There are books about the facts of life out now. And they're probably better at explaining things than you or I would be."

"That's a good idea," Bert admitted.

"I saw one in the rack down at the gift shop the other day, now that you mention it. I can't remember the title but it was just the kind of book we're talking about. I'll walk over there tomorrow and have another look at it."

"Make sure it's not for older kids," your father said.

"Of course. But you know what a good reader Phillip is."

"Yeah. He's always got his nose in something or other." Your father sighed, exhausted to discover yet another new responsibility had crept up on him again. "The book's a good idea, Carol," he said. It was true—the book was a big relief.

"I think so too." She turned over onto one elbow and patted her husband's arm enthusiastically. "Giving him this book, Bert, it's an important occasion. We'll have to find the right moment, do it just right."

"I suppose," he said.

"Seems hard to imagine, doesn't it? Wasn't he just in diapers a little while ago?"

"Not quite," Bert replied.

"Well it seems that way to me."

"Carol, do you think we can get some sleep now?" He turned over onto his side, away from her.

"Goodnight, Dear," your mother said.

But your father was already dozing off and didn't answer her.

JIM CONNELLY SUFFERED a much longer, rougher night than you did. Immersed in so much anguish and shame, he thought he might be drowning. He would rise to the surface of it briefly, gasping for air and then sink more deeply into the abyss of what he'd done. He was filled with self-disgust. If he was going to drown in guilt and shame, the damage was already done. He deserved to feel this bad.

It was this that bothered him most—the irrevocability of what he'd done. He might be physically the same but, inside, he was a changed man. He'd crossed a forbidden barrier; he was someone else now. The fact he looked the same only exaggerated his strangeness, the conclusion that, inside, he would never be the same. He didn't want to be a different man than the one he'd been before. He was desperate to return to who he'd been back then. But this was impossible now. Making love to Rhonda MacLean in the bank vault would now permanently insinuate itself between someone he'd once been and the tormented afterwards of who he'd now become.

"Jim, you're looking very pale. Are you all right?" Betty had asked him when he arrived home, apologizing for being late, feeling certain what he'd done must be visible in his every move. He'd wanted to break down and confess right there and then, because her concern for him seemed so undeserved. He'd wanted to purge himself with tears, the truth, and the extent of his dismay. But he didn't. He knew better than that—he knew he would never be able to justify what he'd done.

"Jim?"

"I don't know," he said. "Maybe I'm coming down with something. Maybe I'm just tired."

He'd survived dinner and the long evening afterwards. In bed a couple of minutes before his wife, he'd turned on the lamp to read. But he'd had to read the same paragraph three times to absorb what it said. When Betty came into the room, he was still staring into the book, not grasping anything. He became aware that she was undressing and he didn't dare look at her. He kept pretending to read as she lifted her pillow to retrieve her nightgown underneath.

She didn't conceal a mild surprise that it was there. "You aren't yourself, are you?" she said as she pulled the garment over her head.

He remembered then that this was Friday night. He and Betty made love on Friday nights. On Friday nights, he would remove her nightgown from its place under her pillow and put it under his, a signal that they were to make love. It was a game they'd played for years, an intimate way of communicating that didn't embarrass them.

Bemused, he gazed at her. He imagined himself saying, "Well, actually, I screwed Rhonda MacLean down at the bank today and I'm just not up to it tonight." This dark and feeble inspiration made him want to retch.

"I'm sorry, Dear," he said instead. "I'm not myself tonight. I need a good night's sleep. I'm sure I'll feel better in the morning."

Now, as Betty snored softly nearby, Connelly lay rigid in their bed so as not to disturb her slumber. Was he being considerate or merely expedient? He didn't trust himself to actually know the difference.

He wished he could close his mind, shut it down for a week or two, deny that he'd gone at Rhonda MacLean like a thirsty man at an oasis. Like his life was a desert and he'd only just discovered it. Like he'd never really known. Even now he felt betrayed by what he was learning about himself. The way, as he dwelled on what a bastard he was, his shame and self-disgust, that he'd begin to remember Rhonda and fucking her at the bank. He'd get hard again under the sheets. He didn't like this much. It seemed to indicate that a part of him, at least, wanted to do it again. No wonder he was drowning. It was all too much to bear. He believed he could shoulder the shame or the desire, but not both of them. Carrying the burden of both would definitely pull him under.

He slept at last near morning. His final notion before slumber was of his innocence as a leaky boat, slipping away from the dock. And there he was on the pier, waving it goodbye, letting it escape, yet wanting to reach out to call it home again.

ELEVEN

. . . Dwight queried us each morning about the status of our assigned cases, making sure we were living up to our gumshoe responsibilities.

"Chuck, what's new on the Clements case?"

"Nothing," muttered Chuck, who was letting it be known he was losing interest in The Skeleton Club.

"C'mon, Chuck. Detectives don't chicken out."

"I'm not chickening out."

"Well there's a mystery there."

Chuck only nodded.

If not for the Mafia Man at the end of July, Skeleton Club Private Investigations Inc. might have folded up due to lack of interest. But the Mafia Man gave it new life and eventually became a pivotal figure in a summer none of us would forget. . .

EMOTIONALLY, YOU KNEW, NIGHT AND DAY are opposites. You already realized night could be torment when there was something on your mind. Whenever you were preoccupied with doubt or uncertainty, night was a place with no way out. But day brought clarity, order, safety. In your experience, day mocked night's resolutions and fancies, then shooed them all away until life resumed its normalcy. No wonder, on the weekend of your falling in love, you were perturbed to discover the same restless butterflies still nesting in your stomach when you awoke on Saturday morning, and Kimberley Smith still the source of so much confusion and delight. All of this despite a gloom in your room perpetrated by a day now cloudy and dismal, in fierce contrast to your yesterday, a conspicuously perfect day of sunshine and warmth—and Kimberley's smiling face.

You supposed, as you lay awake in your Saturday morning bed, that the endlessness of delight confirmed what you felt for Kimberley was love. When people talked about love on television, they used words like "always" and "forever." It was love's endlessness that determined it was love rather than some of its fickle imposters, wasn't it? Wasn't this what everybody thought? If so, you believed this morning that you'd now passed love's first true test. The permanence you felt in your feelings seemed to indicate you'd taken the first enthusiastic step towards the horizon of "always" and "forever," where mistakes were rectified and doubts transformed themselves into certainties.

"Good, you're awake," your mother said, materializing in your doorway, startling you there alone with your poignant longing. "I have to go shopping. I won't be gone long."

"Okay, Mom," you managed to reply.

"You'll have to get your own breakfast. There's a new box of Cheerios in the cupboard."

"Okay." You felt impatient with all of this, with where she was going, with Cheerios, with what you knew was coming next.

"Then I want you to do something with this room."

On Saturday mornings you tidied your room, not because it was untidy, but because it was Saturday. Saturday your room was a mess even when it wasn't.

"Phillip? Did you hear me?"

"Okay, Mom."

She waited at the door. "Well, get up, will you?"

"Mom? Do you mind closing the door?"

She signed deeply and rolled her eyes but did as you asked.

Then, wearing only undershorts, you and your tormented heart clambered out of bed.

"I THOUGHT I SHOULD LET YOU SLEEP," said Betty Connelly that same morning from the kitchen table in the immaculate Connelly bungalow less than two town blocks away.

"Thanks," her husband replied, cautiously drifting into the room.

He'd showered. His hair was wet. He was still pale but it was a clean pallor so colourless he thought he'd become translucent overnight. Connelly felt weak and shaky but supposed that he'd improved. Even a morning as grey as this one provided a fresh perspective of hope. Just surviving the first worst night of his astonishing fall from grace seemed a major triumph to him.

"Are you feeling better, Dear?"

"I think so," he replied. "I didn't sleep well, that's all."

He poured coffee from a percolator on the counter. He set the mug down on the table, remembering to briefly anoint the top of his wife's head with a kiss. Then he sat down across from her to drink his coffee black, holding the mug in both hands, hiding its Bank of Nova Scotia logo and signature from his conscience.

"Bad night," he muttered, feeling this honesty expunged some of his remaining guilt. He would take penance wherever he could find it.

"Must have been a bug of some kind," Betty said. "It's a bad time of year."

"I guess so."

"Are you going for your haircut?"

Bemused by her question, Connelly didn't answer.

"It's the last Saturday of the month, Jim, that's all."

"Oh, right," he said. "No, I think I'll leave it a week."

His wife nodded.

She knew him to be a creature of habit and he felt threatened by this, that her knowledge of him was a booby-trap waiting to trip him up. "I'm going to be okay," he told her then, as if these words would keep him safe.

"Of course you are, Jim," she replied, clearly amused by what he'd said.

HE WAS MISSED at the barber shop, though.

"Jim's usually here on the last Saturday of the month," Basil Grisham remarked at one point, his scissors clacking away at his words as if he was typing them.

Your father was there and so was John MacLean, along with all the others who'd staked out each month's final Saturday morning as their day at the barber shop.

"Jim must be under the weather," someone said.

"There's a flu bug going around," your father announced. "Some of the people down at the store have had it."

He tossed an issue of Life he had been perusing onto a pile of magazines by the door as the men began to discuss how much more influenza there was these days with Canada accepting so many foreigners into the country to live.

"They bring it all in from Asia," someone said.

There were several grunts of assent because everyone knew that.

"Well," said Grisham then. "It's no small thing when Jim Connelly misses his day at the barber shop. He must be pretty sick."

All the men nodded warily. They were the kind of men who've come to believe that chaos can be averted if one recognizes and watches for the small details in life, the ones that dangle like fringe from the sleeves of impending change.

YOU FORCED DOWN some Cheerios—your mother had decided you favoured them even though you didn't—then left them to complain in your stomach. Restless after you tidied your room, you put on your coat and went outside, even though it was much colder than yesterday. The sky was thick with peevish clouds in various hues of grey. In all, the day looked like some shabby parking lot where neighbourhood hoodlums gather, intent on making trouble. The network of gullies, dams and canals you'd constructed yesterday had reassumed their state of ice and crust. You felt deeply disappointed, afraid yesterday's spring and Kimberley's beauty had been some kind of mistake, something you'd conjured up in a moment of vivid imagination.

You put your hood up against a nasty wind and strolled across the street to the church. You climbed the wooden steps and leaned against the stone wall housing them, your elbows feeling the cold of the unrelenting masonry. From here your view of Kimberley's mobile home on the Supertest station lot was unimpaired. You gazed in its direction, wondering where Kimberley was and what she might be doing.

Several minutes passed this way until you noticed her at her window. When you saw her face in the distance, you felt a deep relief.

Neither of you waved. You sensed that waving would vandalize this rich and silent communion. Yes, to wave would be too light. Whatever love was—besides wanting to look at someone endlessly, and then remember it over and over again later—you knew it wasn't light. It felt like it weighed a ton, an ache in your chest and a notion that something could be complete, that this weight was something you carried along the road towards a vaguely perfect destination where you could finally set it down on top of a new beginning.

Even when, much later, after several minutes of gazing back and forth, Kimberley got up to go, neither of you waved. Both of you simply drifted away, Kimberley from her window, you from the steps of the church.

THE NEXT MORNING at Grace United Church, Jim Connelly fervently hoped the Macleans would not show up for Sunday services this week. To come face to face with Rhonda here in the house of God, well, he wasn't prepared for it. But John and Olive arrived and took their pew at the front of the church on the right-hand side of the aisle. Connelly found himself staring at the backs of their heads, feeling like a fugitive soon to be returned to justice. Sometimes Rhonda attended church, but more often she did not. He wondered, in view of her absence today, if she felt even a modicum of the shame that he continued to suffer. Somehow he doubted it. Since Friday he'd come to believe that Rhonda was rather wicked. Wickedness was dangerous. Everyone here on a Sunday morning was well aware of this, along with wickedness's predilection for pleasure.

This morning's service tolled like a bell. Connelly couldn't concentrate on it. Easter was coming and the sermons in recent weeks had been growing more and more morose, an ever-worsening indictment of admonishment and guilt that, in Connelly's state of sorrow, was simply too much to bear. Shutting out the drone of spiritual shame emanating from the pulpit, he reviewed the conclusions he'd reached on how to deal with Rhonda MacLean. It gave him strength, this purposeful strategy, like studying for an examination that hard work would enable him to pass.

He'd have to talk to her, of course. It was likely she'd stay late again Monday, until after Mabel and Blanche left for the day, perhaps to apologize to him, perhaps to attempt to seduce him again. Either way, he'd sit her down in his office, apologize for his bad behaviour the previous Friday, and sternly point out that he was a married man and she was much too young for him. And if these two truths weren't enough, he'd remind her that they lived in a small town with a code of behaviour both of them would do well to respect. What had happened to them last Friday would never happen again. This, he would conclude, was the end of the matter. If necessary, he would tell her how ashamed of himself he was. Surely she'd understand that he was happily married and wanted to preserve his marriage, that now that he had failed himself he must somehow atone for his deeds.

Even if she didn't understand, or didn't want to, what could she possibly say to make him change his mind? This was his trump card—the intensity of his resolve. It wasn't like she could make him do something he didn't want to do. Even if she told someone what had happened between them, well, he'd just deny it. Besides, she probably realized it would put her job in jeopardy. No need for it to go that far. He'd make sure she understood. He had enough common sense to know what was best for both of them.

What secrets we all must have, he mused, glancing at his neighbours in the congregation. Lust, avarice, jealousy. How many secret sins simmered in this stew of humanity around him, posing as a pious congregation? Did any of these people own a dark secret as grave as his own? How much of everyone's innocence here was just the medicine they had to take to make up for what they'd done?

He'd never considered questions like these before. He'd tended to view the practises of others by the standards of his own, including his tendency towards innocence. He felt comforted by this. He was a resilient man. Once time healed his dignity, he'd become the same man he'd always been.

"Thought I might see you at the barber shop yesterday," John MacLean said as he approached him after the service.

"I had a touch of the flu, John," said Connelly as he shook his hand, relieved that he could pretend so well that everything was still the same.

Politely they chatted about what a fine day it had been on Friday, how pleasant it was to know that spring was just around the corner.

"Soon be planting season again," MacLean said with a farmer's certainty about each coming year and what its seasons held for him.

Connelly drew strength from the prosperous farmer. By the time he and MacLean parted company, he felt even more reassured that his feet were squarely set on the certainty of acceptable ground.

AFTER LUNCH THAT DAY, your parents called you down from your room because they wanted to speak with you. As always under these circumstances, you arrived in the living room apprehensively.

Your father was seated in his chair in the corner; your mother was on the couch, smoking a cigarette. It was balanced in her long, slim fingers like a baton. The smoke curled up like a question mark.

"Sit down, Son. We want to talk to you," your father said.

You sat as instructed, anticipating bad news. Were you moving again? Moving away was all that you could wonder about; it was the worst news you could imagine.

In the silence your father seemed to need to collect his thoughts, you noticed a paper bag beside your mother's ashtray on the coffee table. It was a book. You could see its outline inside the flimsy brown paper.

"Your mother and I have been talking," your father began. "We've noticed how fast you're growing up. Next year you'll be in Grade Seven. The year after that, you'll be a teenager . . ."

". . . And you're so mature for your age," your mother interjected, extinguishing her cigarette in the ashtray with such resolve it appeared to be impatience.

After a pregnant pause your father began again. "As we grow older, Son, we realize that life is a series of stages. At certain stages, we have to broaden our knowledge about our responsibilities, so that we can take our place in adulthood."

You felt embarrassment. None of this sounded like your father at all. It was like a speech he'd memorized. You realized you were attending a special ceremony in your honour that you hadn't been warned about. Discovering this, you only wanted it to be over as quickly as possible.

So did your mother, apparently. "What your father's trying to say, Dear, is we've decided you've reached the age when you should know the facts of life. Isn't that right, Bert?" she added as if to make amends for taking over the speech.

"That's right."

"You know what we mean by 'the facts of life?'"

"I think so," you replied.

"The birds and the bees," your father said, waving his hands in the air in an elaborative flourish of flight that only confused you more.

"Men and women and love and babies," your mother said with a sigh.

"Oh."

"It's time you knew all about it."

"Oh."

"So we've bought you a book, Son," your father said. "Carol, show him the book."

She reached for the bag, extracting a thick paperback and handing it to you.

"Thanks," you said uncomfortably, glancing at the cover.

It was called A Young Person's Guide To Love And Dating. There was a photograph of a couple embracing with the title superimposed over the tops of their heads.

"We want you to read this book, Son. Unfortunately you didn't get a chance to grow up on a farm where all of this would be natural to you."

Thoughtfully, you nodded, wondering what about farming was integral to dating.

"And come to us, Dear, if you have any questions afterwards," your mother said.

"Okay. I'll start today."

Your parents nodded.

You began to get up but your mother's voice prevented your escape. "This is an important stage in your life, Phillip. We want you to know that."

"It is, Son," your father echoed soberly.

"Okay," you replied. "Thanks."

"There's stuff in that book you'll have to understand to know how to behave as you grow up."

"Okay." You stood. "I'll start reading it right now."

"Good," your mother said.

"Good," your father echoed.

"Thanks," you said again.

Then you fled with the paperback.

YOU REALIZED THIS BUSINESS WITH THE BOOK

was because you'd been outside talking to Kimberley and Maggie the other day. You knew this book was about love and, if so, it was about you and Kimberley. And that was a relief. You'd now decided that you loved Kimberley—there didn't seem to be any question about it. Everywhere you looked, eyes closed or open, you inevitably saw her face. If that wasn't love, what was?

But the book was a grave disappointment. By suppertime you'd spent hours turning its pages, reading a few chapters, then skipping ahead to see if it was going to get any better. You supposed you'd learned a lot but it didn't seem to explain what you wanted to know. You'd learned how essential it is not to be late on a date, how to mind your manners, why it was important that you helped girls on with their coats. The book had described how to politely answer your date's parents' questions. You'd discovered that love attracted various imposters—crushes, infatuation, and promiscuity. You'd also eventually discovered the chapters your parents no doubt wanted you to read the most, illustrated with clinical blueprints on the act of human procreation, a means of having babies that made little anatomical sense and, according to the book, you wouldn't need until you got married. Were you to carry the book around until your honeymoon? Was that the idea?

The keenness of your disappointment, though, concerned what the book didn't say. Since falling in love with Kimberley, you'd felt oppressed by love's secrecy. The book shared nothing with you about what Kimberley made you feel, or what you wanted to celebrate. You wanted to share the idea of how you felt about Kimberley with someone, as you would share half of a candy bar. The book didn't explain why you felt what you felt. It merely assumed you felt it, then outlined the various responsibilities connected to the feeling. The book said you couldn't have the chocolate bar until you ate your Brussels sprouts.

After four hours of A Young Person's Guide To Love And Dating, you set the book aside to think about what you'd read. But you only felt more muddled. Kimberley's image preoccupied you in ways the facts of life had failed to define. The guide, despite all its information, remained outside of what you felt. The book said you'd want to kiss her, you could count on it. But right now, even trying to imagine kissing her, the notion drifted away. The book hadn't been able to explain just wanting to look at her and wanting her to look back at you. It hadn't mentioned Kimberley's smile and the joy you continued to feel when her smile was smiled at you.

TWELVE

. . . He was tall and stocky in a charcoal suit. He came to town each week on the bus, a fact we discovered during our regular scrutiny of the comings and goings of Colonial Bus Lines.

"Routine surveillance," Dwight had explained, stressing that we should be on hand whenever the bus came in. "You have to check out strangers, see who's coming and going."

The Mafia Man was a compelling visitor. The regularity of his arrival in town, the dark suit, the ominous attaché case he always carried, his dark complexion, and his black moustache were enough to make him mysterious to the detectives in The Skeleton Club. And then there was his barrel chest . . .

BY THE END OF THE NEXT FEW DAYS, Jim Connelly concluded he would never be more than a bobbing cork in the tempest of life. He felt paralyzed by the conclusion and the helplessness it implied. Had it always been this way? Was he condemned to lack of control for the rest of his life? What calm waters had lulled him into the proposition that he was in charge of his own destiny? Why had he not seen the storm on his horizon? Must he now be torn by crest and trough forever, tossed and buffeted by an infinite turbulence? Or would he eventually ride the hurricane out?

He considered mentioning his concerns to Rhonda, then decided not to bother. She wouldn't understand. By now he'd concluded she enjoyed the storms of life in a way he never would. She'd find his doubts and worries laughable. In a way, this convinced him even more of how wicked she could be.

Still, lying here beside her, stinking richly of sex, he supposed he should say something cautious. Make an attempt, at least. "We can't keep doing this on a table in the bank vault, you know," he said at last.

Rhonda snickered. "I find it kind of exciting."

Her youthful carelessness, the bravado that distanced them, compelled him to silence.

"So do you, Mr. Bank Manager. You just won't admit it."

There it was, he thought in the silence. How could she understand? What he considered bad behavior didn't bother her. An affair with a married man. Having sex in a bank vault, surrounded by a small fortune in cash. Connelly knew it wasn't in the same category as screwing on the church altar, but what they'd just done on the bank vault table felt powerfully sacrilegious just the same. God, there were limits, weren't there? What kind of a life would it be without limits?

"You go all cold and quiet after sex, don't you?" Rhonda said.

"I don't mean to," he replied.

"Well I wish you wouldn't, that's all."

He tucked her in closer to him, his arm around her shoulders. "It's this business of being in the bank," he told her.

"You worry too much," she said.

But she'd sniffed out a secret truth. Wanting Rhonda made sense during the wanting stage. Afterwards, though, in the state of fatigued clarity that followed, he felt merely crazy and condemned, incarcerated by his lust. He was two men living in one body, he now believed. One craved risk, desire, and foolishness, the other safety and propitiation. He was a before and after man, before and after Rhonda happened to him, the two versions clearly distinct. The before man, a ghost of propriety past, was ashamed of its hapless twin, the Scroogeful bobbing cork tossed on the tempest of lust.

Forced to acknowledge the new self he'd now become, from the perspective of the man he'd been before, then he felt really crazy. Then he felt really lost.

How brazen they must look, he reflected bitterly. Both of them nearly naked on a table in the vault—careless, lascivious Rhonda nestled against his shoulder under his suit jacket because the vault was chilly today.

"I suppose you're right," she said, breaking into the weave of his thoughts.

"Huh?"

"About making love in the bank."

"It's dangerous, Rhonda."

"I know it is."

She sighed, rising up on one elbow to study him. A corner of his suit jacket fell away, exposing one of her breasts. He glanced at it, feeling the act was sexually hallowed, dismayed that she didn't seem to notice or care.

But she did. "I know you find it exciting," she said impishly. "I just want you to say so."

"Okay, it's exciting. But mostly it's dangerous and uncomfortable."

Satisfied, she nestled into his arms again.

Dangerous and crazy, he reflected. The whole goddamned business. Rhonda's fault that they were here. She was attracted to the precipice. She went willingly to danger; he went there under her influence, bemused, helpless, and fearful.

This explained, in his mind, how he'd travelled from stubborn resolution to giddy surrender so easily. Like making the voyage in a trance. He'd resolved to end the affair; Rhonda had prevented him. He could still hear the echo of his audible gasp a short time ago, only minutes after Blanche and Mabel left for the day, when she'd revealed she hadn't worn underwear to work. Just her garter belt and stockings. Laughing, standing in front of his desk, she'd lifted her dress to show him, wickedly, he thought now, depraved.

He'd glanced away in embarrassment from her tawny pubic thatch, wondering in a hallucinatory way how she'd managed to stay warm all day, shuddering at the apparent inebriation such a thought represented. Shouldn't he have been thinking about why his resolution to end the relationship had already evaporated?

To blame the act of lifting her dress—a strangely wedded marriage of depravity and innocence—for his failure to talk frankly with her the way he'd planned over the past few days was probably disingenuous. His resolve had dissipated before her seductive act, probably in a gradual way. Because he'd wanted her again. He'd gotten up from behind his desk, not knowing what to say, but knowing enough to take her hand and hurry down the hallway to the vault with her, tearing at his clothing along the way, everything rising in him again, his blood, his penis, his carelessness, their lovemaking so frantic and maddening he wanted to remain on its summit forever.

She'd outsmarted him, that was all. She'd given him Monday to weaken, then had gone for the jugular on Tuesday. On Monday he'd been committed to the proper course of action. All day, keeping his distance, he'd remained resolute. When she stayed behind at the end of the day, he'd talk to her and that would be that. But on Monday she contrived to be first to leave the bank. Without explanation, without even a glance in his direction, leaving him behind to feel betrayed, used, dismissed. By Tuesday he was facing the possibility that he wasn't done wanting her yet. She'd outsmarted him by turning his well-planned Monday into Tuesday. Bamboozled, he'd stampeded down the hall to the vault like a bull with a pedigree, relieved and nearly crazy to make love with her again.

Rhonda had planned it all, right down to birth control. She'd brought her diaphragm on Tuesday. This time he'd stayed inside her when she cried out in pleasure. He'd spurted something profoundly needful as deep inside her as he could.

"God," she said afterwards. "You make me just explode."

He didn't know whether to believe her or not. Mostly he felt bad for Betty. Betty never did that, didn't come that way, not when he was inside her. Betty called it a climax and only reached it infrequently, usually when he played with her with his fingers. Betty said this was the way it was for most women. He'd been satisfied with her version until now. But if Rhonda was lying to him, he was determined to believe the lie.

It was time to go and they got off the table to dress.

"I've never done this before," Connelly told her, "you know, cheated on Betty. I never wanted to do something like this."

"You sure wanted to today."

He felt ashamed and angry after her remark. "You know what I mean," he said. "You know what I'm trying to say."

"But I don't want to talk about this," Rhonda cried with startling passion.

"I was just trying to be honest."

"I don't care!"

He gazed at her a moment, repelled that she might cry. Although he felt cruel, the feeling of repulsion remained.

They finished dressing in silence. Connelly had questions but he didn't want to ask them. Did she believe she was in love with him? Was she young enough to fool herself this way? Or was wanting someone enough, even when wanting was less than love?

"I know we'll have to talk eventually," Rhonda said as they prepared to leave the vault. "But not yet. I don't want to be hurt this early."

"Rhonda . . ."

"Please? Can't it wait?"

He didn't think so but he gave in anyway.

"I know what we're doing here," she said. "I know what it means, how little, how much."

She was biting her bottom lip, delicately nibbling at it. To Connelly, she looked beautiful then, frail and anxious, no longer wicked, but someone he was tempted to protect. But he didn't say anything. He walked with her to the front door to let her out, feeling large and clumsy and soiled, sequestered in his silence.

Rhonda attempted to smile and looked all the more vulnerable for it. "So I guess that's it for the old bank vault," she said at the door.

He nodded.

They stood there in silence a moment.

He thought he should say something. "Where do people like you and me go?" he asked.

Her eyes flicked away from his before she answered him. "The usual places, I guess," was what she said.

Then she slipped outside, rounded the corner of the building and disappeared from view.

OUR CLASSMATES AT SCHOOL treated your love for Kimberley with an unexpected reverence. Even Miss Cartwright—controlling the class at the front of the room like a resigned maestro conducting a hopelessly inept orchestra—displayed an unusual tolerance for your love struck distraction. This kind of benevolence was not what you'd expected the first day back at school after the Friday you'd fallen in love. You'd expected torment and torture. The girls chanting, "Phillip and Kimberley sitting in a tree, k-i-s-s-i-n-g." The boys taunting you and jeering, pushing you down in the mud during recess.

Everyone at school soon knew about it, of course. How could we not? How could we not notice how many times you turned around in your seat, located so conspicuously at the front of the class, to glance in Kimberley's direction near the back? How could we not notice those delicate, tender smiles you both exchanged? How could we not detect that delightful tension between certainty and doubt that felt like love to you, that seemed to be written on your face?

As your best friend, I required an official confession, even though I had earlier recognized the signs. You proffered it that afternoon as we walked to my house after school, intent on listening to more of my voluminous collection of records.

"You like Kimberley, don't you?"

"Yeah," you replied, feeling a delightful twist in your belly.

"I mean, you really like Kimberley, don't you?"

"Yeah."

"What's it feel like?" I wanted to know. I needed some of your secret knowledge. As far as I knew only a lucky few understood what love was like.

You were surprised by my question. I could see it on your face. I was a brain, the school genius. How come I wouldn't already know?

"Phil?"

"Butterflies," you said.

"Butterflies?"

"You know, in your stomach."

"And this is good?" I asked.

"Sort of," you replied.

Mostly the butterflies arrived at bedtime, you explained in your own words, when, trying to sleep, you reviewed another day of gazing at Kimberley in wonder, then remembering what you thought you'd seen. The best part about love, you said, was right after dinner, hanging out on the church steps, leaning against or sitting on the stone wall, waiting for Kimberley's face to show up in her window in the mobile home just down the street. The butterflies softened then, their sharp edges blunted, a plea bargain in velvet. You felt stroked on the inside somewhere when she looked at you from her window. Like you were exchanging an oath, your feelings now truly knighted, chivalrous forever. That's how I describe it in your place, remembering what you said.

"HOW'S KIMBERLEY THESE DAYS?" Eldora asked Gertrude a few weeks later. "I haven't seen her for a while."

"She moons. She moons at her window," her mother replied.

"Moons?"

"A boy up the street," Gertrude said with an impatient wave of her hand.

Eldora grinned. "Oh, you mean she's in love. The Barrett boy, I suppose."

Kimberley's mother nodded.

Eldora reached for the teapot, topped up their cups. Both of them drank tea clear; there was no milk or sugar on the coffee table.

"Do you know him? Is he a nice boy?"

Eldora nodded. "Oh, yes," she replied.

"He sits on the steps of the church. She sits at her window. Hours go by. Aach."

Eldora grinned again. "Sounds serious," she remarked.

"Yes," said Gertrude soberly. "Serious. So serious."

"She's growing up, Gertrude."

"Yes. Life moves. Life is . . . treacherous."

"Sometimes," agreed Eldora. "Sometimes it's wonderful."

"It is so serious."

"What? Life?"

"Boys and girls."

"Well, love's a serious business. I've told Kimberley so myself."

"Too serious."

"Oh, Gertrude," said Eldora. "You said it yourself—life moves."

Gertrude only nodded, then shortly changed the subject.

THIRTEEN

. . . "His jacket is always done up," said Dwight inside the dark humidity of our clubhouse. "That means he's probably got a gun. You can almost see it sticking out of the shoulder holster."

Belief and disbelief. We wanted Dwight to be telling the truth and hoped, at the same time, that he was mistaken.

As leader, Dwight opened a new file and called it The Mystery of the Mafia Man. Each of us followed the ominous stranger for more than two weeks, bringing back our reports and suppositions.

He came to town on Tuesdays and Thursdays on the bus that arrived at noon. He departed each evening on the seven-fifteen, after eating in the Tea Room. He always carried a newspaper under his arm and he always wore the same suit, which was shiny in the ass from wear. He called on each business in town each afternoon, never deviating from schedule . . .

WEARING COVERALLS AND A PLAID SHIRT, working gloves and a cap with John Deere monikered on the front, John MacLean strolled into his stable, knowing his daughter was there.

"You're going riding?" he said, not concealing his surprise.

"Yes," Rhonda replied, barely glancing at him, still bending to tighten the cinch.

He'd wanted her to be friendly. But, as always, his daughter pushed him away.

"It's cold," he observed. Here in the stable his breath erupted around each consonant, visible in front of his face. "Pretty cold for the end of April; pretty cold for a princess to go out riding." It was the kind of remark she usually ignored. He was surprised when she answered him.

"I'm getting anxious, Daddy. First ride of the season. I've been looking forward to it."

He stepped closer to the rough boards of the stall, resting his forearms on the wood, inhaling the familiar, wise smells of straw and manure, watching his daughter making adjustments to the gear on her horse. He viewed the animal dispassionately. Joe, one of the more sedate palominos Rhonda sometimes rode, fidgeted gently, regarding her preliminaries with a doglike patience. MacLean could see the horse's breath too, bursting from its nostrils in misty snorts and snickers.

MacLean didn't like horses in the same way that Rhonda did. Although he owned several, he'd never ridden a horse in his life. He preferred to drive out to the distant paddock periodically, where most of the herd ran free. There, behind the wheel of his pick-up, he'd light up his pipe and watch them grazing or bolting or staring back at him. Looking at his horses was his way of reviewing his achievements, as if they defined the vastness of his kingdom, the sacred ground that lay beneath their grateful hooves. Sitting in the paddock with the horses sometimes, not too close, but close enough for comfort, he felt like a soaring falcon, the fields beneath him a testimonial to his accomplishments.

Rhonda, he concluded now, would never know a feeling like that. Rhonda was a woman. Rhonda rode his horses because he said she could.

She was the only family member left who rode. Although she was still an excellent rider, she was not as good as he'd once hoped she'd be. She'd stopped competing early. Janice, her sister, had enjoyed riding for ribbons but, married now, she no longer bothered. And Olive? Well, Olive had been the best. But now she was in retreat, not just from horses, saddles and jumps, but from life itself. Olive, he sometimes thought, might just as well be dead.

Women let him down, defacing all his triumphs with a deep and nagging disappointment. He supposed this was the same for most men. A man worked to build a farm, grew prosperous and respected, but women eroded the satisfaction his successes were supposed to create. Rhonda, as much as Olive, had managed to let him down. He'd been angry with her when she decided to stop competing on the jumps. Not the horsemanship necessarily but because she was so beautiful on horseback or off. He'd been swollen with pride whenever he saw her compete. Like the accomplishment in Rhonda was there for everyone to see, the perfection that had sprung from his married, urgent loins.

But Rhonda was a stubborn as her mother. She often resisted him. Big things, little things. It was why she rode in western gear when he'd told her long ago he preferred her in English style. Even now Joe wore a western saddle arrayed with studs and bits of dangling leather. Rhonda wore chaps, cowboy boots, her suede jacket rippling with fringe.

"Daddy, did you want me for something?"

He didn't answer at first.

"Daddy?"

He shrugged in embarrassment. "I need a date again, Rhonda. The OFA annual meeting is coming up in a few weeks and your mother doesn't want to go."

"Oh, Daddy. What about Janice?"

"Janice is already going with Jim."

She stood there holding the reins in her gloved fist. Even Joe was as still as a statue.

"I don't know why they have to hold the damned thing in the middle of May anyway, just when things are getting so busy," he said then. "But you know I have to go."

"Well, you're president next year. Maybe you should change the date."

He wondered if she was mocking him. She had a talent for it, hiding a bite inside her words. Annoyed, he stepped back from the slivers and crevices in the boards around the stall, as Rhonda began to lead the horse out of the enclosure.

"Maybe Mom will change her mind," she said as she passed.

MacLean didn't reply. He stood there watching Rhonda walk towards the stable door, feeling angry and vaguely needful.

But she turned to him and sighed, apparently defeated. "I'll consider it. Okay?" she said to him.

He followed her out of the barn and watched her mount the horse. "Jesus, it's cold," he said.

She answered him with a cryptic smile, giving him a wave he knew she didn't mean, then rode away.

He watched her a moment or two, wondering where she was going and why, on a day like this, she was going there at all.

I CAME OVER THAT MORNING to throw the baseball around with you, but after a few tentative tosses we gave up because it was too cold. The ball stung when it found the pocket and throwing a baseball in the chilly spring temperatures, sunshine or not, seemed a little too much like work, especially with baseball season still several weeks away.

Shortly we meandered across the street to sit on the church's balustrade, not saying much, just hanging around. Although you'd arranged for me to come over and this was my time with you, I noticed you were hoping Kimberley would check at her window and discover you at the church. Maybe, even with me here, she'd sit at her window a few minutes, letting you see her face in the distance. You loved Kimberley at her window and you on the church steps. Each day you passed some time this way reinforced the exquisite certainty that you were deeply in love. Which was how I would have described it. You'd explained some of this to me again; I thought I understood.

So it was that I saw her face in the window first.

"There's Kimberley," I said, raising my arm to wave.

"We don't wave," you said, clutching my wrist.

"Oh," I said in surprise. "How come?"

"We just don't."

"Oh."

She vanished not long afterwards but soon reappeared with Maggie Mathieson, both of them strolling up the street in our direction. They joined us at the church, just standing around and talking, then taking part in some harmless jostling and teasing that gradually evolved into a game of tag.

You were fast this morning, as fast as you could be. You'd been fast for a couple of years now, loving it, knowing being fast was very good. When Kimberley was It, she couldn't catch you and you shared the satisfaction in this with her, sensing she enjoyed it as much as you did. She'd laugh and complain to Maggie that chasing you was pointless. By then her face was flushed and her eyes were gleaming. She looked beautiful this way, lit up with fun and pleasure. It made love better for you, not just love for Kimberley, but united mysteriously with the joy you felt in your own speed. You let yourself get tagged sometimes, to chase Kimberley again, drawn to her, always drawn to her even in such a harmless game. You tagged Maggie a few times so that she didn't feel left out, but even this was instigated by love. Love made you feel rich and you could afford the philanthropic luxury of kindness attached to it. I remember that game of tag this way. I remember it clearly now.

The game soon warmed us up. Joyful, laughing and overheated, all of us took off our coats and put them on the church steps. The brown grass on which we ran was muddy and slick, but our feet danced over this obstacle as they would in an inspired ballet. Everything felt perfect and extraordinary, I knew. You felt endless with your friends.

"Phillip? You get your clothes muddy and you'll get a licking."

Your mother's voice seemed to come from everywhere, shattering your joy, tearing a fissure through your morning, ripping it in two. I heard you exhale in disappointment and nearly not breathe again.

We all turned and saw her leaning out the front door, one foot inside the house, the other on the rubber mat on the stoop. Her hair was up in curlers and bobby pins, a get-up that didn't confirm that she was angry but made her look as if she was.

I saw you feel a deep embarrassment, color Chinese orange.

"Phillip? Did you hear me?"

"Okay, Mom."

She hesitated a moment, then disappeared inside.

You felt stupid now, not just your mother's warning, the threat of a licking, but what you'd believed about endless joy, or that this time spent with your friends was invulnerable somehow. Now it was all gone, the moment destroyed. I could see it on your face. You weren't fast any longer, your feet had gone heavy again. All of us stood there, sharing this transformation with you. The game of tag was over, its battery dead. Coats were back on. While you battled a deepening gloom, Kimberley and Maggie announced that they had to go.

You swallowed in disappointment until Kimberley smiled at you.

"Don't forget tonight," she said just before she left.

We watched the two girls walk down the street before I mentioned I had to go home too.

"What's this about tonight?" I asked.

"I'm going to Eldora Diamond's for dinner."

"The Cat Woman's?"

"Yeah."

"With your folks?"

"No, just me and Kimberley."

You walked with me across the street in the direction of your house.

"I have to get all dressed up," you explained.

"I thought your parents didn't like the Cat Woman."

"Well . . ." And you didn't know how to explain it, so much had changed during the past few months.

"Is this like a date or something?"

"I don't know," you replied.

It seemed a difficult question to answer. Even A Young Person's Guide To Love And Dating had assumed you knew what a date was and wasn't. Bud Anderson went on dates on Father Knows Best but he was older and his world of dating didn't seem to have much to do with you.

"I don't know," you said at last, "if it's actually a date or not."

"Are you picking her up?"

"Kimberley?"

"Yeah, who else?"

"No. She'll already be there. She's going to help with dinner. Do you have to pick someone up for it to be a date?"

"I think so," I replied.

You considered my verdict a moment. "It really bugs me, Gare, that everyone thinks you know something when no one's ever explained it."

"I know," I said. "But I've got a feeling we haven't seen anything yet."

RHONDA WAS OFF ON A TANGENT, talking about her mother, but Connelly was barely listening. The entwined affinities, empathy, and history between Rhonda and Olive MacLean seemed too complicated to him. As usual, now that sex was over, he'd grown deeply nervous again. It was hard to listen to Rhonda when he was so preoccupied by the nature of his risk. She lay in his arms, her cheek against his chest. As she pattered on about her mother, the words vibrated along his flesh until he was more aware of the touch of her speech than he was its sound.

"So Mom doesn't do much anymore except cook the meals and do the dishes. She spends most of her time in her room. That's why Daddy is always looking for someone to go places with him."

"You'd think she'd want to get out. Why doesn't she go?"

"I think she's had enough. I think she's tired. I think she's finally been overwhelmed."

"Your father's a strong man. It's why he's done so well."

Connelly was beginning to feel sorry for John MacLean. Women were never satisfied: men were either too ambitious or not ambitious enough.

"He wears you down, that's for sure. He overwhelms everyone eventually," Rhonda said.

"Except you."

"Me too, I guess. You know something? I'll probably go to that stupid OFA dinner and annual meeting, if Mom doesn't change her mind."

Connelly gazed from the bed at a series of geographic smudges on the tiles of the ceiling. He not only felt sorry for John MacLean, he felt impatient with Rhonda's youth. "Well he's your father. It won't hurt you to go to a dinner with him, will it?"

"I'm not my father's wife," cried Rhonda with unexpected vehemence.

"Of course not," Connelly said, perturbed by her outburst. "That wasn't what I meant."

"Men don't understand anything, do they? To men, it's all property, isn't it?"

Connelly didn't answer her. She'd asked her questions tonelessly, compliantly, almost in a state of serenity. He wondered if she was learning early that acceptance was the key to serenity. A person grew up. One learned to surrender to life's disappointing inevitabilities. There was no promised land, only a bleak and dingy downtown—which was life. Eventually this kind of slum was good enough. People made the best of it.

"Jim? I'm sorry for what I said. Don't be mad at me."

"Hush," he replied. "I'm not mad at you."

Obligingly she fell silent.

He was grateful for her silence. He wanted to be alone with the feeling that his being here was tragically fanciful. He wanted to worry through his trepidation that he was going to get caught, that this young woman was going to ruin his life. He wanted to keep it to himself. He didn't want to have to explain something as nebulous as his fears to a virtual child like Rhonda who wouldn't understand them.

Excited to see Rhonda when he'd first arrived, wanting to make love to her in a bed for the first time, he hadn't cared how dangerous this setting was. How exposed. Now, though, he felt himself in danger and Rhonda didn't care. Wanting to lollygag in bed, she couldn't see their situation through his eyes. He was alone inside this danger, trespassing on hallowed ground. This was John MacLean's cabin. It was on John MacLean's property, on a point of land where his vast acreage reached the edge of the river. The banker's car was hidden among the trees at the rear of the cabin, but Connelly was convinced it remained visible to any passing boat daring to negotiate the last few melting flows of river ice. John MacLean's cabin, not only by deed and title, but in practise too, as far as he knew.

Rhonda had told him that her parents lived in this cabin for two months not long before she was born, during major renovations to the main house. But it hadn't seen any use since then except during duck hunting season, she said. On the surface of it, what she told him seemed convincing. He could see for himself the lack of upkeep, the way the roadway in was just a track, two parallel pathways with a grassy median separating them.

But there was a horse tethered to the front porch today. No wonder he felt strange. It was like he'd stumbled onto the set of a western movie. Caught at the scene of the crime, it wouldn't be too long before the lynch mob set out to tear him to pieces. It continued to annoy him that Rhonda was oblivious to his risk. Arriving shortly after he had, she'd wanted to build a fire in the fireplace. He'd had to caution her about the smoke.

"I've come here alone and lit a fire," she argued.

"Rhonda," he replied as patiently as he could. "You're not alone this afternoon."

"What about the kerosene heater in the bedroom?"

"That'll be fine," he'd said.

No matter how cautious he was and how reckless she

was, she didn't quarrel with him before sex. Too much lost lovemaking at risk, he supposed. Rhonda liked sex as much as he did, with her at least. If ever they had a fight, he was sure it'd be afterwards, when the guard of their wanting one another was down.

Even Rhonda's enjoyment of sex made him uneasy, though. Was it natural? Was it healthy? Was this how sex was supposed to be? He liked her provocative enthusiasm but was also embarrassed by it. It confirmed their affair was something other than love. When he made his escape from this situation—and he definitely still intended to escape—he was sure the task would be easier because he wasn't in love. Rhonda's ardor for sex was integral to this conclusion.

Connelly glanced at her in the silence, wondering if she'd fallen asleep. Her eyes were closed but he thought she was awake. My God, she's gorgeous, though, he thought. The observation caught in his throat, compelling him to look away. Sometimes gazing at Rhonda this way was like peeking inside Pandora's Box. Magical beauty, he thought, with an ability to shine even here in this gloomy bedroom. Here, the bed squeaked, the night table was stained, as was the small dresser and the wood paneling on the walls. Altogether it was dark and oppressive here with the curtains closed. But Rhonda nonetheless took his breath away.

A new wave of alienation came over him and he felt strange again in this setting, the kerosene heater tsking its disapproval, his clothes folded on an old chair, looking sarcastically formal because hers were tossed on the floor. Riding gear. And he remembered the horse tied up out front.

"Rhonda, I have to go. The later I stay, the harder it'll be to explain where I was."

She didn't reply but moved away from him, an act of immediate, cold disentanglement.

He nearly complained because her abruptness seemed so unfair, but he climbed out of bed in silence and hurriedly began to dress.

"Aren't you coming?" he asked, noticing that she lay

there watching him.

"No." She looked glazed, distant, magical again. "Actually I'm going to lie here a while and smell where you were in my bed."

Her words embarrassed him. He felt inept. "Rhonda," he murmured, "I'm sorry."

She gazed at him a moment. Eventually she shrugged and didn't say anything else.

After he was dressed, he stood awkwardly at the side of the bed, not knowing what to do next.

"You're going to kiss me goodbye, aren't you?"

"Of course," he replied, no longer sure whether this was to mollify her or he'd actually intended to kiss her or not.

But he stumbled around to her side of the bed, located perilously close to the wall. He laid the flat of his hand against the panelling to steady himself and found it astonishingly cold. Winter was still a fossil within the cabin's wooden walls.

When he kissed her, her tongue darted into his mouth and he felt a charge race along the tendons of his body. He started.

She giggled afterwards. "Once a tart always a tart, eh?"

"Don't say things like that," he whispered, rising to his full height, barely two inches below the ceiling. "You're not a tart. I know you're not a tart." Still, his annoyance with her was deep. Even her self-deprecation seemed impudent somehow.

"You don't like me, do you?"

"I'm crazy about you," he said with a sigh.

"But you don't like me."

"Rhonda, I have to go."

"I know."

"This is your father's cabin."

"I know. My father owns everything."

"I have to go."

"So go," she said. "Just go."

He left. He drove the narrow lane back to the concession road that would take him safely home, perturbed by Rhonda's behaviour. But when he reached the intersection, his fretting over his mistress gave way to a deep relief that no one had spotted him. His relief gave way in turn to the lies he must prepare for Betty if she questioned the length of his absence. Saturday afternoons tended to be his own; sometimes she didn't think to ask him what he did while he was gone. But this was something he shouldn't take for granted.

"DON'T MAKE ME ASHAMED of you," your mother said as you left the house to walk to Eldora Diamond's for dinner.

"I won't, Mom," you replied at the door, familiar with this parting instruction. You carried daffodils in one hand. You turned the door knob with the other.

It was still chilly outside. She'd made you wear your winter coat over your blazer and this much clothing felt tight at the shoulders, like you'd been stuffed into a fabric box a little like a coffin. The necktie knotted at your throat felt alien and twisted, wrong, a noose. Your mother had insisted you dress up this way for dinner even while she'd resented it. "She's artsy, Eldora Diamond. Dressing for dinner is putting on the dog, as far as I'm concerned. But that's probably what she'll expect."

You let her remarks pass without comment. Miss Diamond wasn't the point. The point was Kimberley. You just wanted to get going. Had your mother even mentioned once that Kimberley was going to be there, you would have gladly replied. This, you would have discussed enthusiastically. This, you would have shared, if only you'd had the chance.

Girdled in too many layers of tight clothing, you took a shortcut towards Eldora Diamond's home, the pathway a house away, connecting your street with the next. The thick mud that had characterized the path a week ago had at last dried up. Rebelliously you unfastened your heavy coat. "Poor little sausage," you imagined your maternal grandmother saying, you felt so encased by your clothing. It just popped into your mind. "Poor little sausage," you knew she would have said.

You emerged from the path and rounded the corner of

the tiny Meridian library. You passed the barber shop next door. Mr. Grisham was in the barber's chair half turned towards the mirror. You'd seen him here before as he neared the end of his day, using the mirror to study the street he pretended not to watch.

Nervously you trudged on, anxious to see Kimberley, feeling socially inexperienced. Your mother's fault, you thought. Each time she told you to behave it implied you didn't know how. Tonight, with so much at stake, she'd convinced you it was true. The business over the daffodils, your mother fretting about not having tissue paper to wrap them in, then suddenly becoming defiant and settling on foolscap. "Foolscap," she'd muttered with a meaningful glare, "will simply have to do." Because she hadn't wanted to spend the extra money on tissue paper. Like there was some principle at stake in all of this honorable poverty. "You be proud of yourself, Son. You're as good as anyone," she'd said.

Now, as you rang Eldora Diamond's doorbell, you still weren't sure exactly what she'd meant. Still, her attitude, her annoyance had increased your nervousness.

Kimberley answered the door.

"Hi, Phillip."

"Hi, Kimie," you replied, calling her Kimie recently whenever no one was around to hear.

Blushing a little at the formality of it, she took your coat and hung it on a hanger in the closet by the door. You thrust the daffodils at her, pleased when she said thank you as if you'd brought them just for her. She looked so pretty holding the flowers, even wearing a checked apron spattered with flour.

She noticed you glance at the apron. "Eldora's teaching me to cook," she said. "I've learned so much today."

She led you down the hall towards the kitchen. Along the way, one of the cats peeked out of a doorway at you, then dashed away, feline, fleeting, furry. You remembered the Cat Woman gossip and the way you had believed it, and felt ashamed of yourself.

"Hello, Phillip." Your hostess stood at the stove, wearing an apron as smudged as Kimberley's.

"Hello, Miss Diamond," you said.

"Oh my," she replied, taken aback by this. "Please call me Eldora. I have an aunt in Calgary. We call her Miss Diamond."

You smiled when she did.

"Look at you all dressed up. Kimberley and I look like short order cooks in a diner. Why don't you take off your blazer. Just hang it on the back of the chair. It's awfully hot in here. The oven's been on for hours."

"Okay."

"And stuff that tie into the pocket. It looks like it's torturing you."

"Okay."

Kimberley grinned when you caught her eye.

They sat you down at the kitchen table, which was already set. Kimberley and Eldora both talked at once, laughing about what rotten cooks they were. The blind leading the blind, was how Eldora put it. The dinner was soon ready, though—roast beef, roast potatoes, peas and Yorkshire pudding.

"Your father trimmed this roast," Eldora reminded you as she carved the beef.

It was quite pink and fascinated you. You'd never seen rare roast beef before.

"Come to think of it," Eldora added, "your father probably trimmed most of the meat people are eating in town tonight. Have you ever thought about that?"

"No, I haven't," you replied, trying to imagine it.

While you ate the first course, Eldora managed to drag what you knew of your family history out of you. It turned out that she'd visited Port Frances, the place where you were born. She knew South Clarion too. She'd once travelled a great deal, it appeared.

Kimberley served dessert, apple pie with ice cream, but not until Eldora showed you the patchwork repairs to the pastry on the top. "It looks fine to me," you murmured politely.

There was an awkward moment, as you ate your second piece of pie, when you asked Eldora if she had ever sung professionally in the opera. This was what your mother had been told. She'd harrumphed about a professional thinking she was too good for the Meridian Choral Society.

But Eldora was astonished. "In the opera? Good heavens!"

"Just wondered," you said in embarrassment.

She burst into laughter. "Is that one of the stories?" Conspiratorially, she squeezed Kimberley's arm. "Oh no, Dear. I don't sing in the opera. I couldn't carry a tune in a basket and I don't have the bosom for it."

You noticed Kimberley blush. You blushed too, more or less to keep her company.

You offered to help with the dishes afterwards, but Eldora wouldn't hear of it. "Dishes tomorrow," she said. "The night is young."

This, you knew, was something you shouldn't relate to your mother unless you were pressed. Your mother did the dishes as soon as the eating was done, whether there were guests or not. Leaving dirty dishes, she'd said before, was irresponsible and unsanitary.

You helped Kimberley and Eldora clear the table and stack the dishes by the sink. Eldora brought out a brand new game of Monopoly still wrapped in plastic. You supposed it had been purchased just for this evening. You liked Monopoly and your dice were lucky. Even wanting Kimberley to win, you couldn't help the way your token nimbly danced from Chance to Community Chest to the properties you'd amassed, the way you'd played tag that morning, like you'd never slow down long enough to ever have to pay rent.

Eldora conceded defeat at nine o'clock when it was time for you and Kimberley to go home.

Remembering your instructions, you thanked your hostess for a wonderful evening. It came out stiff somehow, sounding insincere and awkward.

"You're welcome," Eldora said with a bit of a knowing smile.

"I had a great time," you added. "It was fun."

"I know you did, Dear," she said, touching your arm.

It was dark as you walked Kimberley home. You were nervous and excited being with her alone. You kept your hands in your coat pockets, as if clenching your fists prevented you from drifting away. Because, as you walked with Kimberley, it felt like you could float. When you glanced at her, seeing how pretty she was, you felt like you'd done all this before, lived your life this way on a previous occasion, that you knew it had some purpose, like you and Kimberley were meant to be this way somehow, that you lived in Meridian for this reason, for this night and this time. It was a wonderful euphoria, believing time and space made sense that night.

But two men approached along the sidewalk, not far from the Supertest station. You knew them as Mr. Connors and Mr. Simpson, so you said hello to them.

"Good evening," one of them said as they passed.

When you glanced back over your shoulder, you discovered they'd both stopped to gaze at you. One of them made a remark you couldn't hear. You realized it probably wasn't a nice remark, when both of the men laughed.

You glanced at Kimberley, perturbed by the laughter, but she didn't say anything.

Still, you didn't float quite the same way the rest of the way to her door. Your euphoria was gone. They'd said something nasty about Kimberley, you were sure of it. What did a nasty remark have to do with perfect time and space?

FOURTEEN

. . . "He's probably sellin' somethin'," said Chuck after one report. "For Chrissakes, he's probably just a salesman."

"Or an extortionist," countered Dwight.

"A what?"

"An extortionist. Extortion is where you go into businesses and make them pay you money so that you don't burn their place down or blow it up."

"Oh shit," said Chuck. "He's probably just selling watches or somethin'."

"In Winstons'? Winstons' don't sell watches."

They argued this way for several minutes . . .

DOZENS OF HANDPICKED VOLUNTEERS showed up on the first Sunday of May to help the Kiwanis Club clean up the site of the Findlay fire. The event was as ceremonial as it was industrious, at times even festive. This was how Eldora Diamond viewed it when she wandered down the street that afternoon to have a look at proceedings.

Those who took part gathered shortly after the conclusion of their respective church services, an arrangement permitting the local ministerial association to open the proceedings with prayers. The United Church blessed the work, the Catholic Church blessed the communal impetus behind the effort, the Presbyterians noted the wisdom and goodness which evolves from tragedy, and the Anglican Church blessed the light lunch its ladies auxiliary and the United Church Women served before work got underway.

Although the Baptists had been invited to take part, they boycotted the event because it was scheduled for a Sunday in spite of their objections. Not even the practical impetus of Sunday's manpower availability could justify working on the Sabbath, as far as the Baptists were concerned. Eldora had caught wind of the controversy twice, once at the grocery store and then while waiting in line at the post office a few days earlier. It wasn't difficult to see that few Meridians cared for the Baptist view. The Meridian Baptist Church, situated equidistantly between Ottawa and the village, wasn't part of Meridian in a true sense anyway, most people said, regardless of its name.

"Trust the Baptists to object," one woman said to another that day in the post office. "Can't compromise for a moment, can they?"

"The Baptists have always been that way," the other woman said. "Always have, always will be."

"Not part of the village at all. I don't know why we bother to invite them to take part."

The weather—nearly perfect for the event, Eldora noted—had rewarded mainstream religion. The day was a tart mixture of sun and cloud, the temperatures relatively cool. Overhead puffs of curious cumulus zipped like furtive witnesses across a blue sky as the throng attacked the Findlay wreckage. Most of the work was accomplished manually. Except for two dump trucks and three pick-ups on hand to carry away the charred boards, timbers, and concrete blocks, the men of Meridian shunned sophisticated equipment and battled the wreckage with crowbars, sledge hammers and their bare hands.

"A communal mood of inspired obligation permeated

the entire event," Eldora wrote in her journal afterwards. "Not only did it motivate the men to tackle the chore fiercely, but it whisked them through the various blessings, the dainty sandwiches served for lunch and the scalding coffee that washed it down. The men were clearly impatient to engage the blight that had scarred the downtown landscape for nearly a year. They were inspired. Here was the opportunity to remove a blemish on the face of the village's history, restoring a status quo the fire had insultingly interrupted.

"I sensed that a feeling of nobility blessed the afternoon. The men labouring in the wreckage derived an unusual energy and single-minded purpose from it. The women on the fringes were aware of this focus too, although the main thrust of their duties was to keep the coffee hot and periodically wipe a heroic, sweaty brow.

"I think all of us along the sidelines—the caste not invited to contribute our labour," she wrote, "the elderly, children, the outsiders—were aware of the prevailing atmosphere of inspired conquest. It felt like a local version of the Crusades. There, in the wreckage, I could see Meridian's knights battling the infidel of shameful tragedy which had entered the village's midst when no one was looking. I sensed, when the wreckage was removed by the end of the day, so too would be the remaining evidence of the passing through of some cancerous heretic. Those who cleaned up the mess fought for moral justice. Virtue, this afternoon, felt like rapture. The men of Meridian were on a mission to erase the mess of what had happened."

AS A CHILD, YOU SENSED the importance in this mission from the sidelines too. You stood with me for a while at the edges of the activity, both of us forbidden to wander onto the site. We noticed the palpable triumph of the men as they worked: our neighbours, your father, the other Kiwanians, the women serving them, including your mother who was part of the Anglican contingent. You, especially— much more than me—felt a powerful force in this victory over blight. It was handsome and seductive, a nobility and solidarity in which you could be gratefully immersed. Here, I know, you felt safe, strong and secure. Here you recognized an inner social circle you could comfortably live inside, where everything was clear, warm, and contained. Here you sensed life promised definition. Here was a place so communally transparent you felt an intense relief that you couldn't run afoul of its clearly defined expectations.

"This is great, isn't it?" you said to me, watching two men with a sledge hammer driving a hole in a charred wall of concrete blocks several yards away.

But, as usual, I was troubled by the tragedy of the Findlays this building represented and didn't hear you speak.

"Gare?"

"Do you remember the night of the fire?" I asked finally.

"Sure."

"We weren't supposed to be here, you know."

"I s'pose not."

"If they'd known what was going to happen, they'd have kept us all home."

"Yeah, I guess so."

I fell silent then, leaving you to think about the rest of it on your own.

But you had to dig inside your memory like the men working with shovels nearby. The incidents of the night of the fire had collapsed in on themselves for you and their horror was buried in rubble. Only last summer, only a year ago, yet you could barely remember the fire. It was so hazy you wondered if it had happened to someone else.

Mrs. Findlay had died, you remembered that much. She died in the dancing flames, pleading, crying, melting, vanishing. Her death seemed to be something worth forgetting in a curative sense. And I supposed you had.

"It was an awful night," you admitted out loud, but more or less to appease the intensity of my memories.

Soberly I nodded. "Do you ever feel like it was sort of our fault?"

"The fire? Are you crazy?"

"Not the fire exactly," I said, "but all that stuff before the fire. You know?"

"Huh?"

I sighed, exasperated with you.

"Nothing was our fault," you said then. "We didn't start the fire. We didn't get the Findlays into trouble."

"I know," I said. "But were you surprised that night? Were you surprised it happened?"

"Sure. Weren't you?"

"In a way, I was. In a way, I wasn't."

"Geez, Gare, whaddyuh talkin' about? I wish you wouldn't do this. You get scratching at things sometimes that make me nervous. I don't get it."

"We should have warned somebody, that's all."

"Huh?"

"You know, that something bad was gonna happen to the Findlays."

"We didn't know anything was gonna happen. What're you talking about?"

"Yes, we did," I said, looking at you for confirmation. "I'll bet the whole town knew something was gonna happen. They had to know."

"Oh c'mon," you protested angrily.

I sensed that I'd flushed you out of hiding inside that state of solidarity you'd felt with the men and women of the village a few moments ago.

"No one knew there was going to be a fire. I mean, c'mon! No one knew anyone was going to die," you were saying.

I gazed at you, trying to believe you.

"We're just kids," you said then, seizing on the fact with a deep desperation. "Whadda we know? Nobody listens to kids. We don't know anything. We're too young to know anything. I think we should just forget about it," you added when I didn't argue with you.

"I wish I could sometimes," I said.

"Well, it was an awful night. I'm glad I don't remember much."

You stood there in silence. There was dust rising from the site of the fire--dust and noise and human camaraderie.

"I gotta go home, Phil," I said shortly.

"I guess."

"I'll see yuh."

"See yuh, Gare."

I felt you watching me walk away, feeling resentful that I'd spoiled your mood, that sense of triumphant inclusion you'd felt earlier while watching the cleanup. When you tried to get it back, the mood, it resisted you. The town's mission here today no longer felt clear or warm or safe, the way it had just moments ago. Now the village's promise of sanctuary seemed fleeting to you, wispy, unconvincing. You felt yourself losing to time—you were a tortoise taking on time's hare. And you weren't convinced at all, as the fable led you to believe, that you could eventually win the race to end your vast confusion. Eventually you mentioned all of this to me, in words of your own choosing. But back then it was hard to describe that peculiar death of hope one gets when one feels pushed to the outside by everybody else's collective aversion to the truth.

JIM CONNELLY—aware that he didn't look like a banker at all on this arduous Sunday afternoon, working in shirtsleeves, his coveralls stained with grime, labouring in the cluttered basement of what had once been Findlay's General Store, shovelling ash, soot, charcoal, and three seasons of rot into wheelbarrows with a half dozen other men—contemplated a dilemma of his own. It was the same issue that had preoccupied him for more than a month and a half now, aggravated today because both his wife and his mistress were present at what had become an important community event.

So far he'd kept his distance from both of them. Enjoying his labours, working up a thick, legitimate sweat, he'd disdained the infrequent pauses that would have drawn him to one of the tables where the women supervised the refreshments. Both Betty and Rhonda were there, stationed several yards apart, doing duty behind different tables. If he approached one of them for a drink, it would clearly represent not going to the other. Betty had territorial rights. He shunned both of them to avoid any awkwardness made likely by his deceitful lust for Rhonda.

Periodically he stopped working to ease the burden on his protesting back and to wipe his brow with the sleeve of his old plaid shirt. Because of his height he was able to peer over the lip of the basement in which he laboured. Noticing both women, he would remember that he wasn't deciding anything. Not even from whom to beg a drink. Stupid, really, he'd already decided. Betty was his wife; certainly it was appropriate to go to her. But if he did, Rhonda would notice it and, well, discomfort might be the least of his problems in the aftermath. Going to Rhonda for a drink was simply out of the question. That kind of unfortunate public announcement would be insanity, whether he worked with her at the bank or not.

Oh, yes, Rhonda had tried to bring refreshment to him at one point, showing up at the lip of the basement, carrying a large pitcher of lemonade. "Drink, Mr. Connelly?" she'd said, that impudent smile on her lips.

He'd been startled to hear her use his last name in this fashion, the basement workplace of grime and sweat such a contrast to the hushed tranquility of the bank. And before he could resist it, a clear memory of her whispers in the cabin yesterday while they were making love had stumbled into his brain. "Oh Jim. Oh Jim, darling." The "Mr. Connelly" address seemed unimaginable now, like a marshmallow made of metal. Never again would they be able to salvage their pre-affair propriety out of the rust of their sexuality.

"No thank you, Rhonda," he'd said, sounding as managerial as he could. He gave his head a curt shake, a warning to keep her distance.

But she was turning away by then and he wasn't sure she saw him.

After that he'd just begun mulling it over again, this business of how he should end his affair with Rhonda. He was sick of mulling it over, yet he did so endlessly. His preoccupation was like a despised melody playing every time he turned on the radio, the same old repetitive verses—the reasons why the affair should end, his resolution to do so, and a nagging doubt that he actually could—rendered in static, hardly a single note out of place. His disappointment in himself contained a vivid imagination. Sometimes he felt as if he'd thrown himself over a cliff, telling himself he'd sprout wings before he crashed at the bottom. So far, though, he'd grown no wings at all; there was only his long and nerve-wracking tumble at the hands of emotional gravity.

He felt like a coward as the afternoon wore on, ignoring both women, not wanting to ignore either of them, but feeling he should, sometimes out of deference to one or the other, but mostly just to escape this day unscathed. Yet he'd find himself watching them sometimes, comparing them and the emotions they inspired. Betty was so attractive, so constant, and he felt guilty betraying her. But Rhonda was so beautiful, so sexual, and he felt deeply jealous when some of the younger men openly flirted with her. He felt damned by his need for both women. This, he decided, was purgatory, the vicious protestant kind, a sense of endless obligation incongruous with the pleasure he had found. He continued to believe his life possessed two halves—one before Rhonda and one after—each half there to torment the other like the quarrelling of spiteful siblings.

At one point he even fastened on the notion that he should work beside Rhonda's father in the wreckage of the fire. This would keep him from harm, from accepting that this man's daughter had become his sexual prey. In the end, though, MacLean had assumed a supervisory role in the cleanup, moving from labourer to labourer, making suggestions and giving instructions. Connelly just kept working in the basement.

Around four, Betty came over to announce she was going home.

"Looks like it's just about finished," she said.

"An hour maybe and then the bulldozer will show up to fill it all in, level it all off."

Betty put her hand on her husband's shoulder. "You've been working hard," she said. "I'm so proud of you."

He hardly heard her words, distracted by the touch of her hand and knowing, in the distance, Rhonda was watching them. He barely managed to nod, feeling ashamed of himself.

"I'll wait dinner," Betty said just before she left.

She'd been gone less than five or ten minutes before Rhonda showed up again with another pitcher of lemonade. "I'll bet you need that drink now," she said, glancing around to verify that no one was within earshot.

"That would be nice," he murmured.

She poured the lemonade into a plastic tumbler she'd brought with her. "I love you, you know," she said as she handed him his lemonade.

He stiffened. "Rhonda . . ."

But people were drifting closer, some of them wanting lemonade as much as he did.

She grinned as she turned away from him.

He knew she'd picked this moment to make her proclamation because he couldn't argue with her here, wouldn't question the depth of her feelings, make something else of her caring, something less.

John MacLean, standing across the ruins from him, caught his eye. Curdy Connelly nodded, drained his glass, picked up his shovel and leaped into the hole in the earth again.

God! he thought nervously, like the truth was written all over his face. Shakily he volleyed the truth of this possibility back and forth like an urgent tennis ball. No. Yes. No. Yes.

Yesterday he'd told Rhonda there'd be no more meetings at her father's cabin. They'd been dressing, getting ready—as he liked to think of it—to make their escape.

"You understand, don't you?" he said. "This is your father's property."

She didn't answer him at first.

He was too distracted to care. Watching her dress in front of him was nearly as exciting as undressing her had been. It was the way, as she tucked herself into her clothing, standing so close to him, that she seemed to be putting herself away for his future use. She wasn't, of course, but he liked the idea of it, that, after sex, as she was dressing, she was actually his.

"Where do we meet then?" she asked at last.

"I get nervous, Rhonda. We're on your father's land, making love in his cabin. You're his daughter. I'm his banker . . ." He stopped at that point. The more the list grew, the more it sounded like nonsense. It sounded like hopeless nonsense.

"Where do we meet then?" she asked again.

"I don't know."

"My father never comes here."

"This time of year, you mean."

"It's not hunting season. It's planting season. He'd never come here."

"Okay," said Connelly. "You understand why I get nervous, though, don't you?"

She nodded.

"It's not the same for you," he added for good measure.

"You mean, because I'm not married?"

"Yes."

"God, this world is stupid," she remarked.

Her non sequitur silenced him. He'd never thought of the world as stupid and had no idea what it had to do with what he'd been trying to say.

"It's here or a motel," she said, as if she'd asked him to pass the salt.

"I'd probably like a motel room," he admitted. "Once we found a place that was safe."

At times he delighted himself by imagining them showering together, spending the entire night, making love in the morning. But the delight was in his fancy only, in knowing it wasn't real, that none of these events was likely to take place.

"Maybe we could go away together some time."

"I don't know, Rhonda. Maybe."

"I like being here with you," she said, moving into his arms. "This cabin is the closest thing I have to my own place."

"Maybe that's the answer. Your own place."

"Daddy would never stand for it," she'd said, shyly turning her face away.

At last Connelly climbed out of the basement when the bulldozer showed up, forced to speak of the devil.

John MacLean was approaching him. When he arrived, he warmly shook Connelly's hand. "I want to thank you, Jim, for your efforts this afternoon."

"My pleasure, John," the banker said. "You and I both know how worthy a cause this is."

MacLean nodded. "You're a good man, Jim."

MacLean's warmth seemed so genuine Connelly felt a renewed shame that he was sleeping with his daughter. MacLean's kindness turned his act of predation into even worse willful trespassing.

The bulldozer started up with a phlegmy, baritone roar and everyone hurried out of the way. Connelly drifted away from MacLean and thoughts of trespassing. What was the point in feeling wrong now that it was clear that's exactly what he was?

THAT EVENING, after supper, you and I returned to the site of the cleanup project to see what had finally been accomplished.

The wreckage of Findlay's General Store was now entirely gone. The bulldozer had filled in the hole in the earth and neatly levelled the ground. A large brown patch of earth, looking extraordinarily naked, helped you to pretend the wreckage and the Findlays had never existed.

"My father says it's going to be a park," you told me.

I said nothing to this. It was as if the burden of the entire village rested squarely on my shoulders.

We should have warned somebody, was what I'd said this afternoon.

Nobody listens to kids, was what you had replied.

We stood there in silence as evening melted down, not saying these things to one another again, but believing them just the same.

FIFTEEN

. . . I sided with Dwight because I needed the excitement. It was vital that the Mafia Man turn out to be a crook. I sensed Skeleton Club Private Investigations Inc. was hanging by a thread and, with it, the fate of my summer. Although I couldn't articulate it then, I was desperate to keep Dwight's detective game alive because it kept us young, tireless and timeless. The instinct to retain my present tense was now overpowering. I wanted to keep my past a tiny beaker, my future as large as a lake, and I wanted to remain secure between the two extremes . . .

"SMALL TOWNS POSSESS a collective character all their own," Eldora wrote in her journal that spring as June approached. "Towns, even cities and regions, tend to cling to a collectively agreed upon perception of knowledge, supposition, suspicion, and contract. Small towns in particular utilize this sense of community to define knowledge, surmise events and opinions, and to be suspicious of trends or developments. Most of all they maintain a contract, a tacit agreement to hide and keep secret what might be threatening to the community's status quo. Is this part of what Karl Jung means when he refers to the collective unconscious? Keeping things hidden for the perceived good of the social unit?"

That spring of 1960 Eldora wrote often about her views

of life in Meridian, her pen dancing over the paper of her notebook. She had no idea where her observations might lead, but she was compelled to report them regardless. It seemed the germ of some creative idea, or a process of reflection. Or maybe, in the end, it was only a distraction.

"Nothing changes much in Meridian these days. I detect that life's propensity for changing very little appeals to everyone. Most residents derive a deep comfort from the village's familiarity, as if there's a profundity in familiarity I haven't learned to understand as yet. There's a pride I perceive here because few people have changed their lives in any significant way. For the people in Meridian there's triumph in keeping the same job or not changing your hairstyle, in clinging stubbornly to an ill-tempered husband or wife, even if only for ritual consistency. Life here becomes a schedule of habits, whether bad or good, that no one wishes to alter. And changing an opinion is simply out of the question."

Dutifully that spring, Eldora reported, "News comes and goes, less a matter of information than a means of justifying an existing point of view. Life, if not perfect, is at least predictable and safe. People here not only count on the predictability but on the fact everyone else is counting on it too. Mores, codes, beliefs, opinions, judgments, decisions, states of acceptance, tolerances, intolerances, pastimes, regrets, jealousies, hatreds, loves and friendships are gratifying mostly because they're permanent. I overheard a woman saying the other day that she supposed life wasn't getting any better but she was grateful that it wasn't getting any worse."

By the end of June, Eldora was reporting data in support of her opinions. "There have been two deaths by natural causes this month, two wakes, two funerals, two burials, two headstones have been erected. There have been a half dozen weddings. The match-ups surprised no one. No one had second thoughts, I gather. No one expressed regret about the family-in-law unions that were going to result. No one travelled far away on their honeymoon and no one took more than one week to do so. None of the brides was pregnant. None of the grooms mourned the end of his bachelorhood."

Eldora wrote: "No one learned something they shouldn't this month. No secrets have been exposed. No one has been seriously ill, although a few of the children have had measles. No one expects much this year, expectation being so difficult to elucidate or defend.

"Beyond the progress of the park where Findlay's General Store was located, to be called Meridian Kiwanis Park, there are no other civic improvements being contemplated at the present time. But people have been painting the trim on their houses. The colours are sober and polite, and it seems they give no offense as a result. Apparently the spring painting binge has inspired other residents here to consider painting as well, once fall arrives and it's cooler again. Meridian isn't a place where contrasts are allowed to last very long. Contrasts are treated like an itch in a private anatomical region no one wants to admit can and does exist."

Later she wrote: "It's as if Meridian waits on the surface of itself this year. Like everyone knows there's a rash just underneath its skin. And if everyone takes the medicine of convention, the rash will go away before it rises to the surface to embarrass everyone. Don't adjust the fine tuning. It's clear for Meridians what's right and wrong, that these two states need no fresher or broader definition. Women, especially wives, will remember their place. Children will be seen and not heard. That's it. Meridian thrives on everyone staying in place. If you challenge place, you must do it behind closed doors. Keep the rash confined under the skin until it goes away.

"So Meridian waits. Because waiting never fails to be the same as itself. Waiting is familiar. Entire lives go by in a state of waiting. And then the people here die."

Eldora's journal speculated that Meridian had its share of secrets. Secrets, she decided, were a philosophy unto themselves. "Secrets are kept less because they are secrets than because they are secrets *from* something. Secrets are about aberrations because there is a state of normalcy inside of which they are construed to be aberrant. I suppose people keep secrets because they fear punishment at the hands of a pervasive virtue, not knowing that virtue too, depending on who is in charge of its definition at the time, is an aberration all its own. No wonder choices are such torture. Smothered by the responsibility of everyone else's choice, when it comes to choosing their own path, it's usually easier not to choose at all."

LIFE WENT ON IN MERIDIAN that spring, for you, for me, for everyone.

Aside from the time she spent speculating in her journal, Eldora continued work on her novel—in the mornings mostly, not long after dawn. Coffee black. Three differently coloured pens: blue for the body, black for her instructions to herself, and red for changes, arrows, disappointments, improvements, and angry, murderous Xs.

You noticed part of the manuscript on her kitchen table one afternoon after school while you and Kimberley were visiting. Eldora soon stuffed it into a file folder, but not before you'd caught a glimpse of her work and wondered what it was. It looked like war to you, a battle fought with words, a hieroglyphic holocaust, a planned offensive, a deployment of troops: blue platoon, black platoon, red squad. But you didn't say anything, your curiosity didn't last. Most things entering your mind that spring slipped out its other side. Your mother said you had a mind like a sieve. Not that you cared. You continued to be lost inside the velvet wasteland of your love for Kimberley Smith.

You sensed she loved you too. Neither of you said so; it seemed convenient not to mention it. The feeling was clear, which seemed to be what was most important. Words about love, you intuited, would be too adult for you—inadequate, ceremonial, litigious, and ultimately negotiable.

You continued to meet privately each day as you had all along, you on the steps of the Anglican church, Kimberley in her window in the mobile home in which she lived. These, you believed, were the most private and splendid moments. In the distance, Kimberley's beauty was throat-catchingly hushed—a perfect whisper, you supposed, in a universe of shouts, cries and sirens you suspected you were special not to prefer.

This long-distance tryst of gazing at one another briefly interrupted the burden of family life for both of you. It kept Kimberley away from the scars tormenting her father, the way much of him had been broken by World War Two, death and more death—one brother, one sister, both parents, even his firstborn son, a victim of exposure on the day of a frantic escape from one European catastrophe to another. Up the street in your home, your mother became newly resentful of your father because he'd gleefully taken up golf. She determined you were probably her best friend when she sat you down to listen to her complaints. It wasn't just the expense, she said, but his passion for the game, this most recent manifestation of his unending self-absorption. Once upon a time it had been fishing. Now it was golf. No half measures for Bert Barrett, she observed ruefully. Politely you inquired if she'd talked to him about this. No, she said. She couldn't. "You know how mad he gets."

Elsewhere that spring Jim Connelly and Rhonda MacLean continued their affair, Connelly impaled on the quandary of wanting it to end and hoping it would continue. That June, in a moment of weakness, in a state of hallucinogenic guilt, he told Rhonda he loved her. She kept telling him she loved him and he couldn't bear the silences afterwards that served as his reply. This wasn't long after the Sunday afternoon in late May when they'd gone to Ottawa, rented a motel room and made love on a bed under a print of autumn leaves that rattled against the wall with the commotion of their passion. They'd come to this room to allay Connelly's fears about continuing to meet in John MacLean's cabin. Afterwards, though, he declared the cabin was better, less complicated than motel rooms, which demanded additional lies or deception and amplified the sounds of their ecstasy, displaying the shocking blemish lust painted on their respectability.

That June, with his crops now in and his livestock grazing on his fields, John MacLean began to wonder why his beautiful daughter wasn't dating anyone. "Why don't you leave Rhonda be?" Olive replied when he asked her about it. MacLean didn't answer his wife. He didn't want to say out loud that he didn't trust his daughter in adulthood to be as responsible as he'd like. Or that sometimes, privately, he hated her independence, swearing that one day soon he'd break it once and for all, not caring why he needed to or why her independence bothered him so much.

As for me, I was haunted that June by the ever-improving site of the park where the Findlay fire had been. Sometimes I took you along when I wanted to stand there in silence at the edges of the property, worrying about my worries.

"It wasn't our fault," you said, "just because we knew there was trouble."

But when I didn't answer you, you doubted I believed this rationalization for a moment.

I know you resented me sometimes for this insistence on our culpability. Why couldn't I let it go, this summer especially, with you and Kimberley in love and the summer ahead holding so much promise?

SIXTEEN

. . . So I volunteered to solve the mystery of the Mafia Man once and for all.

"The key to the whole thing is in his briefcase," I said during a lull in Chuck and Dwight's debate.

"No kidding," said Chuck nastily.

I ignored this. "I'll look in his briefcase. Then we can close the file."

Silence. Shrugs. What I was proposing was uncommonly courageous.

"Okay, Richie," said Dwight after a long hesitation. "I guess you've got the assignment . . ."

BY JUNE YOU AND KIMBERLEY—and a haplessly conventional interpretation of the precociousness in what was taking place between you that couldn't help but tag along— where being noticed and appraised by some of the people of Meridian. You were only partially aware of this attention, catching a glimpse of it sometimes out of the corner of your eye. Too preoccupied with Kimberley and too young to believe you could make the village curious, you ignored a growing fascination by the community witnesses watching you with Kimberley.

"What a fucking waste!" a man named Mitch McKee said

as he glimpsed you through the window of Basil's Barber Shop one afternoon after school, while you and Kimberley strolled by on your way to Eldora's house.

A couple of other men in the shop that afternoon joined McKee at the window and, with grunts of mutual assent, validated his opinion.

These were not the kind of men you noticed at this stage of your life. They were known to be careless men, the kind who watch the passing of each day with a leer of envy and defeat. They were weeds in a delicate garden never harvested, now so used to being unwanted they could hardly remember what a harvest was. They were jealous of and lusted after the many opportunities they felt they'd been denied.

"It's a boy sent out to do a man's job," said McKee to his appreciative audience.

Offended by McKee's language, Basil Grisham glanced up from the head of hair he was cutting and gazed at you briefly as you passed. He frowned until you and Kimberley passed from view.

"Jailbait, Mitch," one of the other men was saying.

"Might be worth a month or two in jail for a night with a virgin like that."

The men laughed heartily, not noticing or caring that Grisham did not join in.

Gradually, now that you were out of sight, they returned to their seats, picking up magazines, glancing at their watches, remembering to light a cigarette or cast a furtive, admiring glance at themselves in the large mirror on Grisham's wall.

Grisham worked in silence, resigned to the nature of his business and the way a businessman couldn't be fussy about whom his customers were. The men of Meridian had congregated in like-minded groups in his barber shop from the very beginning, usually according to their status. This was Wednesday, the traditional afternoon when the town's coarser elements visited his barber shop. They were all labourers, hired hands, or lay-abouts.

McKee was a mechanic at the GMC car dealership. He

was known as a good technician, but he was as rough around the edges as his fingernails were dirty. He serviced Grisham's Pontiac and Grisham cut his hair. On the street, however, they greeted one another with nothing more than a curt nod. Grisham felt superior to McKee; both men pretended not to care.

As the scissors clicked with ancient competence in his fingers in the silence of the barber shop, Grisham supposed he understood the envy beneath McKee's remarks, even if he didn't care for the way the mechanic had expressed it. Grisham often saw you and the Smith girl pass these days. People remarked about it now and then because the Smiths remained an enigma and you were the son of a respected man. Sometimes they commented on your incongruity. Although you were mature for your age, most viewed your romance with the Smith girl as a mismatch.

Grisham thought so too. This conclusion shared a room with his envy of your youth. Not that he wanted to be young again. No, it wasn't that exactly. He supposed youth was something a man his age wanted to tour now and then, mostly to plug some holes in it from which a vague but persistent regret occasionally leaked. He wanted to have another go at his past, take events out, put other events in. He admired the look of the Smith girl, regretted how she filled your youth in a way she hadn't been part of his. It was all right to feel this way, he supposed, to believe there was an imaginary way to come to terms with his regret. In contrast to observations by the likes of Mitch McKee, what could be more benign than wishing he'd had the company of that kind of girl in his youth? It wasn't lechery to recognize something you'd missed. It wasn't lechery to wonder what it might be like to be a young boy like you.

Still, sometimes Grisham felt a mild annoyance about you and Kimberley, like both of you were unfair, some kind of cruel riddle in time. To the barber, the Smith girl seemed here by mistake, being so young while he was so old, a second chance denied him while it was bestowed by fate on you.

He glanced into his mirror and caught his mechanic's

eye. McKee was grinning at him with mysterious insolence. Grisham flicked his gaze away, afraid McKee was reading his mind, transforming his regret into the fruits he could grow in his own dirty mind. Grisham flushed a little at the implied insult. But it bothered him afterwards that McKee might suspect he was a man with an unfilled cavity. Or that the Smith girl was a filling of opportunity it still embarrassed him to crave.

ELDORA NOTICED A VARIATION of the same mismatch herself that afternoon, but she felt sad about it. There was no envy, no personal regret in her, just an unexpected clairvoyance that you and Kimberley would not last. At some point soon you would not fit the puzzle you fitted now. Love wasn't enough to keep you knitted in place. Although love felt invincible sometimes, it could not be strong enough to repel the siege of time and space. Eldora had learned this once or twice herself many years ago.

She stood at the kitchen table, watching you and Kimberley outside. You sat side by side at a picnic table in her back yard, drinking lemonade. It was shady at the table; the leaves you'd raked last autumn had returned with a lush vehemence to the tree branches. Watching you, Eldora was moved by your innocence. She loved Kimberley, liked you, and sometimes felt inspired by the intensity of your chaste romance. But gazing at you now, she knew it must ultimately fail. And the poignancy in this failure touched her deeply.

"How long until summer vacation now?" she asked as she joined you at the table.

"Three and a half weeks," you replied.

"Then what?"

"Swimming, baseball, the usual stuff, I guess."

"What about you, Kimberley?"

"The same, I think. I hear there's a girls softball team starting up."

"What about your parents, Phillip? Are they going away?"

"No, not that I've heard."

You'd been told that money was tight this year. Your mother had complained that your father planned to golf. "Could be a long summer," she'd said, crushing a cigarette butt to death in an ashtray at her elbow.

Kimberley's parents, all of you knew, couldn't get away either. They were as imprisoned by the commerce of the gas pumps as your parents were going to be by your father's new passion for golf.

"You'll have to make your own fun around here, I suppose," said Eldora.

"Sure," you replied. "Meridian's great in the summer."

Eldora said nothing, although she didn't agree. She planned to be away for all of August and was looking forward to it. Meridian felt more oppressive than usual. She wasn't sure exactly why.

"I'll be away in August," she told you and Kimberley. "When I get back, Phillip, you'll be a foot taller, you'll be singing baritone and Kimberley . . . ." Here she had to pause. "Well who knows what terrific thing you'll be."

"Just good old Kimberley. I guess that's what I'll be."

You smiled at one another, jointly happy with this conclusion.

But Eldora couldn't share your verdict of permanence. It was Kimberley, she realized, three years older than you, who was going to change. Eldora could see the faint outline of her bra, knew her breasts were still growing. She wore a t-shirt at this moment that didn't hide them very well. Physically, at least, she was miles ahead of you.

Next year, Eldora speculated with a guilty shudder, Kimberley would start dating, really dating, turning for a goodnight kiss on her doorstep. And the year after that? Out with boys in cars, resisting, not resisting, contemplating hors d'oeuvres of lust, sampling, not sampling, comparing some anxious young man's palate with the conditioned ambivalence of her own. Meanwhile, you'd be left behind by all of this experimentation, sentenced to your own time, you own shy place in things, merely on the verge of the hormonal madness of puberty.

After you left, after Eldora watched you go, she remained preoccupied by what you and Kimberley must lose, the kind of innocent love she sometimes saw on both of your faces. To Eldora, your feelings resisted greed or gain; they didn't want to harm anyone. Your caring seemed emotionally pure, unsullied by definitions that make carefree love so difficult.

All of this was precisely why she knew it wouldn't last. The rules of adult love were based on different needs: expectation, obligation, religious ritual. Once you and Kimberley let these adult strangers in, they would crush your innocence the way they did for everyone. Loss of innocence might be inherent to the process of growing up, but Eldora knew it was often cruel. You'd have to give yourselves up to the cult of human sacrifice. Much of whom you might have become would be cut away permanently upon the altar of adulthood.

YOUR CLASSMATE GERALD CONNELLY noticed something special about you and Kimberley that June too. He wondered about it for a day or two, as was his way—reflective, reclusive, ponderous.

"What is it, Gerald?" his mother asked him finally, when she noticed him doodling at the kitchen table one afternoon where she was preparing dinner.

Mother and son were close. They talked often. Betty Connelly was there to listen, her husband Jim was not. He was busy down at the bank.

"C'mon, son, what's on your mind?"

He gazed at her a moment, searching for a way to begin. "Can kids my age be in love?" he asked at last.

Betty had been peeling and washing potatoes. She put down her peeler and wiped her hands on her apron, then sat down at the table across from him.

"I suppose they can," she replied, feeling a tug of something like jealousy whisper over her heart. "What makes you ask?"

"A couple of kids at school," he said. "Phillip Barrett and Kimberley Smith. They're in my class. You know the ones I mean?"

Betty nodded. "What about them?"

Gerald shrugged, some of what he was saying vaguely embarrassing to him. "He sits at the front, she sits near the back. He turns around and smiles at her. She smiles back. So I just wondered, you know?"

"Must be hard on their school work," his mother said.

Gerald shrugged again. "I've heard Kimberley's going to skip Grade Seven."

"Oh? Well, she's older. Maybe that's why."

"I was just curious, that's all."

"Well," said Betty. "At your age it's called a crush. I suppose it's a little like love. Crushes are kind of like rehearsals for a concert, Gerald. You know what I mean?"

"I guess so."

"They're like music lessons or rehearsals. You practice love to get ready for the big concert. Your father and me? That's the concert."

"What does it feel like?"

"The rehearsal?"

"Yeah."

"It feels like love, I guess," she replied. "It just doesn't last very long, that's all."

"But what does it feel like?" Gerald persisted.

"Oh boy," his mother said with a bit of a chuckle. "Don't you ask some questions!"

"I'm just curious, that's all."

Betty thought for a moment. "I'm not sure I can help you, Dear. Let's just say, when it happens to you, you'll know. I'm afraid that's the best I can do right now. Is that okay?"

"Sure."

"So Phillip and Kimberley have a big crush on one another, do they?" she asked just before she got up to work on dinner again.

"I think so," her son replied.

"Hmm," said Betty. "I wonder what Phillip's mum thinks about that, with Kimberley being so much older."

Gerald could only shrug.

"Never mind," said Betty, getting up to run the tap into the potato pot. "I'm sure it'll pass."

But after Gerald left the kitchen, she kept thinking about what she'd learned from her son. She kept thinking about your mother, trying to imagine, in a state of subdued delight, how her musical rival was dealing with a girl who looked like Kimberley Smith having a crush on her only son.

"WELL, IF IT ISN'T LOVER-BOY," a voice jeered from the bleachers at the ballpark a few nights later.

You heard the words clearly but, strolling with me towards the canteen for a bag of chips and a drink, you clearly didn't realize at first that they were directed at you.

"Hey Lover-boy! I was talking to you!"

This time you turned and three teenagers, obviously high school seniors, leaped down from the bleachers and came towards you.

You hesitated a moment, then strode towards the canteen. These young men were strangers to you. I could see you wanted nothing to do with them.

You were here at the ballpark because your father and the rest of the Meridian Marauders were engaged in a softball practice on the nearby diamond, the same diamond where you and I and the rest of our little league team had recently begun preparing for the coming season. It was still early—the evening sun was still bright and high in the sky. Some clouds on the distant horizon had turned pink at the edges of its rays. It was warm, June perfect, too nice an evening for trouble.

"Where yuh goin', Lover-boy?"

Smoothly the three high school kids surrounded us.

"You talkin' to me?" you asked, your voice cracking as you spoke.

"You talkin' to me?" one of the older kids whined in parody.

His friends laughed. He was their leader. Everything he said or did was supposed to be funny.

Your adversary was no taller than you but you knew he was much older, a hood. His hair was black, slicked into a jelly roll. He had sideburns like Elvis Presley and wore a white t-shirt. A package of Export As bulged from a pocket and a box of matches clung for dear life from its lip.

You stood there in silence, stunned that you were being accosted in this way. Older kids had always ignored you. What unhappy aberration, what cruel twist of fate had now altered this fact for you?

"Where's your girlfriend, Lover-boy?"

"Huh?"

"Huh?" the greaseball mimicked.

All of us stood there in a cluster.

"Hear you're quite the lover-boy," the greaseball said.

"I don't know what you're talkin' about. I don't even know you."

"Well I know you, fuckface. And I know your girlfriend."

Your stomach knotted in fear. Your mouth had gone dry.

"And I wanna know what a fuckfaced punk like you is doing with a girl with tits like that."

"C'mon, Gary," you said to me. "We have to get goin'."

But your assailant had other ideas. Without warning he pushed you on the chest. It was a powerful blow and you tumbled to the grass. In one fluid motion, the greaser straddled you, pinning your arms to the ground with his knees and sitting on your belly.

"Hey, c'mon," you cried.

He was much stronger than you and your terror increased. Your senses filled up with feelings and observations, all of them acute. You smelled the scent of green grass and earth, and felt the dampness in the ground yesterday's rain had created. And the kid pinning you there smelled too, of sweat and grease and advantage, merciless advantage. You felt the focus of your life sharpen with painful clarity.

Fear had its partners too—first a sense of inadequacy, then your tragic acceptance. You ceased struggling. Whatever was coming next seemed powerfully inevitable.

I made a move to escape, to seek out your father who was fielding balls on the diamond, but the other two high school students grabbed me by the arm, imprisoning me there. I didn't struggle much either. I felt it written all over my face, the same sense of hopeless inevitability you felt as you lay pinned to the ground.

"Thought a lover-boy like you would be tougher'n this," your adversary said, his face so close to yours you could smell stale tobacco on his breath. "Thought a guy with a girlfriend like yours wouldn't be such a weakling."

You didn't reply.

With a menacing tenderness, he gently slapped your cheek.

"Whaddyuh say, fuckface?"

"You should pick on someone your own age," you suggested at last.

He seemed to contemplate this a moment, recognizing its ethical truth, but you sensed something more powerful than fairness was needling him. He didn't move an inch.

But he didn't say anything for the moment either. You'd reached an impasse; you could feel it in the air, see it on his face. As he kept you pinned to the ground, not knowing what to do next, not knowing where to go from here, it occurred to both of you that he'd begun to look ridiculous. Somehow he'd reached the point where he must relent.

"Oh, fuck this," he said to his friends. "This guy's nothin'. Just a big nothin'." He clutched a handful of grass and dropped it lazily on your face. Then, abruptly, he let you up.

"See yuh around, Lover-boy," he said as he and his friends slipped away.

But you and I knew there was no way for him to save face, no way to change anything he'd said.

"You all right?" I asked.

"Yeah. What a jerk."

You brushed grass and dirt from your clothing. Turning, you noticed your father gazing at you from the other side of the bleachers.

"I think your father saw what happened," I said. "Part of it, anyway."

"Yeah, I guess so."

"How come he didn't come over?"

"I don't know," you replied. "I think he wants me to fight my own battles. That's what he did when he was my age."

"Screw that," I said. "Those kids were a lot older'n us. And they outnumbered us."

"I know," you said.

"Screw that," I said. "I hate crap like that."

"Me too," you admitted.

"And I hate that there has to be an unfair code. Like there's only one way of doing things—stick up for yourself or die. You know what it means, Phil?"

"What?"

"It means we're on our own; that's what it means."

Soberly you nodded, although I'm not sure you actually understood.

THE NEXT NIGHT, during an exhibition game against the Panthers, Robbie Bennett threw a wild pitch that ricocheted off home plate, evaded your catcher's padding and struck you in the genitals. The resulting pain arrived like the slash of a dull, rusty knife.

You groaned, futilely clutched yourself, and collapsed, vaguely aware of the contrast of an unchanged world around you, the dust behind the plate billowing upwards, the mesh backstop spinning wildly, the sky sinking down to crush you in your suffering.

You nearly passed out, seeing darkness at the edge of a starburst all around you. But you swam away from this, holding back unconsciousness. You heard and saw in fragments, like your brain had poor reception. There were kids laughing—you could hear them—not meaning to be cruel but succumbing to thoughtlessness. You could see your father's face against the blue sky overhead, asking, "Are you all right, Phillip?" But of course you couldn't be and couldn't answer him. Then your teammates showed up, more faces, and as you twisted your gaze away, they were transformed into a gaggle of legs and sneakers. In the distance you saw the Panthers batter move away in a state of sympathetic disdain.

Amidst all of this throbbing confusion, you remembered Kimberley. You found her usual place in the stands where she sat with Maggie Mathieson. You saw her coming down the steps towards you, her face pale with alarm.

"No," you gasped in her direction. "It's okay. I'm all right."

She came no closer, knowing you were addressing her. Your eyes touched. You could see she was torn between concern for your injury and respect for your request. She stood in this state of ambivalence for a very long time. And you tried to smile at her.

With the assistance of your father and a couple of helpful teammates, you gained your feet.

"You're all right," your father said like he was telling you to be.

Shakily you nodded.

"Walk it off then," he said. "Just walk it off. It's part of being a catcher, son."

"Okay, Dad," you said.

You began to stumble around the diamond in ever widening circles, your hands on your hips, the dust dancing around your sneakers, the air feeling hot and dirty and dry in a way it never had before.

Gradually, as the pain eased, you found the will to glance into the bleachers again. You must have smiled at her because Kimberley smiled back.

Your father thought you could finish the game. You supposed later that he was right; you hit a double into right field during the second to last inning.

"PHILLIP'S GIRLFRIEND comes to all of his ball games and practices," your father mentioned to your mother that night.

They were in bed and the light was off. Your father felt the bedroom was a safe place to talk. He'd said as much more than once.

"I'll give her one thing," he added. "She's loyal. None of the other players have girlfriends in the stands."

"It's Little League," your mother said as if this explained everything.

"I know," mused her husband, scratching himself under the sheets.

"You may as well get used to it, Dear," your mother said. "Girls are going to happen to a boy like Phillip."

"I guess so."

Gravely your mother paused. "Do you think you should call her his girlfriend? Phillip's pretty young. It doesn't seem like the right word somehow."

"Huh," your father said. "It's the one that comes to mind. I mean, you've seen her, Carol. She's pretty mature, you know."

"Oh come now," your mother said.

"Back in high school, I would've thought she was a knockout."

"Oh, Bert, c'mon. In high school?"

"Damn right," your father replied.

There was a dark and thoughtful silence. "I'll have to take a closer look," your mother said.

Satisfied, Bert didn't comment further.

"You're not trying to tell me we should be concerned, are you?" your mother asked shortly.

"No, not really. But I'm glad you're going to take a closer look. I think you'll be surprised."

"Oh, Bert, they're classmates, still in Grade Six."

"She'd older than Phillip, Dear."

"How old can she be?"

"Old enough to have tits."

"Bert! For God's sake!"

They fell silent again, this time for several minutes.

"You thought I was a knockout in high school," Carol murmured eventually.

"I still do," your father said.

"Huh! A moment ago, I had the impression you might be distracted by the girls your son brings home when he grows up."

"Oh, Carol," your father said, reaching for her.

Gradually, cautiously, they found the accord they needed to make love.

SEVENTEEN

. . . That Thursday afternoon, I "tailed" the Mafia Man as he travelled from store to store. At Fargo's, he glanced at me as if in recognition and I made matters worse, I suppose, by clumsily turning to the comic book rack, as if I'd been caught doing something I shouldn't. Behind me, I heard him ask what was now a familiar question: "Need anything next week?"

Mr. Fargo said he didn't.

It was becoming apparent that Chuck was probably right, that the Mafia Man was just a salesman and not a crook at all. But I stuck with him anyway, following him into Winston's.

There was no one else in the store, just me and the Mafia Man and Buck Winston. I knew Buck Winston from a distance and didn't care for him much. You'd see him at the occasional ballgame or going into The Tea Room or just hanging around with friends. He was like the rest of the older kids, pretending to be hoods, always swearing and spitting and lighting a cigarette, or pushing and shoving and catcalling at girls . . .

"I WANT TO MAKE LOVE at the bank again," Rhonda said out of the blue.

"Oh Rhonda, Jesus," Connelly replied. "Why?"

"It excites me." She giggled then and bit him gently where her face was tucked against his chest.

He wondered if the bite would leave a mark. He hated it when she left marks on his flesh. Like she wanted Betty to see them, to discover she'd put them there.

He thought about going, leaving her here in the cabin, getting home early this Saturday, as if to do so would shrink the lie his Saturday afternoons had become. But he didn't move. He laid there in the gloom of the cabin bedroom, hearing birds outside the window, remembering the sunshine dappling the leaves on the trees outside, something he'd noticed earlier before he'd drawn the curtains. She'd placed her leg over his and he liked it. It was warm and all the covers were in a tangle at the foot of the bed. He liked this too, being naked, connected and lazily replete. Strange, he realized, how he liked all of this even during those times he didn't like Rhonda very much, or disliked some of her moods after they were finished making love.

"So?" she said.

"So what?"

"At the bank? For old time's sake?"

"It's too dangerous."

"I don't care," she said.

"Well I do," he replied.

"You have to make it up to me."

"Make what up to you?"

"Planning your vacation and leaving me behind."

"I can't help that, Rhonda. I have a family. I owe them a vacation."

"You owe me something too, for fucking you so well."

He no longer felt replete. Now he felt uneasy. Her mood, her petulance. The shocking things she sometimes said. It was becoming less and less subtle, the way she put the squeeze on him, the way she described their affair, the invectives she sometimes used. Still, he knew and understood what she was sulking about. He'd told her he was taking two weeks' vacation with his family at the end of July and she'd asked if they could get away for a weekend somehow, her and him. He'd explained he didn't think so, not before he went away with his family.

She'd laid there in his arms, not seeming to mind at first. Now, he supposed, she'd had time to think about it, to become annoyed with him.

"How often do you make love to Betty?" she asked.

"Huh?"

"How often do you make love to Betty now that you're banging me?"

"Jesus, Rhonda, stop talking like that about us. You and me. It's not fair to either one of us."

"I'm sorry, Jim," she said, giving in easily, yet unconvincingly.

He kissed her on the forehead. "That's okay," he said.

"But I want to know," she told him.

"Why?"

"Because I'm in love with you."

He was besieged by guilt at this moment. Her love felt like an attack in an endless battle, as if he was caught up in a war he couldn't get out of.

"Jim? It's okay. I just need to know."

"I can't have her getting suspicious," he murmured listlessly, feeling the remorse that gathers at the edge of some large inevitability.

"I know," said Rhonda. "I'm not that stupid."

"I don't think we should talk about this."

"I do."

"I don't."

"Oh, c'mon. I'm not going to get too mad, if that's what you think."

"Do you think I want you to be hurt?"

She didn't answer him.

In the silence he decided he probably should reply. Grudgingly he supposed she had some right to know. Serve her right, perhaps.

"Friday nights," he said.

"Friday nights? Really?"

"That's what I said."

"Every Friday night?"

"No, not every Friday night."

She was up on one elbow now, bare breasts lolling against his chest, a look of surprise and irony around her eyes. "I see. Not every Friday night. Just on Friday nights when she might be getting suspicious."

"Look, I don't want to talk about this," he complained. "What the hell did you expect me to say?"

She snickered and cuddled in close again. "I thought it might be Tuesday nights. Or Wednesdays maybe. Some night when there's a gap between you and me. We're Saturdays. Friday nights seems kind of close. Like Christmas Eve and Christmas Day, you know? Do you open your presents Christmas Eve as well as Christmas Day?"

"This is a stupid conversation," he said.

But he didn't move out of her embrace, still compelled to stay, to be touched by her warm, exciting flesh. God, was wanting someone this way separate from the rest of human experience? Was it outside logic or reason or safety? Did it have a life of its own?

"I'll tell you one thing," Rhonda said after a moment or two. "If you were married to me, it wouldn't be some certain night in the week. It'd be whenever and wherever we felt like it, as often as we wanted."

Although he didn't believe her, her words excited him. "But we're not married," he said, so that it wouldn't show.

"Tell it to him," she said, glancing down his belly to where his cock grew in her hand.

IN THE END, HE AGREED to another tryst in the bank vault.

"What day?" he'd said.

"Tuesday."

"Any particular reason for Tuesday?"

"Because it's not Friday or Saturday," she'd replied. "Believe me, I'll make it worth your while."

Her words, now that it was Tuesday, had excited him often all day long. After Blanche and Mabel departed, however, he grew newly benumbed by risk and foreboding. After Rhonda watched her co-workers leave for the day, she sat down at her desk and turned to face his office. They gazed at one another through his open door. She crossed her legs. He watched her, glancing up her skirt. This felt normal. But so did his trepidation.

He checked each corner of the bank, searching for witnesses behind the counter, under desks, even in the washroom. At the window, he studied the street, looking for passing pedestrians who might be peering back at him with just enough imagination to know what he was shortly going to do.

The risk seemed to heighten his anticipation. Maybe Rhonda knew this better than he did. She was patient with him. She waited at her desk while he patrolled the bank, ensuring when they went to the vault they would not be caught. This conveyed to Connelly that she too enjoyed this delay in the lovemaking they had planned.

He returned to his office a moment, glancing at the school photo of Gerald that Betty had framed for him. He put the picture face down on his desk. The notion of Gerald hearing about his affair bothered him deeply. Lately he'd been thinking about this often, how his son would hate him if word ever got out. Not just on his own account either. Betty would see to it that Gerald hated him forever, which, to Connelly, was only just. It was the price he must ultimately pay for what he now believed was some kind of insidious weakness.

"I don't want to do this," he said as he left his office.

"Yes you do," said Rhonda.

But he stood there a long moment longer, feeling doubtful, remembering the day in March, now so ethereal in his recollection, when he'd first succumbed to what he now considered an inexplicable passion of need and shame. The sunbeams dancing at the edge of the narrow hallway leading to the vault. The odour of the bank air, stale and ancient. The looming walls, the bleak stillness at the mouth of the vault, the safety deposit boxes gleaming in the distance, their sheen like a wall of sneering grins. He stood there remembering this, yet not sure if it had been that way at all.

Rhonda got up and calmly took his hand. Taking his hand was how she always launched them on their journey towards making love. Like a little girl, he sometimes thought, her fingers narrow and absurdly short inside the envelope of his giant grip. Like Aphrodite too: as old as lust itself, confident and sure of herself. They passed down the narrow hallway, Rhonda leading them hand in hand. Together they passed through the dancing sunbeams he recalled from three months before.

In the vault, she knelt down on the floor to unbuckle his trousers. When he was exposed, she sucked on him.

I'll make it worth your while, she'd said.

He disliked enjoying this.

The first time, a few weeks ago, he'd had to be talked into it. Like someone other than the two of them was going to know and disapprove. She'd said she loved him after she moved her mouth away. He'd said he loved her too, mostly because he didn't know what else to say. He was not an inventive man; he didn't know how to describe delight. He liked mostly to be calm because it required no inspiration.

"I want to be on top," Rhonda said as she embraced him at the edge of the table.

In an out of body way, he only nodded.

I'll make it worth your while.

He laid down on the table, feeling the chill of it on his buttocks. He watched her undress nearby, still startled by her beauty when she presented it to him this way. Yet even the pleasure of this filled him with guilt and doubt.

On the table, she straddled him and said what she often said as she impaled herself on him. "Oh, God, what can I do? I'm such a little whore."

He'd given up arguing with her over remarks like these. He couldn't explain how they embarrassed him. This shame was something tragic she'd learned from the world in which they lived. He sensed he was as greedy to possess all of their shame—hers as well as his—as he was this sexual pleasure.

"You like me on top, don't you." Rhonda said as she moved on him.

"Yes, you know I do," he gasped.

Her breasts were red and wet where he played with them. He was rough sometimes this way, feeling guilty afterwards that he'd temporarily scarred her flesh.

They orgasmed with cries and pleas, first her, then him. It echoed against the vault's dead metal and concrete, then died abruptly like a crib-deathed child.

Rhonda told him that she loved him.

"I love you too," he said.

The vault seemed colder and darker now that they were done. But Connelly felt safer as they cleaned themselves of sex and restored their clothing again.

"I'm such a little whore," Rhonda said once more before he could raise a finger to her lips to prevent it. "That's what you do to me, you make a whore of me."

But Connelly doubted this. Maybe love was what was between them after all. Maybe they only made an excuse of one another for feeling what they shouldn't feel.

THE LAST HALF HOUR of Connelly's working day was mostly fabrication: The extra work he'd told Betty would keep him at the bank until six; the open ledger on his desk and the way he sat in front of it, holding a pen in case someone came to the door to catch him working; feeling hollow again now that Rhonda was gone and believing that he must, for the sake of everyone, end this hopeless affair; believing he didn't know which of his two selves was real and which was the devilish shadow pressed up against him from behind like a deviant in a crowd. These were the ideas he considered while pretending to work.

MAGGIE MATHIESON AND I became an item not long before the beginning of summer vacation. You were happy with this—I know the arrangement felt like symmetry to you. Not much was said, even when you asked me how it had come about, wanting to share the delight of love with me.

"Proximity," I replied after a moment's thought.

"What?"

"Proximity."

"I don't know what that means, Gary," you admitted.

"All of us hanging around together," I said. "All of us being friends."

"Oh," you said, not quite getting it yet.

But I know you felt the symmetry in your relationship with your friends, the comfort in its solidarity. You felt it most powerfully in early July when the four of us swam out to the raft in Brannigan's Cove one afternoon. The water was still cold, summer still young, and all of us complained and gasped as we swam the distance between shore and the raft.

Shivering and hugging ourselves, we dried our wet bodies on the raft in a sun that hiccoughed ambivalently between swiftly passing clouds.

"The river isn't ready for swimming yet," I said with a baleful glance in your direction.

"Couple more weeks maybe," you replied.

This was your river, its seasonal moods belonged to you. You respected them and anticipated them. Maggie and Kimberley were newcomers to Brannigan's Cove. Even I didn't share your experience with this place. To us, you felt like the host. Even symmetry, this afternoon, seemed to need a leader.

No wonder everything was perfect. I sensed we were your three favourite people and I knew this place was one of your favourite haunts. In this way, all of us were symmetrically in love, symmetrically at home in a symmetrical setting.

You laid down on the smooth, wooden planks and gazed at us, smiling in benevolence like a patient, kindly monarch, while the raft rocked and rolled on the water, its drums licked and caressed by the sensual green affections of the breeze-bothered river.

"I keep thinking," said Maggie, "that we have to swim back. That's what I keep thinking. No matter what, it's going to be cold again."

"Me too," said Kimberley. "That's what I keep thinking too." She smiled at you afterwards with one of those smiles you'd come to think of as a wink.

"It'll warm up," you said. "In a week or so it'll be gorgeous."

"Geez," I muttered. "You mean we have to stay out here for a week?"

You punched me gently on the arm.

I reclined happily on the raft too. The girls sat cross-legged, like two gamblers in an alley, about to deal a hand of cards.

You didn't say as much as the rest of us did. You wanted to savour this afternoon in delicious silence. You tucked your hands behind your head and watched the sun find patches of blue sky between the commuting clouds. Your flesh sang in the warmth of the sun and you'd never felt so happy. You watched me being blonde, already turning pink. You saw Maggie grow more freckles, her summer bumper crop. Kimberley tanned like you, both of you turning brown. Maggie and I were hearts and diamonds, you and Kimberley were clubs and spades. It seemed everyone here was mystically connected to the person they cared about most. And all of us seemed well shuffled into this complete, symmetrical deck.

You and your friends: we were still giddy because school was now recessed.

"No Miss Cartwright," you said.

"No homework," added Kimberley

"No arithmetic." This from Maggie.

My turn. "By the end of summer we'll be looking forward to going back to school."

I was right and all of you knew it, but you groaned at me anyway.

While we relaxed on the raft, you swam only long enough to get wet and chilled, then you climbed the ladder and shook yourself like a dog, spraying us. Even the resulting howls of outrage seemed perfect in some way.

As the afternoon leaked by, you listened to us, the stories we told, our ideas for the future. But you didn't say much yourself—afraid, I know, that it would interrupt this perfect now. You didn't care about the future, didn't want to remember an inadequate past. When you glimpsed the differences among the four of us, you didn't acknowledge them: me so pale in the sunshine, Maggie so freckled and young compared to Kimberley. You resisted difference because it might lead to imperfection. When you noticed Kimberley had breasts, that she was less of a child, you turned away from this, not wanting it to be true. The girls wore the same style of bathing suit, brightly coloured with a short skirt around the hips—this made them the same in your manipulated perception.

You were so happy that afternoon, in love with Kimberley, in love with your life and your friends. Summer stretched out before you like a long, golden hallway. Somewhere at the end, you sensed there was an immaculate vista in which your numbered days would reveal they were numberless. That day in Brannigan's Cove you glimpsed immortality. It was, I think, your finest moment of joyful innocence.

THE BLISS OF LOVE and happiness continued after that day. You began to imagine you could contain it inside a definition and, in this way, hold onto it forever.

"Caring about people should have numbers," you told us a few nights later.

All of us sat at the top of the bleachers at the ballpark where the Meridian Marauders were battling their rivals from Adelaideville. No one was nearby. Although the stands were fairly crowded, most Meridians had gathered along the baselines when they couldn't get near home plate. Here, at the end of the bleachers, it was dark, like a closet at the edge of the living room field of play.

"You know what I mean?" you asked when no one answered you.

Kimberley just smiled. I glanced at you because I sensed you were going to embarrass me.

"Okay, whaddyuh mean?" asked Maggie.

"Like a measurement," you said.

"I don't get it," said Maggie.

"He means measuring caring with numbers," I explained. "Right?"

"Huh?" said Maggie.

"Oh, never mind," you said, too embarrassed to go on, too embarrassed to actually stop.

"C'mon, Phil," I said. "You may as well finish it now."

"Go ahead," said Kimberley.

"Okay. Let's say liking your best friend is one. And liking your brother and sister is two."

Maggie and I were nodding; we each had brothers and sisters.

"And liking someone like a girlfriend is, well, you know, three."

We waited.

"So I guess loving someone is four. You see what I mean?"

"Like someone you'd marry if you were old enough?" asked Maggie. "That's four?"

"Yeah," you said, flushing. "I guess so."

"So, you like Gary one?" said Maggie.

"Well, sure," you replied.

"And you like me one?"

"Sure."

"But you mean you like Kimberley three?"

You glanced at the object of your affections. You felt butterflies, a new intoxication in the revelation that you were going to tell the truth.

"Is that what you're saying?" persisted Maggie. "You mean you like Kimberley three?"

Even in the darkness, you could see Kimberley was blushing.

"Phillip?"

"Well, not exactly," you stammered.

Maggie's prosecution could not be stopped. "You mean

you don't like Kimberley three?"

You realized you were trapped. Glancing at Kimberley as she began to look at you, you knew you had to forge ahead, so there would be no misunderstanding.

"No," you said in a voice strangled of its breath. "I like Kimberley four."

The resulting silence was so oppressive you thought you were going to die. The ballgame, the cries of the crowd, the catcalls to the players, the smack of the ball in the catcher's mitt, the grunt of the umpire behind the plate, all this seemed some distance away, distorted, out of reach.

Gradually you turned to see Kimberley's face. Shyly she looked at you and gently smiled.

"Geez, Phil," I said to no one in particular, embarrassed by your foolishness.

Ultimately, though, it was all right after that for you. My words didn't matter. Maggie didn't matter. It was Kimberley's smile that mattered. It was all right after that.

EIGHTEEN

. . . *I loitered near the door while the Mafia Man went up to Buck at the counter.*

"Where's your dad?" said the Mafia Man.

"Under the weather again," replied Buck.

The Mafia Man put his briefcase on the counter and snapped it open. "I've got a proof of your ad for next week," he said.

Nervously, I moved closer, intent on the open briefcase and the answers I was sure lay inside. There was an aisle that ran by the counter. It would take only a few seconds to stroll by ignored and glance inside the Mafia Man's briefcase. I started towards them.

But the Mafia Man turned, his eyes as black as death. "Hey, Kid, you following me?"

I stopped in my tracks. "Huh?"

"You following me? Everywhere I go today, you're hangin' around."

I just stood there and trembled.

"Can I help you with somethin'?" Buck Winston asked, imitating the Mafia Man's curious menace.

While shopping with her, I'd heard my mother's response to this question a dozen times. I mimicked it with as much self-assurance as I could muster. "Just lookin', thanks," I said.

"Well, go look somewhere else, you fucking little asshole."

I gaped at Buck, aghast.

He lunged towards me. "Get out of here before I kick your arse."
I bolted for the door, hearing them complaining behind me.
"That kid's been doggin' me all afternoon."
"Just a little asshole," said Buck.
Then the door closed behind me and I was safe again . . .

FOR MORE THAN A DECADE it had been Basil Grisham's habit to close his barber shop for two weeks at the end of June so that he and his wife Florence could take their vacation before school let out for the summer. Childless, they travelled each year to a lodge they favoured in an area just north of the Madawaska Valley. Here they took advantage of the peace and quiet July and August—the height of the Canadian vacation season—would have denied them.

Accustomed to this, the men of Meridian who liked to have their hair cut at the end of June crowded into the barber shop as soon as he returned. Overdue for their June trims and destined to be slightly early for their cuts at the end of July, they forgave Grisham this interruption in ritual each year at the beginning of summer. His return was normally festive, like a resumption of good health after a period of illness. Grisham's "h'lo" as his regulars came in. Everyone inquiring if he'd had a pleasant holiday. It was an agreeable tradition. Normally, though, it took a week after his return for these men to harvest the local news and information Grisham relayed as village conduit.

His return in 1960 was especially festive on the first Saturday of July because the official opening of Meridian Kiwanis Park on the site of the old Findlay building was set for the next day. The men at Grisham's that morning—Jim Connelly, John MacLean, your father, and most of the other regulars—felt pleased with themselves that the park had been completed. The blemish of the Findlay fire could soon be forgotten, entombed beneath a pleasing network of lawns, gardens, benches, and pathways.

"You know something?" said John MacLean to the assembly in the barber shop. "Once we open the park, a lot of us will be wondering what to do with ourselves for a while. Last year we had the centennial. This year the park. After the ribbon cutting tomorrow, well, I don't know. There's a chance we might be bored."

There was a collective murmur of agreement.

"I think you're right, John," said Don Stuart. "I was just saying to Blanche last week, 'what's going to need our attention next?'"

"There's always something," someone said. "If things aren't getting better, you can rest assured they're probably getting worse."

Again, there was general agreement. No one in the barber shop could argue with that.

Connelly was already in the chair, his trim nearly complete. For the past few months he'd been showing up early and sometimes he was already gone by the time MacLean and some of the others arrived. MacLean found himself pondering this new habit today as the other men talked among themselves. His banker was quieter these days too, as if something troubled him.

"How're things with you, Jim?" asked MacLean.

The question startled Connelly, mired the way he was in a deep reverie of tension and anticipation as his Saturday appointment with Rhonda at MacLean's cabin drew nearer.

His gaze met MacLean's through the medium of Basil Grisham's mirror. "Just fine, John," he said. "Looking forward to two weeks off."

"I'll bet you are," said John MacLean. "I hear you're going away."

"Prince Edward County," Connelly replied.

Gradually all the men had stopped to listen to this exchange. All of them believed Connelly wasn't himself these days: quieter, more sober, sometimes even distant. Because he was their banker, they searched for clues. They feared economic disaster almost endlessly. If Connelly was worried, maybe they should worry too. If he was too loyal to the bank, he might not have their best interests at heart.

Connelly left shortly afterwards. Barely had he departed than the men began to share their observations on the matter. George Manson, a prosperous farmer in his own right, reported that he'd had the temerity to ask Connelly just the other day if things were going all right.

"What'd he say?" asked Stuart.

"Just that he needed a vacation. It's been a busy time at the bank."

"Hmmm," said Stuart thoughtfully. "Blanche hasn't mentioned anything out of the ordinary."

"Management priorities," I suppose," said MacLean, enjoying once again his gift for bringing aimless speculation to some kind of formal close. The men looked up to him and he was aware of this. "I'm sure it's nothing to worry about."

Sure enough, the men relaxed, including your father who was next in line to be sheared.

"Phillip was in the other day," Grisham told him as he took his seat in the barber's chair. "First time Phillip's come in on his own. He's growing up fast, Bert."

"Like a weed," your father replied.

"How old is he now?"

"Eleven."

"Eleven going on sixteen," the barber said. "He didn't want the brushcut this year. Nosiree. Short back and sides, he said. Let it grow on top."

Your father forced a laugh. "I know. We had quite the talk about that this year. Said he didn't want a brushcut this summer and that was that. He's changing a lot, I guess. Kids grow up. They get their own opinions. They begin to get stubborn."

"Kids get like that on their way to being men," Don Stuart said from his chair by the door. "We were all the same, weren't we?"

Most of the men agreed.

Your father felt better for this. He'd been angry during the discussion about your haircut, not about your hair so much, but about how defiant you'd been. And Carol had taken your side. "Let him have his hair the way he wants it," she'd said. "He's growing up." Your father felt betrayed by this, like he was losing control of you.

"Growing up's one thing," your father said to the men in the barber shop. "But there's a responsibility that goes along with it."

"Absolutely right," said John MacLean.

"You still have to respect your elders," your father added.

"It's that Smith girl making him grow up so fast," George Manson said with a meaningful laugh, just as your father was feeling better.

There were guffaws of acknowledgment all around.

Deeply embarrassed, your father didn't like it and didn't join in. He realized at that moment how tired he was of hearing about the Smith girl and what a young knockout she was. To him, it made the entire family look foolish, especially you.

But John MacLean had noticed your father's discomfort reflected in the mirror. "C'mon, fellas," he said. "He's a good-looking kid, Bert's boy." When that silenced everyone, he added directly to your father, "It looks like you've got yourself a ladies' man there, Bert."

"Maybe so," your father said, not feeling very much better.

He felt the silence afterwards, the way the men were watching him. He didn't like silence, the way it slipped outside his grasp, outside his control. He'd never trusted silence like this, the kind perpetrated by peers. It left him to drift all by himself on a sea of speculation. He felt defensive, his dignity offended.

"Smith girl or no Smith girl, Phillip's been well raised. He knows how to behave." As he said this, your father searched the mirror for argument on the faces of the other men.

There was none.

John MacLean nodded slightly, clearly in approval.

"Nice to see your family getting more use out of that cabin of yours on the point, John," George Manson said then, noticing the nod.

MacLean gaped at him, puzzled by the remark.

"I see Rhonda's horse tied up there on Saturday afternoons sometimes," the other farmer explained.

"Oh, you mean when she's riding?"

"Sure."

"She stops there for a break," MacLean said, immediately annoyed with himself that he'd felt compelled to explain his daughter's behaviour on his land.

Everyone felt the tension and silence descend again. Even Grisham noticed it and grew a little apprehensive. Like a host at an otherwise well-planned party, he wondered what was wrong with his customers' collective mood.

Everyone found solace in their private thoughts, George Manson especially. He contemplated Rhonda MacLean and how, quite recently, he thought he'd seen a car parked in the grove at the edge of the MacLean cabin a couple of Saturdays ago, when he'd been passing in his boat. Rhonda's horse had been tethered out front but the metallic glint he'd seen likely was a car. Like someone intended to hide it from view, which was something to think about.

That day, the sighting had been inconclusive; the grove's foliage was summer dense. Over time, though, he'd convinced himself this was what he'd seen. It was fun to toy with the notion that it was a car and, if so, that Rhonda was meeting someone in the cabin on the sly. Manson wasn't a fool. If the meeting was taking place on the sly, then the man Rhonda was meeting was as married as a man can get. And wouldn't that be something, the lucky sonofabitch? One of these Saturdays, he'd promised himself, curiosity would get the better of him and he'd cruise in closer to shore to have a better look. A man liked to know, just on general principle, if Rhonda MacLean was up to anything.

For his part, MacLean was secretly angry at Manson's unprovoked intrusion into his affairs. Like your father, he too was bothered by silence, its potential for imagination and its resistance to control. Manson's remarks had touched a nerve. He'd been wondering himself what his daughter was up to these days. As far as he knew she wasn't dating anyone and he'd begun to wonder if she was seeing someone she shouldn't. He believed he knew what she was like. If Rhonda brought shame on the family name, it would torture him. Rhonda knew this as well as anyone.

In the silence of the barber shop, Grisham's scissors clacked loudly in the curls of your father's hair. Grisham sensed the change of mood that had enveloped the room. Like some new crisis was now impending, something bleak, a kind of dark foreshadowing that Meridian—and all it stood for—was vaguely threatened again.

No rest for the wicked, Grisham thought as he brushed hair from your father's neck.

When your father climbed out of the chair and Grisham called out, "Who's next?" his voice carried like an alarm in the uncharacteristically silent shop.

THE NEXT DAY most of the village showed up for the official opening of Meridian Kiwanis Park. It was warm and sunny, and this was reason enough for the human crush spilling out of the park and onto the streets the Kiwanians had blocked off for the event.

"Geez," you said to me, standing beside you in the crowd. "The whole town must be here, Gare."

"Half of it, anyway," I admitted with a shrug.

Your father had anticipated this kind of crowd; he'd told your mother so. "It's more than just the opening of a park," he said. "It's getting over that awful tragedy last year. Everyone in town feels the same way," he'd added for emphasis.

You sensed a mood of closure yourself, as you stood there in the throng. You imagined hearing the whisper of the turning page as Meridian finished reading the chapter about the Findlay fire. Now the community could "move onwards," as John MacLean put it just before he and three other Kiwanians, manipulating a large pair of gleaming scissors, cut a long red ribbon that drifted lazily to the new sod, accompanied by a spirited round of applause.

As you had the day of the cleanup a couple of months earlier on this same site, you felt a comforting solidarity with the crowd watching the proceedings. Again you felt protected by something socially larger than yourself, by its rules, standards, and expectations, in place to keep you from harm.

This time, if not magnified, the feeling was reinforced because everyone you cared about was here. Your father, in a striking blue blazer and grey pants, stood with several other Kiwanians on the dignitary side of the ribbon, actually helping to hold it steady just before the cutting. He'd never been able to hide these moments when he felt proud. As he gathered alongside men like Joe Langley, the impressively tall and moustached Jim Connelly, and John MacLean himself, your father stood erect, his barrel chest puffed out, parting the lapels of his best blazer.

Your mother was nearby, across the horseshoe of spectators from you. Her smile came and went in intensity, waxing when she found her husband who, because of his role in the proceedings, seemed at last to have arrived—a fact she'd mentioned to you beforehand so that you'd know enough to be proud of him too—then waning cautiously when she looked in your direction. Even on a day as auspicious as this one, she remained vigilant over your behaviour.

Kimberley was there too, not far away from your mother, although they didn't seem to notice their proximity. Kimberley, most of all, made you feel giddy with certainty and the sense that you belonged. She stood with her mother, her friend Maggie, and Eldora Diamond, all of them across the new park from you. You and Kimberley hadn't arranged to witness the ceremony from this vantage point, but you took full advantage of it from time to time, smiling at one another, seemingly unnoticed by the otherwise preoccupied crowd.

I didn't say much as the park was officially opened. I continued to suffer a deep guilt over the Findlay fire, still believing something could have been done to prevent it. To me, a bombastic ceremony wouldn't alter the nature of the tragedy.

You still regretted the way I kept remembering things you'd managed to forget. If I could let the memory go, and the guilt, you believed I'd feel embraced by the village the way that you felt embraced today.

"That was a nice ceremony," you said when it was all over and the crowd began to disperse, as the dignitaries gathered in a cluster to shake each other's hands. "Whaddyuh think, Gare?"

"Sort of like a funeral," I replied.

"You think so?"

I didn't answer you, pondering privately my interpretation of the day's significance. It was clear to us now that you regarded the Findlay tragedy from a different point of view than I did. There was no need to argue or explain.

As you drifted towards your parents who were still chatting on the park lawns with other important Meridians, you turned to me to ask me if I'd noticed Maggie and Kimberley. I heard you sigh and felt your dismay. I was in the act of vanishing away from the crowd. I looked back once and saw you turning in a circle, still looking for me. Soon I was gone and you didn't see me again. When you asked me about it later, I said I'd just wanted to go home. I said it in a way that ensured that you believed me.

NINETEEN

. . . *Dwight closed the file on the Mafia Man, but not until he'd explained to all of us that the man in the dark suit was obviously an advertising representative for one of the area's newspapers.*

"Jeezus," said Chuck. "I told you guys he was just a salesman."

We all nodded in the dim light of the clubhouse, giving Chuck his due.

"This is getting dumb," he said. "Some detective agency. Nothing ever happens."

For the moment there was no adequate reply. Dwight and I exchanged glances.

It was August now and summer had cooled. Irving swayed gently to the music of a strong breeze coming in the clubhouse window. I sensed that things were close to being over.

But Dwight finally broke the silence. "Looks like Richie's done some of the groundwork on our next case," he said.

Chuck muttered an invective. "Don't you guys ever give up?"

"Let's call it The Case of the Vanishing Winstons," Dwight said, paying him no attention. "Richie, I'm putting some of your Mafia Man notes into the new file."

"You mean the Buck Winston part?"

He nodded, raising his hand to reposition his disintegrating spectacles . . .

HOT. HUMID. CONNELLY lay on the bed beside Rhonda, where both of them were bathed in sweat. He wondered for a moment if he would suffocate. The heat, the sex, the thick and heavy shroud of risk that continued to imprison them. Even this cabin setting felt strangled in the humidity, its walls perspiring in the heat. Connelly gasped for breath. Something about Rhonda and still being here with her frankly frightened him. Like it was about to crush him somehow.

"So when do you leave on vacation?" she was asking.

"Monday."

"You won't be dropping in at the bank?"

"No. I'm officially on vacation right now."

"And you'll be gone for two weeks?"

"Yes."

"It'll be three weeks then before we can meet again here."

"I guess so," he admitted cryptically.

They lay on the bare mattress today, sheets and blankets in disarray at the foot of the bed or tangled on the floor. Naked, they felt no breeze, although they anticipated one. Connelly, in particular, longed for a pleasant gust, the refuge of an oasis. Rhonda was pressing in on him, like she might smother him.

They'd made almost desperate love several minutes ago. Connelly was convinced the desperation had been Rhonda's. By the time he'd felt it, he knew it was an infection and she was its carrier. Yet he felt confused. Even smothered by her love, three weeks seemed a very long time to not make love with her. He wasn't tired of Rhonda yet, although he often wanted to be.

"Are you going to miss me?" she asked, as if she sensed his thoughts.

"Yes," he replied truthfully. "Are you going to miss me?"

"Stupid question," was all she said.

"Well, you asked me."

"We're different that way," she said. "I need to know things more than you do. I know this business of you and me means more to me than you."

"Not true," he said. "I'm just not as free as you are."

She couldn't argue with this—his words silenced her.

He took a moment to consider the nature of his regret. Until now he honestly hadn't admitted what it would mean to him to not be naked with her for three weeks. He felt a petulance over the loss that, once acknowledged, grew surprisingly deep.

"I'm going to miss you very much," he confessed, knowing to say so was tactically foolish even while it was the truth.

He supposed she deserved to see him open up one small vein. When the affair was over, she could look back on it and know the dilemma of his marriage was what had been at fault, not the solace they found in each other's arms.

Almost from the outset—faced with the risk to his marriage and his status in the community, the potential that existed for his personal ruin—he'd enjoyed imagining Rhonda finding someone else on whom to shower her sexual favours. Now, though, faced with three weeks of sexual deprivation, the possibility of her change of heart filled him with unexpected loss. He felt betrayed by this. It reminded him he still didn't know whom he actually was.

"I can't wait for the day you realize how much you really love me," Rhonda said shortly.

"I've said so, haven't I?"

"But you've never believed it. It's just something you say."

"C'mon, Rhonda."

"Anyway," she added with murky calm, "come that day, you'll want to marry me."

He turned to her, unable to conceal that he was alarmed by her words.

"All in good time," she said, an ironic smile on her lips.

"Rhonda, I have a son, a family."

"So where are you going, anyway?" she asked, ignoring his words.

"Huh?"

"On vacation."

"Oh. Prince Edward County."

"Is it far from here?"

"Between two and three hours."

"We could meet somewhere in between, couldn't we? Isn't Kingston down there somewhere?"

"Jesus, Rhonda, how am I supposed to explain traipsing off to Kingston by myself? What would we do in Kingston?"

"Get a room, make love in the shower, have a nice dinner out, be noticed by strangers who would see we're in love."

"Jesus," he said again. "Fine if they were all strangers. Why risk it?"

"Do you know Kingston well?"

"What's the difference? How would I explain a trip to Kingston alone to Betty and Gerald?"

"You'd think of something."

He sighed in exasperation. "Why would we want to risk something like that?"

"Because you'll miss me."

While appalled by her self-assurance, it also amused him. "Pretty cocky, aren't you?"

"About this, I am."

He said nothing. He knew, by Saturday, he'd be wanting her again. But he also knew he would never acquiesce to her proposal.

She was watching him think his thoughts. "Stop looking so trapped," she cried. "I hate it when you look trapped."

"Rhonda, how can I help . . . ?"

". . . Shush," she instructed sternly.

He obeyed. Of late, he'd begun to obey her in the same way he obeyed Betty—to keep the peace, to ensure that events in his life took place as innocuously as possible, keeping him from harm, keeping him hidden from a treacherous world.

As they talked, she'd begun playing with his cock, distractedly at first, then with more intensity. He'd been only dimly aware that he was erect again, their conversation distracting him from the predictable assent of his sexuality.

Rhonda glided along the mattress, planing over the

perspiration along his body. Soiled though he was, she took him into her mouth.

"Jesus," he whispered, surprised, aggrieved, delighted, getting ready to protest.

She drew on him a few times, then moved her mouth away to glance into the face of his pleasure. "Don't be too sure you won't want to marry me someday," she said with a wicked certainty.

"For God's sake, Rhonda."

But she only laughed and returned to what she'd been doing.

He let himself disappear inside the exquisite storm of pleasure caused by her stroking tongue.

"YOU KNOW KIMBERLEY isn't my real name, don't you?"

She said this from where she sat on the stone wall at the edge of your property. Her legs, bare and brown, dangled from the precipice. She was wearing her pink shorts and white sneakers. She smiled at you and it struck you that she'd never looked more beautiful.

You noticed this from where you crouched beside your bicycle. It was turned upside down on the cracked driveway asphalt. You'd been oiling its chain and wheels when Kimberley had come along, but now that the job was done, you kept spinning the back wheel, turning the pedals with your hands, then applying the brake. Pretending to test them, pretending to be busy, pretending to have an excuse for the pleasure you felt in being here alone with her, the two of you together in the quickly descending dusk. Like enjoying these few moments would require an explanation to someone somewhere somehow on the outside of your inner self.

"What I mean is Kimberley is my real name now," she was telling you. "But it wasn't when I was born."

"What was your name when you were born? What did they call you then?"

"Elsa."

"Elsa," you repeated thoughtfully. "That's a nice name too, you know. It has a nice sound to it."

She smiled.

"Why did your name get switched?"

"Because we were German and now we're Canadian."

"You mean because of the war?"

"I guess so," she said with a shrug. "It's complicated."

"Sorry," you said, not really apologizing to Kimberley, but to a tedious world around you.

You were tired of hearing about the war. When your father talked with other men about it, it sounded like bragging to you, their voicing of an opinion they were never going to change. The more they talked about the war, the less you understood it, their need to recount it, the way they connected war to a purpose you couldn't imagine.

"War seems pretty stupid. I wish they'd shut up about it."

"I know," was her response. "Me too, I guess."

You grinned, the war forgotten. With Kimberley here, the evening was transformed from the boring possibility it had been before her arrival. There was no ballgame scheduled, I had declined to come over, and your prospects had looked grim. Now, with Kimberley here, it had evolved into something miraculous. The two of you in the dusk, alone, feeling special together. A warm joy gathered along your flesh—inside and outside—and you felt the marvelous flattery of some vague possibility. You felt blessed by good fortune, endorsed, sponsored, approved of in a rich and exciting way.

"It's getting pretty dark," said Kimberley. "How can you see what you're doing?"

"I can't," you admitted with a chuckle. "I'm just fooling around."

"Oh."

You gazed at her helplessly, shy and inadequate.

"You could sit up here beside me," she ventured. "I have to go home soon."

"Okay."

You inverted your bicycle and leaned it against the wall a few feet away. Then you hopped onto the cool stone beside her. Kimberley took your hand and held it in a secret, unseen place between her thigh and yours.

"What a great night," she said. "It's warm and perfect."

"You're not kidding," you said, thinking it might be the best night of your life.

You grew shy together here. You held hands limply, unused to touching one another. Her hand in yours, unstroked and still, felt like the most exciting sensation you'd ever know.

"Does Gary still like Maggie?" she asked you suddenly.

"I think so," you replied hesitantly.

In fact, you weren't certain. These days I wasn't around as much and, when I was, I seemed preoccupied and distant.

"Maggie thinks he doesn't."

"Oh yeah?"

"She's only seen him a couple of times and he was different."

"He was away on vacation for a few days. I dunno."

"Gary's strange," Kimberley said without malice.

"Yeah. Because he's so smart. Sometimes he thinks too much, you know?"

"It's just that it was nice when he liked Maggie."

"It kinda made things perfect," you admitted, blushing hotly.

This quieted both of you for a time. You sat there in the darkness, listening to the crickets, watching bats swooping among the evening's lush harvest of insects.

"Gary's skipping Grade Seven," Kimberley said.

"What?"

"They're putting him in Grade Eight this fall."

"What?"

"Didn't you know?"

"No. He hasn't mentioned it."

"He told Maggie he is."

"Oh."

You felt disappointed and betrayed. You'd be left behind while I escaped the odious Miss Cartwright. No longer in class together, helping one another along, what would happen then?

"Me too," whispered Kimberley. "I guess you knew I'm

skipping too, didn't you?"

This time your pain was even deeper. You gazed at her in dismay and hurt.

"Phillip?"

"I didn't know," you cried, feeling dizzy with the news, like the world had tilted away from its own horizon.

Kimberley squeezed your hand in reassurance but the sadness you felt lingered on. It was easy to imagine the hopelessness you'd feel sitting in class next fall and not being able to glance at Kimberley or enjoy the perfect balance of having her glancing back at you.

"Do you have to skip?"

"I guess so."

"Even if you don't want to?"

"Yes. Everyone thinks I should, because my marks are good and I'm older."

"It's just stupid," you muttered bitterly.

"It'll be all right," Kimberley said, squeezing your hand again.

"Gary's right," you said. "He says the world's too bossy, especially where kids are concerned. Always telling us what's good for us even if it's not."

Kimberley nodded. You knew there was nothing she could say.

"Kimie? When you're in Grade Eight, will you still, you know . . . ?"

". . . Yes," she said. "I will."

Your face turned hot again, the pleasure in your relief. Your love for her felt too frantic to be kept secret. If you didn't find a way to tell her how much you cared, the knowledge, privately endured, would crush you like an egg.

"I have to go soon," Kimberley said.

The time had come to speak, you knew. Perfect, imperfect night was hanging in the balance.

"Kimie? You remember that night when I said, well, you know, that I liked you number four?"

"Yes."

"It was, uh, really true, you know."

She leaned towards you and kissed you on the cheek. You felt a curiously complex sensation of happiness that was hungry and full, both at the same time.

"I love you, Kimie," you whispered.

"I love you too," she said.

She held your hand a moment longer then let go of it, as if all opportunity was now gone. "I have to go," she said as she hopped down from the stone wall.

"Okay."

"Goodnight, Phillip."

"Goodnight, Kimie."

You spun around on the rough concrete to watch her walk down the street. You watched her until she vanished into the darkness.

You felt miserable, yet happy, and somehow cheated by both sensations. Like you could hear the ticking of time, its remorseless progress at a moment you wished it would stop. Yet, instinctively, you knew time failed everyone. As a divider and issuer of goods, time wasn't going to let you hold onto this favourite moment to enjoy it a little longer; time belonged to everyone and divided up its profits accordingly. No matter how fine the love of this, your moment, felt, it was a booty you sensed you must share with everyone else. The trouble with having love, you intuited at this moment, was that once you acknowledged it, it was only a matter of time until someone took it away.

YOUR MOTHER HAPPENED to enter the kitchen and happened to glance out the window as Kimberley kissed your cheek. Surprised to be so territorially affronted, she didn't turn on the light but hid in the darkness for a few moments, watching you until Kimberley left. Then, succumbing to a inexplicable fatigue, she pulled out a kitchen chair and sat down in the gloom.

Although she felt ashamed of it, everything about life now seemed somehow your fault. You were the focal point of several varying tragedies. She couldn't name the tragedies but she felt them regardless. She considered time in the way you had—its knots and the failure of human fingers to untie them. At this moment, for your mother, the past didn't seem like it evolved smoothly into the present, and the present didn't promise a fair or just future. It was all knots and tangles instead. She'd wanted things in the past; the present, in not providing them, had failed her. The future was opaque with limited promise. So there she was, faced with her knots and her own fumbling fingers. Was this the nature of life? Her own inadequacy, a gift for mistakes, the power of life to contrive incidents outside her control? Were these the knots she could not untie? If so, why did it seem for the moment that you—her son—were at fault?

She couldn't answer her questions and pushed them away. She found comfort in a more specific kind of fretting. She was going to lose you someday soon to some version of Kimberley Smith. She felt jealous, not just anticipating your going, but because you might discover something joyful she'd managed to miss herself. Loss of you and loss through you. The mirror she used to see herself was casting a rebellious reflection.

The Smith girl. In the darkness she might have been any young girl with a bit of a crush on you. But your mother had been troubled ever since the day your father and the others had cut the ribbon at Meridian Kiwanis Park. She'd noticed the Smith girl that day and had been surprised by her maturity, exactly as her husband had predicted. She'd observed a pretty young woman when she'd expected to see a girl. She'd concluded right away that Kimberley Smith was much too old for you.

Nor had the smiles that passed between you and Kimberley that day ameliorated her discomfort. Your apparent preoccupation with one another only aggravated your mother's notion that you were giving up your childhood without her permission.

"The Smith girl was up to see Phillip earlier tonight. I caught her kissing him on the cheek," she told your father after you were safely up in bed.

"Caught her?"

"I saw it from the kitchen window."

Soberly Bert nodded.

"She's too old for Phillip, isn't she?"

He kept nodding. "The whole town's talking."

"Oh, Bert, the whole town?"

"You know what I mean, Carol."

"Huh," she murmured, torn by this piece of news. "You'd think they'd have other things to talk about than a little boy and his girlfriend."

"Well, we're talking about it, aren't we?"

"That's different; we're his parents." She lit a cigarette. "So what's the town saying? Is she a little trollop or just mature for her age? She doesn't have a reputation, does she?"

"No, I've seen her at Phillip's ballgames. It isn't that exactly. The town's not saying anything nasty. It's just that they're saying anything at all."

"Well what are they saying?"

He sighed. "It came up last time I was at the barber shop."

"What did they say?"

"Little remarks about Phillip being a ladies' man."

"Oh Bert, for God's sake. He's tall for his age, that's all."

"I know. And remarks about what a little knockout she is."

"She is pretty," your mother remarked grimly.

"It's a variety of things, I guess," your father said at last. "She's good looking, she's mature, her family is German, and it's likely they're Jews."

"So everybody's curious."

"I guess so."

"Well how do you feel about all of this?"

"A little embarrassed. I can't put my finger on it, Carol. It's like Phillip's getting a reputation and it's not his fault."

"Do you think we should talk to Phillip about this?"

"I don't know," he said with a shrug. "I'll tell you one thing: I'll feel a lot better about it when it all goes away."

"And until then?"

"I suppose we just keep an eye on our son."

"We do that anyway. You and I are responsible parents."

"Well, a closer eye, Carol. You know something? It's like the people in this town don't realize how well we've brought Phillip up, how well behaved he is. When I hear comments about the Smith girl, I want to put a sign around his neck to remind everyone that Phillip's a good boy."

"Well, I don't like the idea of some girl ruining his reputation, whether she's a nice girl or not."

"I know. It's hard to understand, this whole business. As far as I know, he hasn't done anything wrong. But the way the town is making fun of him, well, it's embarrassing."

"We have to live here, Bert."

"That's just it."

They considered this conclusion in silence until Bert glanced at his watch. He wished they could arrive at a consensus so that they could go to bed.

"I guess all we can do is keep an eye on the situation and try not to worry," his wife said, sensing her husband's impatience. "I have faith in Phillip. He wouldn't do anything knowingly that would reflect badly on the family. You don't think so, do you?"

"I hope not," your father replied.

"I'll bet it's completely innocent," your mother said. "We don't want to blow this out of proportion, Bert."

"No," he said, getting up. "We don't. But if she's kissing him on the cheek, the situation will bear watching."

As he left the room, your mother remembered Kimberley's kiss. She sat there on the sofa, lit another cigarette, and fumbled with the knots she'd discovered in the flow of time.

TWENTY

... *"What about the Winstons?" said Chuck.*

"There's something fishy going on."

"Like what?"

"Okay," said Dwight. "Like Buck's looking after the store these days. Like his old man's just a drunk and they've been seen fighting, him and Buck. Like no one goes to the store anymore."

"So what?"

"Like the cops were there Saturday night, my old man says, and he said Buck's old man is hitting his old lady and stuff like that."

"I don't know, Dwight," I said.

"Yeah," said Chuck. "What's it got to do with us?"

"It's the perfect case for The Skeleton Club. We keep an eye on things in case something terrible happens."

"Like what?"

"Well, in case Mr. Winston is hitting Mrs. Winston around. I mean that's a terrible thing. Don't you guys think so?" He studied us one by one.

There was no moral alternative, not even for Chuck. We all said "yeah" to a man ...

YOU WERE TO INVITE ME ALONG, this was the plan. But when you called to ask me, I didn't want to go.

"You never want to do anything anymore, Gare," you complained.

I didn't feel like talking. "I play baseball," I said listlessly.

"Yeah, but you don't want to hang around with us anymore. How come? Are you mad at us for something?"

"No. I've been busy, that's all."

"Doin' what?"

I sighed. It crackled in the telephone. "I have to go now," I said.

Which only made you feel more desperate. You'd be losing me in the fall when I skipped Grade Seven. Now was too early for me to vanish, as far as you were concerned. "Wait a sec, Gare. Are we still friends?"

"Yeah, we're still friends."

"Best friends?"

"Yeah, best friends."

"Well, gee," you said, relieved but still confused. "Are you going to tell me what's going on?"

"I can't explain it," I said. "Look, I have to go. I'll see yuh. Okay?" I hung up.

There'd been music in the background, as there often was at my house, and you knew I was playing my records. You supposed, as you hung up the receiver, that I was creating my own music charts again. I liked to type up my own top twenty, then play the songs I'd selected in order from the bottom to number one. Then, after I'd played the number one song, I'd roll dice, the results moving songs up or down the chart, according to the whims of fate and a complex arithmetical system I'd tried to explain to you once but you still didn't understand. The game bored you, but it was important to me which songs had the good fortune to make their way to the top of my chart. I had my favourites, I explained. They gave me something to root for. Sometimes I'd play my top twenty all afternoon long, as if I could doggedly make it relevant. It was a way I escaped the troubles I saw swirling around my life and the town in which I lived it.

You'd asked me one day, fed up with the game, if how it

all worked out actually mattered. "I don't get it," you'd said.

"I know you don't," I replied.

All of which was why, on a sunny Sunday afternoon near the end of July, you ended up going without me on an outing to a nearby beach with Kimberley and her mother. No Gary to even up the sides, as you found yourself sandwiched between Kimberley and Maggie in the back seat of Mrs. Smith's car, the only male, your legs tangled up and cramping on the convex imposition of the old Ford's transmission.

Maggie, as distressed as you were by my absence, waited until Mrs. Smith and Eldora Diamond were talking in the front seat before she asked quietly why I couldn't come.

"I don't know," you murmured. "He said he was busy."

Kimberley took your hand, holding it where it couldn't be seen between her leg and yours.

Maggie swallowed. Both of you could see she was disappointed.

It wasn't like you were going far, just ten miles down the highway towards Ottawa, to a small bay in the river offering a tiny stretch of beach popular to some of the area residents during the summer months. It wasn't Brannigan's Cove, that was for sure. You'd been at this beach twice before, once with friends and once with your mother and her friends. You'd found it crowded with strangers and the mandatory list of rules strangers usually demanded. Here—it was called Black Water Bay—you were required to swim inside the ropes because the river current on the other side of the buoys gradually accelerated towards a series of rapids a mile or so away. Even a handy snack bar and the hospitality of a sandy beach couldn't justify the squeals and shouts of strangers and the rules that they required. Better to go to Brannigan's Cove where you could swim freely by yourself.

Accordingly, you felt ambivalent and apprehensive as you drove to Black Water Bay. I had let you down; Maggie was disappointed; your destination was foreign and disquieting. Even holding Kimberley's hand in the back seat couldn't prevent the discomfort you felt with everything else, with the tear you'd now discovered in the perfect summer fabric you'd thought unblemished only a few weeks earlier.

Kimberley detected this. "Are you okay?" she whispered.

"Sure," you said automatically.

She gave your hand a squeeze. Kimberley wasn't fooled.

Mostly you'd dreaded meeting Kimberley's parents. You'd walked down the street to the mobile home feeling a deep trepidation, a beach towel coiled around your neck, wearing your bathing suit and a clean t-shirt, your mother's instructions to remember your "pleases" and "thank-yous" a tiresome echo in your thoughts. Like it was a forgone conclusion Kimberley's parents wouldn't approve of you.

Once you arrived, though, it hadn't been so bad. Eldora had been there and Eldora was a comfort. So much so that you endured a persistent and inexplicable difficulty in remembering that Eldora wasn't Kimberley's mother, that the wrinkled, rather stern other woman with the short grey hair and thick accent was actually Kimberley's mother.

On the way down the street you'd realized you feared her father most. Partly your mother's doing again. She'd warned you this morning that he was "miserable." You'd seen him at the gas pumps yourself from time to time, frowning into space as if space was frowning back, neither one of them intending to give in. But when you arrived, the gas station was closed and Kimberley's father was lying down.

It was hot and busy when you reached Black Water Bay. Mrs. Smith complained about this but Eldora said they could make the best of it. Resigned to the crowds, you, your chaperones, and your friends negotiated a path through sprawling sunbathers and their picnic baskets and blankets, winding your way through a group of boisterous teenagers intently tossing a baseball back and forth. Eventually you found a spot some distance from the beach, close to a patch of shade where the two adults could set up their chairs. Kimberley had brought a new badminton set along and here, away from the crowds, there was room to erect the net.

"We're going to swim, aren't we?" you asked after you'd

233

set up the net. "We'll be hot if we play badminton."

You'd already removed your shirt and ticklish ribbons of sweat trickled down your back and belly.

"Mom doesn't want us to swim," Kimberley announced with a blush of embarrassment.

"Oh?"

"She doesn't want us to get the back seat wet."

"Oh."

Yet Kimberley and Maggie wore bathing suits as well. Confused by this, you felt a familiar resentment, not with Kimberley's mother exclusively, but with the more general adult preoccupation with silly rules and directives. "I brought a towel," you said half-heartedly.

"C'mon, Phillip, we don't have to swim," said Maggie.

You glanced at Kimberley, noticing she blushed more deeply. You smiled in reassurance. "I like badminton," you said. "Badminton is fun."

But it was hot for badminton. Maggie capitulated early. She borrowed your towel and spread it out not far from where Eldora and Mrs. Smith conversed in the shade. You were happier then. You and Kimberley could climb inside the exclusive bubble permitting you to be together, oblivious to everyone else. Inside this perfect happiness, you batted the foolish white bird back and forth over the delicate net, laughing and making a chaste love of gazes and knowing grins.

"WHAT IS HIS AGE?" asked Gertrude of Eldora at one point after Maggie slipped off to the canteen to purchase a chocolate bar.

"I don't know exactly," replied Eldora. "Eleven or twelve, I guess."

"So young. Kimberley is fourteen."

"I know."

Both women fell silent, watching you and Kimberley at the badminton net, resting for a few minutes, talking through the mesh.

"They're such good friends," Eldora said, hoping that it

helped.

"She still sits at her window. He still sits on the church steps."

"Really? After all this time?"

"When they are not together."

"They're really close, Gertrude. It's a rare kind of friendship."

"Too close maybe."

"It won't last forever," Eldora said, knowing she sounded disappointed. "I think they're sweet together. What they have is so precious. It's so rare."

But Gertrude didn't answer.

Maggie was on her way back, nibbling on a Crispy Crunch.

"I thought he would be older," Gertrude said.

Eldora could see her friend was deeply troubled. But with Maggie within earshot, she couldn't pursue the matter further.

FOR YEARS NOW, since her childhood, the same question—"Do you have a minute?"—the same request, the same interruption, the same command performance.

"Rhonda? Do you have a minute?"

Her father's voice, disembodied—it didn't call out so much as broadcast itself through the rooms of the house from his headquarters in his study.

Rhonda, on her way to the kitchen, now four paces beyond his doorway, had long ago given up choice. She stopped, turned, obeyed, retracing her steps. She hesitated a moment before she entered his room.

"Sit down," he said this time, as she entered his domain.

She sat down.

He was drinking an expensive scotch and working. His hand held a pen, silver and black, that whispered across several columns in a thick ledger. He didn't look up for the moment.

While Rhonda waited, she felt faintly lost in time, like déjà vu, events taking place over and over again, this scene a tarnished segment in a long- running play. Boldly she gazed at him while he worked, noting how the demeanor he hoped was imposing was compromised by the height and girth of the chair in which he sat. What was it her sister, Janice, had called him when they were younger, when the huge chair dwarfed and mocked him? "The monkey in the blanket?" Yes, that was it, although it had seemed funnier and more apropos when they were little girls than it did now.

"Daddy, what is it?" Rhonda asked.

"I'll be with you in a minute," he said without looking up. He'd lost his place in the network of columns. He used his finger to find it again.

"Is there something wrong?"

This time he glanced at her. "I just want to talk to you," he said. "Give me a minute, will you?"

Rhonda sighed in the silence. She didn't like this room. It was too much his, connected to his fatherhood, which was sometimes generous, frequently indifferent, too often selfish and cruel. Man and study seemed one, deriving artifice from one another, as if incongruity was acceptable only when both parties agreed to it. There were expansive shelves of books, for instance—some of them bound in leather—although her father never read anything thicker than a newspaper. Heavy burgundy drapes framed the tall window but they were dusty at the tops because he never drew them closed to open them again. To Rhonda the room was a private movie set, with even less function than that. Perhaps the decanter of scotch and single tumbler had the most usefulness here, along with the accompanying ice bucket. Perhaps the set was for a movie about a glass of scotch and a pair of flirtatious ice cubes tinkling in his glass.

As far as Rhonda knew, her father only used his study to sit alone with the decanter of scotch. Or to do his books, pay his bills, and tally up his profits. Or, back then, when she and Janice were younger, he brought his daughters here, closing the door behind them before he exacted punishment on them. A spanking, always a spanking on their bare rear ends. Then an atonement, saying he felt sorry for having to spank them, still holding them over his knees, stroking their buttocks gently to heal the damage he'd caused; once, in

Rhonda's case, lifting her up to his lips, bending to gently kiss her stinging flesh. Was it memory or just something she imagined? Sometimes she wasn't certain.

Strange what she could remember clearly and what was now a blur. Hard to get a fix on the spanking and the stroking, but a framed portrait of a champion Aberdeen-angus bull on the wall behind him remained vivid even now. She would stare at it while she was being punished until it swam clearly into focus. It existed in a dimension all its own, something that resisted the mist of her tears and humiliation. The bull had something to do with her pain in a way her father did not, with its prize ribbon pinned to its harness, bovine stupidity honoured and photographed. Occasionally she still dreamed of the Aberdeen-angus, waking up just before dawn in a sheen of sweat and terror.

Her father put down his pen. "So," he said.

"What is it, Daddy?"

"I just wanted to talk, that's all. I don't see you much these days."

"You saw me at dinner."

"I mean privately," he replied. "A man and his daughter catching up on things."

Rhonda didn't comment. What was she supposed to say? What was she supposed to do? What did he really want? She realized at this moment how little she trusted him, how much she hated the extent of his control over everyone.

She turned to his open window as if she could snatch a breath. A balmy, damp breeze whispered through the screen. She noticed casually that the window was propped open with a hardbound copy of Frenchman's Creek. The book was badly warped.

"How's it going at the bank?" her father asked.

"Fine. It doesn't change much. Most days are the same as one another."

"Connelly good to work for?"

"Fine," she replied, gazing at him intently to freeze her face into obligatory indifference. "A little stuffy, but fine."

"He's a good man."

Rhonda nodded. "Old-fashioned."

"Good trait in a banker, as far as I'm concerned. We don't need someone flighty managing a bank."

"I suppose not."

MacLean drained his glass of what remained of his scotch. "You're awfully quiet these days."

"I am?"

"Well, yes. You go to the bank and come home, go to the bank and come home. You don't seem to do much else with your time."

"Still waters running deep?"

"Don't put words in my mouth."

Rhonda shrugged. "I just don't know what to say. I keep to myself. I ride more than I used to. It's been years since I've enjoyed riding so much."

"Well, that's good. But whatever happened to your social life?"

"You mean dating?"

"Sure. Dating and friends. Parties. Dances. You're the most eligible young woman around here. I should be beating young bucks away from the door with a broom handle. Instead I've got this career girl wallflower on my hands."

"I'm taking a holiday," Rhonda said. "Dating for the sake of it, well, I guess I've outgrown it. Are people asking questions in town?"

"No. Why would they?"

"I just wondered. We're having this talk, after all. I know Meridian, Daddy. It watches me like a hawk. And I know you worry what people think, more than I do, anyway."

His eyes narrowed. "You're a MacLean," he said.

Rhonda felt strangely embarrassed by his conventional ignorance. "I'm also what you would call a little whore," she imagined herself saying in reply.

"You've become hard to talk to, Rhonda," he said then. "You're still my baby girl, you still live at home. I just wondered how things were going for you."

"Are you suggesting it's time I left home?"

"Of course not," he replied. "Where would you go?"

"I meant get my own place."

"Where?"

"Not in Meridian, that's for sure. Ottawa, I guess."

He sighed impatiently. "I think not, Rhonda. That isn't how we do things. Your sister didn't leave home until she got married."

"Family ties," Rhonda said drily. "You couldn't keep your eye on me if I had my own place, could you?"

"Do I need to? Would I need to?"

"You've always thought so," she replied. "You're old-fashioned too."

"Too?"

"Like Mr. Connelly."

"You've done well by it, Rhonda." He cleared his throat. "Just so there's no misunderstanding, there'll be no apartment in Ottawa. You're a MacLean. We're family. We stay at the homestead until there's a valid reason to leave."

"Would you stop me?"

"Of course I would." He said this calmly, then fell silent, studying her. "Why do you try to provoke me, Rhonda?" he asked at last. "You have so much because of me." He continued to gaze at her, spinning his empty glass in his stubby fingertips.

Rhonda gazed back at him, craving a moment of defiance that would defeat him once and for all. Yet she didn't believe such an opportunity could ever exist and she fell back on ritual discretion. "I have no plans to leave," she heard herself say, "unless you're throwing me out."

"Don't be ridiculous."

"I was just joking, Daddy. For God's sake!"

He studied her thoughtfully. "I wish we could talk without arguing," he said.

"I wish you trusted me."

"Trust is something you earn."

"I'm not a little girl anymore, Daddy. Give me some credit for growing up."

He said nothing to this.

"Can I go now?"

"Of course," her father said. "I just wanted to talk to my baby girl. I wasn't intending to quarrel. Even when a man's children grow up, he wants them to have a good life and be proud to be part of the family."

"I have no complaints," Rhonda said before she left the room.

AFTER SHE DEPARTED, MacLean poured himself another scotch and dwelled on his version of what they'd said. Of course, she was lying to him. MacLean believed Rhonda was a consummate liar; it seemed she'd always been. He longed to punish her for this, the way he had when she was younger, reminding her not to be so snotty.

It had been years since the last time; he remembered it clearly. Sixteen when he'd bared her ass and spanked her that last time. She'd surprised him that night with her spunk. She'd reared up out of his lap and slapped him harshly across the face, tears in her eyes and a deep, scarlet blush on her cheeks. She'd slapped him so hard his lip bled. By the time he'd recovered from the force of the blow, the shock and challenge in it, she'd already fled the room. Angry and embarrassed, taunted by her spunk, he'd gone right after her.

He found her with Olive that time, crying to her mother. He'd approached them and Olive screamed at him not to come any closer. Dismayed, he stood there and listened to his wife's terms. Olive told him if he ever touched either of their daughters again, she'd leave him on the spot and take both girls with her.

He'd been furious at first—the three of them now in alliance against him. But he'd given in that night. Outnumbered and betrayed, he'd adhered to the terms of Olive's truce.

Now MacLean sat at his desk, drinking, feeling betrayed again. As he drank and brooded in the silence, he felt comforted by a welcome quiet rage. It nursed him through the bruises of the times he felt he'd failed.

TWENTY-ONE

. . . "And what about Buck?" said Dwight. "He acts like a hood. Maybe he really is."

Well, none of us liked Buck and this was a challenge we couldn't ignore. And Buck had called me an asshole. By extension, he'd insulted our entire Skeleton Club operation.

"Then it's settled?" said Dwight.

We all nodded. We began working on the Winston case that very same evening . . .

YOU ENCOUNTERED KIMBERLEY'S MOTHER again a few days after the outing at Black Water Bay. You were dismayed and instantly apprehensive. She'd only just turned up the walk towards the door of your home as you came outside, and although you glanced in her direction, you didn't recognize her at first. But when you did, a second afterwards, you felt convicted of some crime. Perhaps it was the way the two of you abruptly halted, sharing the same guilty surprise. Kimberley's mother. Was she to be another antagonist in the life you felt was now perfect?

Your thoughts flashed back to the previous Sunday and the excursion to Black Water Bay, in a review of the afternoon's events during which you might have offended her in some way. What offended adults wasn't always clear; it was difficult to know at times how and when you'd managed it. Yet it seemed impossible that she could have a complaint she might want to share with your mother. If you'd disappointed her in some way, you had no idea how.

"Hello, Phillip," Mrs. Smith said after she'd regained her composure.

"Hello, Mrs. Smith.

"Your mother is home?"

"Yes. She's inside."

"This is good," Kimberley's mother said with a force you found disconcerting.

You'd run out of conversation. An awkward silence ensued. You stood there on the sidewalk, not knowing what else to say. She seemed stern and preoccupied. You were conscious of how much taller than her you were. You felt impertinent because of it, like you were inadvertently blocking her way. The awkward silence between you grew brittle and precarious.

To end this uncomfortable gridlock, you blurted the first thing to come to mind. "I'm going downtown to meet my best friend, Gary," you said.

"I see," said Mrs. Smith, sternly accepting your confession.

You felt stupid and unexpectedly ashamed. It brought a blush to your cheeks, filling you with a vague remorse.

A few more hapless heartbeats passed in which you didn't know what to do. Then you heard your mother's voice behind you on the stoop.

"Phillip? I thought you were going downtown to meet Gary."

You turned to her. "I am."

"Well, shouldn't you be going?"

"Well, uh, sure," you replied, feeling new embarrassment.

"And Phillip?"

"Yes?"

"Don't be late for dinner.

"I won't, Mom," you said, recognizing that, in warning you about dinner, your mother was strutting her stuff for Mrs. Smith. You were never late for dinner—the penalty for such a transgression had been worked out years ago.

You tried to smile at Mrs. Smith as you turned to go, perhaps in some kind of apology, but she was veering around you by then and didn't see it on your face.

"Please come in, Mrs. Smith," you heard your mother say.

Still shaken by all that had just transpired, you glanced over your shoulder as both women entered the house. You felt an inexplicable urge to run. Bad luck, adult judgment, fate's treachery, you remembered, could sprint up on you with blinding speed. Perhaps if you started now, you could outrun it for a change.

"HE IS AN ATTRACTIVE BOY," Mrs. Smith told your mother.

"Thank you," she replied.

"Very polite."

"Thank you."

The two women sat on your parents' fraying sofa, one at either end. Your mother had set out tea and some Peek Frean shortbread cookies on the coffee table. These were so perfectly placed they were as much an obstacle as a hospitable gesture, a boundary through the no-man's land of the middle of the couch.

"He is young, shy."

"But mature for his age."

"Yes," conceded Mrs. Smith, although the word slid downwards in the end towards the "but" she didn't include. "What is his age?"

"Eleven."

Soberly Mrs. Smith nodded. "Kimberley is fourteen."

"A young woman then."

"Yes. This is what we have: a boy and a young woman."

"Kimberley is very pretty. I've seen her from a distance."

"Yes. Being pretty will help her, I think."

Your mother didn't know how to reply to this

observation. Truth put so bluntly betrayed convention and she wasn't used to it.

"Soon, I hope, my daughter will see boys her own age—young men."

"I'm sure she will."

"In a town like this . . ."

". . . Yes, people talk."

Mrs. Smith nodded. "Phillip and Kimberley are so serious together."

"You think so?"

"Yes. Too serious for both of them. This is my opinion."

"It worries you?"

"Yes. A little. I wonder what will happen."

"My husband and I have discussed it, now that you mention it, Mrs. Smith," your mother admitted.

"Gertrude. Call me Gertrude."

"Okay, uh, Gertrude. My husband and I have been concerned."

"This is good. Parents should be vigilant."

"Absolutely. Vigilance is essential."

Mrs. Smith nodded. "Perhaps we are aware of similar things, that Phillip is too young. And Kimberley? I hope Kimberley wants to see boys her own age soon. We are new to this country. Her life lies ahead. It is important that she see boys her own age. We want her to have a good life."

"Of course."

"She should see young men her own age. This would be normal."

"Sooner than later, I guess."

"I do not understand."

"You'd rather Kimberley began to see boys her own age soon. Not later on."

"Yes. This is true."

They fell silent to sip their tea.

"It's because they are so serious," Mrs. Smith said with a sigh. "Perhaps if they could be friends instead."

"Yes, friends without the romance," your mother said.

"Without the crush on one another."

"Yes. Such a serious crush. Your son is too young for Kimberley to have such a serious crush."

"My husband and I feel the same way. We don't want it to be serious either. I guess there's been talk. They're seen together so much. And Kimberley is so obviously a young woman now."

"She is a good girl," Mrs. Smith said, wanting there to be no misunderstanding. "She would not shame her parents."

"And Phillip's a good boy. I'm sure it's innocent enough. Both of them, I mean."

"Yes," said Mrs. Smith.

"But perhaps they need a break from one another."

"Yes. I did not know Phillip is so young."

"He's mature for his age. They're in the same grade at school."

"Until the fall," explained Mrs. Smith. "Kimberley will study Grade Eight this fall."

"Oh, that's good," your mother said.

Mrs. Smith nodded.

"These things pass."

"But they are too serious. I do not mean to interfere."

"But we have a responsibility, Gertrude."

"Yes, this is so."

"I'll talk this over with my husband. I'll see what we can do."

The two women nodded in agreement, pleased with their accord.

"YOUR MOTHER VISITED MY MOTHER this afternoon," you told Kimberley that evening at the ballpark."

"She did?"

"Didn't she tell you?"

"No."

The two of you gazed in silence at the antics on the ball diamond. The lights were on and the field was dusty with drought. Sounds, motion, catcalls, all of these were absorbed into a deep, arid stillness. The ethereal nature of the ballgame was an aggravating reminder that being here with Kimberley felt mostly imaginary, that the world outside of you was so vividly real—out there, elsewhere—in a place where you and Kimberley would be convicted of being a mistake.

You felt nervous and vulnerable. Apprehension washed over you in waves, compromising your contentment at being alone with Kimberley; she sat beside you, being alone here with you.

You sat in your usual spot at the end of the bleachers where it was darker, away from the crowds who remained faithful to their Marauders and clustered around the areas between home plate and first and third base. Kimberley was holding your hand, her touch still gently exciting. Holding hands with Kimberley made you wish that life had an emotional point, a purpose that granted wishes. You didn't want to understand such an emotional point—you just wanted it to be there, a happy destination awaiting you at the end of the uncertainty of waiting.

Maggie had been at the game previously but, when I hadn't showed up, she'd decided to go home. I was still a mystery to all of you these days. You could feel me pulling back—I was aware of something broken in our lives you didn't know about. I needed to back away until the rest of you caught up.

So Maggie had stayed only for the first inning. "Where's your father?" she had asked not long after the game began.

"He's not pitching tonight," you said.

"I know. But he's not even on the bench."

She was right. Your father never missed a Marauders game.

You shrugged. "I guess he had some important stuff to do. I don't know," you had said, concealing a powerful uneasiness because the difference in something, in anything, often was a threat.

You were just as glad that Maggie was gone because this moment of privacy with Kimberley filled you with so much hope. You still felt vulnerable but you had the strength to hope no one noticed how happy you were in time to decide you didn't deserve it.

"I wish I knew what was going on," you said, squeezing Kimberley's hand.

"You mean your mom and my mom?"

"Yeah. And my parents wanting me to come to the game tonight. Usually I have to ask for permission. And then my father staying home. All that stuff. Like they're up to something and they wanted me out of the house."

"Maybe our mothers are going to be friends. I'll bet it's nothing."

"I hope so."

"Don't worry," Kimberley said. "We haven't done anything wrong."

"I know. It's not that. It's just . . ." and you had to struggle to find the words . . . "that everything's so perfect. Right now, this summer, it's perfect. I just want it to stay that way."

"Me too," said Kimberley.

You glanced at her and blushed. "Kimie?"

"I know," she said with an embarrassed impatience. "You don't have to say anything. It's the same for me, you know."

And she rested her cheek against your shoulder so that you knew she meant it. Now you smelled shampoo. This fine and affectionate moment moved deeply into your memory and, for a long time afterwards, for you, the scent of shampoo was the scent of love itself.

This should have banished your trepidation. In fact it nearly did. Yet the happier you became the more you were afraid. Because your happiness depended on the benevolence of someone else. It was clear your parents wielded a power over everything you did. It seemed happiness was conditional on their approval of it.

YOUR FATHER WAS SMOKING a cigarette and watching television when you arrived home, his leg slung over the arm of his chair. When he turned to you he neither smiled nor said hello. Although he wasn't a man for greetings, your apprehension deepened. You glanced away from his gaze.

"Did we win?" he asked, surprising you with the question.

"Huh?"

"The game," he said impatiently. "Did we beat them?"

You felt stupid and inadequate, caught in an unexpected trap. You realized with some alarm that you didn't know for sure.

"I think so," you replied hastily, seizing on the only highlight you remembered from the game. "Ben Gillis hit a home run."

Your father nodded.

"How come you weren't at the game?" you asked.

"I had some things to take care of," your father replied before turning away.

You went into the kitchen for a drink of water and found your mother at the stove, heating up her milk. You considered asking her if something was wrong but decided to hold your tongue. Sometimes questions like that awoke the sleeping dog that bit your hand.

"It's bedtime, Phillip," she said.

"I know."

In bed in the darkness a few minutes later, you remained apprehensive. When your mother came upstairs to lean in your doorway, the hall light blazing behind her, you realized you'd been expecting her all along. She was smoking and held her cigarette in her right hand, an ashtray in her left. Her pose seemed eerily familiar, like you'd already lived this forthcoming scene clairvoyantly.

"Are you awake?" she asked.

"Yes."

She came right out with it. "You father and I want you to spend some time on the farm with your grandparents this summer."

Despair arrived with numbing force. Here it was, the unhappy, ill-defined event that you'd been dreading most of the day. It was a miscarriage of justice and you knew it. Tried, convicted, sentenced. Your feelings trampled by an unfair world. Convicted of wanting nothing to change, imposed change was to be your sentence.

"When?" you managed to ask, trying to conceal your hurt.

"Tomorrow."

"Gee, Mom. Tomorrow?"

"You're going for two weeks."

"How come?"

She remained backlit, her face in shadow until she inhaled on her cigarette and its red coal cast a brief, brimstone glow over her cheeks and nose. "You need a break from Meridian even if your father and I can't have one this year."

"I like Meridian, Mom."

But she went on anyway, as if she hadn't heard what you'd said. "We talked to your grandmother tonight. They think it's a great idea. Two weeks on a farm will be a great experience for you."

"Can't I stay here?"

"Phillip, I don't want an argument. Your father and I know what's best for you even if you don't understand it at the time."

"What about my friends?"

She sighed. And you knew for sure all of this was about Kimberley. Her mother's visit. Decisions arrived at. Like there was something wrong with you that might be wrong with Kimberley.

"Gary will still be here when you get back," your mother was saying, pretending that I mattered more than Kimberley did.

"Two weeks is a long time," you said, believing it was long enough to destroy the rest of your summer with Kimberley.

"Oh, Phillip, it is not. Besides, think of the adventure of it. Your first time travelling on a bus yourself. Helping out on a farm. You'll end up loving it. You lived there when you were a baby. It'll be like coming home. I think it's going to make all of us—the Barretts—much closer."

You didn't even try to counter her remarks. There was no point; it was already too late. You knew you'd have to go; your masters had already decided. Your stomach felt sick and you were close to tears. Worse yet, you knew your disappointment wouldn't matter to them, that nothing was going to change, even though you were suffering. Your parents, you realized, were never wrong because their idea of parenthood didn't acknowledge they could be wrong. This time they were mistaken—their judgment was impaired—but although you believed this devoutly, it wouldn't matter in any way. Intending to keep you away from Kimberley, there was no question in their minds that they were justified in doing so.

"Phillip?"

An acorn of sad helplessness had formed in your throat. It ached. When you answered her, you did so with sheer force of will. "Okay, Mom."

"Get a good night's sleep. We don't want you arriving in Port Frances all tired and cranky."

"Okay, Mom."

Then she was gone.

The hall light went out a moment later and you were grateful for it. At last you could let yourself cry in the thick hiding-place of darkness. You cried yourself to sleep in a rage of bitter sadness over love and powerlessness.

BEFORE YOU AND YOUR MOTHER left for the bus terminal next morning, she let you call me to tell me where you'd be.

"Just Gary," she said sternly, lingering near the telephone to make certain you did what you were told.

When I came on the line, you explained where you were going and how long you'd be away. Then, not caring if you were breaking the rules or not, or whether or not you would be punished, you asked a favour of me.

"Tell Kimie for me, will you, Gare? Or tell Maggie to tell Kimie?"

"Okay," I said.

"You promise?"

"I promise."

After this, your mother's patience was at an end. "That's enough, Phillip," she snapped. "You're going to miss your bus."

TWENTY-TWO

. . . *It was our most complex investigation. Dwight divided us into two teams. Billy and Chuck were responsible for counting the number of customers that went into Winston's each day, cataloguing what they purchased. Dwight and I took over at mid-afternoon and our function was to watch the place after hours, focusing on the Winstons' living quarters above the store, at least until we had to go home to bed.*

We studied the Winstons carefully until the middle of August, alternately bored and intrigued by the assignment. The number of customers and what they purchased, carelessly reported by Billy and Chuck, didn't tell us much because we had no prior figures for comparison; in the end, we embraced Dwight's blind assertion that, indeed, business was falling off badly.

It wasn't difficult, though, to verify that things were not going well in the Winston household above the store. Dwight and I heard three violent arguments ourselves during the course of our investigation. Sitting outside their windows in the gathering darkness, we'd discover we were holding our breaths at the unpleasantness. And, once, we ran home to my house in a panic when we heard the breaking of glass. On another occasion, Buck startled us in the darkness when he ran out the side door of the store not far from where we hid, heading down the street. We were astonished because both Dwight and I could see that he was crying.

During our surveillance, we recorded each sighting of each member

251

of the family. We saw Buck half a dozen times. His father, drunk, staggering, and unshaven, only twice. Mrs. Winston not at all. Dwight speculated at headquarters that Mrs. Winston might be a prisoner. This time, not even Chuck could find a way to argue. We all sensed, in some way or other, that Dwight was close to being right . . .

AFTER YOUR GRANDMOTHER retrieved you from the Port Frances bus terminal, packing you and your luggage into her large Pontiac, she escaped from the downtown core of the city as quickly as she could, driving with a desperate intensity in the direction of the farm a few miles beyond the city outskirts where you were to be imprisoned for two weeks.

You sensed your father's mother felt at risk outside the rural environment in which she had lived her entire life. She complained about the delay at each stoplight then, when the light turned green, she lurched away from the intersection, the steering wheel gripped fiercely in both hands. She sped down each traffic-cluttered street, her foot grinding down on the accelerator, and she didn't even glance at you while driving the city avenues. The two of you gazed in silence through the bug-spattered windshield, passing your respective versions of this urban tension back and forth between you as if it might burn your hands. Finally, when she reached the uneven concession road leading in the direction of the farm, she settled down, relieved to be on familiar turf.

You remembered this road from the previous Christmas when you'd visited here with your parents. Back then, though, the landscape had been snow covered, the barns, houses, and abutting lanes hushed by winter and the still reverence of Christmas. Today the route was much more alive. Fields of corn and paddocks of livestock came into view on both sides of the road, a pattern broken intermittently by a pair of gleaming railway tracks. Sheep, the occasional horse, and fields of grazing Holsteins waited around each bend. The green of the crops was encouraging, although the earth looked dry and thirsty.

Still, you felt awkward with this woman. You felt trapped

inside the moment when you'd met her at the bus terminal, the two of you virtual strangers.

"You've gotten bigger," she'd said as you climbed down from the bus. "Could've used you at haying time."

It was difficult to know what she had meant by this, whether it was intended as a compliment or as an undisguised lament. You merely smiled and shrugged, not knowing how else to respond.

She was a tall woman, and stocky. Your father had described her often as a "tough old bird" and you were inclined to feel fearful of her. She didn't smile very much. You'd seen this in adults before, their faces lined by worry or the burdensome responsibility of remaining implacable.

The contrast between this grandmother and your mother's mother was pronounced. The latter, at the beginning of a visit, would beam broadly, embracing you happily whenever you encountered one another after a long absence. This grandmother didn't even offer to shake hands.

You'd brought only one suitcase. The driver winced as he dragged its bulging bulk out of the belly of the bus, plopping it on the asphalt a pace or two away from the back wheels.

"That yours?" your grandmother asked, gesturing in its direction.

"Yes."

"Well we'd better take it with us, don't you think?"

"I guess so," you replied, wanting to reward her remark with a smile, the urge dying away when you noticed her stern expression.

She didn't help you with the heavy suitcase. She hurried ahead to open the trunk, then stood by the gaping cavity, waiting for you to drag it the last few steps to the car, puffing in exertion.

"You staying two weeks or two years?" she remarked as you struggled to lift the suitcase into the trunk.

"Just two weeks," you replied, in case she wasn't kidding.

"Have you eaten anything?"

"I had a sandwich on the bus."

She nodded and ordered you into the car.

As she'd embarked on her frenzied escape from the city, you'd remembered something your mother had said about her mother-in-law: that she spent most of her days on the second concession, maintaining her narrow mind.

"You'll be expected to help out with some chores," your grandmother mentioned now as their farm came into view on your left.

"Sure," you replied. "That'll be fine."

"Your father and his brothers did."

"I know."

She glanced at you then in mild surprise, as if she'd now fully realized that you were the son of a father and the father was her son. No orphan, you, nor foster child she'd adopted inadvertently after a chance encounter at the bus terminal, but blood related and family, like it or not.

"How is your father these days?" she wanted to know.

"Fine."

She didn't ask about your mother. You'd been told a number of times that your grandmother hadn't approved of the marriage, maintaining quite bluntly that your mother was "too delicate to be a farmer's wife." You had no idea if this remained her opinion, adults being so polite about their various points of antagonism. Sometimes the adult mind seemed a dishonest place to you, where politeness possessed more virtue than actual principle did, and where appearing to care mattered more than the actual caring itself.

Meanwhile the car turned up the long lane towards the house where you tried to imagine your father growing up. You'd failed in this fancy last Christmas and you couldn't conceive of it now. His childhood stories were legends to him as well as you, but they widened the gap between father and son instead of narrowing it. No matter where your childhood went, it would be a less provocative journey than your father's had been—this was what you had come to believe.

"We need rain," your grandmother said as she directed the Pontiac up the lane, racing its own cloud of dust towards the house.

She parked in front of the garage, although its door was raised in readiness.

"There's your grandfather," she said with a cursory nod in his direction, before she climbed out of the car.

He'd been kneeling among the tomato plants in their large vegetable garden, but as you slipped out of the car he stood up to look at you, leaning on his hoe. He was a small man, much thinner than his wife, barely even the same height. He seemed at first to be smiling but, as you gazed at him more carefully, you realized he was merely squinting because the sun was in his eyes. You raised your arm to wave but he turned away at that moment, back to his gardening, not noticing. Husband and wife didn't bother to greet one another. Your father's father didn't look up again until after you'd gone inside.

"We'll want some help in the garden while you're here," your grandmother said.

"Sure."

"Unless it doesn't rain and everything dies, of course."

She said this with a kind of terrible calm and you glanced at the broad, unbroken blue sky, noticing the dust the car wheels had raised still wafting in parched confusion in the crisply warm, summery air.

THE BARRETT HOMESTEAD possessed a familiar farmhouse smell. When you'd lived in South Clarion, many of your parents' friends had been farmers. Visiting them, you'd grown to recognize the aroma of rich mustiness in their homes, an insistent combination of hay and straw, herbs and fruit, and a not always subtle trace of animal manure. Noticing it now—the ghostliness of the aroma—you realized your own house, beyond the acrid weight of cigarette smoke, seemed sterilized; it possessed no scent at all.

Your grandmother showed you to your room, navigating the narrow stairs ahead of you while you struggled along behind, grasping the heavy suitcase with both hands. When you finally caught up to her, she told you to change, unpack and put your other clothes in the dresser.

"Okay," you said.

Abruptly she left you there to do what she had asked, precisely, without dissent, without hesitation.

You didn't need any encouragement to change your trousers. Your mother had insisted that you wear your Sunday pants on the bus. Primarily made of wool, these were winter trousers, the only good pair that still fit you properly. Too warm and dark for summer, they'd absorbed the intense sunlight beaming in through each bus window, cruelly prickling your flesh during the three-hour trip from Meridian. Bad enough that you didn't want to go in the first place, that you were travelling alone for the first time, strangers glancing at you in seemingly hostile speculation. The wool trousers had served as a pivotal ingredient in the torture.

You closed your bedroom door, opened your suitcase, changed your clothes, then put everything else away. It didn't take you very long and, afterwards, you sat on the edge of the bed, gazing out the window, a sad yearning in your heart that wouldn't let you go.

Mostly it was missing Kimberley. Me too, you told me later, and your favourite haunts in Meridian. But when you imagined two weeks away from Kimberley, the pain grew so fierce, your betrayal so deep, you felt that you would die if you didn't squeeze it from your thoughts. Your view of suffering of this kind differed from your parents' view and only alienated you further. Sometimes you felt your parents considered suffering a noble duty, the pride you were supposed to feel in doing a job you didn't like. But to you it felt like grief, a state of mourning so intense it nudged you towards the precipice of panic.

Guilty and torn because you knew what was expected of you, you felt compelled in some ritual way to try and do your duty. When you felt angry with your parents, it filled you with shame. You couldn't quite believe they'd intended to be mean. Your parents were usually right. It was possible this entire escapade only reflected their good intentions. You doubted they understood how much you missed Kimberley, that two weeks without seeing her was an unimaginably long time. Besides, what in loving Kimberley could they conclude was wrong?

Sitting on the edge of the bed, you took a series of deep breaths, trying to compose yourself. There was a refreshing breeze drifting in the window, billowing a pair of gauzy white curtains. In the distance between the dancing curtains, you could make out the main barn and a network of fields stretching some distance beyond. A lane running north divided the fields in half. Perhaps when you found time to go exploring, you wouldn't feel so sad. Sad and hurt and angry wasn't how you wanted to feel.

AT SUPPER YOUR GRANDPARENTS didn't say very much and you knew that this was normal. The meal had a mechanical aspect even more pronounced than what you were used to at home. Eating was a chore to be overcome before moving on to the next. It was as if your grandparents, living on this farm so isolated from the news of the world and from its own vicinity, already knew what there was to know about one another and they had nothing further to say on the subject.

"What grade do you go into this fall?" your grandmother asked you midway through the meal.

"Grade Seven."

"You like school?"

"Oh, sure."

Nothing else was said. The silence was filled by the clatter of tableware on porcelain, the clack of your grandfather's false teeth on slices of overcooked roast beef.

Afterwards he went into the living room and turned on the television.

You offered to help with the dishes but your grandmother wouldn't let you. "Woman's work," she said, "and you can tell your mother I said so." But she allowed you to clear the table with her; at least this wasn't seen as a crack in the foundation of tradition.

After she was done, she watched a quiz show with you and her husband. Then, when the program was over, she left the room and didn't return. Shortly, from behind a closed door at the eastern extremity of the house where they'd put up the Christmas tree last year, you heard her playing the piano. She played like your father, you noticed: faltering, hesitant, going back over each bar until she'd mastered it.

You went to bed before dark. Night, you knew, would intensify your loneliness but you wanted to get it over with. Climbing into bed and gazing out the window, watching dusk gradually smother the last few moments of daylight, you let yourself cry silently. You wept, wondering what you were doing here, wondering if Kimberley's caring would vanish in your absence. Thinking of Kimberley was both bitter and sweet. While missing her was physically painful—it gathered in your stomach like a thick, barbed lump—your memories of time spent with her earlier this summer provided a mitigating solace.

You favoured your memory of the night a couple of weeks ago, when she'd told you that she loved you, sitting with her on the broad stone wall at the edge of your driveway. You kept recalling this moment, replaying it in your mind, viewing it from different angles, like a mysterious, yet perfect sculpture. You stopped crying, comforted by this and other memories. Recalling Kimberley's love, you realized, would help you make it through these two weeks. And if there was a God, nothing would be changed when you arrived home at last.

YOU ENDURED, YOUR DAYS from that point onwards regulated by periods of work and solitary play. In the morning you did your chores, starting in the barn where your grandfather did the milking. There, using a pitchfork, you carried straw and cow manure from the gutters of the stalls to a large pile in the barnyard just outside the door. Except for occasional instruction, your grandfather remained silent during the hour or so you spent with him in the barn. He was preoccupied by the news he heard on the radio, making sense of what was said despite a persistent buzz and crackle of interference your perception could not penetrate. When something of interest caught his attention, he'd cock his head in the radio's direction, grunt in satisfaction or spit on the cement floor in disgust. Then he'd go on as if none of it actually mattered.

At first you found this work unpleasant, the odor offensive, countless flies annoying, the humidity in the barn bathing you in sweat. Then, as one day became another and gratefully another, you accommodated the work's predictability, numbed by its familiar changelessness. Here too, you relied on secret reflections about Kimberley to get you through your responsibilities.

After an hour or two in the barn each day, you were dispatched to the large vegetable garden where you worked with your grandmother, weeding, hoeing, raking or picking what was ripe. Raspberries, cucumbers, green and yellow beans were collected in baskets and lined up on the stoop by the kitchen door. Carrots were thinned or pests were removed from the leaves of tomato and potato plants. The weeds you yanked out of the hard dry earth snapped at the stems but were raked to the garden edge and collected in a sugar bag.

You showed your grandmother a couple of blisters on your hands the third day of your visit.

"Huh," she said with a frown. "City hands, I see."

You wanted to tell her that Meridian was just a village, not a city by any stretch, but wisely kept silent. Children splitting hairs, you knew, would certainly try her patience. And when the blisters progressed into calluses, you grew vaguely proud of them.

Lunch on the farm was a much larger meal than you were used to—vegetables, preserves, meats, breads, even pies for dessert—but you soon grew used to this. Your grandmother opined a couple of times that you were too thin.

"Just like your father," she said, "when he was a boy." But in spite of the food you consumed—you were often hungry and knew better than to refuse anything placed in front of you—you remained gaunt in defiance of her.

Your afternoons were your own. You enjoyed walking the long lane towards the northern boundary of the farm. Along the way, fields of corn, timothy, and alfalfa snoozed in the sunshine on either side. Cedar rail fences abutted the lane but wild shrubs and saplings had overwhelmed the ancient timbers; the growth was now an integral part of the fencing along the way.

Your destination on these walks was a small woods at the end of the lane. Here, stands of immature birches and maples guarded a rise you adopted as your own. On this secluded hummock, you whiled away the hours, watching birds come and go or staring at cotton batten puffs of cloud drifting across the sky. This place reminded you most of lying on the raft in Brannigan's Cove and you pilgrimaged here each day because it helped you feel less alien. Although your grandmother lamented daily that the need for rain was growing desperate, your hummock in the woods seemed to appreciate the drought. The parched soil was warm and dry, an entomologist's delight. It was alive with marching ants, with nomadic beetles and crickets. Time passed calmly here, your loneliness endurable.

You noticed a ground hog sitting on its haunches in one of your grandfather's fallow fields one day that first week. It was stationed at the lip of its den, listening, looking, and smelling for inevitable danger. As you drew closer, it heard the sound of your approach, glanced at you a moment, then fled back inside the earth. You continued on your way.

"You should take the twenty-two and shoot him," your grandfather said at supper that evening when you mentioned this sighting.

You gaped at him in surprise.

"You ever use a rifle?"

"No."

"Maybe it's time you learned."

"I don't want that kind of responsibility, Seymour," your grandmother said then. "What if he ends up shooting himself."

"No reason for him to shoot himself. Just shoot the goddamned ground hog. I don't have time to do it myself."

"No, Seymour. And that's the end of it."

He glanced at her a moment, deciding whether or not to give in. "Suit yourself," he muttered, knowing it was settled.

Forgotten during this exchange, you felt relieved when the subject was dropped. Over the years, when adults suggested how you might injure yourself, it had become a kind of whammy, a psychokinetic truth. How many times had you been burned by something scalding after you'd been warned that it was hot? How many times had you tripped on a scatter rug after you'd been warned to watch your step? More times than you wanted to remember. Now that it had been mentioned you might shoot yourself, it seemed reasonably probable that indeed you would, if you were provided a firearm.

After the debate about the rifle, your grandparents fell silent for the rest of the meal. By now you'd realized they didn't like one another very much. It was clear they slept in separate bedrooms, as revealing an indication as any you could imagine.

After-supper ritual resumed. Your grandfather watched television and your grandmother disappeared to play her piano. You watched television sparingly, bored by what your grandfather preferred. It never occurred to him to ask you what you might like to see.

In bed early each night, you kept your date with Kimberley and the memories she inspired. And as each day passed, you accepted more and more that, in sentencing you to this visit, your parents had betrayed you knowingly.

ON THE FOLLOWING SUNDAY—a day marking the approximate halfway point of your exile, you realized joyfully—your aunts, uncles and cousins arrived for a visit shortly after the mid-day meal. At first you wondered in some embarrassment if the occasion was in your honour, which made you feel awkward and self-conscious, but soon you discovered this gathering took place nearly every Sunday of the year.

They arrived in two cars, up the long, dusty lane. The same two uncles—your father's brothers—their wives and six cousins, four boys and two girls, all of whom you'd seen last Christmas, piled out of the cars with the routine efficiency of a military drill. As soon as they arrived, a shady section of the yard was prepared. Lawn chairs were removed from the trunks of the cars and from a corner inside the garage, and a circle formed not far from the front of the house. There the adults sat down, your uncles lit cigarettes, and you and the other children took your places on the grass nearby.

There was no opportunity for play with your cousins. For the next hour or so, you sat among the adults, virtually in silence, speaking only when spoken to. Although you sensed the other children were as bored by the proceedings as you were, all of you went along with the ritual, sitting on the grass at the fringes of the adult conversation, suffering in patient silence.

Your presence here was noted within the context of the previous Christmas, good-natured reference made to the injuries you'd sustained when you'd been struck in the forehead by your new electric train. You laughed along with this anecdote in some embarrassment, relieved when your relatives dropped the subject to ask politely after your parents. You replied, just as politely, that both your parents were fine.

This done, you were subsequently ignored. The rest of the conversation reverted to the need for rain, the drought's impact on this year's harvest, and some scandal that had taken place that morning at church where all of them, save your grandfather, had been in attendance. The nature of the scandal eluded you, their church a mystery to you. You had been scarcely aware it was Sunday until, following your chores in the barn this morning and expecting to toil in the garden the way you usually did, you'd discovered your grandmother was gone without a word or explanation. When she materialized in time for lunch, she was wearing a hat and suit, and you realized she'd been at services.

As you sat on the lawn in silence, ignored by your cousins, you felt alien and intrusive. It struck you that Port Frances was their home in the way that Meridian was yours, a separate world with its own events and purpose. You were a foreigner here in the way your father was. You were his proxy today, condemned on this visit to wear the mantle of the prodigal son. Whatever had driven your father away, you felt you wore his reasons as well, only because you were his son.

Your grandmother served iced tea from a large pitcher and the ordeal continued. Snatches of conversation, nervous laughter, painful silences. When your cousins were mentioned, it was by name, in the third person, as if they weren't there to answer for themselves. Such remarks were directed at your grandmother while your grandfather was ignored. She was the matriarch here: all conversation was for her benefit, presented to her as tribute.

No one asked whether you were enjoying your visit. No one asked why you were here. It was as if your return to the fold contained no mystery or the mystery had already been solved. The visit tolled by, each second passing with a monastic bong. You felt more and more alien and more and more inclined to be proud of it. In your silence you nursed a private defiance about how wonderful Meridian was, how much sweeter your life than theirs. But while your defiance felt satisfying at times, your alien status aggravated your homesickness. You could not escape your persistent yearning to be back home again.

There'd been no embraces or handshakes when your uncles arrived and there were none when they departed. The visit came to an end with astonishing abruptness. Someone mentioned that they should be going and everyone suddenly stood up. Lawn chairs vanished and everyone climbed into their car. Although the visitors all waved as the vehicles headed back down the lane, it was, in your mind, a gesture of relief. Your grandparents folded up their chairs and stowed them back in the garage before the two cars had barely reached the concession road.

You stood there alone as the departing automobiles turned west towards the city. You were puzzled by what had transpired and how little purpose the get-together had seemed to possess. By the time the dust settled on the lane again, it was easy to convince yourself the visit had hardly taken place at all.

YOUR MOTHER TELEPHONED later that afternoon and spoke to your grandmother first.

"Yes, he's been fine. No trouble."

A pause to digest the next question.

"Oh, yes. Helping Seymour down at the barn. Working in the garden with me."

Pause.

"Very polite. Like his father was. Minds his manners."

A longer pause this time.

"I thought on the Monday morning, a week from tomorrow. There's a bus at ten after nine. That's right."

Pause.

"Gets in around noon or so."

Arrangements for your return—you felt a joyful relief. You'd been on the farm so long by now, you'd begun to fear that you'd never be going home. And you fretted that something complacent in your heart or something lazy in your soul had begun to accept this fact.

Your grandmother called you to the phone.

"Hi, Phillip," your mother said.

"Hi, Mom."

"How are you doing, Dear?"

"Fine."

"Are you being a big help?"

"Oh sure."

"What've you been doing?"

"I help in the garden and down at the barn." Cross-referencing your answers with what your grandmother had said.

"That's good."

"What's new in Meridian?" you asked as cautiously as you could.

"Not much. Your father's golfing. Nothing changes here, you know that."

Although you felt a desperate need to ask about Kimberley, you knew this was out of the question. Fearing behaving anxiously would prolong your exile here, you didn't even ask about me. It left you with little to say. The gulf between life on the farm and the one you lived back home had widened.

"You're enjoying yourself, I hope," your mother said sternly.

"Oh sure," you replied carefully.

"No sulking or complaining."

"No, Mom."

"It must be interesting for you, Phillip. This is a whole new experience for you."

"That's true," you said.

"Well, Dear, I have to get going. You know this is long distance."

"Sure."

"Your father says 'hi.'"

"Okay."

"And we'll see you a week from tomorrow. Okay?"

"All right."

She said goodbye and hung up.

Afterwards you went outside and stood a few moments on the stoop. Eight more nights, you thought. And you felt newly forlorn again, angry with yourself. Now that the opportunity was gone, you regretted not admitting how much you missed Meridian and me and Kimberley. You felt impotent and self-betrayed. You hadn't stood up for yourself. And growing angrier still, you doubted it would have mattered if you had. You seized this conclusion in your jaws and mauled it like a tiger. No matter how unfair it was, there were things you weren't permitted to feel. You'd been told to be helpful, to enjoy yourself. That you seemed to be doing so was all that your mother had wanted to know.

You took several deep breaths and waited for your anger to pass.

"Eight nights, Kimie," you whispered out loud, to hear yourself say the words.

You felt better then, less vaguely ashamed of yourself. Thinking of Kimberley, life grew forgivable again. You felt hopeful once more, knowing if she still cared for you, if nothing had changed in your absence, everything would be all right, the way it had been before.

"I DON'T THINK you should be in there, Phillip," your grandmother said when you mentioned the next day that you'd discovered a large shed of old coaches and sleighs some distance from the rest of the farm's main buildings.

"Oh?"

"It's cluttered and dangerous. You could hurt yourself. If there's one building on this farm I wouldn't care if it burned down, it's that one. Why Seymour insists on keeping all that junk is beyond me."

Soberly you nodded, conveying an understanding you didn't possess. What did she mean? That you weren't allowed in there or that you should be careful when you were?

Puzzled, you went back outside to draw your own conclusions. The shed hadn't been locked, although the latch had been stiff. Stiff or not, eventually you'd opened the door and slipped inside. Okay, you'd been warned of the dangers. It wasn't the same as actually being forbidden to play in there.

The trouble was you'd been fascinated immediately by this large, stale-smelling shed that was blissfully disconnected from the tiresome regularity of the rest of the farm. Here among the large assortment of old carriages, buggies and sleighs—many of them stacked one upon another so that they could all fit inside, some of the sleighs standing on their ends, their runners rusting towards the ceiling—an enticing history lurked in every corner. The shed was dusty and full of cobwebs. It smelled of dry wood, aging steel, decaying canvas and shredding cloth—an intriguing combination, enticing in its contrast from the more familiar odours of manure and sweat. Cool and chock-full of imaginative possibility, it was a perfect hiding place from the arduous futility your stay on the farm had become.

The buggies intrigued you most. You'd watched variations of these vehicles parade down Meridian's main street last summer during the centennial celebrations. You'd felt captured by history that day, everyone lined up along the street in traditional costume, buggy wheels squeaking and horses clomping by in exotic procession, exploding out of history book photographs with an unexpected realism. Being here in this giant closet of buggies and sleighs, Meridian seemed closer again: Meridian and Kimberley and your concept of them both as home.

This hiding place abetted your favourite fantasy. Recently you'd begun to imagine Kimberley could share your perception. You pretended she could see you here on the farm through the lens of your eyes. Pretending she sat before a screen where she could see what you could see, you didn't miss her as much. When you walked the lane to your hill, you'd imagine she shared the vista that you enjoyed. Here in this small barn of buggies and sleighs, you explored the artifacts together, you and Kimberley. During this game you felt less lonely: the love you shared was less threatened.

You began to visit the barn every afternoon despite your grandmother's warning. Although you'd decided it hadn't been precisely forbidden, you came here cautiously, locked inside a purgatory of rationalization. Was defiance truly defiant when it probably wasn't necessary?

Cautious or not, on the Wednesday before you were to go home, a hot, muggy, clumsy day that finally threatened rain, you tripped over a section of floorboard as you slipped between two buggies. Off balance, you fell against a runner on one of the sleighs, cutting your arm on a jagged piece of metal.

"Oh, shit," you said aloud, less concerned with your injury than with fate's perfidy again.

With a frightened clarity, you realized, as your arm began to bleed, that you were going to be punished, that you had been a fool to believe you could return to Meridian entirely unscathed. You gazed at the blood and the gash in your arm, aware that it would have to be bandaged. You cursed again before reluctantly heading for the house, your fingers trying futilely to hold back the blood. If you stained your clothing, you'd be in more trouble, you knew that much for certain.

Your grandmother sighed in some annoyance when she saw what you had done. Retrieving a first aid kit from a cupboard over the refrigerator, she set about repairing the damage.

"It isn't very deep," she said, dabbing disinfectant on the cut.

You winced.

"Oh c'mon, Phillip. Does it hurt that much?"

"The iodine," you replied, embarrassed by her disdain.

She placed ointment on the cut, then wrapped it in gauze and adhesive.

"Okay," she said when she was done. "You'll live."

"Thanks," you replied. "I'm sorry I cut myself."

"How did it happen?" she asked, looking you straight in the eye.

"I tripped."

"Where?"

You hesitated, tempted to lie, but knowing if you did, it would only make matters worse. "In the barn with the sleighs and carriages," you confessed.

"I thought as much," your grandmother said.

"It'll be okay," you told her, partly to reassure her, but mostly because her calm seemed menacing to you. You could feel her growing angry and, with it, getting larger. She was a stocky, unyielding woman. You were going to have to pay.

"I told you not play in there, didn't I?"

"I wasn't sure," you whispered weakly.

Her eyes were dark as death. "You know damn well I

did, Phillip."

"I guess I got confused," you stammered.

"What will your parents think?"

Having no answer for this, you didn't reply.

"I won't tolerate disobedience while you're staying here with me. I don't know what you get away with at home, but you won't get away with it here."

Again you held your tongue. She was confusing you again. What was she actually angry about? Which act were you to defend? Going into the shed? Cutting yourself? Or living in Meridian outside her control?

"Go up to your room," she said with a tired sigh. "I'll be up in a moment."

"Grandma?"

"Get going," she said.

She was five minutes locating the belt she likely hadn't used in years. When she arrived carrying it in her hand, you were only mildly surprised that this was going to happen to you. Although it seemed to be a mistake, another miscarriage of justice, it was predictable as well. Sometimes life moved inexorably towards punishment and pain, regardless of what you did to sidestep it.

"Grandma?" you said. "I'm sorry. I didn't mean to disobey you. I didn't understand exactly that I shouldn't be in there."

"What nonsense!" she replied. "I told you to stay out of there. And you're accident prone, Phillip. Someone has to teach you not to be so clumsy."

"Grandma? Please?"

"That's enough," she snapped. "We all have to take our medicine. Begging never helped anyone."

Ashamed, you fell silent.

She told you to pull down your trousers and undershorts, then instructed you to lean over the side of the bed. After you did so, she struck you five times on the bare buttocks with the flat of the belt.

You grunted at the pain of the first blow, steeled yourself against the others. Outrage, rich and stubborn, prevented you from crying out.

"Pull up your pants," your grandmother said when she was done.

You turned your back to her to comply with her instructions. You didn't face her again until you'd covered up.

"You won't disobey me after this, will you?" she said.

"No, Grandma."

"And you'll stay away from that barn?"

"Yes," you said. "I promise."

"Don't come down until supper. I want you to think about what disobedience means and what it brings you."

You nodded and she left you there alone.

YOU STOOD BY THE BED for several minutes, feeling different about yourself. Your forearm ached and your buttocks smarted, but these receding agonies continued to give way to a welcome anger. It was a cold anger you'd never experienced before, emotionless and stubborn, defiantly nourishing.

You propped your pillow against the headboard and stretched out on the bed, gazing out the window, keeping your face frozen and blank. You noticed that at last it had begun to rain, rewarding your mood somehow that it was going to drizzle for the rest of the day. Punishment, bitterness, and drizzle seemed made for one another.

For two and a half hours before supper, you laid on the bed, staring rigidly out the window, letting a vengeful anger simmer in your heart. Not just for your grandmother, but for your parents as well for cruelly banishing you to this place. Your exile here had no justification; it was clear you hadn't done anything wrong where Kimberley was concerned.

When you returned, you promised yourself, you would make certain you were different. No more fear or pain when you returned to Meridian. Anger was stronger than pain. This calm, unceasing rage, you knew, would keep your various pieces together, even you and Kimberley. You repeated promises to yourself like sacred oaths, over and over again to keep them memorized. When you climbed off the bus on

Monday, you'd never be frightened again. You'd be angry instead. Anger would keep you strong to resist your powerlessness. You believed you'd be different now: stronger, smarter, angrier. Thanks to your grandmother's licking, you believed life was less than you'd once thought it was. It wasn't a matter of imagination, of feeling anything, or even coasting along. Life, you now decided, was a matter of skill, the skill people employed to ensure that they survived.

THE REST OF YOUR STAY at your grandparents' farm took place without incident. Your injury healed quickly. You remained polite and helpful. On sunny days—now that it had found the will, it rained three of the five remaining days—you walked the lane to your favourite hummock, where you gazed at the distant sky, nursing your defiance and resolve.

At night you yearned for Kimberley. Just Kimberley now. Not Meridian so much. Not your parents; not even me. Just Kimberley who seemed connected to how you now viewed yourself. She was an instrument in your resolve.

On the day before you left, your aunts, uncles, and cousins visited again. Everything about the event was the same, except that you were different now, pleased, no longer disappointed that they were going to remain strangers. Except for Kimberley, you didn't need anyone. It filled you with delight that you didn't care about any of them, that your polite behaviour prevented them from even noticing that you'd changed.

As arranged, your grandmother put you on the early bus the next day. Again there was no embrace and she didn't shake your hand. When you politely thanked her for everything, she said you were always welcome. Privately you hoped you'd never have to come back.

You waved at her through the window of the bus as it pulled out of the terminal, proud of the skill you detected in such an artful gesture. When she waved back, you suspected it was in the spirit of a similar artfulness. You settled in for the long ride home, nursing your new anger, feeding your new defiance.

TWENTY-THREE

. . . *Whenever something infamous happens, people record it in their memories by recalling where they were and what they were doing at the precise moment the disaster occurred. I'm no different. I know exactly where I was and what I was up to when I heard the news about the fire at Winstons' store. It was dark and getting late, and I was lying on my bed, reading a Blackhawk comic, when people showed up at the front door to tell my father. I left my room to better hear what was being said.*

"The Winston place is going up!"

"Oh my God! The Winstons?"

"Yeah. It's burning pretty good."

"The fire department there yet?"

"No, but they've been called."

Burning buildings in our village didn't have much of a chance. Fire trucks had to travel from the next town more than ten miles down the highway.

The Winstons. I climbed out of bed.

The entire village was there, or so it seemed to me. Dwight, Billy, Chuck, their dads, their mums, dozens, even hundreds of others . . .

EVENTS TOOK PLACE IN MERIDIAN, of course, while you were away. The world from which you were separated continuing to breathe, to live, to happen. Events, rituals and unnoticed inspirations. The usual. The slightly unusual. Life.

I kept my promise to convey to Kimberley that you'd been sent away for two weeks. I called Maggie and Maggie, in turn, called Kimberley. Perplexed by the lack of warning, the three of us met at the ballpark on the day after you vanished, as intrigued by the development of your absence as we were disappointed. For me, the conspiracy in your being gone was somewhat exciting, a verification that the adult society in which I lived was as imperfect and devious as I suspected.

Gathering on the bleachers that evening for a Marauders game, the three of us found everything the same as it always was, but only superficially so, which clearly emphasized your absence. The warm up before the game took on an unusual poignancy; the dusty, noisy infield was ethereal, the behaviour of the players strangely silly and irrelevant, the swagger in their bodies now parody, as they flicked the softball back and forth, crying words of encouragement to one another in some foolish ceremony lacking substance. Streaking in the glow of the bright lights, as shiny as a badge, the ball smacked into each leather glove underneath the lights blazing down on the field, an orb given social virtue it was now clear it didn't deserve.

This was how it looked to me, how I thought it must feel to Kimberley too, already yearning for your return.

I knew the two girls must understand that leaving Kimberley behind hadn't been your choice. "You see," I said, "he sounded pretty unhappy when I talked to him on the phone."

"You mean, he didn't want to go?" asked Kimberley.

"Nah. He sounded . . . trapped, if you know what I mean."

Soberly both girls nodded.

"He wanted to make sure I got the message to you, Kimberley. That's the main thing for sure."

"Okay," she said solemnly.

"So where did they send him?" asked Maggie.

I explained about your grandparents' farm, how far away from Meridian I understood it to be. "He'll be gone for two weeks, I guess," I added.

"Two weeks! That's just about the whole rest of the summer," Kimberley cried, not hiding her distress. "What if he forgets all about us?"

"Not Phil," I said. "Not you, Kimberley."

"Phillip really likes you," added Maggie, touching her friend on the arm.

"My mother did this, you know," Kimberley proclaimed then.

I glanced at her in surprise. Maggie too.

"My mother visited his mother the day before he left. Phillip told me so that night."

"Oh, Kim," said Maggie. "That doesn't mean anything. Maybe it's just coincidence." She glanced at me as if I might confirm her opinion.

But I couldn't do it. I was now certain events like your banishment had a more sinister reason than either of the girls understood, although the reason itself—its specifics—eluded me.

"Gary, don't you think so, that it could be coincidence?"

I shook my head. "This town," I said. "Sometimes I hate this town."

Neither girl said anything.

I knew they were perplexed by my words. I knew they didn't understand in the way that you didn't understand, that it was a bigger conspiracy than the seemingly innocuous events which coalesce to make conspiracies take shape.

"This town," I muttered. "It has its own idea of things, you know? It has its own version. Then, if something happens that doesn't fit the version, well then they get together to force it to change until it fits. Like the townspeople can make everything the same as themselves, Like there's only one way of doing things. You see what I mean?"

"I think so," Kimberley said, glancing at Maggie for support.

But Maggie shook her head in exasperation. "Are you saying the whole town sent Phillip away? Why would the town do that?"

"Not the town, exactly," I replied in frustration. "They didn't have a meeting about it or anything. I just mean, when you live in a town like this, you have to become the town. You do what the town expects, or else."

"That's just stupid," Maggie said. "Why would the town want Phillip to stay on a farm for two weeks?"

"Well, it didn't. Not exactly. It's really hard to explain. It's not as stupid as you think. You guys are just used to accepting things the way they are, that's all. You're just used to believing the town is right because the town says it's right."

Both girls gaped at me. I knew then I'd never be able to make them see what I was talking about.

"It's called the status quo," I said more or less to myself. "Things not changing, things not being allowed to change. Everyone not understanding the different things other people might want to do."

"Gosh," Maggie complained. "Why do you have to make so much of things? It makes you hard to like, you know."

"Yeah, I'll bet it does," I said, disappointed in her words. "What about you, Kimberley? Do you see what I mean?"

Kimberley shrugged. "I don't care about the town. I don't want to make so much out of it. I just miss Phillip. I think it should be a simple thing, missing someone."

I felt I understood her words. But I found myself frowning at my two companions, alienated by their complacency.

"Why do you have to make such a big deal out of everything, Gary?" Maggie snapped at last.

"Well, shit," I muttered. "Because it's a big deal to me, I guess."

"And don't swear," added Maggie. "Swearing just makes it more stupid."

I laughed hollowly. Now who was being stupid? I wondered angrily.

We sat a long time in silence on the bleachers.

"I feel bad, that's all," Kimberley said shortly, directing her admission at me.

"Yeah, I know."

"Kim, it'll be okay," said Maggie. "You just miss him, that's all."

"I don't think my mother likes Phillip."

"How come?" asked Maggie.

"I don't know."

"Has she said anything?"

"No."

"Well then," said Maggie with a gesture of helplessness.

"But she hasn't said anything good either. We don't talk that much about stuff like this. But you have to wonder when she goes to see Phillip's mother and then Phillip's sent away, if she had something to do with it."

"Maybe he was going away anyway. Maybe he knew about it all along and didn't want to say anything."

"I don't think so," I murmured, fearing Maggie's words would sadden Kimberley further. "I told you how he sounded on the phone. He was upset. I heard it in his voice."

"If you say so," said Maggie.

"Are you going to talk to your mom?" I asked Kimberley.

She shrugged. "I think I should talk to Eldora."

I nodded. Maggie did too. Talking to Eldora made a great deal of sense to both of us.

"I just want everything to be the same when Phillip gets back," Kimberley said with a bit of a blush.

"Well, uh, sure," I said, knowing what she meant.

"I think I'll talk to Eldora," confirmed Kimberley.

"Good idea," I said. "To hell with the rest of this town."

"Oh shut up," said Maggie.

I fell silent after that, nursing what was now a powerful frustration. I hated being so suspicious when I had to be suspicious all by myself. And what was the point in being smart when the majority of the world was too stupid to know what smart was? This wasn't arrogance, I believed, when it was such a fair question. Who was crazy, after all: me or everyone else? Or was there a place in the middle where hardly anyone was crazy at all? In the middle of life, between me and the people I knew, I wanted to believe there was a place that contained more truth. There had to be a place of truth, I thought, or else I'd end up crazy after all. Or dishonest, anyway.

ELDORA WAS BUSILY PACKING the next day when Kimberley dropped by to see her. They shared a cream soda at her kitchen table, uncomfortable in the August humidity, noticing the skies were threatening on the other side of the window. Although the rain was needed, its imminence felt oppressive. The air was thick and still.

"I'm glad I'm getting to see you before I go away," Eldora told her young friend.

Kimberley smiled at this but the smile was bleak. Eldora noticed she still looked pretty, even suffering from sadness.

"Where are you going again?"

"Pardon?"

"Where are you going on vacation?"

"Oh," she said. "Toronto."

"For a whole month?"

"Yes. I've got so many people to see."

"I'm going to miss you, Eldora. Everybody's going to be away."

"I know. I'm going to miss you too. I'll be telling all my friends about this wonderful young woman I know back home, what a good friend she is. Don't you worry about being forgotten."

As usual Kimberley blushed, but it disappeared quickly, it's heat forlorn and weak.

"I'll bring you something from Toronto, a memento," Eldora said.

"That's really nice," said Kimberley, not brightening very much.

Eldora grimaced. Until Kimberley arrived, she'd been preoccupied with her packing and the anticipation she felt at leaving Meridian for a while. Now she felt slightly ashamed, like she was letting her young friend down. Kimberley probably missed you a great deal by now.

"I know about Phillip being away," she said then.

Kimberley nodded.

"And I know you must miss him."

Kimberley kept nodding.

"I'll bet he misses you too."

"I hope so."

"Well of course he does," said Eldora. She touched her young friend's hand reassuringly.

"Two weeks is a long time," said Kimberley. "It seems like forever."

"I know."

"I don't think my mother likes Phillip."

"Oh, Kimberley. Your mother thinks he's a nice boy. She told me so."

Apparently puzzled by this news, Kimberley said nothing.

"She hasn't told you?"

"No."

"Well, maybe that's because she also thinks he's a little young for you. He is, you know."

"What does age have to do with anything?" Kimberley said calmly.

"Well, not much, I guess. But girls mature faster than boys and you've already got a head start. Down the road a bit it'll matter more than it does now."

Soberly Kimberly nodded. "But what's the rush?" she said. "It could have waited until it mattered."

Eldora considered the truth in this observation and didn't know what to say to it. "It's just the way life is," she suggested at last. "We change. You'll like older boys—you won't be able to help it."

"I like Phillip, Eldora. Things should be left to happen the way they happen. People shouldn't interfere. They should just let nature take its course."

"I suppose that's true," Eldora admitted. "Do you think there's been interference?"

Kimberley nodded. "It looks like my mother and Phillip's mother arranged to send him away for two weeks. They got together the day before he left."

"I see."

"Didn't you know?"

Eldora shook her head. "Your mom hasn't mentioned it. Anyway, you shouldn't assume things, Kimberley. Parents try to do the right thing, regardless. They mean well, you know;

they really do."

"I'm not so sure," said Kimberley.

"I see."

"I mean, if it was so right, Eldora, I wouldn't miss him so much, would I?"

"I don't know, Dear. I'm sorry. I don't know what else to say. I wish I could be more help."

They sat there a time in silence. Eldora wondered if even she had underestimated the extent of Kimberley's caring. And she couldn't think of anything to say that wouldn't sound banal or patronizing.

"If it's meant to work out, it will," she said, confirming she was out of ideas.

"Gary says it's the town, you know."

"Gary?"

"Phillip's best friend, Gary Burnside."

"Oh yes."

"He says it's the town."

"And what does he mean by that?"

"He says the town has rules and people are supposed to fit the rules."

"And don't you and Phillip fit the rules?"

"I don't know. I don't see why we wouldn't."

"Well," said Eldora carefully, "there you go. If this friend of Phillip's thinks it's a conspiracy, it doesn't mean it is."

"I know," said Kimberley. "But he might be right that towns have rules and you have to obey them because you're part of the town. You'd think they'd tell you the rules so you'd know how not to break them."

"Oh, Kimberley, just forget about the town and its rules. This fellow Gary is probably just making too much of things."

"You think so?"

"Was he the astronaut last Halloween?"

Kimberley nodded.

"Well, young people Gary's age shouldn't dwell on things like that."

"So it's true? Could Gary be right?"

Eldora hesitated—what could she say that would be true, that wouldn't be a lie? "To a certain extent," she said, "as far as it goes. But you'll feel better about this when Phillip gets back. Everything will get back to normal; you'll see."

"I hope so," Kimberley said.

"You and Phillip have something special, you know. I've seen it myself. You'll always remember how special this was, Kimberley, even when it isn't special any longer."

"But I don't need to remember, Eldora. It's happening right now."

"But now, the present, just doesn't last. We'd get bored if things didn't change."

"But I'm not bored yet," said Kimberley. "Besides, isn't whether I'm bored or not—whether I should be bored or not—kind of up to me?"

"I suppose so," Eldora said.

"It's just because we're kids, isn't it, that people interfere?"

"I'm afraid so," Eldora admitted. "But that's how we all grow up. And most of us survive the experience."

ON THE SATURDAY BEFORE THE MONDAY of your return, John MacLean watched Rhonda ride away from his stable in the drizzle and decided without premeditation that he'd run out of patience. It was a calm revelation and he arrived at it with certainty. He stood under the eaves of the main barn, protected from the rain, wearing coveralls and boots caked with cow manure. He stood there until she vanished over the fields and he thought about what he would do, vaguely excited by the prospect of taking control again.

Riding in the rain, he mused. Not for a princess like Rhonda. She could only be going to meet a man she shouldn't be meeting. Only this would bring her outside in such weather. Indeed, she would never have done the same thing for him. And, where the family was concerned, this was treachery. He felt a mild curiosity over the identity of the man, partly because of the risk to the family name; mostly, though, what enraged him was that Rhonda found her lover worth riding to in the rain.

Yet MacLean was in no hurry. He could afford to wait an hour or so. He knew where she was going and why—that busybody, George Manson, had cleared that up a month ago in the barber shop. So what was another hour after all this time when the trap needed to be perfectly set?

He sighed at the edge of the gentle drizzle, feeling pleasantly angry. His senses were on edge, their hunger keen. He slipped a work glove from his left hand and reached into the falling rain, letting the rain caress his flesh. Turning his hand this way and that in the warm, delicate raindrops, he felt calm and powerful. He stood there for several minutes, turning his hand back and forth in the rain, before he went back inside.

IT HAD BEEN THREE WEEKS since their last lovemaking and Connelly and Rhonda had seen to it that they were frantic for one another. For one thing, he'd resisted the temptation to slip away from his family to meet her while he was on vacation, as she'd proposed three weeks before. He'd remained in Prince Edward County the entire two weeks, toying with the notion that he didn't want her any longer.

This lasted until the Monday morning he returned, when he quickly succumbed to the aggravating anticipation their proximity in the bank inspired. They practiced their accustomed professional distance, letting it enhance the flavour of their lust, further spiced each day by risky little smiles and hungry glances.

On the Wednesday, Rhonda passed him a note. "The vault? Today? Please?"

"No," he wrote back. "Saturday. I'll make it up to you."

She didn't seem to mind his response. For her too, he suspected, this game of rising expectations was as exciting as sex itself.

On Friday she wrote him another note. "I'm going to tear you to pieces tomorrow," it said.

"I can hardly wait," he wrote back.

Connelly was positioned by the front window in the cabin when she galloped up. He watched her tie her palomino to a veranda post, wanting her to look up and see him there. But she'd worn a dark slicker over her shirt and jodhpurs, and a hat she removed to shake the rain from it, and, preoccupied, she didn't look up at him.

He was deeply disappointed. He'd wanted her to see, before she came inside, that he was a different man, already hard and anxious, not nervous this time in the slightest. He'd wanted her to know that today's tryst, free of its usual apprehension, was the destination in which their affair had been headed all along.

He met her just inside the door.

"Oh, Jim, it's been so long," she said.

But he didn't say anything back; in fact he couldn't reply, intent as he was on taking her right there where she stood against the closing door.

They made love inside the applause of the rattling, rickety door, not so much removing their clothing as sweeping it aside, simply getting it out of the way. They made love inside her slicker, up against the door, the urgency of Connelly's thrusts pushing Rhonda up on her toes.

She cried and yelped and urged him on, clawing at this flesh.

It was fast and very complete. It left both of them crying out and breathless afterwards.

SHORTLY JOHN MACLEAN told the two men who worked for him on Saturday and Sunday mornings that he had an errand to run. He gave them an extra instruction or two, told them he'd be back in an hour or so, then left, heading for his truck. Inside the cab, he took a moment to fill his pipe, tossing the pouch of Blue Amphora on the dash after he was done. He enjoyed a couple of rich, thoughtful puffs, squinting through the raindrops on the windshield. Although the drizzle had stopped, the sky remained grey and thick. With a farmer's expertise, he knew more rain would fall before this day was done.

He started the engine, feeling calm, resolute, and inspired. He enjoyed his righteous indignation—a man liked his mission to be holy: a devout crusade. Then he drove away at last, acknowledging only one fear: that Rhonda might let him down by being as innocent as she claimed. Although he doubted this, the possibility persisted like a tiny, nagging child. He turned on the radio to catch the two o'clock news as he drove towards his cabin, but he didn't absorb much of it, preoccupied the way he was by how good and how bad he felt.

THEY'D MADE LOVE TWICE and the joy was out of his system—Connelly grew apprehensive again. Still lying naked next to Rhonda in the cabin bedroom he knew so well, he glanced at his lover carefully, disappointed by how quickly want and need had fallen away. She lay in his arms, easily, peacefully, not feeling, he supposed, the emptiness that he felt.

"I missed you while you were away."

"I missed you too," he said.

"I was angry, you know." Rhonda nipped at his chest, as if this would resolve her annoyance.

"Angry?" Connelly winced at the bite in her teeth and her words.

"Because Betty got to go away with you for two weeks and I didn't."

"Betty and I are married. I have a son."

But she said nothing to his ritual litany of obligation.

"You wouldn't betray me, would you, Rhonda?"

"What do you mean?"

"Blow the whistle on us?"

"You mean tell Betty?"

"Anyone," he said emphatically, although it was Betty he meant mostly.

She sighed unconvincingly. "No, I wouldn't tell anyone."

Still, he laid there wondering if she was lying to him. And then he wondered if he should get going soon because to leave would make him safe. And finally, as he always did, he wondered how he was going to get himself out of this terrible mess.

MACLEAN RECOGNIZED CONNELLY'S CAR right away; he'd seen it so many times before—at Kiwanis meetings, parked in Connelly's driveway, even at church on Sunday mornings; yes, not far from the house of God. It was a Ford Galaxie, a family man's car, the kind that suited a banker who went to church every Sunday with his family.

MacLean wasn't as surprised as he thought he should be. Connelly worked with his daughter—a seduction made perfect sense. Proximity and temptation, an acknowledged antidote to some men's repressed desperation. Rhonda knew how to exploit this kind of desperation. She had an instinct: a gift, a talent. "Oh, Jim," MacLean concluded, disappointed in his friend. "When Rhonda takes your breath away, it's hard to get it back."

MacLean parked some distance from the cabin on the other side of a gentle knoll and approached on foot, veering away from the grove where Connelly had parked his car. He heard Joe, Rhonda's horse, nicker and shake his mane, and he caught a glimpse of the horse's hindquarters around the corner of the cabin boards.

Connelly, he kept reflecting as he crept closer to the wall at the rear of the cabin. MacLean felt more than disappointment now; he felt a curiously bitter elation. It was the kind of triumphant amusement that would have been even more profound had Rhonda's lover been a clergyman, a saint or an apostle. Strange, he realized, that he felt triumph when nobility was brought down to size, that he felt uplifted because hypocrisy had won the day, exposing the hopeless weakness inside most lofty ideals.

MacLean crouched at the edge of the cabin until his legs began to ache, trying to discern words in the distant murmur of their bedroom conversation. Was Connelly fucking her right now? Would someone cry out? Or were they planning the necessary deception fucking Rhonda required? How do you do it, Jim? What do you tell Betty when you get home today, smelling of Rhonda's sex, covered with her lust?

MacLean waited another uncomfortable thirty minutes for the banker to emerge and walk towards his car. Just to be absolutely certain, so that there was no mistake. Then, after Connelly drove away without a glance in his direction, the farmer crept cautiously back over the hill to his waiting truck. As he turned the key in the ignition, it began to drizzle again, forming a delicate mist on the windshield.

MACLEAN LET HIS DAUGHTER put away her gear and finish administering to her horse later that afternoon before he stepped out of the shadows near the stable. He knew this would startle her, but surprise was to be part of her punishment. It was integral to his need for revenge.

But when she turned and discovered him there, she showed no astonishment. Instead she grunted in resignation as if what would happen next reflected inevitability itself.

They stood there for a moment in silence, staring at one another.

Rhonda's gaze faltered first. "You startled me," she murmured as she moved to leave the stall.

The horse consumed some high quality oats from a pail she'd placed before him on the floor and the sound of his chewing was loud and incongruous in the silence.

Calmly MacLean approached, barring her way, partially forcing her towards the edge of the stall. "Lousy day for a ride," he said.

She nodded. "It rained off and on."

MacLean felt calm and strong, confident and justified.

They were alone. The morning men had all gone home, their work for the day complete. He'd watched her for several minutes here in the stable, growing calmer and more sure of himself as she gradually assumed the state of fragility he required of her. The more fragile she became, the more sure he was of his mastery over his daughter.

"Daddy, is something wrong?"

He'd taught her to call him Daddy. He liked it. She didn't, he knew, because she'd told him so some time ago. It was a childish name—she'd said she was much too old for it. But he'd insisted until, at last, she'd given in. Well partially, anyway. You couldn't entirely win with Rhonda. Sometimes, as a means of address, she transformed it into parody.

"Daddy?"

He hesitated a moment, to stretch it out a little longer, to let her begin to suspect what he knew. Then, "Connelly," he said at last.

His daughter didn't blink.

"It's Connelly, I see," he said. "I'm surprised that it's Jim Connelly. I guess I thought he was smarter than that. I'm not surprised at you, of course. But Connelly? Wondering who it was, I never would have thought of him."

"Daddy . . ."

"He's a married man, Rhonda. But then that wouldn't matter to a little whore like you, would it?"

She didn't react to this.

"A liar and a cheat and a whore," he said coldly.

Silence.

"Aren't you going to say something?" he demanded.

She sighed. "What are you going to do?" she asked.

This infuriated him, her lack of emotion, her failure to embark on a moral debate he wanted to win.

"You and Connelly, was this just to spite me? Was Connelly just a way to hurt me?"

"I didn't think it was any of your business."

"You're a MacLean," he said. "Of course it's my business."

"A MacLean and a little whore," she mocked, stealing the accusation for herself.

"Are you proud of it?"

"Just stuck with your limited vocabulary," she replied boldly, tiredly.

"That's stupid, Rhonda," he said. "You don't have to behave the way you do."

'Are you convincing me or yourself?" she said then, trying to stare him down.

"Don't provoke me," he said. "You know that you'll be sorry."

They stood there a time in silence, like a script in intermission.

"Well? What have you got to say for yourself?" he demanded at last.

"Nobody knows about Jim and me," she said then, her voice tired and flat.

"Well, I know about it."

"We're in love," his daughter said.

"The hell, you are. It's over."

Neither of them moved. Rhonda didn't argue; she seemed to have little life.

"I'll handle this," he said. "You know I'll handle this."

"You handle everything," she said with a hopeless shrug.

"You're goddamned right I do."

"Can I go now?"

"Not 'til I'm done with you."

"Well," she said with a tiny smile, "what are you waiting for? Want to know what it was like, what fucking Jim Connelly was like?"

He stepped forward and slapped her across the face with the back of his hand. "You goddamned little whore," he cried as she fell backwards against the wall of the stall.

Silence. She regained her balance and stood up straight, facing him again. Her hand reached for the cheek where his blow had landed, then hesitated and dropped to her side. She stood almost at attention.

MacLean's fury intensified. Watching her cheek turn pink, he found himself wishing he'd used his fist. To make her cry out. To make her understand.

"What's wrong with you?" he said. "What in God's name is wrong with you?"

"You ought to know," she replied calmly. "You made me what I am."

MacLean's rage exploded then. He pushed her hard at the shoulders, just above her breasts. She stumbled against the wall of the stall and fell to the floor. Some dust in the straw danced upwards into the gloom, like a dreary shroud.

She had to be punished, he knew. She had to be taught a lesson. In charge of who she was, MacLean advanced on his daughter, his flesh tingling with need and fury.

TWENTY-FOUR

. . . The building was completely drenched in flames and smoke billowed into the sky. I could smell that stench peculiar to the burning of a human dwelling, the acrid odour I will forever associate with the destruction of something built by man. And the crackling fury of the flames was so loud people had to shout to be heard.

For a time, everyone milled around on the street, safely away from the heat. Then people began to wonder if the Winstons were away. Someone ran towards the alley, returning shortly to say their car was parked near the building, melting, cracking, parts of it dissolving in the heat from the inferno beside it.

"Oh my god," a woman cried . . .

THE MONDAY MORNING YOU RETURNED to Meridian, John MacLean telephoned the bank. Blanche Stuart took the call and MacLean explained that Rhonda was ill and wouldn't be in to work for a few days.

"It's not serious, is it?" Blanche asked dutifully.

"No, not life threatening or anything." He chuckled after this remark, before adding, "But don't expect her in for a while."

"Okay. I'll tell Mr. Connelly."

"I'd appreciate it," said MacLean.

Before he hung up, Blanche inquired after Olive and

MacLean inquired after Blanche's husband, Don. Both said their spouses were fine. That done, they said their goodbyes.

Blanche told Jim Connelly right away that MacLean had called and what it was about.

"He didn't sound worried, did he?"

"No," replied Blanche. "You know John MacLean, always cheerful."

Connelly forced a smile. "Thank you, Blanche," he said.

He watched her return to her wicket, wondering a little apprehensively why Rhonda hadn't called in herself, why John MacLean, his biggest customer, hadn't spoken to him personally, the way he usually did.

He missed Rhonda already, this being Monday morning. Monday was the day he felt satisfied with her. It was a satisfaction that tended to grow each week, a pleasant secret he enjoyed until Saturday, which was the satiation of the journey to each week's end.

YOUR MOTHER WAS THERE to meet you when your bus pulled in. You recognized the car, then noticed her standing near the brick terminal where the angle of the sun couldn't reach her sliver of shade. You were glad she'd brought the car. You'd anticipated lugging your large suitcase home in the vicious heat, being asked to hurry up because it was so humid and hot.

Saturday's rain had departed like a rationed refreshment, failing to interrupt these oppressive first dog days of summer. The drizzle had magnified the moist electricity and friction buzzing in the air. You expected a thunderstorm—the kind that rips a day in two and drives a wedge between summer and autumn.

Your mother hugged you as you stepped down from the bus. Her embrace made you impatient—you didn't trust her any longer. Soon she pulled away from you, held you at arm's length and inspected you for blemishes. You endured this hopeless moment with tolerant defiance.

"Where are your good pants?" she asked, frowning.

"In the suitcase," you replied. "It was too hot to wear them on the bus. They itch like crazy and make me sweat."

"I suppose so," she said with a sigh. "That's wool on a hot day. They'll be wrinkled, they'll need pressing." She considered this a moment, then managed a solemn smile. "You need new summer pants, I'm afraid, but with school coming . . . oh, I wish we had more money."

"I'm sorry, Mom," you said, mostly out of habit.

While the driver located your suitcase, you glanced around the terminal. How new and strange it felt. Your mood of resolve and defiance had changed your view of the place. Despite the heat of the day, Meridian shivered in the chill of whom you'd now become. The anger you'd felt for days continued unabated.

"I don't imagine your grandmother made you a sandwich for the bus, did she?" your mother asked after you forced your suitcase into the trunk.

"No."

"So you haven't had anything to eat?"

"No."

She peered into the gloom of the terminal. A small lunch bar there was empty even though it was still the lunch hour.

"She's a thoughtless old woman," your mother said.

"I know," you replied, although your mother didn't seem to hear you.

"Would you like a hamburger because we're glad to have you home?"

"Sure," you replied. "A hamburger would be great."

"My treat," she added, as if you had money of your own.

She ordered your hamburger, a soft drink, and a coffee from someone she knew behind the counter, a man named Johnny. She wasn't hungry herself, she said as you both sat down.

"What happened to your arm?" she asked, noticing the bandage—now significantly smaller than the original had been—taped to your tanned flesh.

"I slipped and cut it on a piece of metal."

"Oh, Phillip, you're so accident prone."

Deftly you agreed. "Grandmother Barrett says I'm clumsy."

"I can just hear her," your mother said.

You nodded, the injury forever equated with the licking you'd received afterwards. "It wasn't serious," you said. "It didn't hurt very much."

"Okay," she said.

You were relieved when she didn't pursue the subject further. You didn't intend to tell her how the accident had happened, that you'd been convicted of disobedience and been given the strap for it. These were secrets now, integral to your anger and defiance. You'd discovered the usefulness of secrets, sorrows, and pain. They were to be your education in surviving life.

"How were your grandparents?"

"Fine."

Your mother lit a cigarette. "Did you enjoy yourself?"

"It was okay."

"You didn't sulk the whole time, did you?"

"No, Mom."

"I thought, once you got there, you'd make the best of it."

"I did."

"But you don't want to be a farmer when you grow up, do you?" she said with a coy smile.

"I don't think so, Mom," you said with an artful shake of your head.

"I hated the farm, Phillip. Your father and I were stuck out there alone. Winter, spring, summer. Working morning and night. It was worse after you were born. It was miserable."

Eventually your hamburger arrived. The man who brought it, who looked Italian, topped up your mother's coffee. She said, "Thank you," without looking at him.

You felt a tension here you didn't understand, between the man and your mother. Adult stuff, you decided. You felt alone and outnumbered, so separate now from the adults that you knew. Gary would understand, you thought, remembering things I had said in the recent past. It was them versus you, you versus them, you concluded.

"Can I ask you something, Mom?"

"Sure." But she sounded cautious.

"If you hated the farm, why'd I have to go there for two weeks?"

"I wanted to talk to you about that," your mother said.

You waited. The hamburger was sawdust in your mouth.

"To be honest, we wanted to get you away from the Smith girl for a couple of weeks."

"Kimberley," you said, brave enough to say her name. "What's wrong with Kimberley?"

"Well, nothing's wrong with her, Phillip. But she's fourteen. She's too old for you."

You didn't reply. Fourteen? You hadn't known; Kimberley had never mentioned it. Older, was all she'd said. But then, the way you were in love, what difference did her age make?

"Her mum was concerned. Your father and I too."

"About what?"

She signed impatiently. "About you being only eleven and her being fourteen."

"I don't get it," you said. "What does age have to do with it?"

Your mother fished for and lit another cigarette. "Honestly, Phillip," she said at last, "you two look like Mutt and Jeff. You don't want people making fun of you, do you?"

"Why would they do that?"

"Because she's a young woman and you're still virtually a child."

You found it hard to believe that people would have time to be making fun of you. You couldn't understand why they'd even care.

"You look perplexed, Phillip."

"I'm sorry, mom. I just don't get it."

She gazed at you strangely. "Your father's heard comments. Down at the barber shop, for instance."

This news astonished you. The discussion you'd heard at the barber shop, whenever you were there, had always seemed important. It was impossible that the men who gathered there to talk about vital issues had noticed you and Kimberley at all. "So what?" you wanted to cry in disappointment.

While your mother embellished the news that there'd been comments at the barber shop with who was there, who'd said what, and how embarrassed your father had been, you barely heard a word. What difference did it make now that you knew people were so stupid? And what if Kimberley had been told what you were being told? God, what if it turned out that you never knew for sure what Kimberley was being told, that you didn't get to talk to her about it? What then?

"Well, what have you got to say for yourself?" you heard your mother say.

"Kimberley's my best friend," you answered carefully.

"I thought Gary was your best friend."

"It's not the same thing."

Thoughtfully your mother smoked the last of her cigarette, then crushed it to death in the ashtray. You finished your hamburger, forcing it down.

"Someday," your mother said then, "you'll understand this better than you do now. Right now, because you don't understand it the way your parents do, it doesn't seem fair. But someday it'll make more sense. Someday you could find yourself in exactly the same situation with children of your own."

"I still don't get it, Mom."

"Maybe so. But your father and I know what's best for you. You know we only want what's best for you, don't you?"

"I guess so," you replied to give her the answer she wanted.

"This is a small town, Phillip. You live here and Kimberley lives here. You can be friends. We don't want you to snub her. We just want you to see a lot less of one another, that's all. Best friends come and go at your age. She's older. She'll get tired of you—she'll get interested in older boys. And you'll get interested in girls your own age. She's going into Grade Eight in the fall. You'll only be in Grade Seven. You'll see her at school. But you can't hang around with her the way you did before. That has come to an end."

Hearing this, you seethed with fury. She didn't understand anything. But you nodded as if in understanding, as if in agreement.

"Life isn't fair sometimes," your mother said then. "But later it makes more sense. That's what parents are for, to help you through the bumps while you're growing up, while you're learning what life's about."

Sitting across from her, the hamburger a lump in your belly, you didn't believe any of this. She was lying, you realized, even if she didn't know she was. Well, you could lie too. You nodded—and in the nod you were telling a lie of your own.

"You understand what this means, Phillip?"

You nodded again.

"We want you to take a break from Kimberley for the rest of the summer. That's what it boils down to. Okay?"

Nodding, still nodding, you hated everyone for what they didn't understand about you and Kimberley.

"She's too old for you, Phillip."

"Okay," you said, not listening any longer. There was so much to be angry about, you could hardly sort it out. A litany of reasons for anger. Boy, if you knew the licking I got because you sent me away.

"You're such a good boy, Phillip."

It was divine, your master stroke. "I know," you said with a mischievous grin.

She was delighted.

But you sat there wondering how she could be fooled by this devious ploy, unless she wanted to be.

"I suppose you'd like to go home," she said.

"I want to call Gary."

"I'll bet. You'll want to tell him all about your adventures."

"I sure will," you said, bringing your fingers to your mouth in case you suddenly laughed. Strange that personal, private anger could hang out so well with mirth.

She patted your hand on the table. "Do you want to pay the check for me, if I give you the money?"

"Sure," you said with a smile, pretending this foolish boon still meant something to you, the way it had such a long time ago.

YOU PUT OFF AS LONG AS YOU COULD the slow, potentially heartbreaking walk across the street to the church steps where you could check Kimberley's window. Two reasons to demur: the powerful threat of disappointment and the pains you must take to ensure your mother didn't grow suspicious when you left the yard.

You'd called me and told me you were back, as soon as you arrived home from the bus station, arranging to meet me at Brannigan's Cove the next day and hoping I would know enough to call Maggie so that she, in turn, would know enough to call Kimberley. If the sequence unfolded in this way, you prayed that Kimberley would still care.

Afterwards, masking your impatience and trepidation, you played some records in your room while you slowly unpacked your things. It was heartbreak music—Conway Twitty, Roy Orbison—but the melodies didn't penetrate the intensity of your angst. All you wanted to do was cross the street to the church, then, once there, gaze down the street to Kimberley's window and celebrate seeing her face.

Finally, when your mother was preoccupied at last and you could stand the delay no longer, you slipped out of the house, strolled across the street and climbed onto the concrete ledge of the church's balustrade. Immersed in your hopeful vigil, you sat in the heat and humidity and let the afternoon transpire. Now and then a car passed on the street. Insects came and went, settling on your flesh before departing again. Birds called and flew from perch to perch. You noticed these events with resentment, aware the world went on just fine without you, living its own life, leaving this new, angry you behind, some unacknowledged stranger shut outside, forgotten.

As time passed you grew increasingly fretful. Had you been too subtle with me? Had I not called Maggie? What if Maggie was too busy to call Kimberley? What if Kimberley was away and couldn't get to her window? What if she no longer cared enough to even bother? This last possibility was agony. There was no doubt your parents had placed you on the skewer, but perhaps life itself happily turned the crank. Kimberley's change of heart seemed deeply plausible. If you couldn't overcome life's unfairness, how then could Kimberley?

You felt a bitter shame that you'd spent so much of your life to this point in a delirium of innocent faith. It had been a stupid, sleepy way to pass your time. Unprepared for treachery, you'd remained thick and puzzled, its easy victim. Why, then, should Kimberley appear in her window when all she'd been gazing upon previously was this unusually foolish child? Life didn't reward fools; everyone knew that. You'd failed in life somehow. Kimberley might know that now.

You would have to live life differently from now on, you determined, as you waited on the church steps. It wasn't nearly enough to have expectations. In a world as treacherous as this one, you'd have to look after your own interests, take responsibility for them yourself. It was a conclusion that filled you with anger, that cried out for some kind of revenge. It wasn't enough to be smarter—someone must pay for keeping you stupid for so long.

You must have wandered through this network of conclusions more than a dozen times, gazing down the street at Kimberley's window. The cruel world moved happily along, oblivious to your feelings, not caring about your needs. Then, at some point, as you glanced again at the mobile home, you discovered with a leap of joy that she was at her window.

You gazed at one another, then smiled across the distance. You nodded, hoping she could understand the relief you wished to convey. And what a relief it was, so deep it couldn't figure out how to celebrate. Yet your joy felt different than how you'd imagined it would feel. This time joy wasn't simply joy and nothing more. Now it was something to defend, requiring a commitment from you to last. You would have to fight for it. To ensure somehow it could last, you would need some kind of control. Empowered by Kimberley's smile, you began to consider seriously how to protect your joy, now that your love was forbidden and was threatened by enemies.

JOHN MACLEAN ARRIVED at the bank just as Mabel and Blanche were preparing to leave for the day. He tapped a knuckle on the glass in the door, peering around the gold lettering to confirm that he'd been heard. Neither woman was surprised to see him there—he'd visited the bank on other occasions when it was officially closed.

"I wondered if I might see Jim for a few moments," he said to Mabel after she let him inside.

Connelly glanced up in his office, vaguely surprised to see him there. He watched as MacLean wiped his brow with a handkerchief while he commented on the heat. It was clear the tellers were leaving so Connelly got up and walked to the door to let them out, feeling somewhat apprehensive and deeply tired of the feeling. When MacLean made him nervous these days, he automatically believed it was Rhonda's fault.

"I need a minute of your time, Jim."

"Of course, John," said the banker. "You're always welcome here."

Mabel and Blanche departed. He closed and locked the door. He gestured towards his office and MacLean headed in that direction.

Later Connelly would not remember what pleasantries they exchanged as MacLean sat down in his office, or how he walked around his desk to sit down facing him. Later it would seem that time began only when MacLean came abruptly to the point.

"I know about you and Rhonda," the farmer said, gazing at him with an expression of sad disgust.

TWENTY-FIVE

. . . I don't know where Buck Winston came from. First he wasn't there and then he was. Everything seemed to be happening all at once now. In the distance we could hear the sirens as the fire trucks approached along the highway. And the roar of the flames had increased as more and more of the building disintegrated in the fire.

Buck ran from onlooker to onlooker. "My mother," he cried, his face contorted in fear and despair. "Have you seen my mother?"

And though people reached out for him, perhaps to hold or comfort him, he danced away from them, further up the line of helpless witnesses, asking the same desperate question.

I suppose we saw her at the same time, all of us, the entire village, moments before the fire trucks arrived. If that's so, the entire village must wonder if, for a few brief moments, it shared a glimpse of hell.

Mrs. Winston came out of the flames, witchlike, a small human inferno, at the side door of the building where the stairs led up to the Winston apartment. There was a moment, so short, in which she seemed to be alive, seemed to be reaching for the door, then she began to dissolve like a candle in the flames encircling her, in the flames that seemed to belong to her alone. I heard and was part of the screams and cries of horror . . .

TO HIS DISMAY AND SHAME, it occurred to Connelly that he might cry, that he might break down or shatter. He felt naked before Meridian's most influential citizen. MacLean's words kept echoing in his ears. I know about you and Rhonda. And there he was, exposed and completely vulnerable. He wished he could be a child again, permitted to weep until he could be comforted and magically forgiven, appropriated once again into the familiar realm of safety he'd lived outside of for so long.

Yet, to behave like a child at this moment would only shame him further. Knowing this, accepting it, he controlled the impulse to break down and gradually smothered it. He hung his head, trying to convince himself he was dreaming, but this long moment of silence was too desperate to be fancy. Rhonda's father sat not far from him, gazing at him with a baleful calm more powerful than rage could ever be. All along, having imagined this moment many times previously, Connelly had believed he would simply deny it. Now that the time had arrived, he knew it was too late.

A great breath of air escaped Connelly's lips—he heard it leaving his body. This sigh, he realized, was profound relief. Relief obliterated everything, even the misery he knew must lie ahead for him. He'd been dancing around the flames for so long that falling into the fire felt gratefully inevitable. Like the flames could purify him, could burn away his guilt.

"Take your time," said MacLean. "And don't offend me by lying."

"I won't," Connelly managed to say. "I'll just tell you that I'm sorry."

"I imagine you are," the farmer said.

Connelly nodded with a pathetic sincerity. "For what it's worth, I've been sorry all along. Day after weary day I've been sorry. I couldn't get out of it, couldn't find a way to escape." He wanted to confess more, explain and keep explaining. But it was beginning to sound like babbling. How could an apology fail so completely?

"Thank you for not denying it," MacLean said. "That would have embarrassed us both."

"Did Rhonda tell you?" Connelly hoped she had—the

betrayal he would feel would give him back some dignity.

"No. But she didn't deny it either."

"I see."

"Saw your car at my cabin. Saw you come outside and drive away."

The cabin. John MacLean's cabin. Connelly swallowed, feeling even more ashamed. Trespassing on a man's property seemed worse somehow, more unforgiveable than lusting after his young daughter. "John," he said, "I'm sorry."

The ensuing silence was long. It appeared neither one of them knew where to go from here.

Connelly imagined spewing a thousand sorries that would make everything all right but this, he knew, was impossible.

"Are you in love with her?" MacLean asked shortly. Then, with an irritated flick of his hand, he waved his question away. "You'd be a goddamned fool if you were."

"I love Betty, my son, Gerald. I wouldn't want to lose them."

MacLean gazed at him thoughtfully.

"Who else knows?" asked Connelly, not caring about the desperation in his voice.

"No one," MacLean replied adamantly. "And I mean that."

"Thank you," Connelly said.

"Jesus, Jim, I thought you were smarter than this. You're a good man, you have influence in the community. People respect you, look up to you. You must know that."

Connelly didn't know how to respond, although he'd considered these facts himself many times before. It was hard to know what to say when he felt so much relief. And MacLean's genteel behaviour only shamed him more. Such calm was disturbing. Connelly was at a loss. Didn't MacLean care about his daughter the way other fathers did? Did reality contain less passion than passion reality? Who did MacLean blame for this—the man who couldn't resist or the daughter who couldn't be resisted?

"Look, Jim," said MacLean, as if he'd read his mind. "This is hard for me to say, but I know what Rhonda's like.

That's the brutal truth of it. She's my daughter but I know what she can be like."

Connelly nodded, a fresh gust of relief swirling over the dunes of his soul. "It just happened, John," he said. "It just kept happening. I wanted to end it, but it just kept happening. I thought I'd go crazy."

MacLean held up his hand, embarrassed by these admissions. "Well, you've found your way out," he said. "I've handled the situation."

Connelly nodded. He thought he might weep again, so exonerated did he feel.

"There are larger issues at stake here," MacLean was telling him. "This is a small town. Betty and Gerald. Your future here. I'd like to slap you silly but what would it achieve?"

"You must hate me," Connelly murmured.

MacLean considered this with some amusement. "We're adults here," he said at last. "You were a damned fool, though, I'll say that much."

"I know. It's just that Rhonda is your daughter. I could have shown more restraint. I could have resisted better."

"This is the last time I'm going to say this, Jim, because it embarrasses me too much. A man has his pride where his family's concerned. But I know what Rhonda's like. Any other man but you, Jim, well, I don't know . . ."

In the silence, remembering that Rhonda believed she loved him, Connelly felt a fresh wave of guilt at conspiring in this way with her father. But the feeling quickly passed inside the force of his relief. And Rhonda? To ask how she was taking all of this would be a mistake. Even politeness would convey an ambivalence in his caring for Rhonda he couldn't risk.

"Will Rhonda . . . ?"

". . . Rhonda won't do anything," MacLean said with calm assurance. "I've handled everything."

Connelly knew enough to nod, to accept this assertion as the truth.

"You're not the only banker I know, Jim. I've pulled some strings with your superiors. Rhonda will be transferred to a branch in Ottawa, beginning next Monday. They'll be sending someone to replace her here in a week or so. Until then, Rhonda is under the weather. And, don't worry, your superiors aren't suspicious. I invented an excuse they could understand. That part is none of your business. Most important to you, your reputation remains untarnished."

Mildly surprised that MacLean had such influence, Connelly only nodded. The man sitting across from him was even more formidable than he already believed him to be. Connelly accepted this. John MacLean was probably right about everything. Where Rhonda was concerned, Connelly knew he'd been a goddamned fool.

MacLean gazed at him in silence, waiting.

"I don't deserve this, I suppose, but thank you, John, for your understanding," the banker said. "You must realize how ashamed I am."

MacLean shrugged. "It'll do you good, Connelly, to feel ashamed a while. But I know, down deep, you're a good man. You may have shown some weakness, but we also know you're important to this community. You've been a goddamned fool—you could have ruined your life. The town would've had a heyday with this, you know. And Betty? Well, I don't even want to think about it."

Compliantly Connelly nodded. He was mystified by the depth of his relief, the way he came alive in this state of forgiveness and absolution. Like there was a place called normal, population everyone, which, when you lost your way, was there to be found again. If you were lucky and if you cared enough to find your way back home, that is.

At the same time, though, the devil in him tempted him one last time. An image of the love he'd made with Rhonda only two days previously passed through his mind. He felt a mild regret that lovemaking with this kind of urgency would never happen to him again. Standing at a fork in the road, he turned away from this regret, enticed in a permanent way by the depth of his relief.

"My god, John. I owe you so much for your understanding and

forgiveness."

"I'm an understanding man," MacLean said without irony. "Of course, if you take up with Rhonda again, you won't get another chance. I'll destroy you." He sighed. "You understand why, don't you? A man who'd make the same mistake twice . . ."

". . . I wouldn't do that," Connelly said. "I'm not that much of a fool."

"Just wanted it on the record," MacLean said, rising. "Beyond that, it's going to be our little secret. Okay?"

"I'm sorry, John, for letting it happen. I can't even come up with the proper words to describe the way I feel. I'm so ashamed of myself."

"I know that," replied MacLean.

Connelly walked him to the door. Awkwardly, the two men stood there a moment, not knowing what else to do now that they'd reached this kind of accord. One or the other of them offered to shake hands. This was familiar ground, safe, predictable.

"Remember," MacLean said just before he left. "If you go near Rhonda again, I'll run you out of town."

"You have my word on it, John," Connelly replied, deeply aggrieved.

MacLean nodded, then quickly slipped out the door.

Connelly locked it behind him and watched him walk away. He realized then the nature of what they shared—the burden of knowing Rhonda embarrassed them both. He stood at the door a moment longer, hardly remembering how he'd succumbed. What had he been looking for? he wondered with a shudder. It would not occur to him for many years to blame himself for Rhonda with the same vehemence with which he blamed her.

"MY," BETTY CONNELLY SAID a half hour later, when her husband called from the bank, "you sound awfully chipper. I thought with this heat . . ."

". . . I do?"

"Well, yes, Dear, you do."

He hesitated. He didn't feel real at this moment. Relief made him wary, like he was a careless someone else he should carefully watch.

"Jim?"

"I guess I'm glad the day is over," he said with an awkward chuckle.

"Oh this heat," his wife said. "I think we need a storm."

"Probably in a day or two," he suggested, still feeling like two men, one talking to his wife, the other smirking sardonically at his guilty sibling.

She asked him if he was leaving for the day.

"Yes," he replied. "I thought I'd pop into the Red & White and get some steaks and charcoal. I thought I'd barbecue tonight. I was thinking how hot the kitchen would be for cooking, you know?"

He hated that everything he said had a duplicity about it, the truth in his words and the lies. How long would he have to watch himself this way, being cautious about what he said because he was two men, not one?

"Well, aren't you thoughtful!" his wife was saying.

"I'd better hurry, Betty, before the store closes."

"Okay. See you soon," she said.

His euphoria of relief persisted throughout dinner and into the evening, although the feeling of watching himself from some great distance continued. He didn't know what he celebrated most: being convicted without punishment or escaping Rhonda at last. He felt like he'd won the sweepstakes with a ticket he'd forgotten that he purchased. Like something must go wrong to offset the imbalance of his good fortune.

Later, around two a.m., he woke up covered in sweat, frightened by a series of sleep-shimmered worries that had eroded the depth of his relief while he was slumbering. Wide awake, he laid there a long time in the heat and humidity, staring at the ceiling, feeling trapped inside this domestic, darkened bedroom where Betty snored gently beside him. He resisted moving or slipping out of bed in case he disturbed his wife. He felt so fragile. It was easy to imagine one thing leading to another—Betty waking and asking him what was wrong, him finally telling her the truth after a series of awkward evasions. Something in him wished to confess and he was terrified by this. Was it because he'd received such a light sentence for his crime? Was this why he wanted to make it up to someone? Did he need someone else to know he was truly sorry, that his remorse was no invention, that it was astonishingly deep?

Stupid, he decided. He couldn't confess. He would have to put up with it until this particular madness of shame eventually evaporated. It was possible he'd be able to look John MacLean in the eye someday, wasn't it? Forgive his indebtedness to the other man's understanding and forgiveness? That was it, wasn't it? Wouldn't MacLean have terms? What form would payment take? How many installments would there be? Although he felt ungrateful for it, it seemed clear there was an implied infinity in the debt. Rhonda's words: My father owns everything. My father controls us all.

Connelly sweated it out, now doubtful that he was going to get away with the affair unscathed. And Rhonda? He was tempted to worry about her. What would she have to endure to convince her father that she was sorry? Thinking of Rhonda now, Connelly felt the deep wash of his first real sense of loss—her beauty, her desirability, her willingness. Now he felt torn between relief and loss, acknowledging the pleasures that were truly lost to him. He was going to miss her intense lovemaking, the desperate way he'd sometimes wanted her, the pleasure she'd given him as he satisfied his needs.

He continued to stare at the ceiling. Perhaps he should seek a transfer through the bank. Betty would be disappointed, but if they moved far enough away he wouldn't have to fear the endless possibility that Rhonda might tell someone what they'd done, that John MacLean might change his mind, that the next time he saw Rhonda, even at a distance, he'd feel regret again. But how would he explain a transfer to Betty who loved Meridian so much? God, he'd been naïve to think he could escape his bad behaviour so easily.

Was he making too much of this? Night was such a bleak and nasty time in which to be alone with guilt. Night had so much talent for exaggerating the truth and distorting everyone's lies. He wished he could escape night's talent for asking so many questions. For a few fleeting moments with Rhonda he had loved life. Loving life was a private affair—it was hard to imagine loving life now when his freedoms were clearly a long and bitter negotiation with everybody else. Was this how life transpired? By the time you asked the question—life or appearances—was it too late to choose life as the answer?

Dawn came, then gradually wheezed into day. He didn't sleep. Too many hopeless worries, to many frightening choices. He felt like the marble in a game of bagatelle, encased in plastic, directed here and there among the plastic obstacles of society's formidable ruins.

I MET YOU, PHILLIP, AT BRANNIGAN'S COVE later that same morning. It remained hot and humid. You wanted to talk to me privately and the anticipated afternoon heat ensured that several of the village kids would arrive here to swim sometime after lunch, intruding on our conversation.

"Have you seen Kimberley?" you asked me after you emerged from the warm river to climb onto the raft.

Strange to be here in the morning—I squinted into the angular sun. "No, not since just after you left," I said. "Have you?"

"Yesterday," you replied. "I saw her in her window. I was over at the church."

Although it was only mid-morning, a strong breeze had begun to come up. There was a harsh chop on the water that rocked the drums of the raft. It was a hot wind, even off the water. By afternoon, we knew, everyone would be sweltering.

"Do you think she still likes me the same?"

"I don't know," I replied. "I guess so, if she was at the

window. She seemed to like you the same the last time I talked to her."

You wished you could be sure of this. Your doubts and the heat had made it difficult to sleep last night. Doubt was relentless—it was always stronger than certainty.

"My parents are being so stupid," you said. "And Kimberley's mother too."

I nodded. "I guess you know what Meridian's like now, don't you?"

"I didn't want to go to my grandparents' farm for two weeks, I'll tell you that much, Gare."

You told me about the licking, the Sunday visits of your cousins, your sense of exile.

I took it all in, not showing any surprise.

"I sure missed Kimberley. I didn't get to tell her where I was going. That just made it worse."

"I know."

"It was because of Kimberley, you know. That's why they sent me away."

"Yeah. I thought as much."

"My mother says we look like Mutt and Jeff."

"This town," I murmured.

You swatted at a horsefly on your leg, missed it, then watched it get caught in the powerful breeze and disappear towards shore.

"Meridian isn't the same without Kimberley," you admitted. "If I had to choose between Meridian and Kimberley, I'd choose Kimberley."

"Yeah, me too, if I was you."

You felt good about my reply. It implied I understood, truly understood.

"So whaddyuh think I should do?" you asked.

"I don't know, Phil."

"My parents don't want me to see her. But I have to. Do you think I should?"

I shrugged. I knew it was a tough one, what you were up against.

"I could get into a lot of trouble."

"Yeah."

"I'll bet Eldora would know what do do."

"She's away," I said.

"'Til when?"

"All this month, I hear."

"Geez," was all you said, the news aggravating how abandoned you felt.

"Does Kimberley know it's our parents?" you asked.

"Yeah, I think so."

"Is she as mad as I am?"

I shrugged. I couldn't say for sure.

"I have to talk to her, Gare. That's one of the things I gotta find out. You could help me."

"Maybe," I said. "But you could get into a lot of trouble, Phil."

You gazed at me a moment, suddenly aware that I didn't get punished or scolded as often as you did. "Do you get lickings, Gare?"

"No."

"Wonder why I do," you said.

But I didn't reply because I didn't know.

"So whaddyuh think?" you asked.

"About what?"

"Helping me out a bit? You could call Maggie and get her to call Kimie. Then I could meet her and we could talk about things."

"When?"

"When what?"

"When do you want to meet her? Where?"

"At the ballpark? Right after lunch? Whaddyuh say?"

"Okay."

"Besides, what difference does it make?" you said. "I'm in trouble anyway."

"That's the way it is sometimes," I said, feeling bad for you.

TWENTY-SIX

. . . The loudest scream was Buck's. "Motherrrr!"

He tried to run to her, but the men of the village—one of them my father—wrestled with him, trying to hold him back.

"No, Buck," someone shouted. "It's too late."

But he didn't want to hear.

I watched him struggling to break free. I watched as his shirt ripped away in tatters, as his trousers let go at the waist and fell down around his knees. His jeans and some of the men finally combined to drag him to the ground where he was pinned, embraced, imprisoned, some confusing amalgam of victim and survivor.

At last I turned away. The image of Mrs. Winston melting in the flames was all I could see and I raised my hands to my face to try to block out the memory. I discovered then that I was crying . . .

KIMBERLEY WAS ALREADY WAITING for you when you arrived at the ballpark. Seeing her in the distance as you approached, you noticed she shimmered in the heat. Or was it in the anticipation and admiration of your gaze? She sat in your usual place at the top of the bleachers, the afternoon wrapped around her like a protective package, as if she was something precious.

Two weeks without seeing her and the fact that she'd

shown up filled you with delight. You hurried across the field towards the bleachers.

Meeting Kimberley was defiance. Meeting Kimberley was forbidden. But it was also right and innocent, and you realized quite clearly that you intended to stand your ground. Kimberley too, it seemed, because she was here to meet you.

Your mother had asked at lunch where you'd been this morning.

"Brannigan's Cove," you said.

"With Gary?"

You nodded.

"Just Gary?"

"Yes," you said with a sigh. "No one else was there."

She fell silent after this.

You sat there angrily, disapproving of her because you knew you now must lie. You blamed her for making you angry and ashamed.

"I'm s'posed to meet him at the ballpark after lunch. We may go swimming again, if that's all right. It's so hot, you know?"

She'd gazed at you a moment before she supposed this would be all right.

Now sensing your arrival, Kimberley turned and waved. Nervously you waved back. It wasn't the day that was perfect, but Kimberley herself. You understood this at this moment with some broad clarity inside your soul.

The day was changing. The wind had fallen back to a cloying whisper and the sky had thickened with clouds since your swim this morning with me at Brannigan's Cove. What little sunshine remained now gasped through a thick humidity like it suffered from emphysema. No wonder you perspired. The heat, the humidity, the ten-minute walk from home, these first few important minutes with Kimberley. Beads of sweat collected on your forehead. You felt electric as you climbed the bleachers towards her and she smiled at you.

"Hi, Kimie."

"Hi, Phillip."

You sat beside her on the bleachers, gazing at her in

casual awe, knowing without doubt that you still loved her as deeply as you had before. You felt a profound relief that she looked so much the same, so pretty and familiar.

"What?" she said, blushing at this scrutiny.

"I missed you, Kimie," you said boldly, not shy about it any longer.

"I missed you too," she said, her blush deepening.

"You're my favourite person of everyone. I don't care who knows it."

Embarrassed, she looked away.

You grew apprehensive again. Her hands were clasped together and you wondered why she didn't take your hand the way she usually did. She hadn't replied that you were her favourite person. Had something changed after all? Had Kimberley given in?

"I'm not supposed to see you," you told her then.

"I know."

"It's stupid."

"I know," she said again.

"Have your parents said anything?"

"No."

"How come?"

"I don't know," she said.

"I don't get it," you murmured more or less to yourself.

"What did your parents tell you?" Kimberley asked.

"My mother says you're too old for me. She says we look like Mutt and Jeff."

"Maybe I am. Too old for you, I mean."

"What?" you demanded. "Who says?"

But she didn't answer you.

"They're crazy. You're not too old for me."

"I will be some day, I guess. I think that's what they mean."

"You're giving in, aren't you?" you cried disconsolately. "You think they're right, don't you?" You felt angry with her, ashamed to discover that she might not share your resolve. I'd warned you about this that morning on the raft—blaming Kimberley for what the town wanted from you, thinking it was what Kimberley wanted too.

At last Kimberley took your hand. "Not in my feelings," she replied with a sigh.

"You mean your feelings are still the same? Nothing's changed?" You wanted clarity, no rounded edges. You wanted to sweep away any kind of doubt.

"Inside, nothing's changed, Phillip," she replied calmly. "That's the important thing."

"But we're not supposed to see one another."

"I know."

"Well what are we going to do?"

Kimberley didn't know.

"I hate them for this, you know."

"They don't mean anything by it, Phillip."

"Yes, they do," you said. "When they don't understand something, they just lay down their stupid law."

Kimberley gazed at you, still holding your hand. "What do we care what they do, if everything's the same inside for you and me?"

"It just makes it more unfair," you replied. "It just makes it more wrong of them. You see that, don't you?"

"But we can't do anything about it. And some day it won't matter."

"Yes, it will," you replied, frustrated by her calm and the way she didn't understand as well as you did. "I'm going to feel like this forever," you added passionately.

She looked at you serenely, happily squeezing your hand. "Maybe you will and maybe you won't," she said, her words separate from the pleasure on her face.

"It's true, Kimie. I know it's true," you sputtered in confusion.

"Well then we can keep it secret. We can just know the truth. We can see one another now and then and know we have this secret."

"No," you cried in desperation. "I don't want to keep it secret. What good is that? That's what they want to happen. They want everything to be a secret."

Kimberley sighed. "Well, there's nothing else we can do,

Phillip."

"Yes, there is," you said, knowing an important moment had arrived.

"Like what?"

You tried to organize your thoughts. You'd been thinking about a solution each night you were away. Only now, back in Meridian, did your plan take concrete shape.

"Like what, Phillip?" Kimberley prompted.

"Kimie, we could run away."

"Oh, Phillip," she said, dismayed and disappointed. "We could not."

"Yes, we could."

"Where would we go?"

"Someplace else."

"Oh, Phillip. Wouldn't it be better to try to talk to our folks? Maybe Eldora would help."

"Nah. They wouldn't listen. They don't change their minds when it means they're going to be wrong."

"What about Eldora?"

"Eldora's away."

"We could wait until she gets back."

"When's that gonna be? Not 'til the end of summer."

"Oh, Phillip."

You wished she'd stop saying that—Oh, Phillip, she kept saying. It made your idea—and you—seem silly. You fell silent again. Petulant, angry and hurt, you felt betrayed by everyone. It wasn't difficult to imagine that Kimberley was betraying you too. Even if she didn't intend to.

"It's more important to know what's true inside," she was saying.

"No, it's not. I think we should run away."

"But where would we go and what would we do when we got there?"

"What difference would it make as long as we did it?"

"They'd just find us, you know," she said.

"But they'd have to take us seriously, wouldn't they?"

"They'd probably just be mad."

"Yeah, but they'd see it was important too."

"Maybe," she said, not sounding very certain.

"Do you want to?"

"What? Run away?"

"Yeah."

"I don't think so," she replied. "It's a dumb idea, Phillip."

Your disappointment was so deep it was like drowning in molasses.

"Then I'll go myself," you cried. "I'll just run away myself." You gazed at her intently then, waiting for her response.

She didn't answer until she saw the expectation on your face. "I wouldn't like that," she said. "I'd have to miss you all over again."

"Well, shit," you said helplessly. "We're not getting anywhere."

Kimberley only shrugged.

"Well, I'm going to do it," you said at last. "Because they're wrong and they don't understand anything. I have to do something or I'll go crazy."

"But it wouldn't make sense. We wouldn't have anything then."

"We don't have anything now."

"Yes we do. We still have each other, don't we?"

"Ah, what's the point?" you said. "I'll go by myself."

A long time passed in silence. You sensed you'd hurt her feelings and you were puzzled by this. With all that you had said, couldn't Kimberley see how much you cared for her?

"When?" she asked at last, the question so hushed you barely heard it.

You hadn't had time to consider this yet, but you wanted to answer her. "Later this afternoon," you said. "I'll need to get some stuff together."

"It's supposed to storm."

"I don't care."

"I don't think it'll work, Phillip."

"Well, I'm gonna do it anyway."

More silence, longer this time.

Eventually she glanced at her watch. "I'd better get going."

"I'll meet you here at four o'clock," you told her. "Bring some food and your stuff."

She let go of your hand and stood up. "What if I can't get away?"

Controlling your desperation, you fell back on disdain, feeling cruel and hating it but compelled to force her hand anyway. "Then, like I said, I'll go myself."

"Oh Phillip," she said sadly.

"I know what I have to do, Kimie."

She studied you a moment; you hoped she was believing you. "I'll see yuh," she said at last, turning away to go.

"Four o'clock," you said coldly at her departing back.

You watched her walk away. You watched her cross the outfield of the other ball diamond, the dirt road near the rink, and disappear around the corner of a deserted livestock building.

You felt stubborn and afraid you'd badly hurt her feelings. Not wanting to let go of your anger and resolve, though, it was torture to sit there wondering if you'd ever see her again.

LATER YOU PUT TOGETHER a couple of peanut butter sandwiches while your mother was lying down. "Oh, this humidity," she'd complained on her way upstairs to her bed. She frequently napped in the afternoon, always proffering an excuse for it.

You'd been preparing a complicated story about how your afternoon was going to transpire, but now you didn't need it and felt almost disappointed. It seemed integral to your new defiance that you be clever and dispassionately shrewd. You wanted to be bad to demonstrate your commitment to yourself. Bad was the word in your mind. Bad was what you wanted to be.

Instead, with an ear for her waking in the still dampness of the house, you hurriedly made your sandwiches, wrapping them in wax paper and stuffing them into a small lunch bag. You contemplated taking a change of clothes but decided against it, not wanting to disturb your mother by poking around in your room. And your resolve grew stronger when you considered departing with nothing more than what you wore on your back. Two gooey sandwiches and all the money you had in the world – two dollars and ten cents – would have to be enough.

You slipped out of the house early, before your mother could awake, arriving at the ballpark well before four. There you resisted the temptation to consider what you would miss most when you departed Meridian. It was enough to know you'd miss the village, but if Kimberley went with you most of what you now cared about would be leaving by your side.

Four o'clock came and went, and Kimberley didn't arrive. Sitting on the bleachers as the minutes gradually ticked by, you grew more and more frustrated. What kind of world was this, constructed mostly of betrayal?

As you waited, the day grew still. The clouds overhead gathered into a thicker mass. There was a hushed electricity in the air—nature rubbing its hands together, the heat of its action crackling with friction. It seemed a perfect day for vivid resolution. If Kimberley didn't show up by four-thirty, you'd show them all, you thought. Even her. You'd leave by yourself and maybe you'd die before you reached where you were going. They'd all be sorry then, weeping in despair as they filed by your tragic coffin. They'd know then how unfair they'd been. They'd all be sorry then for what they'd done to you.

It was almost five when Kimberley arrived to allay a new ambivalence. You'd begun to wonder if there was any point in running away if Kimberley didn't show up. If Kimberley let you down, you'd have to face the fact that she didn't love you as much as she had before. What would be the point of running away then? There wouldn't be anything then to be defiant about.

"I didn't think you were coming," you muttered as Kimberley climbed the bleachers.

She sat down beside you. "I wasn't going to," she admitted. "I don't think this is a good idea, Phillip. I was hoping you'd change your mind."

"You didn't bring anything," you said, ignoring this. "You're not going, are you?"

Her expression was forlorn but stern, a sisterly combination of love and impatience that made you feel foolish. "You shouldn't go either," she said.

"You got any better ideas?"

"It's going to storm."

You contemplated this. A new breeze, damp and restless, tousled her hair. Behind her, the sky had grown sullen with clouds, although it remained unpleasantly warm.

"I don't care if it storms," you said at last.

"They'll just find us and then we'll be in trouble."

Her point of view was reasonable, which only made you more resentful. "I don't care," you said.

"And when they catch us, they won't even let us be friends."

You didn't know what to say to this. You felt trapped by everything—Kimberley's logic, the immense power your parents possessed, the unfairness in their decree, even your own decision to run away. Yes, this latter as much as anything, was ensnared by principle and ideology.

"Kimie," you said at last, trying to be patient. "We have to make them see they're wrong. Don't you think so?"

"It won't work, Phillip."

"Why not?"

"Nothing we do on purpose will make them change their minds."

"All the more reason to run away then," you said, knowing she was right.

"They'll just find us."

"Not if we're smart."

Mired in your unhappy gridlock, you sat in silence for a time.

At last you turned to her, your heart pounding. "Are you going with me or not?"

"It won't work, Phillip."

Your disappointment ached. You couldn't look at her face. "You don't care about me as much as I care about you, do you?"

"I do so," she whispered crestfallen.

Although you felt sorry for what you'd said, you couldn't acknowledge it. Not now. You felt compelled to press her further, even knowing you were being unfair.

"I'm going now," you said, getting to your feet.

She noticed and reached for the brown bag of heat-blemished sandwiches, handing it to you, not looking at you.

"If you don't come with me, I'll know you don't care about me as much as I care about you," you said as you snatched the bag from her hands.

She didn't reply. She gazed into the distance in wounded resignation. You knew you'd hurt her feelings.

Feeling sorry and mean, you nonetheless felt right. Although you were angry with yourself that things had gone so far, it seemed clear to you that you couldn't go back. All of this was part of your punishment, inevitable, inescapable.

"To hell with it," you said as you dropped angrily from the bleachers to the ground. You glanced up at her once more, then, before you could change your mind, started across the field towards the woods beyond. In a vague way, you knew this would take you south. You'd gone this way with me one day earlier this spring. Like you'd been preparing for this voyage even way back then.

Several yards later, you turned around again, to glance one last time at Kimberley, whether in love or anger or both, you didn't know. You discovered with a gush of triumph that she was following you. You waited for her in the weeds at the edge of the woods, to give her time to catch up.

ALTHOUGH KIMBERLEY LET YOU take her hand as you entered the trees at the edge of the ballpark, she continued to convey her reluctance in her silence and the slump of her shoulders. You considered challenging her hesitation as you trudged through the woods, but the words required to do so were elusive. You knew how she felt; she knew how you felt—there wasn't much more to be said.

Gradually you felt spoiled and guilty about her change of heart. You'd coerced her with your accusations about how she didn't care and now you felt responsible for her. In a way, she'd become a burden, the fragile victim of your unkind tactics. Preoccupied by this, you fell silent in the growing turbulence of the waning afternoon. How to be sorry for what you'd done; how to change things back to the way they'd been scant hours before; how to stop blaming Kimberley for what was clearly your fault: you had no answers in the helpless brew of your anger. As you picked a route through the woods, across four empty fields, along a narrow path through another small woods, then along the shoreline of a creek, you moved automatically, resenting Kimberley's reluctance and how you weren't making good time. The more she slowed you down, the more responsible you felt and the more your own doubts about the mission increased. And you hated yourself for feeling this way.

It had occurred to you that it would grow dark in a few hours. Where would you take shelter when darkness fell? To make matters worse, the threatening storm now seemed a certainty. The wind continued to increase and the sky kept growing darker. The clouds soon peered down on you like a choir of menacing faces. It all demanded so much strength—the approaching storm, impending night, Kimberley's reluctance, and your continuing regret that you'd convinced her to come along. Not wanting to give in, you clung in desperation to the conclusion that you'd been given no alternative. You were here, exposed in the countryside because your parents must see the injustice of keeping you and Kimberley apart. This was the only way, you felt, to make them face the unfairness in their edict. With a sense of secret embarrassment, you realized that your cry of pain and outrage had been your only destination after all. Once it was heard by your parents, you doubted at this moment that it would trigger their understanding.

At times you glanced at your watch, knowing it was too late to turn back in time to make amends. You felt frightened and betrayed by how quickly the hours passed. Now trapped by your own childish defiance, you stumbled relentlessly on, clinging to Kimberley's hand, knowing you tugged her more deeply into the crater of a tragic mistake. Not knowing what else to do, you kept walking into the storm.

THE STORM ARRIVED A FEW MOMENTS LATER with a sudden and unusual fury. You could see in the distance the dirt road you and I had taken several months previously. As you veered away from the shore of the creek to head in that direction, the storm came down upon you with a terrifying violence, like a drunk falling in through the doorway, unexpected, mean and misshapen. Harmlessly booming on the distant horizon one moment earlier, the storm now charged in your direction, lashing out at you in an incomprehensible temper.

The wind rose to a virtual gale. Daylight collapsed in the face of a dense, pulsating darkness. There was a loud and terrifying crack of thunder and a buzzing arc of lightning that soon reoccurred with increasing frequency. Across the field on the other side of the road, a thick, seething curtain of rain hurried towards you. The heat and humidity you had endured for several days suddenly fell away, as if something had pulled the plug at the bottom of the thermometer.

"Phillip?" Kimberley cried against the fury of the wind. "We have to go back."

"No," you shouted. "It's too late! It's too far!"

In the silence following this short debate, the rain arrived overhead, angling towards you on the wind, lashing your bodies coldly. More thunder boomed and lightning exploded in the air.

"Phillip? Please! We have to go back!"

"No," you shouted again. "I know a place. It's off the road. It's not as far. We'll go there."

"Phillip? Please?" She'd let go of your hand and was tugging on your arm.

"I know this place, Kimie. We'll hide there until the

storm passes, then we'll go home. I promise."

The wind, having already ridden over you, was diminishing but you still had to shout to be heard over the intense hiss of the rain. Both of you were drenched. Kimberley's hair was plastered to her scalp and raindrops streamed down her face. Her t-shirt clung to her body like a layer of cotton flesh. Your own trousers felt heavy and cold, your sneakers sodden. Everything was flesh and skin, your clothing glued so tightly to you, it revealed the bone and muscle underneath. The paper bag in which you'd stashed your sandwiches disintegrated in the rain. When the food inside tumbled to the ground, you left it there, ruined.

Kimberley was rooted to this exposed place in the field, unable to move.

"Kimie?" you cried in desperation. "Trust me, will yuh? I know where we are. There's a place down the road. We can get out of the storm there. I know how to get in."

Gazing at the horizon and its endless storm, she didn't seem to hear you.

Feeling desperate and sorry, guilty and breathless, you clutched her hand more tightly and began to tug her across the field in the direction of the road.

You did know a place. It was an abandoned farmhouse you and I had discovered some distance down the road that carefree day before summer when we'd gone exploring. You'd have to turn left on the road to reach it, taking you further away from Meridian, but the dilapidated structure wasn't far from here, much closer than the village. Yet your recollection seemed dreamlike and you regretted not being more certain. As you hurried Kimberley across the field in the driving rain, you felt adrift. You felt fate held you in its complex, woven whimsy.

You could see the farmhouse in your mind, the window you and I had slipped through, your sneakers disturbing the glass on the floor, long ago broken. You recalled a fascinating detritus of ruined, abandoned furniture, the odds and ends of household junk. Had you been preparing for this storm and this night with Kimberley all along or did it just seem that way?

It was dark and the air was very cold by the time you reached the gravel road. The rain still fell in torrents, and thunder and lightning punctured an indigo horizon as if the day was now at war.

Kimberley hesitated at the side of the road. "This must go to Meridian," she cried above the storm.

"Kimie, it's too far in the storm. We'll take shelter until the storm's done and then we'll take this road back home. I know where we are. It's all that we can do."

Considering your words, she peered into your face, as if wondering whether it was wise to trust you any longer.

You felt pierced by another jagged bolt of guilt and responsibility. She looked so forlorn and soaked, and she'd wrapped her arms around herself in an effort to keep warm. Her bottom lip trembled, she was shivering so fiercely.

Why was it now so cold? When you exhaled, you could see your breath, like winter had returned and it would be a very long time before you were warm again.

You pleaded with her guiltily. "Kimie? Trust me. It's all we can do."

"Okay," she said at last, when you took her hand again.

As you looked at her, you felt a profound rush of love that clung to your guilt. It was a strange but powerful partnership.

"Kimie?" you blurted then. "I'm sorry I made you come with me. I'm sorry about the storm."

Vaguely she nodded. "I know," she replied. "I know you're sorry, Phillip."

But she seemed far away from you, beyond rescue, beyond hope.

ON THE WAY TO YOUR DESTINATION, you passed an occupied farmhouse on the opposite side of the road, announcing itself with a large, brilliant light improvised at the top of a rough pole at the end of the lane. You and Kimberley passed through its glare like moths, glancing in the direction of the house a hundred yards up the lane, deeply tempted to approach it and give yourselves up to its warmth. But you resisted, hesitating at the end of the roadway, holding Kimberley's hand in the heavy rainfall.

"I don't know," you said.

Kimberley said nothing at all.

You sensed, if you walked up the long driveway and knocked on the door, someone would take you in. But your parents would know you and Kimberley were together. Maybe if you waited out the storm you would be able to get home separately and you'd get away with your mistake. After a moment, you continued on your way.

When you reached the abandoned farmhouse a few minutes later, the rain had eased. But a premature, eerie night encased you and the derelict building was ghostly at the edge of the road.

"This is it, Kimie," you said as you tugged her forward. "This is the place."

You slipped through the same window you and I had used last spring. Then, with grit and broken glass complaining under your feet, you helped Kimberley inside.

"It's awfully dark," she said.

"I know," you admitted. "But it's dry."

"What do we do now?" she asked as you stood inside the eerie structure. "I'm freezing."

"Me too." You stood there helplessly, feeling inadequate, puzzled by what should come next.

"We'll get pneumonia," Kimberley said.

"Just stay here by the window," you said. "I'm going to see what's useful. There's all kinds of stuff lying around. Maybe I can find a blanket or something."

"God, Phillip, can't we just go home?"

Not knowing what to say and wishing you'd brought a flashlight, you left her by the window, stumbling deeper into the room, using your sneakered toes to detect objects on the floor. You were shivering too, though not as fiercely as Kimberley. Why was it so cold? Wasn't it still summer?

"Phillip?"

"I'm right here," you called over your shoulder.

"It's so dark," she said.

"I'll be right back," you told her.

"Don't go far," she said.

You found a couch. When you reached out to define its shape with your hands, it tipped and struck the floor with a startling thump. You remembered from the previous spring that it had only three of its four legs.

"What're you doing?" called Kimberley.

"I've found a couch," you replied, still exploring it with your fingers. "And I've found a blanket here on the arm."

"Is it dirty?"

"I'll shake it out," you said.

The blanket amazed you—it seemed miraculously providential. Never mind how much junk you'd found here last spring. Then again, it was like you'd done all of this before, that this was why you knew the blanket would be here. There was something about this night that seemed inexorable. You felt hopeless to resist its inevitability.

"Phillip?"

"I'm going to shake out the blanket," you said.

And you did so before she could reply, snapping it in front of you several times with as much force as you could muster.

"You could wrap yourself in this blanket," you said.

"We have to get out of these wet clothes, Phillip. It's cold."

"I guess so," you replied, feeling awkward about her suggestion.

"If we don't, we'll get sick."

Something in her voice. Like she'd taken control of the situation, like she was now wiser than you'd ever be.

"Yes," you thought you said.

"Phillip? I'm so cold, so tired."

"I'm sorry, Kimie," you said. "I'm sorry about everything."

She didn't answer you.

You stood there becoming more and more accustomed to the darkness. You could make out vague shadows, the shapes of walls, doorways and broken furniture, nearby a tattered kitchen chair, its plastic covering hanging in ribbons.

"We'll have to hang our clothes on that chair," said Kimberley. "They won't dry but we'll be able to warm up."

"I guess so," you replied, still embarrassed by her new ability to take charge.

"We'll have to wrap up in the blanket. Lie on the couch." She hesitated a moment, then added, "We'll have to keep each other warm, Phillip."

"I guess so." Your words caught in your throat.

As you stood there, the hiss of the rain increased again and there was another clap of thunder. You imagined a Cyclops fuming outside your cave.

"Just 'til we get warm, Phillip. No one will know if we don't tell them."

"All right," you replied.

"You wouldn't tell anybody, would you, Phillip?"

"No," you said, now realizing she meant the two of you would be naked. "Would you?" you asked, deeply embarrassed.

"No."

She began to undress, then abruptly stopped. "Geez, Phillip, don't look at me," she said.

"Sorry," you stammered awkwardly, turning your back to her. "I wasn't thinking."

You could hear her removing her clothing behind you. You heard her place its various pieces on the back of the kitchen chair. You heard the couch thump against the floor as she laid down on it. You heard the rustle of the blanket as she covered herself.

"I'm covered now," she said, her voice disembodied in the darkness.

"Don't look at me either," you warned her, now deeply self-conscious.

"My eyes are closed," she said.

You undressed with your back to the couch, then hung your clothing where she'd hung hers. Naked, you backed towards the couch and heard her throw back the blanket. As you turned, you caught a glimpse of her flesh, pale and unbroken in the darkness. The couch thumped again as you laid down beside her and she covered you with her blanket.

Her flesh felt dangerously cold, like it didn't have any pieces. She tucked the blanket tightly around you and the scent of mould and rot drifted to your nostrils. Sighing as if she had to do everything, Kimberley positioned your arm around her shoulders, then tucked herself inside a place she'd discovered against your chest. You were uncomfortably aware of yourself touching her cold flesh.

"Are you getting warm yet," she asked, giggling in embarrassment.

"Not yet."

"I'm not shivering so much," she reported.

"That's good."

"It'll take a while to warm up, you know. This is okay, isn't it?"

"Yeah, it's okay," you said.

"You won't tell anyone about this, will you?"

"I won't, Kimie, I swear."

"Not even Gary?"

"Not even Gary," you replied.

As both of you fell silent, you tried to forget you were naked here. Both of you were so cold, it didn't seem like nudity.

"When the storm stops, we'll get dressed and go home. We can say we got lost," she said shortly.

"That's a good idea," you replied. "I'm sorry, Kimie. I guess you were right all along."

"They'll be looking for us now. We'll be in trouble when we get home."

"I know."

There it was, the verdict and the sentence. You fell silent accepting it.

Her breath whispered over your shoulder, warming your

flesh. You'd stopped shivering. You smelled her shampoo and felt the wash of love it inspired, in the way the scent had married itself to love that first time a few weeks before.

"I think we'll get through this, Kimie. I mean, it's kind of an accident, right?"

"I hope so," she replied.

The storm was abating again, gradually. You felt drowsy and calm, convinced in some inexplicable way that everything would be all right. A long time passed this way in silence, the two of you warming each other with your naked bodies, your private despair and guilt gradually evolving into hope.

"Are you okay, Kimie?" you whispered at some point.

When she didn't answer, you realized she was asleep. You supposed you should stay awake to keep her from possible harm. But you grew heavy-lidded too, unsuccessfully battling your drowsiness, drifting gratefully and helplessly towards a slumber of your own.

As you dozed, it all became a dream, your running away, the storm, Kimberley lying next to you. As a dream your circumstance was harmless; reality melted away. Comfortable in Kimberley's embrace, you vanished into a pleasant, deep sleep.

TWENTY-SEVEN

. . . I don't know when someone thought to wonder where Mr. Winston was. Maybe later that night. Maybe a day or so afterwards, when his body didn't turn up in the ash and rubble. At any rate, to my knowledge, Mr. Winston was never seen again . . .

IT WAS PROBABLE you and Kimberley were missing just before the storm arrived, but it wasn't clear until the height of the storm that the two of you were likely missing together. Both of your households—yours directly across from the church and the mobile home a few hundred yards further down the street on the Supertest service station lot—were required to unravel the mystery of your absences separately. The detective work commenced by telephone just after six o'clock, when everyone was sitting down to dinner.

By then Karl Smith had switched off the gas pumps, locked up the service station repair bays and entered the mobile home where, as usual, he would be served his dinner. By then your father had closed up Red & White Food Lockers (Joe Langley had already left for the day) and driven home, expecting to be fed as well. By then, in both residences, your respective mothers toiled at the kitchen stove, irascible in these last, intense moments of the day's humidity, separately annoyed that their respective children were not yet home for supper.

"WE'RE GOING TO GET A STORM," Bert Barrett said when he arrived home, carrying a paper bag containing two packages of emergency candles he'd purchased where he worked. "In case the power goes off," he explained. "I think it's going to be a dandy."

Angrily your mother glanced over her shoulder at him, snapping the knobs on the stove to the Off position with furious twists of her fingers. "Well, your son's not home yet," she announced.

Your father scowled, then stood there helplessly.

"He'd better have a damned good excuse for this," your mother fumed. "He's getting just a little too big for his britches, if you ask me. We'll be nipping this in the bud, let me tell you."

Your father remained in the doorway, torn by confusion and the rising anger he would need to maintain a solidarity with his wife. "What's he been up to, Carol?" he asked. "He's only been home a little more than a day."

She shrugged. "Well, nothing specific since he got back. That's not what I mean. I'm just talking about this business with the Smith girl and everything."

"Oh? I thought you worked that out with him."

"I did."

Bert remained confused.

"You know what I'm talking about," his wife said. "Too big for his britches this summer, that's all. The lack of consideration. The Smith girl business. And now, all of a sudden, he's late for supper. It's just lack of consideration, that's all it is."

"Overdue for a licking, I suppose," your father said calmly. He moved deeper into the kitchen to take his seat at the table. "Just on general principle," he added.

"Well, what do you think we should do?"

"Eat our food before it gets cold. Maybe, if he goes

without his supper, he'll learn to be on time."

It was enough for the moment. Silently your mother served your father and then herself from three pots on the stove. Fried chicken, potatoes, canned peas, a gravy that had gone lumpy.

Your father enjoyed his food—his plate was piled in layers.

"He'll get caught in the storm," your mother said, picking up her fork.

"Serves him right," your father muttered around a mouthful of mashed potatoes.

"Oh, Bert, I could just throttle him."

"Well, you're right. It's time to teach him some consideration for others."

They fell silent again, finishing their dinner without a word.

IN THE MOBILE HOME down the street, though, Kimberley's mother was worried. Her daughter had never missed a meal without prior arrangement. She expressed her concern in German, out of deference to her husband.

Karl listened as he ate his meal.

Gertrude, too worried to eat, got up from the small table and looked up the Mathieson's number in the telephone book. "I call Maggie," she said while her husband ploughed into his dinner of sausage, roast potatoes and sauerkraut.

Maggie was as helpful as she could be. No, Kimberley wasn't there, Mrs. Smith. No, she hadn't seen Kimberley since this morning. But she'd mentioned that she was going to meet Phillip Barrett that afternoon at the ballpark.

After she hung up, Gertrude stood by the telephone, rifling through the directory again, looking for your number. Although she was still quite worried, disappointment and anger now crept into this emotion. She wished now that she'd mentioned her concerns about you to Karl, the ones she'd told your mother about the day that they'd had tea. Karl had no idea that you and Kimberley were too close, in his wife's opinion, or that your mother had agreed to find a way to separate you from Kimberley for a while because she thought you were too close too. Gertrude had kept all of this to herself because it was an issue she believed was concluded. She hadn't even thought it necessary to forbid Kimberley to see you. Sadly she realized this inadequacy was something else she would have to explain to her husband.

It took time to be sure he completely understood. It was six-thirty by the time Gertrude dialed your home. The line was busy and she hung up in frustration.

Karl had pushed his empty plate away and now fumbled in his shirt pocket for his oil-stained package of Players. He didn't say anything, although he studiously watched his wife.

A fierce and sudden gust of wind rocked the mobile home. The Smiths glanced out the window and realized the storm was now upon them.

"So she's with the Barrett boy?" Karl asked at last.

Gertrude nodded. "Yes, I think that's where she is."

Karl cursed angrily.

YOUR TELEPHONE WAS BUSY because your mother had called my home. I was forthcoming too, although it took some mediation: first a conversation with my mother, then another with my father. Eventually I revealed that I hadn't seen you since morning, but I admitted that you'd arranged to meet Kimberley that afternoon at the ballpark.

After she hung up, your mother was in a rage that grew in ferocity as she explained everything to your father.

"You mean he's with the Smith girl now?" your father asked, gesturing to the storm outside. "In the middle of this?"

"Probably," your mother cried. "And you know what this means, don't you? It means Phillip lied to me. He said he'd stay away from her and then, telling me he was going swimming again with Gary, he arranged to meet her this afternoon."

The phone rang.

"That had better be him," your mother said as she hurried to answer it.

But it was Gertrude Smith. Mostly your mother just

listened. She apologized twice, embarrassed and ashamed. Then, tired of being sorry when Kimberley had a role in the situation too, her voice grew colder and sharper as they found a polite, conciliatory way to hang up on one another.

"Oh, Bert," your mother said, on the verge of tears. "I'm so embarrassed."

"What is it, Carol? Was that Mrs. Smith on the phone?"

"Yes," your mother murmured, drifting towards fretful silence.

"Tell me what's going on, for crying out loud," your father shouted, hitting his fist on the table. The dishes, knives and forks rattled in response.

"Bert! Don't yell at me, for god's sake!"

He scowled a moment but got hold of himself. "Okay. Just tell me what's going on."

Your mother explained that the Smith girl hadn't shown up for dinner either—that it was likely the two of you were somewhere out there together.

"What?" your father raged. "I'll beat him black and blue."

The storm outside your house was worsening. The wind shook nearby tree limbs, and branches clawed at the walls, like they were trying to break in. Rain slammed the windows, splashing down each pane in a silvery torrent. It had been light outside a few moments ago, but now it was black as pitch, as if night had arrived by leaping the hurdle of twilight. Thunder boomed like dynamite. Lightning strobed the sky.

"We have to find them, Bert," your mother said, glancing out the kitchen window.

"Jesus! And on a night like this." Your father slammed his fist on the table again.

"Karl Smith wants to go with you, if you go looking for them," your mother now reported.

"Oh, Christ! The man hardly speaks any English."

"Bert, it's his daughter."

"Irresponsible little tart, is more like it."

"Bert!"

He held up his hands to fend her off.

For a long moment your parents stared at one another in

surprise and indignation.

"On a night like this," Bert complained bitterly. "When I find him, well, Phillip's got some serious explaining to do."

AT SOME POINT, while he was preparing to go out, your father decided he and Karl Smith were going to need some help.

"Help?" said Carol, now sitting at the kitchen table with an instant coffee and a cigarette.

"Yes," Bert replied irritably. "We can't cover the whole village ourselves, me and some guy that can't speak English. Not in a storm like this."

"You mean the police?"

"No, Carol. Not the police," he replied, momentarily surprised. "All we need is sirens and flashing lights. This is embarrassing enough without that."

"Well, who then?"

Bert glanced outside again, where the storm remained eerie, wind-crazed and unnaturally dark. Lightning flashed frequently, each clap of thunder deep and long.

"Bert?"

"I'll make some calls. I'm a Kiwanian," your father said.

"Oh, Bert," your mother said, butting out one cigarette and fishing for another. "The whole town will know about it."

"Well, what if our son is in danger?"

"You don't really think so, do you?"

"I don't know. How the hell would I know?"

"Who are you going to call?"

"Friends," he replied. "Joe Langley, Basil Grisham. John MacLean, I guess. John and I see eye to eye on family matters. He knows this town better than anybody. People look up to him. He'll know who else to ask."

"Oh, Bert."

"Oh Bert, what?"

"The whole town'll know about this tomorrow."

"I know. I know. But under the circumstances, what choice do we have?"

Your mother said nothing to this.

"Damn him! If he's all right, I'll kill him, I swear to God, I will."

"Now, Bert," your mother said.

But he was headed for the telephone to make his calls.

All the men agreed to meet at the Supertest station right away. Even John MacLean. In fact, as Bert had anticipated, MacLean offered to call in some extra troops.

"What if something has happened to them?" Carol asked him when he was done. "The Smith girl—she's very pretty. Phillip's young—she could convince him of anything, I'll bet."

"Stop it, Carol."

"I keep imagining them in the river, lost in the dark somewhere, caught by the storm, hit by lightning or something, all because of . . ."

". . . Carol, that's enough!"

She fell silent.

Her husband did too. He didn't want to think about some bad accident or crime—it was too distressing to imagine. Misbehaviour on your part made much more sense. And anger, familiar and known, implied he still had some control over the situation and himself. If he let worry replace his fury, he wasn't certain he'd know what to do any longer, the way he seemed to know now.

He glanced out the window again, muttered an expletive, then buttoned up his jacket. "I think the storm's letting up a bit. I'd better get going," he said.

"Be careful, Bert," your mother said.

He nodded, then left the house without a further word.

BETTY ANSWERED THE TELEPHONE in the kitchen at the Connelly residence. Her husband heard it ring from the living room, then kept listening as she said, "Hello?" Her silence afterwards re-aggravated his apprehension.

His nerves had been frayed all day. Lack of sleep and too much aimless wondering. Wondering if Blanche or Mabel might be suspicious about him and Rhonda MacLean, if they might guess he was the reason Rhonda had been transferred.

Wondering if there might be gossip in the village and Betty would hear of it.

All day long he'd felt the same knot of apprehension . . .

"I see," Betty said gravely in the background.

. . . What had happened to his initial feeling of relief that the Rhonda problem was over? Dissolved, he supposed, in the conclusion that his life was never going to be the same now that he'd had the affair with her, regardless of his apparent escape from punishment. What was it people said? Once you broke a bone, the limb was never quite the same? Now that the cast of his infidelity had been removed, he doubted he would ever regain the perfect health he'd enjoyed before the injury . . .

"Okay," Betty said. "But you can explain this to Jim himself."

. . . And John MacLean—not Betty, not Rhonda—was the man in whose debt he now lived his life. It was MacLean who had the power to set his injuries to throbbing with residual pain, if this was what Rhonda's father chose to do.

"Jim?"

He turned, vaguely alarmed.

Betty leaned in his direction, holding the receiver in front of her. "It's John MacLean," she said.

Christ! What now? Had MacLean reconsidered? Was he going to blow the whistle?

He moved to the telephone in two long strides, taking the receiver from his wife, smiling apologetically. What had MacLean been talking to her about?

"Hi, John," he said.

"Hello, Jim."

Connelly considered a pleasantry or two but couldn't manage it now. There was a short, awkward silence.

"Bert Barrett called me a few minutes ago," MacLean said then. "His boy and the Smith girl haven't come home for dinner."

"You mean they're out in the storm?" He felt betrayed by the incongruous relief he felt, but it was a powerful feeling just the same.

"We're putting together a bit of a search party. Bert's

called some people. I've called Don Stuart and George Manson. We're meeting at the Supertest station. I thought you should be there, Jim."

"Of course. Of course. When?"

"Right now," MacLean replied.

"I'm on my way."

"Good."

"This is awful, John," he began.

But MacLean had hung up on him.

NOT LONG AFTERWARDS, as the storm abated, Gladys Pendleton called her Thursday night playing partner, Blanche Stuart, to ask her to make some chocolate brownies for their bridge club get-together two nights hence.

"I thought I'd call before the thunder came back," said Gladys. "During the worst of the storm, I couldn't hear myself think."

"I know. Wasn't it terrible?"

"Been a while since we had a storm like this," said Gladys. "Fred thought we'd lose the hydro for sure."

"I know," said Blanche. "But listen, Don's out in it right now, if you can believe it. John MacLean called and said there's two kids missing, the Barrett boy and the Smith girl. Neither one of them came home for supper."

"What?"

"Yes. Can you imagine? Don's on his way to the Supertest station right now. They're going to organize a search party from there, I guess. Their parents must be worried sick."

"Wait a minute, Blanche," said Gladys. "Fred said he saw two kids down at the end of our lane during the storm. He said he caught a glimpse of them in that ridiculous light he put up down there."

"When was this?" asked Blanche.

"Well, I'm not sure exactly. At the height of the storm, he said."

"Oh, my," said Blanche.

"Yes. He thought they might be headed for the old Kennedy place. To tell you the truth, I didn't pay much attention at the time. Fred invents these things sometimes—you know how he is."

Politely Blanche declined the bait. "Way out there?" she said instead.

"Yes."

"Whatever would they be doing out in a storm like this?"

"God only knows," Gladys remarked. "Kids are a peck of trouble, if you ask me. These days especially."

"Gladys, I'd better go. I'm going to try to call Don and the other men. I'll call you back, okay?"

BY THIS TIME you and Kimberley were asleep. You stirred at one point, but only long enough to partly remember where you were and to wonder if the storm was over. You thought you heard a buzz of lightning and resounding boom of thunder, but it might have been a memory or even a dream. The sound of the rain still falling in torrents, pummeling the roof and draining from the old building's broken eaves, all of this seemed to be happening to someone else.

Perhaps you opened your eyes, perhaps you didn't. If you realized where you were, this knowledge was dreamlike and vague. Kimberley still lay beside you, her head nestled against your chest, and you thought you both might still be naked, but this didn't seem possible. All your senses were drunk with slumber, the deep darkness, the warmth and comfort here, an odour of mildew and dust in the material of your blanket that you couldn't quite place.

A feeble inner voice suggested you should wake up, that something important was at stake, but you were too sleepy to listen. And if Kimberley lay against you, defining your comfort now, you felt as safe as you would have felt inside a womb. Was this her breath, her breathing whispering along your shoulder? Was this her leg covering one of yours, as light and rich as satin?

You couldn't answer this, falling back into slumber. Lost

in space and time, you felt only comfort in the fibres of Kimberley's embrace. The envelope of sleep gradually enclosed you again. Your slumber grew very deep.

YOUR FATHER ARRIVED at the Supertest station first, where he and Karl Smith endured an awkward few moments of near silence before Joe Langley arrived with Basil Grisham. During these few moments, neither man apologized to the other and neither expressed any blame for the other's child about what had already happened. Yet both of them knew the other was as embarrassed and angry as they were. They did not shake hands. Instead, they paced in the service station's repair bay, at some distance from one another, divided by language and unwilling to debate who was mostly to blame, son or daughter, child or young woman.

It was an awkwardness passed on to the other men as each of them arrived. Even John MacLean, used to taking charge, didn't quite know initially how to begin a search for two missing youngsters under circumstances such as these. He did, however, place a hand on your father's shoulder and assure him both children were probably all right.

There was some conversation about Kimberley and Phillip's favourite haunts.

"Brannigan's Cove and the ballpark," your father said, "although where they'd take shelter there, I have no idea."

All the men were present by then, wearing oilskin raincoats and carrying powerful flashlights. When they turned to Karl Smith, in case he had anything to add, the unhappy German merely shrugged, embarrassing everyone. It was an awkward moment in which Karl Smith seemed extremely foolish, in which his daughter seemed foolish too, because they didn't know one another well, even though they were family. But the telephone in the repair bay jangled like an alarm and the awkwardness began to ease as each gave up on the feeling that the dragon they'd come to slay was something to blush about, or the notion that its jagged scales resembled pieces of their own flesh that had somehow turned on them.

"You'd better get that, Jim," MacLean told Connelly, gesturing towards the telephone. "It could be important."

The banker hesitated a moment, then hurried to do what he'd been told. When he lifted the receiver, smudged with grease and grime, his "Hello?" came out phlegmy, with no authority.

"I was calling for Don Stuart," said Blanche.

"Blanche? It's Jim Connelly."

"Oh, Mr. Connelly. So you're down there with the others?"

"Yes. What can I do for you?"

"Has everyone left yet?" she asked.

"No," said Connelly, glancing at the other men listening nearby. "We were just about to go."

"I think the two kids were spotted earlier tonight," Blanche said. She took a couple of minutes to relate what Gladys Pendleton had told her.

Connelly thanked her and quickly hung up.

"That was Blanche, Don. Apparently Fred Pendleton saw two kids down at the end of his lane, maybe a couple of hours ago. The storm was pretty bad at that point, so he thought they might be headed for the old Kennedy place to take shelter."

"Jesus," George Manson said. "What the hell were they doing way out there?"

"The old Kennedy place?" your father said irritably. "Where's that?"

"It's an abandoned homestead just up the road from Fred's," MacLean answered.

"Damn," your father said. "Why would they go there, if Fred and Gladys were home?" He glanced at Karl Smith, as if his daughter was to blame for his confusion.

All of the men looked away, embarrassed, wondering what it meant.

"At least we know where to start," said MacLean. "The storm's letting up. They might even be on their way back along the road by now, headed towards town. I suggest we all go that way now. If we don't find them, we can fan out from there."

"These kids are going to have some explaining to do," your father said with a gruff passion, for the benefit of the other men, especially Karl Smith.

There were nods of acknowledgment and grunts of understanding. There was a bond between all of them now, the kind of certainty they derived from concern, adventure, judgments, verdicts, or important resolutions.

"Just follow my truck, Bert," said MacLean. "I know the place."

As a group, they went outside and climbed into their vehicles, ready to see the rest of the search through. Basil Grisham—feeling somehow, without reason of any kind, that he knew Kimberley much better than her own father did—invited Karl Smith to travel with him and Joe Langley. In the deep darkness of the departing storm, the men from the village drove out of the service station lot and sped in single file down the rain-blackened highway.

YOU AND KIMBERLEY slept soundly in a night whose falling was now complete. The storm had moved eastward finally, leaving behind a deep, exaggerated silence. Had you been awake, all you would have heard in the abandoned Kennedy house was the sound of you and Kimberley breathing, your mingled breaths, a temporary peace.

Then the men from Meridian kicked in the front door, ripping both hinges easily from the rotting frame.

In the split second of waking that followed, you wondered if the storm had returned, or if the house was caving in around you. In guilt and remorse, you even wondered if seeking refuge here had caused the structure's imminent collapse.

Kimberley cried out in terror and astonishment.

You glimpsed trembling, fidgeting flashlight beams moving in your direction.

"They're here," someone said.

And another man said, "That's them, all right."

One by one the flashlight beams darted back and forth along the floor, penetrating hidden crevices in the old, dark house, until, eventually, all of them located you on the couch.

Kimberley cried out again at the brilliance of the dancing lights, then hid her face under the dirty blanket.

Forgetting that you were naked, wanting to defend Kimberley, you slipped out of her embrace, out from under the blanket and stood up. The couch thumped loudly on the floor. As you stood there, you realized you should be afraid.

"Jesus Christ!" someone said as a flashlight beam passed over your exposed body.

Silence then, followed shortly by laughter, politely stifled.

The men behind their flashlight beams had no substance. They were as dark as the darkness behind and around them.

Two men—one of them Kimberley's father, that silent, scowling man from the Supertest station you'd only ever seen in the distance, and someone short and bald enough to be Basil Grisham—shoved you roughly aside. In one deft movement, they reached for Kimberley, lifting her up inside the mildewy blanket to carry her away.

She cried out as they reached for her but fell silent as she was taken from the house.

"Kimie?" you cried in a voice that was broken and weak.

But she didn't answer you.

With Kimberley gone, you suddenly grew aware of how naked you were. You cupped your hands in front of your genitals, shielding them from the insistent flashlight beams and the men so dark behind them.

"Kill the goddamned lights!" It was your father's voice.

The lights went out.

And of course, you remembered hopelessly, your father would be here. At this moment it seemed you'd anticipated him all along.

Nothing seemed to be happening. It was as if no one had figured out exactly what to do. In the distance, you heard a car engine come to life and you knew this was the sound of Kimberley being taken away, of Kimberley leaving you behind. Something in you wished the blanket had been clean, a wish arriving out of some nonsensical nowhere, conceited with irrelevance.

"Dad?"

But your father didn't answer. Instead you heard the sudden squeal as he pulled his belt from his trouser loops.

"Dad?" you said, frightened, sorry, frantic. "Our clothes were wet, it was cold."

"Damn you," your father roared as he came at you out of the darkness from his place among his peers.

You entered into agony. You entered into shame.

Barry Grills

TWENTY-EIGHT

. . . *Billy and Chuck never returned to Skeleton Club headquarters and, somehow, I didn't expect them to. But on Tuesday morning, Dwight came by and we walked once by the smoldering ruins of the Winston place. I know we felt jointly guilty somehow, although we would have been hard-pressed to explain why.*

The surprising thing is that we said nothing to one another. The dismemberment of The Skeleton Club was achieved in silence. I discovered a few days later, for instance, that the clubhouse was empty, that Dwight had taken Irving and his little box of files home with him.

For my part, I went through an angry sadness for a few days. It wasn't Dwight. Not Billy or Chuck. Not even the Winston tragedy exactly. Just invisible fate and treacherous time. I knew my present was leaking into that beaker of the past that was now as large as a barrel or vat. And the lake that had been my future now hardly seemed a pond.

Angrily I dismantled the crude offices of Skeleton Club Private Investigations Inc. and burned the cardboard in the incinerator in our back yard.

The rest of August eventually passed, a different August than all the others before it and all the Augusts since. This one whimpered like a dog someone has brutally beaten with a stick. Disappointment can be a beating sometimes. That September, and ever afterwards, nothing was the same again.

AT SOME POINT LATER that summer, or early in the autumn, you decided that embarrassment is more powerful than love. What else could you conclude? Kimberley was no longer your friend, and your mother and father were divided by an impenetrable hush whenever either of them mentioned "the night of the storm." Like everything about that night could ultimately be blamed on the whimsy of nature—the night of the storm. The night of the storm.

You spent the few weeks until school resumed confined to your home. Even I wasn't permitted to visit you. Your mother said I was an accomplice and she no longer trusted me. For the first few days of your confinement, you were content to remain in your room. The licking that night in the wake of the storm had been more vicious than most – bruises and cuts in the flesh of your buttocks that your mother treated with salves and disinfectant, and a stern clucking of her tongue.

"How could you do this to yourself?" she said that night as she applied the first bandages.

You didn't feel you were expected to answer her.

As the days passed, your need to explain what you were doing in the abandoned house remained powerful, but your parents didn't want to talk about it and you were compelled to silence. Your father didn't explain anything either, although he brooded constantly. Sometimes, at the dinner table or when you were watching television with him, you'd catch him gazing at you as if he wondered who you were. Then, caught, he'd turn away as soon as you looked at him, resuming his silence. Knowing he was still angry, you managed to avoid him whenever you could. You possessed a new respect for the range of his fury.

Your mother didn't mention the incident until nearly a week afterwards. By then you were used to the silence interrupted only when you were told to clean your room or cut the grass. She brought the topic up at last while you sat at the kitchen table with a cushion on your chair, eating lunch.

She stood at the sink, her back to you, where she'd been wiping crumbs from the countertop. She'd been going at it furiously but now ceased to move.

"You and Kimberley were naked, Phillip," she said suddenly, without turning around.

Her words shattered a silence broken only by your careful slurping of your soup and the insistent click of the second hand travelling the face of the kitchen clock.

She turned before you could respond. "You were naked," she repeated.

"We were soaked, Mom. It was cold."

She contemplated you a moment, then left the kitchen.

You nearly called after her—you needed to explain, to be believed—but some anger of your own resisted explaining any further.

As the days passed and summer continued to die, your house assumed an atmosphere of ill health, as if the night of the storm had infected it terminally. Your parents maintained a distance even from each other, arguing at times over petty issues—why the ham was salty one Sunday, what should or shouldn't be watched on television that night, what was to be done about your father's shirts, which he said had too much starch in their collars.

At night, sometimes, if you were still awake, you'd hear them talking on the other side of their bedroom door. Now and then a voice would be raised to a rasp (your mother or your father, you were never sure which one) and one would hush the other desperately. You knew they were discussing what you'd done to them, that they were using you to argue, to blame one another for something.

The first few days of your physical repair, spent mostly in your bedroom, gave you time to sort out your feelings, what would be easy to resolve and what would be difficult. You supposed you'd deserved your punishment, not the being naked with Kimberley, but the things your anger had made you do—the running away, the wanting to punish someone for your broken heart. Even so, in a vague way, you were ashamed of what you'd done to your parents. It was an accessible remorse and it came to you easily.

But what you'd done to Kimberley haunted you more deeply. Nor was there any means to make it up to her. You'd coerced her into going with you that day and now, as far as you knew, she lived in a state of suffering similar to your own. Your defiance that day had exploded in your face, not only injuring you, but Kimberley as well. You felt so heartsick about this—and how you couldn't see her to apologize—you sometimes fell to weeping, knowing some of this sadness was love. It couldn't all be embarrassment.

The rest of your anger was directed mostly at the other men of Meridian, who'd witnessed your nakedness and punishment. Someday you'd show them all—their malevolent collective—through accomplishment of some kind. In quiet fury, you would rise up in some way and prove your worth. Then all of them would understand how wrong they'd been about you. You'd show them a thing or two, you said. I didn't think it would matter to Meridian but I didn't have the heart to argue with you.

Eventually your mother gave permission for you to leave your yard and cross the street to the church. "Just don't tell your father," she said as you went out. "And if someone comes along, you have to come back home immediately."

"Anyone?" you asked.

"Anyone at all," she said.

From the church steps you gazed down the street to Kimberley's window, hoping if her face appeared, she would realize how sorry you were and how much you still cared for her. And if she was there, you'd know she still cared for you too. Together you would prove love was stronger than embarrassment after all. But the curtains on Kimberley's window remained tightly drawn. No matter how many times you crossed the street, her face was never there. You didn't give up trying until sometime after school began. Gradually, by then, you had begun to feel humiliated because you cared so much. I didn't know how to argue this conclusion with you back then. I didn't know how to tell you that caring is rarely wrong.

YOUR PARENTS LIFTED YOUR CURFEW on the first day of school, more or less out of necessity. The ballpark and Brannigan's Cove remained off limits but they relented where I was concerned, permitting you to visit my home after school, as long as you were home by five.

Being with me distracted you from everything that had gone wrong. While you listened to my records, you played a game of my invention that I called Geography. Using a thick stamp album my family had given me for my birthday, I'd select a country at random and we'd take turns locating it on a large world map tacked to my bedroom wall, as quickly as we could. I usually won. I remained much more focused than you, I secretly believed, on geography and everything else.

At school you didn't see me much now that I was in Grade Eight, in a classroom across the hall. At recess you and the other boys in your grade played scrub on one ball diamond while I competed on another with my new, older peers. After school and on Saturdays, though, our friendship was renewed.

You didn't see Kimberley much either during the hours spent in school, except in the distance sometimes, at recess. Across the hall with me, in Grade Eight, she remained her universe away, like someone you hardly knew. One drizzly recess that September, when it was too wet to play ball, you noticed her several yards away, talking to some other Grade Eight girls. Unexpectedly it all came over you again—the need to make amends, to know you were forgiven.

You stood there staring at her, silently pleading with her to turn and look at you. If she did, she'd know from your face that you still cared for her. But she didn't glance at you and you turned away angrily. You felt stupid caring for someone you presumed was now unwilling or unable to care back.

Your father took you to Basil Grisham for a haircut early one Saturday morning in mid-September. He wanted to get the job done before the other Saturday regulars arrived, you knew. The barber was curt with you and didn't say much to your father either, beyond telling you to sit up straighter as he silently cut your hair. Thanks to the night of the storm, you knew he didn't like you any longer.

You encountered Jim Connelly as well, two Saturdays running, as he walked towards you along the sidewalk downtown. He still attracted you—his great height and his elegant moustache, the way he carried himself so proudly— but he wouldn't look at you as you approached.

"Hello, Mr. Connelly," you said, somewhat annoyed, hoping he would be shamed by your politeness.

He didn't answer you.

The second time you encountered him this way, you didn't speak to him either. This seemed a solution of some kind until time healed your wounds.

You never saw John MacLean again or any of the other men, not even Joe Langley, your father's boss. Your father felt it was best, for the time being, that you stay out of the store.

One brilliantly sunny Saturday afternoon, while you and I were walking along the road on the other side of the river, on the verge of that October, we encountered Rhonda MacLean not far from the MacLean farm. She startled both of us as she crested the top of a nearby hill, dressed in striking western garb, riding a snorting palomino. She reined in a few yards away and silently stared down at us, especially at you.

You and I, not knowing what else to do, silently stared back.

"Who's she?" you whispered to me.

"Rhonda MacLean," I whispered back.

She must have heard this exchange, but she didn't say anything. She just kept staring at you as if she could turn you to stone, or as if she knew you from somewhere, or as if . . . I can't say for sure.

You could see that she was beautiful, but her beauty seemed to be backing away from everything, fading into a background of visible and tawdry sadness.

How long did the three of us remain motionless and

silent this way? It seemed a very long time, like we'd been caught doing something we shouldn't; not just you and me, but Rhonda MacLean as well. I suspected we all shared some integral knowledge. Life lay broken in various pieces for us now, and I couldn't say for certain exactly what we shared, or what we were to do with the wisdom we had gained. Still the bond between the three of us, especially you and her, was palpable at that moment.

Then urged by the snorting and puffing horse, which was anxious to get going again, she departed, galloping up the hill, fringe and leather flying in the breeze, leaving us there to begin doubting she'd actually been there at all.

You finally ran into Eldora Diamond one Saturday in early October on the new sidewalk they'd constructed not far from Meridian Kiwanis Park. Eldora, to your deep relief, behaved in the same way as she always had.

Smiling broadly, she stopped to talk to you. "Hello, Phillip. I haven't seen you in ages."

"Hi, Eldora," you said.

She asked you about school and nodded approvingly when you replied that it was fine. She asked after your parents. You said they were fine. Then you stood there smiling at one another, not knowing what to do next. It came over you quickly then—the need to mention Kimberley, to say her name out loud to another living person.

"Do you see Kimberley much?"

Eldora's smile faltered then quickly regained its composure. "No, not as much," she said.

"Oh," was all you could say.

"You're a nice boy, Phillip."

"Thank you," you replied. "And you're a nice lady." It was true—there was a lump in your throat.

"Well, thank you," she said with a grin, although her smile seemed rather sad.

Then, startling you, she leaned close and kissed you on the cheek. Afterwards, without a word, she departed, leaving you there on the new sidewalk, confused by what she'd done.

A FEW DAYS LATER, your mother shedding tears, your parents announced that you were moving back home to Port Frances at the end of the month. You were astonished. The school year had begun; had they forgotten? You'd never moved in the middle of a school year before. You almost asked them about this, but managed to keep silent. It wasn't a surprise, not really, to be leaving Meridian in the wake of the night of the storm. Although the news made you angry, you couldn't escape the probability that the move was your fault alone. And no one ever said anything to convince you otherwise.

You helped with the move this time. Taller and stronger now — you'd been growing in the past few months — you could carry your share of boxes nearly as well as the adult men.

I came over to say goodbye. We crossed the street to the church and sat on the stone balustrade of the steps together, feeling mutually awkward about the ceremony of farewell.

You glanced down at the mobile home on the Supertest service station lot, perhaps mostly from habit, not really caring this time if Kimberley would ever be there. Kimberley's curtains were still closed, the way they always were.

"It's Halloween," I remarked.

"Yeah. You going out?"

"Nah. I'm too old for it, thank goodness."

"Me too. Besides, we'll probably still be moving, you know, unloading at the other end."

I nodded.

In all this time, since the night of the storm, I hadn't mentioned Kimberley much, or what had happened to you. And so you were surprised, I know, when I asked, "Is Kimberley ever at her window?"

"Nah, not anymore," you replied after a moment's hesitation.

"I thought not," I said. "Probably trying to forget what happened."

"Maybe," you admitted uncomfortably.

"You too, I guess."

"Why would I want to forget?"

351

"Because it's easier," I said. "Besides, you won't have to remember. I'm going to remember for you."

You just looked at me—I don't think you understood what I might have meant. Nor how could you know I would keep my promise. Neither of us could.

After this, we embarked on our clumsy goodbyes. You promised me you'd come back to visit me someday soon. Then, a few minutes later, you pulled out of Meridian, your father driving a truck he'd rented in Ottawa, your mother and you in the car that followed him down the street. I waved goodbye and you waved goodbye back. Children. We were children then.

Life meanders. You never returned to Meridian and we didn't see each other again for exactly half a century, until just before you died.

AFTERWORD: THE SKELETON CLUB
by Phillip Barrett

Back then, that summer, we called ourselves The Skeleton Club. There were four of us, each of us points of a compass, different but the same. We were eleven years old and going into Grade Six, and there was something tenuous about our relationship, as if different and same argued gently inside us for sole proprietorship of our souls. It was the summer of our lives when we knew for the first time that we were beings on the move and there is a powerful force in the world called change.

The skeleton that served as our mascot belonged to Dwight who was albino blonde and wore horn-rimmed glasses endlessly wrapped in white tape at one joint or another, or right in the middle just above his nose. Dwight was tall and bookish, thin, with a gravely intelligent mind. We knew he took advanced tutoring in subjects like algebra but this was something he refused to admit; he was shame-faced enough in the classroom whenever he turned in one hundred per cent, which was nearly all the time.

The skeleton, about a foot long, was the same colour as Dwight's hair, its plastic yellowing here and there in tantalizingly bleached authenticity. It wouldn't stand, couldn't sit, but there was an eyebolt fastened to the top of the skull so that Irving—we called him Irving—could swing from a cord on a nearby tree branch or from the light fixture in Dwight's bedroom.

The club was actually born that spring, while the last restless days of school were still unfolding, when all of us spent more time looking out the window where the sun was greening the grass than we did with our books. Just Dwight and me at first; we were The Skeleton Club. Then Chuck joined, fat Chuck who never wore bluejeans and who took the oath of secrecy in the woods behind the school, wearing an expression of tolerant disdain, Irving held by a string in one hand over his head, his other hand placed over his heart, mumbling "I swear" in embarrassment at the end of the ceremony. Billy, Chuck's cousin, also joined The Skeleton Club because Billy belonged to whatever Chuck did. Billy was fat as well, though not as fat as Chuck. In obesity too, he could only attempt to catch up to his older cousin.

Of course you'd have to know our village, the way Highway Sixteen hurried through it as if it couldn't wait to leave town, stores on both sides of the street, barely a dozen in all, not counting the car dealership and the ball diamond at the west end of town. You'd have to know there was a river that was only a river from April until May, before it shrank to a creek again. And you'd have to know most of the houses were constructed on streets running diagonally to the highway, except for my house and a half dozen others located directly along the road, all of them fronted by paint-peeling porches where people sat most summer evenings to watch the traffic go by.

We thought we understood the village well. We'd been there forever; no one seemed to move in and no one ever left. We'd learned there were stores that were amenable to kids, others where we weren't as welcome. We didn't go into Stedman's, for instance, unless our mothers were with us. We didn't go into the restaurant that everyone called The Tea Room because that was where the teenagers hung out. We didn't go into D'Angelo's either, where the Colonial bus pulled in a couple of times a day, because Mr. D'Angelo wasn't partial to kids. And we never went into Winston's, the feed and implement store, because it was getting terribly rundown and there wasn't much to look at anymore.

But Fargo's was a different matter. It was headquarters for all the kids in town. At Fargo's you could stand in front of the magazine rack and leaf through the comics after you bought your gum or a bag of chips and a soft drink. In summer, some of us would sit on the steps outside, deciding what we were going to do that day. Mr. Fargo kept his eye on us, a pair of glasses sagging professorially on his nose, but there was a twinkle in his gaze and he whistled the same hymn day after day, hour after hour. Jesu, Joy Of Man's Desiring.

I lived just a few doors up the street and his steps were one of my ritual haunts.

"Mornin', Richie," he'd say to me some days, squinting in the sunlight, ready to sweep the concrete for the day.

"Hello, Mr. Fargo."

"Dust from the traffic," he'd say. "It just keeps comin' back."

I nodded. Chores and dust. One seemed to create the other. I suspected even then that this was a repetition in life I would know as long as I lived.

After school let out, The Skeleton Club evolved into something more than the casual meeting it had been while we were still in the classroom. We decided we needed a clubhouse and were given permission to use a portion of our porch that stretched around the side of the house. We scrounged an assortment of dilapidated materials, including an old bathroom door my father had removed a couple of years before and had consigned to the garage and three or four cardboard boxes—the large kind with White Swan written on the side—from Brown's Groceteria, around the corner from Fargo's. We barricaded the end of the porch, cut in a window, painted Skeleton Club on the cardboard walls and moved inside where we sweltered in the humid July sunshine.

Here, Irving presided over every imagining, dangling mutely from a bolt on the porch where my mother had once hung a planter of geraniums.

It was my idea to make The Skeleton Club a detective agency, a suggestion I raised a day or two after the clubhouse was completed.

"A detective agency," mocked Chuck. "Jeezus."

"Wait a minute," said Dwight. "Why not? Like The Hardy Boys."

"Like The Secret Seven," said Billy.

"Yeah," I said.

Chuck looked each of us over, aware the tide of opinion was running against him. "I suppose so," he said at last.

"Skeleton Club Private Investigations," I suggested.

"Incorporated," added Dwight. "It helps at tax time to be incorporated."

We looked at him in awe; Dwight seemed aware of complexities in life the rest of us would never understand.

"We'll need business cards," he said in the silence.

And we all nodded solemnly.

There was some question of what Skeleton Club Private Investigations Inc. would do exactly, raised, of course, by Chuck.

"Solve mysteries," I explained.

"What mysteries?"

"Any that come up," I replied, glancing at Dwight for help.

"Like what?" persisted Chuck. "I mean, shit . . ."

"They're usually right under our noses," Dwight said calmly, as if he'd been a detective before. "Things look innocent on the surface, but underneath . . ." and his voice trailed off mysteriously.

But what are we going to do?" cried Chuck, now hopelessly frustrated by the lack of specifics in our conversation.

"We follow people," said Dwight. "We take notes on what they say, what they do, where they go."

"You mean grown-ups?"

"Yeah."

"What if they get pissed off?"

"Then we know they've got something to hide."

Silence. This was a notion we hadn't considered before. Grown-ups with something to hide. Secrets. Troubles. Perhaps even lies they told one another. At that moment I was painfully aware that I'd believed forever that adults didn't lie. Dwight, it was now apparent, suffered from no such illusion.

"It's not like on television," Dwight was saying. "All that shooting, murders and stuff. Being a detective is more like, uh, just work. You watch what goes on and make a lot of notes. You just keep an eye on things."

We painted another sign on the side of the clubhouse that afternoon. Skeleton Club Private Investigations, Inc. And Dwight typed our business cards that night, distributing them the next day at our first caseload meeting.

Our July string of cases was heavy but not very exciting. We found out what Old Man Clapp kept in his barn at the edge of the creek, namely ancient newspapers and magazines. We discovered that Mrs. Durbin went to the doctor every week, although we could not explain this apparent excess, and that Mrs. Elkins's regular rendezvous at Reverend Howard's home was for a weekly game of bridge with Mrs. Howard and her two sisters.

Nonetheless, we met every day but Sunday in the clubhouse on my porch, Irving dangling silently nearby. Dwight now handled our various cases, assuming the role of chief of detectives. He read his notes and ours out loud, chastising Chuck for his sloppy penmanship, then filed the details of each case in a small metal box he'd brought from home. He gave each case a title and insisted that they be referred to by name. Old Man Clapp's newspaper collection, for example, became The Case of the Forbidden Barn. Even Chuck contributed a title for the Elkins case: The Mystery of Elkins's Bridge.

Dwight queried us each morning about the status of our

assigned cases, making sure we were living up to our gumshoe responsibilities.

"Chuck, what's new on the Clements case?"

"Nothing," muttered Chuck, who was letting it be known he was losing interest in The Skeleton Club.

"C'mon, Chuck. Detectives don't chicken out."

"I'm not chickening out."

"Well there's a mystery there."

Chuck only nodded.

If not for the Mafia Man at the end of July, Skeleton Club Private Investigations Inc. might have folded up due to lack of interest. But the Mafia Man gave it new life and eventually became a pivotal figure in a summer none of us would forget.

He was tall and stocky in a charcoal suit. He came to town each week on the bus, a fact we discovered during our regular scrutiny of the comings and goings of Colonial Bus Lines.

"Routine surveillance," Dwight had explained, stressing that we should be on hand whenever the bus came in. "You have to check out strangers, see who's coming and going."

The Mafia Man was a compelling visitor. The regularity of his arrival in town, the dark suit, the ominous attaché case he always carried, his dark complexion, and his black moustache were enough to make him mysterious to the detectives in The Skeleton Club. And then there was his barrel chest.

"His jacket is always done up," said Dwight inside the dark humidity of our clubhouse. "That means he's probably got a gun. You can almost see it sticking out of the shoulder holster."

Belief and disbelief. We wanted Dwight to be telling the truth and hoped, at the same time, that he was mistaken.

As leader, Dwight opened a new file and called it The Mystery of the Mafia Man. Each of us followed the ominous stranger for more than two weeks, bringing back our reports and suppositions.

He came to town on Tuesdays and Thursdays on the bus that arrived at noon. He departed each evening on the seven-fifteen, after eating in the Tea Room. He always carried a newspaper under his arm and he always wore the same suit, which was shiny in the ass from wear. He called on each business in town each afternoon, never deviating from schedule.

"He's probably sellin' somethin'," said Chuck after one report. "For Chrissakes, he's probably just a salesman."

"Or an extortionist," countered Dwight.

"A what?"

"An extortionist. Extortion is where you go into businesses and make them pay you money so that you don't burn their place down or blow it up."

"Oh shit," said Chuck. "He's probably just selling watches or somethin'."

"In Winstons'? Winstons' don't sell watches."

They argued this way for several minutes.

I sided with Dwight because I needed the excitement. It was vital that the Mafia Man turn out to be a crook. I sensed Skeleton Club Private Investigations Inc. was hanging by a thread and, with it, the fate of my summer. Although I couldn't articulate it then, I was desperate to keep Dwight's detective game alive because it kept us young, tireless and timeless. The instinct to retain my present tense was now overpowering. I wanted to keep my past a tiny beaker, my future as large as a lake, and I wanted to remain secure between the two extremes.

So I volunteered to solve the mystery of the Mafia Man once and for all.

"The key to the whole thing is in his briefcase," I said during a lull in Chuck and Dwight's debate.

"No kidding," said Chuck nastily.

I ignored this. "I'll look in his briefcase. Then we can close the file."

Silence. Shrugs. What I was proposing was uncommonly courageous.

"Okay, Richie," said Dwight after a long hesitation. "I guess you've got the assignment."

That Thursday afternoon, I "tailed" the Mafia Man as he travelled from store to store. At Fargo's, he glanced at me as if in recognition and I made matters worse, I suppose, by clumsily turning to the comic book rack, as if I'd been caught doing something I shouldn't. Behind me, I heard him ask what was now a familiar question: "Need anything next week?"

Mr. Fargo said he didn't.

It was becoming apparent that Chuck was probably right, that the Mafia Man was just a salesman and not a crook at all. But I stuck with him anyway, following him into Winston's.

There was no one else in the store, just me and the Mafia Man and Buck Winston. I knew Buck Winston from a distance and didn't care for him much. You'd see him at the occasional ballgame or going into The Tea Room or just hanging around with friends. He was like the rest of the older kids, pretending to be hoods, always swearing and spitting and lighting a cigarette, or pushing and shoving and catcalling at girls.

I loitered near the door while the Mafia Man went up to Buck at the counter.

"Where's your dad?" said the Mafia Man.

"Under the weather again," replied Buck.

The Mafia Man put his briefcase on the counter and snapped it open. "I've got a proof of your ad for next week," he said.

Nervously, I moved closer, intent on the open briefcase and the answers I was sure lay inside. There was an aisle that ran by the counter. It would take only a few seconds to stroll by ignored and glance inside the Mafia Man's briefcase. I started towards them.

But the Mafia Man turned, his eyes as black as death. "Hey, Kid, you following me?"

I stopped in my tracks. "Huh?"

"You following me? Everywhere I go today, you're hangin' around."

I just stood there and trembled.

"Can I help you with somethin'?" Buck Winston asked,

imitating the Mafia Man's curious menace.

While shopping with her, I'd heard my mother's response to this question a dozen times. I mimicked it with as much self-assurance as I could muster. "Just lookin', thanks," I said.

"Well, go look somewhere else, you fucking little asshole."

I gaped at Buck, aghast.

He lunged towards me. "Get out of here before I kick your arse."

I bolted for the door, hearing them complaining behind me.

"That kid's been doggin' me all afternoon."

"Just a little asshole," said Buck.

Then the door closed behind me and I was safe again.

Dwight closed the file on the Mafia Man, but not until he'd explained to all of us that the man in the dark suit was obviously an advertising representative for one of the area's newspapers.

"Jeezus," said Chuck. "I told you guys he was just a salesman."

We all nodded in the dim light of the clubhouse, giving Chuck his due.

"This is getting dumb," he said. "Some detective agency. Nothing ever happens."

For the moment there was no adequate reply. Dwight and I exchanged glances.

It was August now and summer had cooled. Irving swayed gently to the music of a strong breeze coming in the clubhouse window. I sensed that things were close to being over.

But Dwight finally broke the silence. "Looks like Richie's done some of the groundwork on our next case," he said.

Chuck muttered an invective. "Don't you guys ever give up?"

"Let's call it The Case of the Vanishing Winstons," Dwight said, paying him no attention. "Richie, I'm putting some of your Mafia Man notes into the new file."

"You mean the Buck Winston part?"

He nodded, raising his hand to reposition his disintegrating spectacles.

"What about the Winstons?" said Chuck.

"There's something fishy going on."

"Like what?"

"Okay," said Dwight. "Like Buck's looking after the store these days. Like his old man's just a drunk and they've been seen fighting, him and Buck. Like no one goes to the store anymore."

"So what?"

"Like the cops were there Saturday night, my old man says, and he said Buck's old man is hitting his old lady and stuff like that."

"I don't know, Dwight," I said.

"Yeah," said Chuck. "What's it got to do with us?"

"It's the perfect case for The Skeleton Club. We keep an eye on things in case something terrible happens."

"Like what?"

"Well, in case Mr. Winston is hitting Mrs. Winston around. I mean that's a terrible thing. Don't you guys think so?" He studied us one by one.

There was no moral alternative, not even for Chuck. We all said "yeah" to a man.

"And what about Buck?" said Dwight. "He acts like a hood. Maybe he really is."

Well, none of us liked Buck and this was a challenge we couldn't ignore. And Buck had called me an asshole. By extension, he'd insulted our entire Skeleton Club operation.

"Then it's settled?" said Dwight.

We all nodded. We began working on the Winston case that very same evening.

It was our most complicated investigation. Dwight divided us into two teams. Billy and Chuck were responsible for counting the number of customers that went into Winston's each day, cataloguing what they purchased. Dwight and I took over at mid-afternoon and our function was to watch the place after hours, focusing on the Winstons' living quarters above the store, at least until we had to go home to bed.

We studied the Winstons carefully until the middle of

August, alternately bored and intrigued by the assignment. The number of customers and what they purchased, carelessly reported by Billy and Chuck, didn't tell us much because we had no prior figures for comparison; in the end, we embraced Dwight's blind assertion that, indeed, business was falling off badly.

It wasn't difficult, though, to verify that things were not going well in the Winston household above the store. Dwight and I heard three violent arguments ourselves during the course of our investigation. Sitting outside their windows in the gathering darkness, we'd discover we were holding our breaths at the unpleasantness. And, once, we ran home to my house in a panic when we heard the breaking of glass. On another occasion, Buck startled us in the darkness when he ran out the side door of the store not far from where we hid, heading down the street. We were astonished because both Dwight and I could see that he was crying.

During our surveillance, we recorded each sighting of each member of the family. We saw Buck half a dozen times. His father, drunk, staggering, and unshaven, only twice. Mrs. Winston not at all. Dwight speculated at headquarters that Mrs. Winston might be a prisoner. This time, not even Chuck could find a way to argue. We all sensed, in some way or other, that Dwight was close to being right.

Whenever something infamous happens, people record it in their memories by recalling where they were and what they were doing at the precise moment the disaster occurred. I'm no different. I know exactly where I was and what I was up to when I heard the news about the fire at Winstons' store. It was dark and getting late, and I was lying on my bed, reading a Blackhawk comic, when people showed up at the front door to tell my father. I left my room to better hear what was being said.

"The Winston place is going up!"

"Oh my God! The Winstons?"

"Yeah. It's burning pretty good."

"The fire department there yet?"

"No, but they've been called."

Burning buildings in our village didn't have much of a chance. Fire trucks had to travel from the next town more than ten miles down the highway.

The Winstons. I climbed out of bed.

The entire village was there, or so it seemed to me. Dwight, Billy, Chuck, their dads, their mums, dozens, even hundreds of others.

The building was completely drenched in flames and smoke billowed into the sky. I could smell that stench peculiar to the burning of a human dwelling, the acrid odor I will forever associate with the destruction of something built by man. And the crackling fury of the flames was so loud people had to shout to be heard.

For a time, everyone milled around on the street, safely away from the heat. Then people began to wonder if the Winstons were away. Someone ran towards the alley, returning shortly to say their car was parked near the building, melting, cracking, parts of it dissolving in the heat from the inferno beside it.

"Oh my god," a woman cried.

I don't know where Buck Winston came from. First he wasn't there and then he was. Everything seemed to be happening all at once now. In the distance we could hear the sirens as the fire trucks approached along the highway. And the roar of the flames had increased as more and more of the building disintegrated in the fire.

Buck ran from onlooker to onlooker. "My mother," he cried, his face contorted in fear and despair. "Have you seen my mother?"

And though people reached out for him, perhaps to hold or comfort him, he danced away from them, further up the line of helpless witnesses, asking the same desperate question.

I suppose we saw her at the same time, all of us, the entire village, moments before the fire trucks arrived. If that's so, the entire village must wonder if, for a few brief moments, it shared a glimpse of hell.

Mrs. Winston came out of the flames, witchlike, a small inferno herself, at the side door of the building where the stairs led up to the Winston apartment. There was a moment, so short, in which she seemed to be alive, seemed to be reaching for the door; then she began to dissolve like a candle in the flames around her, the flames that seemed to belong to her alone. I heard and was part of the screams and cries of horror.

The loudest scream was Buck's. "Motherrrr!"

He tried to run to her, but the men of the village—one of them my father—wrestled with him, trying to hold him back.

"No, Buck," someone shouted. "It's too late."

But he didn't want to hear.

I watched him struggling to break free. I watched as his shirt ripped away in tatters, as his trousers let go at the waist and fell down around his knees. His jeans and some of the men finally combined to drag him to the ground where he was pinned, embraced, imprisoned, some confusing amalgam of victim and survivor.

At last I turned away. The image of Mrs. Winston melting in the flames was all I could see and I raised my hands to my face to try to block out the memory. I discovered then that I was crying.

I don't know when someone thought to wonder where Mr. Winston was. Maybe later that night. Maybe a day or so afterwards, when his body didn't turn up in the ash and rubble. At any rate, to my knowledge, Mr. Winston was never seen again.

Billy and Chuck never returned to Skeleton Club headquarters and, somehow, I didn't expect them to. But on Tuesday morning, Dwight came by and we walked once by the smouldering ruins of the Winston place. I know we felt jointly guilty somehow, although we would have been hard-pressed to explain why.

The surprising thing is that we said nothing to one another. The dismemberment of The Skeleton Club was achieved in silence. I discovered a few days later, for instance, that the clubhouse was empty, that Dwight had taken Irving and his little box of files home with him.

For my part, I went through an angry sadness for a few days. It wasn't Dwight. Not Billy or Chuck. Not even the Winston tragedy exactly. Just invisible fate and treacherous time. I knew my present was leaking into that beaker of the past that was now as large as a barrel or vat. And the lake that had been my future now hardly seemed a pond.

Angrily I dismantled the crude offices of Skeleton Club Private Investigations Inc. and burned the cardboard in the incinerator in our back yard.

The rest of August eventually passed, a different August than all the others before it and all the Augusts since. This one whimpered like a dog someone has brutally beaten with a stick. Disappointment can be a beating sometimes. That September, and ever afterwards, nothing was the same again.

ABOUT THE AUTHOR

Barry Grills is a former chair of The Writers' Union of Canada and the Book and Periodical Council. His short stories have appeared in various literary magazines and anthologies, including *Best Canadian Stories*. His critically acclaimed memoir, *Every Wolf's Howl*, won an Alberta Book Award for its publisher, Freehand Books. His first Fluid Grouse Enterprises book, *Roadkill*, was a finalist in both the Next Generation Indie Book Awards and the Whistler Independent Book Awards. He is also the author of three musical biographies on the lives and careers of Anne Murray, Alanis Morissette and Céline Dion. His work on an updated version of Dion's life, co-authored with Jim Brown, was the source for a CBC television movie. He currently lives and works in North Bay, Ontario, Canada.